THE PRINCESS'S CHOSEN

Inheritance of Hunger - Book Two

KATHRYN MOON

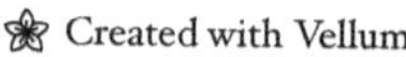 Created with Vellum

This is a Reverse Harem Paranormal Romance and is not suited for those under the age of 18.

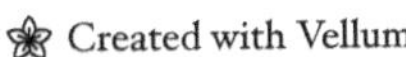 Created with Vellum

For Desiree,
for drawing all the threads together with me

CONTENTS

THE PRINCESS'S CHOSEN

INHERITANCE OF HUNGER
BOOK TWO

BY KATHRYN MOON

1.
BRYONY

"Mmm, yessss..."

I winced as my knife scratched against the porcelain dish, wondering if I was imagining the piercing stare of my grandmother flick in my direction from the other end of the dining table.

"Ohhhh, yes! Yes!"

Cosmo sat to my left, his shoulders shaking as he stared down at his plate with wide eyes and a smile pinned between his teeth. Camellia was slouched in her chair at the center of the right side of the table. Her Chosen Sam was kissing her shoulder and holding a bunch of grapes over her lips, while Igor had his face buried between her legs, where she'd thrust him beneath the dining table after the soup course.

Lady Pru watched the scene with an amused interest and an avid appetite for our steak and kidney pies, while the rest of my Chosen tried to remain impassive, uncertain where to put their gazes.

"Ahh! Ah, yes, finally!" Camellia cried, accidentally taking a grape into her mouth at the precise same moment as her climax, so that she came while choking lightly, her knees banging into the underside of the table and making the dishes rattle.

Candlelight shimmered, and for the first time since Camellia decided she had to be 'served' at our dinner, I watched with interest, waiting to see what the Hunger would do.

There was a great groan from under the table, and Sam moaned and shuddered against Camellia, who spat the grape on the table. There was no transformation I could see, and I realized as Sam began to palm at Camellia's breast and rut against her side—almost falling off his chair—that she'd put the magic directly back into them.

My stare turned to my grandmother at last, meeting her eyes across the miles of table. Was that *really* what she wanted from me? A useless display of carnal satisfaction?

"Take it to the hallway, Camellia," Grandmother said, with a weary sigh.

Camellia giggled, but Sam at least did us the favor of dragging my sister up out of her chair and hauling her toward the nearest hall, Igor chasing after them on his hands and knees with his pants hanging loose. Their grunts and moans started up again a few moments later, and Lady Pru snorted into her napkin as Wendell took a deep gulp of his wine, his eyes sliding to me with sympathy in his stare.

"How long do you plan on visiting, Grandmother?" I asked.

"Are we unwelcome, Bryony?"

Yes. "Of course not. Only unexpected. I wish you had come to see the festival too," I said.

Grandmother hummed and took a bite of her pie, her head shaking. "Dusty common festivals aren't really my form of entertainment, *dear*."

I gritted my teeth, fingers clenching around the handle of my knife, wishing I could reach for Owen, who frowned at her dismissal.

"And how was your journey?" I asked instead.

"Rough," my grandmother growled. "The roads are bad and... you know I approve of Camellia's appetite—" There was a great exclamation from the hall as if in emphasis. "But it does grow tiresome when confined in the carriage."

I resisted the urge to make a disgusted face, and instead hummed and took a slow bite of food. "We noted the condition of the roads on our own travels," I said mildly.

Grandmother raised an eyebrow. "And yet, you decided to forgo taxes?"

I set down my fork and knife and folded my hands into my lap where my grandmother wouldn't see me wringing them. "I observed that the condition of our people was much worse."

The other occupants at the table, and even the guards in the room, seemed to watch us like opponents in a sporting match, eyes volleying back and forth, waiting to see who scored next.

"Is that so?" Grandmother asked, frowning. I nodded, and she turned her focus to her meal. "I see. We'll discuss this more tomorrow. Do you have a young woman who can attend me this evening?"

I glanced at Lady Pru, who took the initiative. "We do, Your Majesty. I'll see to it now if I might be excused."

Grandmother and I both nodded in answer, and Lady Pru left the table with a quiet squeak of her chair on the tile.

"Is there anything I can do for you?" I asked, studying my grandmother carefully. Even in the warm candlelight, she did look...weary. It wasn't a quick journey from the capital to here, and if I'd been trapped in a carriage with Camellia and two of her Chosen, I was sure I'd look much worse.

"No, dear," Grandmother answered, less snappishly. "Nothing a good soak and a decent sleep can't do. Now explain to me why you need two stewards."

"The council appointed Daniel Farraque," I said, glancing around the room and realizing the man in question was missing, for once, which was strange for him. "I appointed Lady Prudence. She suits me better, and Farraque manages the laborious end."

"Well, the palace looks decent enough. Last I heard, it was nearly uninhabitable," Grandmother murmured, looking up again with her eyes narrowed. "You manage festivals and repairing the castle, but not the roads?"

I couldn't restrain the laugh in my chest, and I shook my head. "Honestly, I haven't spent a dime outside of my own pocket. I'll explain it all in the morning."

"Oh, will you?"

We stared at one another, the room watching the silent battle of wills. Since when did I stand up to my grandmother, even in this passive challenge? *Since you've learned her faults and found your own strengths*, I thought, wishing I could go to one of my Chosen and settle myself into their lap.

There was a male moan from the hallway, and I shook myself, glancing at Owen and holding out my hand. His eyebrows rose, but he stood obediently from his seat and moved to mine, taking my place when I stood and gestured for him. His arms wrapped around my waist, and I released a long sigh as I sank into his chest, settling my plate on my own lap and offering him a bite. It wasn't orgasms at the dinner table in full view of my grandmother, but it was what *I* wanted in the moment. Owen kissed my temple as I took my own bite, his hands soothing at my back.

"Tomorrow it is. I've had enough of willful young women," Grandmother muttered.

❧

I WOKE the next morning as Cosmo rolled me over his chest to land between him and Wendell, ready to fall asleep straight away again, when I heard the door and looked up with eyes narrowed.

"Where are you off to?" I croaked, watching Owen attempting and failing to tiptoe out of the room.

He gave me a sheepish grin and shrugged. "I wanted to go and check on the new horses. We still don't have a proper groomsman—"

I sighed and relaxed back into the heap of warm flesh surrounding me, waving my fingers at him. "That's fine. Say hello to them for me. Love you."

"Love you, Mistress," Owen called back, and I found myself grinning as I snuggled into Wendell's chest, pulling Cosmo's arm tighter around me.

"How long do we have until the battle axe comes to find you?" Thao asked from Wendell's other side, his arm stretching over to cup my bottom where it was tucked between Wen and Cosmo's hips.

It took me a moment to sort through the words, and then I snorted against Wendell's chest. "Don't call her that...not where she might hear you, anyway. I don't know. Camellia will be asleep late, she always was the last to rise. And then she'll turn up wherever she thinks she's least wanted." I frowned at myself and huffed, turning on my back to glare up at the ceiling. "She's my sister... I wish I liked her better."

"Her performance last night was designed to irritate you," Wendell mumbled.

"She wants the crown?" Cosmo asked.

"I don't know. Maybe. She likes being better at the Hunger than me."

"She's not better. That was a highly unoriginal display. The one in the hall was worse, and I had a direct view," Thao said.

I opened my mouth to ask and then thought better of it. "I think...I think I should be prepared for anything."

"Your grandmother still doubts you have the Hunger, doesn't she?" Wendell asked, and I nodded. "Do we need to prove it to her?"

I blew out a long breath between pursed lips and then wiggled my way up into sitting, digging my fingers through tangled strands, until Cosmo sat up too and started to comb gently through them, making me sigh. "I've been trying to sort through that. I don't object to being open with my affection and interest for you all. And we haven't really tried to hide our activities around the palace. But if my grandmother wants me to be Camellia, I never will manage to satisfy her. I desire you all, I crave you, I plan on satisfying us *all* but—"

"But your priorities are to your kingdom and people, just as they should be," Thao growled, rolling his face into the pillow, the sheet on his back slipping down to reveal his perfectly rounded ass. Wendell's hand found mine and Cosmo's chin rested on my shoulder, all three of us taking a moment to admire the perfection. "Stop it," Thao said, laugh muffled.

"The only thing you need to prove to your grandmother is that you *do* serve Kimmery, exactly as you are," Cosmo murmured, kissing my earlobe and making me shiver. "I'm not sure that requires a live demonstration, but..."

"But if it does, you consent?" I asked, laughing and craning my neck to make room for him to cover it in nipping kisses.

"If I might be excused, I have some objection to letting the old crone watch me," Thao said, turning again and exhaling, Wendell taking care of brushing his silky hair back. "Wendell is very pretty to watch though."

Wendell laughed and grinned at me with a shrug. "For

Kimmery, I suppose I might be pressed upon," he said, leaning in and brushing his mouth against mine.

I accepted the kiss and then started to make my way out of the bed, my nightgown tangling around my knees as I crawled out.

"That's transparent, you know. I don't know why you bother," Thao called.

"Because it makes her feel nice," Cosmo answered for me. "And because it feels good when we lick her through the lace on her breasts."

I tried to glare at him, but all I managed was getting a good look at them piled together, Wendell's washed out beauty nestled between their warmed earth tones. *I could always just stay in bed with them and make Grandmother come to find me*, my thoughts suggested helpfully. It wasn't a bad idea, but I shrugged it off.

"Has anyone seen where Farraque got off to? He vanished after we arrived back at the palace, and I haven't seen him since."

"Missing him?" Thao asked, dry and sarcastic, leaning heavily into Wendell's side, his hand sliding under the covers in Cosmo's direction. In the back of my head, I wondered what it would mean for Wendell and Thao to include Cosmo in their sex, and if it was something I needed to worry about. It would have to wait for the moment. They were all grown men, and for all I knew, it'd already been discussed.

"No, but considering how he likes to be underfoot, I'm feeling a little suspicious," I said.

"I have a theory," Wendell offered, glancing between a smirking Thao and a panting Cosmo, a soft smile on his lips. "I think he's avoiding your sister. He's unmarried and you're not claiming him. If she sets her eye on him, she may end up Choosing him, and then his role for the council is spoiled."

"We should, mmph, we should set them up," Cosmo said, grunting and falling back into the pillows, revealing the bounce of the sheets over his lap.

"I feel like I'm being set up," I said, wetting my lips and watching Cosmo start to squirm.

"Do you know how to suck cock?" Thao asked me, Wendell

throwing back the sheets to reveal Thao's fist around Cosmo's dark length, Cosmo's hips doing the work of thrusting.

"I have a *little* instruction," I murmured, my feet drawing me back to the bed, eyes on the liquid seeping at the end of Cosmo's cock.

❧

"THERE YOU ARE," Grandmother snapped as I appeared in the doorway of an eastern study that overlooked the woods.

Cosmo's hand was in mine, his smile still loose and cheeks flushed from the attention we'd served him this morning. Mine probably were too for that matter, and I'd decided I could dress as I usually did around the palace—corsetless and in a dress that offered easier access for my Chosen.

Grandmother seemed to freeze for a moment, looking me over again more thoroughly, her eyebrows raising and shoulders softening slowly.

"You look...well. Is this average infatuation or..."

"Or the Hunger?" I asked, helping myself to a seat on the couch, Cosmo making us a plate from the foods laid out over the table for my grandmother. It was a little bit of a dull palette for my usual breakfast, but we'd left our own breakfast with Wen and Thao in the bedroom.

"Would you be disappointed if I said it was both?" I asked as Cosmo moved to sit next to me, feeding me a slice of toast with jam.

"Not if that was the truth," Grandmother answered.

Her hawkish stare didn't have the same effect as it once had, still piercing but not injuring me like only a couple months ago.

"I've grown fond of my Chosen since I met them, and with that grew the Hunger," I said, and Cosmo's arm stretched across my shoulders.

"Fond? Bryony, the Hunger is more than *fondness*," Grandmother scoffed. "That's not how we work."

"No, but it's how *I* work," I said, glaring back at her. "Believe me, it surprised me too. But this is not just infatuation."

"I am glad if you're enjoying yourself here on your little sojourn in the north, playing at commanding our council—"

I sat forward, fingers digging into the cushions beneath me. "What do you want, Grandmother? Me to prove it to you?"

"Of course I do, you silly girl! This is the fate of our kingdom we are discussing," Grandmother answered a laugh. "I see Camellia's faults, don't think I don't. But if she has the power, then she can *rule*."

"Rule? Like Mother does?! From inside her bedroom? You won't live forever, Grandmother, and I've seen Mother leave her chambers three times in the past *year*. Who is *ruling* this kingdom?"

"Bryony!"

I gasped, and my eyes dropped to my lap, discovering my hands clenched to fists in my lap, only then feeling the bite of my nails in my own flesh. My face was hot, and my pulse was loud in my own ears.

"Show her," Cosmo whispered gently, his palm spread over my spine. "It's all right."

"Perhaps the young man might leave so we may speak privately, granddaughter," my grandmother said in a low warning tone.

I glanced up into Cosmo's gentle stare, his brow tangled with concern, lips still swollen from my kisses. I snatched the plate from his hand and smashed it down against the floor, my grandmother gasping as it cracked and shattered between our feet. Cosmo only smiled and fell into me as I grasped at his collar, pulling him in for a deep, demanding kiss, drinking him down in great gulps as my grandmother snarled my name across the table from us. Cosmo moaned and melted into me, his arms wrapping around my waist, pressing me to the arm of the couch we were seated on, ready to drag me under him.

He tasted sweet like the jam, and he was so willing, willing to do anything I asked for any reason, even behave this way in front of my grandmother, the dowager queen. Cosmo made it easy at every step for me to care for him, as happy to please me as Owen was, always careful to note my needs. I wanted to do the same for him from this moment on.

I sighed, and the Hunger was threaded through as Cosmo licked into my mouth, warming my veins and clinging to both our skin. I eased away from the kiss slowly, lowering one hand down to the floor and forcing the magic out of me with a soft push. It didn't go as easily as when I came, like the Hunger knew it hadn't *really* been satisfied with just a kiss, and it left me with a heavier, drowsy feeling as it bled out of me.

And then my grandmother gasped, porcelain clinking together, edges repairing with little chimes and scratches as Cosmo and I settled with me stretched beneath him on the couch. He raised his head, winking at me as I blushed, and then he rolled to fit against the back of the couch. I propped my head up on the heel of my hand and looked to my grandmother. Her eyes were on the floor.

"What have you—How did you do that?" Grandmother asked, leaning slowly forward to lift the plate from the floor.

Not only had I repaired the plate, replacing the pink rose pattern with silver and gold vines and blossoms, I'd also accidentally turned the crumbs of toast and jam into a pile of fresh strawberries.

"How did you think we repaired the palace?" I asked, trying not to smirk at the openly shocked expression that washed over my grandmother's face. She paled and sank back into her chair, the plate of strawberries resting in her lap.

"Our magic..." She lifted a strawberry up, running a thumb over the seeds and the bright green leaves.

"You didn't know?" I asked, watching her marvel at the simple fruit. Not that I'd *known* I could make strawberries out of jam, only that I knew the Hunger could create seemingly out of its own whims.

Grandmother raised the berry to her lips, eyes widening as she took a bite and juice spilled onto her lip. She hummed and stared down at the fruit in her hand and then back at me. "I want you to tell me everything that's happened since you arrived in the north, Bryony."

2.
BRYONY

"I wish I'd seen it before," Grandmother murmured, staring up at the glass roof of the greenhouse. "Not that I don't believe you, dear," she said, patting the back of my hand.

One palace tour and my relationship with my grandmother had transformed practically full circle. At least enough so that when she called me 'dear,' it didn't sound like she was thinking of strangling me.

"I understand it's hard to believe," I said.

Grandmother held my arm for support, the long journey through the palace tiring her by the time we'd reached the greenhouse. Cosmo was still with us, and Thao and Wendell were outside chasing geese in their tiger forms for sport.

"I still don't really understand how it works," I admitted. "Was I the cause of the rainstorm that hit the north after the festival? Or did I affect the fields differently?"

"Did you choose the design?" Grandmother asked absently, pointing out the panels of stained glass that lit up the plants of the greenhouse floor with colored rays of light.

"Mm? No, those are new. I don't really notice when most things happen. I just throw the magic out so it doesn't force my Chosen," I said.

"*Force* them? Bryony, the role of the Chosen is one of honor."

"The only choice in the matter is *ours*, Grandmother! It isn't right! Especially not when our magic can make them aroused."

"You are still very prudish for all your accomplishments," Grandmother muttered, shaking her head.

Cosmo snorted, perched on the ledge by a large fern with his sketchbook in his lap, eyes glancing up as he grinned at me.

"You disagree, young man?" Grandmother snapped.

"Prudish isn't a word I'd use for my princess, Your Majesty," Cosmo said with a respectful dip of his head. "She simply puts great store in the comfort of others before herself."

I bounced nervously on my toes as Grandmother stared at Cosmo with her usual, fierce squint.

"Mm. I suppose." I beamed at Cosmo briefly before sobering as Grandmother turned to stare at me again. "I still have concerns. You can't simply storm over the council—"

"But, Grandmother—"

"You have no right to speak over me, and you know it," Grandmother said, stilling my tongue with an arch of her brow. "But I think I'd like to be present for a meeting regarding the taxes. We can't waive them indefinitely; you know this. However, the council may have reigned with too much freedom here in the north. I've found Lord Roderick an amenable and reasonable man in the past, but he is still only a man, and they tend to be creatures of ego."

I refrained from commenting, but I caught Cosmo's smile out of the corner of my eye.

"You haven't taken their little spy into bed, have you?"

"Ugh. No, Grandmother."

"Hmm. Yes, I suppose that's not something we have to worry about with you, is it? That's convenient. I was never as ruled by my Hunger as your sister and mother are, but I still found myself in a few vulnerable positions when it made demands against my better judgment," Grandmother said softly, sliding free of my offered arm and moving to take a seat at the tea-table under a large exotic palm.

I blinked, watching her slow movements and stiff posture as she sank down into the chair. "Vulnerable positions?" I asked, frowning.

"Mmm? Oh, never mind that. If you *do* decide to bed him, you make him *yours*. It's easy enough to win devotion from men," Grandmother said with a wave of her hand.

"Bryony excels at it," Cosmo murmured, grinning at me.

"Does she? Yes, that's good." My grandmother nodded absently, staring around the greenhouse. She looked tired, and a little frail, and I remembered how the days of traveling had left me aching. It must've been worse for her.

"Would you like me to call for tea, Grandmother?" I asked.

"Call for Lady Prudence. The company of the youth tires me," Grandmother said, adding bite to her tone and a glare in her eyes, but for once, I knew she was teasing. "Bring your tigers in. Are they docile in their forms?"

"Thao is more docile as a tiger than a man," I said, grinning and making Grandmother chuckle. I went to one of the open windows as Cosmo went into the hall to send the maid after Lady Pru.

"Oh, don't whistle, Bryony. How unladylike."

"You taught me to whistle, Grandmother."

"For the *dogs*, Bryony."

I kept my back turned to her as I smirked and watched Wendell and Thao loping toward us. I thought they were a little *like* dogs in their animal forms, although I knew that might easily change if it needed to. I went to the door and stood with it open, smiling as Thao and Wendell entered, leaning their vast shoulders heavily into me and marking up my skirt with dust and grass.

"I think the dowager queen wants to pet you," I whispered.

Thao huffed, but Wendell padded directly toward my grandmother, drawing out an uncharacteristic giggle as he dropped his massive head on her knee.

❦

"You look happy," Wendell said as we walked back toward my rooms together, Thao on his left and Cosmo on my right. Wendell leaned over, kissing my temple and making me pause to lean into the touch. "I'm glad to see that."

"It all went better than expected," I said, nodding.

"And we learned that Bryony can use her magic outside of just her climax," Cosmo added. "You know...Aric might be able to help you learn more control."

I tucked my hands into my skirt, but Cosmo caught one up

and raised it to his lips, grazing a kiss over the back of my knuckles.

"You haven't told him."

"He thinks I don't possess the Hunger," I said, nodding. "And he is...glad of it. He trusts me for that reason."

"You can be trusted *with* the Hunger, Bryony," Wendell said softly. "You've used it for weeks, and all for the betterment of the—"

"Of the palace, and the grounds. And yes, some of it I used for the people. We hope. I just..."

"His opinion shouldn't matter to you anyway. It's good to have a sorcerer, of course. But he's also a *rogue*. Couldn't we find someone to perform magic that won't insult you when it pleases them?" Thao rattled off.

A stone of discomfort lodged in my throat, and I looked down to the tile in the hallway to watch my steps, my cheeks flushing. Since when were our tiles edged with roses and doves?

Wendell shifted at my side, and Thao grunted and then hissed. "But if you respect him then..." Thao floundered then. "No, I can't lie. I think he's rude and obstinate, and if he had any sense at all, he'd be here with you."

I laughed, and the tension binding me up loosened as I smiled at Thao. "Thank you. I do respect him, and I respect that his priorities and his principals stand in the way of—"

We'd arrived at my suite, stepping inside past the stationed guard, and then stopping still at the picture before me.

"Mmm that's it, let me taste you."

Owen was sprawled out on the settee, his skin flushed and clothes rumpled, his body pressed hard to the back of the couch. His brow was furrowed, dewed with sweat, and I couldn't tell if he was trying to get away until his hand clenched on one of the cushions, trying to drag himself to the corner.

Between his spread thighs knelt my sister.

Owen whined as he stared at me, chest heaving and eyes glassy. "Bryony..."

Two steps in and I stopped again, my sister's hand reaching for the open fly of Owen's pants, where his cock was swollen and starting to rise toward her. Her other hand was gripping tight to his trembling thigh, holding him open for her.

"Camellia!"

Owen scooted away, gasping, and then stilled as Camellia's fingers tightened.

"Bryony. There you are. You left me a plaything," Camellia said, glancing over her shoulder at me. "He's so resistant, how do you manage him?"

"Get. Up," I growled, hands clenching. My chest burned and my thighs tensed, urging me to leap across the room and tear into my sister.

"No. Let me have him. You weren't paying any attention to him anyway," Camellia said with an absurd pout. "Look at that cock, Bry-Bry, it deserves a good riding."

"He is *my* Chosen," I hissed, shoulders rising. I wished I could transform into a tiger at that moment. I would've gladly clawed my sister's hand right off. I wanted to.

"You are such a—"

"*Let him go!*"

I didn't realize the Hunger had risen until I unleashed it with a wave of my arm as I tried to grab for Camellia. Instead, she was thrown backward and to the left, sliding across the carpet with an annoyed screech, her robes falling open over her chest. My arms were spread wide as if I could block the rest of my Chosen from her sight, and they moved with me toward Owen, who panted and swooned forward. Owen's face pressed into my skirts, his arms wrapping around my thighs, but it wasn't desire. He was shaking, and I made sure that I wasn't holding magic in my hands as I lowered them to his shoulders.

"Oh for goodness' sake, Bryony, it was only a little bit of sucking I wanted!" Camellia snarled, rising from the floor. "But well done, I suppose. I didn't really think you had the Hunger after all."

"Touching one of the Chosen is forbidden," I warned her, my hands holding Owen close as I refused to take my eyes off her in case she tried to use her magic again. She'd been forcing him. *My* Chosen. My *Owen*, who was too sweet to see what my sister was up to until it was too late.

"Pfffft, we are *sisters*," Camellia said as Cresswell and the guard from the door stepped into the room.

"Your Highness," Cresswell started, frowning as he glanced around the room.

"I want her out of my suite. Why did you admit her?" I snapped to the other man.

"If I can't have one you've claimed, at least let me have the dark guard. He is *exotic* isn't he?" Camellia purred up at Cresswell.

I couldn't *breathe*. My eyes darted down to Owen and then glanced in panic at my Chosen behind me, and finally to Cresswell, whose expression hardened in the face of my sister's hot gaze.

"Head of Royal Guard is exempt from the duty of the Chosen, Your Highness," Cresswell said, words low as he delivered a stiff bow to Camellia.

The panic ebbed and I sighed, my knees trembling and body aching. I wanted to fall to the couch cushions with Owen and wrap myself around him, but I refused to take lower ground than Camellia. There was a hollow ache gnawing my gut, the Hunger expressing its frustration with being used but not fed.

"Fine," Camellia sighed, hands on her narrow hips as she stared at the other guard for a long beat. "You'll do."

"Camellia, out!" I cried, ready to lunge for her until Owen leaned in and squeezed me.

"Yes, Your Highness," the guard breathed, with wide eyes on Camellia's breasts before shifting them nervously to Cresswell.

My Head Guard nodded once and then stepped aside out of the way of the door, arching a warning brow at the guard, who accepted Camellia's offered hand and used it to drag her from the room. My sister sent me a swift, bitter smile, and then Cresswell shut the door in her face.

Owen sighed and shuddered against me, and I crumpled at last, my giant loving man scooping me up and pulling me to his chest.

"I'm so sorry," he breathed in my ear. "You know I would never—"

"Owen, I know," I said, voice strangled, my shaking hands combing through his thick strands. "She had no right."

"I didn't realize—with you it's always been..."

I leaned back, taking Owen's face in my hands. He was pale now, brow still furrowed, but he lifted his chin to me eagerly, both of us breathing shakily into the kiss.

"I didn't want her," he said. "But I..."

"I know. I know, Owen." I pressed a long kiss to his temple. There was simply no question of Owen approaching Camellia in that way.

Cosmo sank down at our side, a hand on each of us, soothing at our backs, but Owen stiffened at the touch and Cosmo pulled his hand away as I shook my head at him.

"Cresswell, I don't want Princess Camellia anywhere near my or my Chosen's suites. I don't want her anywhere near them, period," I added in a hiss.

"I'll inform the rest of the guard," Cresswell murmured.

He shifted out of the corner of my eye and my hand flew out in his direction. "Not now! Not...just..." I swallowed hard, and Owen let me shift to face Cresswell. "I don't want Camellia to catch you in the halls. If she'll force my Chosen to respond, there's no reason why she wouldn't attempt with you too."

"I am..." Cresswell hesitated and glanced between me and Wendell. "I may be more resistant. I am a shifter."

Had I known that? I didn't think so and Cresswell looked nervous to admit it, so maybe he was unregistered like Wendell and apparently *many* of my citizens.

"We don't know for sure," I said, looking up at Wendell who crouched at my side.

"You can test it on me, if you need to," Wendell offered gently. "If Thao and I can ignore a push like that, it'll only be Cosmo and Owen who have to be careful while she's here."

I wanted to bare my teeth and growl at the idea that *any* of my Chosen needed to be cautious in my court. That Camellia would even *dare* to attempt such a thing made me want to race into the hall and tear at her hair.

"I don't think I can right now," I admitted softly, raising a hand for them to see the way it shook. Wendell's brows jumped and he caught my hand in his, drawing it to his lips to kiss the back of it firmly.

"The Hunger wears on you when you use it without—"

"Feeding it," I finished for him, nodding.

"What is your second nature?" Thao asked Cresswell, frowning.

"Oh...a—a grizzly bear," Cresswell said softly.

He was the odd man out in the room, watching us all with interest. And yet I understood in a private and separate part of my mind, that I didn't have room for at the moment, that I had felt almost as strongly opposed to my sister touching him as I did for any of the others. But as Cresswell had said, he was exempt as my Head Guard. I liked him, and I didn't want Camellia to waste him down to almost nothing like her other Chosen.

"Bryony," Owen whispered, hands cupping my waist. "I think...I think I'm just going to go make myself a bath."

I whipped back to him, taking in the slump of his shoulders and the downward tilt of his eyes. "Can I...?" I bit my lip and squared my shoulders, rising up from Owen's lap and then taking his hands firmly in mine. "We're going into the bedroom," I said to the others.

Owen was mine, and I was every bit as much his. If he needed anything right now, even simply a hand to hold, I intended on being there.

"We'll be here," Cosmo said with a nod.

"If we leave the room, we'll go as our second natures," Thao said. "I will bite her hand off before letting her touch me or Wendell."

I sighed and nodded, strangely relieved by the offer, and then I moved to guide Owen toward the bedroom.

"You don't need to stay," he said, eyes not meeting mine after we stepped inside and I shut the door behind him.

I hesitated in place, watching Owen's bunched back as he moved for the screen that hid the tub. "I'll go if you want."

"I..." Owen sighed and shook his head, turning and wearing an open tangle of confusion. "I don't want to be aroused right now, but I don't want you to leave either."

Good, instructions. I wanted those in the moment. "I can be...unarousing," I said, nodding.

Owen's lips twitched. "I'm not sure about that, Mistress." He said the word so fondly it made my chest ache.

I hurried to join him, running behind the screen to start the water in the tub, sliding between it and the wall to perch myself on the windowsill there, twitching the curtains to cover it so that no one would spy us from outside the castle.

"I can be chaste, at least," I said, testing the temperature of the water and ignoring the picture of Owen stripping out of his clothes out of the corner of my eyes.

"I came up here to change before going to find you," he said, nearly whispering. "I didn't think to refuse her when she knocked on the door."

"I continuously underestimate the depths Camellia will sink to, just to appease her own impulses," I growled at the water. "If I'd known, I would've warned you or prepared the guards."

"Which of these is yours?" Owen asked, and I looked to find him naked down to his toes and examining the array of bottles on a small shelf by the end of the tub.

"Mm, I like these two best," I said, leaning forward and tapping a small gold and glass bottle of violet oil as well as a small pot of an herbal blend the maid had recommended. I added them to the water under Owen's supervision, stirring my hand through it as the tub began to fill.

We stood in the quiet rush of water together, not touching, not speaking. There was a rising anger burning in my chest, and while the vast majority of it was for Camellia and her actions, there was a tiny morsel I didn't understand that was more painful and reserved for Owen.

He lowered himself into the water as I stared down at my hands gripping the ledge of the golden tub.

"I should've stopped it," Owen said.

I shook my head. "This is Camellia, Owen. You're not to blame."

"I knew she was being too flirtatious," Owen said. "I just assumed... You always worried over using your Hunger on me, Bryony, but it was nothing like that. Your magic asked for what I already wanted to give. When I tried to stand up and leave, and she grabbed my leg, it *hurt*."

I busied myself by grabbing a soft cloth and dipping it into the water, moving to kneel behind Owen so I could wash his back as he curled forward with his arms around his knees.

"It never felt good, but it also didn't stop my body from reacting. If you hadn't walked in when you did —"

"Owen, I'm so sorry," I breathed, leaning into the edge of the tub, feeling the press of the ledge digging uncomfortably into my chest.

"Bryony, why are you apologizing?"

"Why did you?" I cried, the cloth slapping into the water as Owen twisted to face me. "This wasn't your fault! I should've known to be more careful. She hurt you! She would've, could've done more if Grandmother hadn't let me leave when she did."

"Shhh," Owen murmured, dripping hands reaching for me. "Nothing *really* happened. I didn't let her kiss me."

"You shouldn't be comforting me," I moaned. "I'm comforting you!"

"You're shaking, Bryony," Owen said, kissing my forehead. "You'd better join me."

I should've refused and gone back to washing him, but I stood and wrestled myself out of my dress and slip and stockings, sliding eagerly into the water and leaning into Owen's side, my face tucked against his neck.

"I love you," Owen whispered.

"I love you too."

"No magic would change that I am yours."

I sighed and kissed Owen's pulse, nodding. The sting in my chest softened, and I wrapped my arms around his shoulders, the pair of us resting together in the water. It was warm there, especially with Owen next to me, and the weariness of expending magic I hadn't earned weighed heavily on my eyelids.

"Still...I will make Camellia pay for daring to try to steal you from me," I growled, eyes falling shut.

"I think Thao would say it's the gentleman who defends the lady's honor," Owen said. "But for myself, I wouldn't mind watching you show her her place."

"You *are* mine."

"Yours, always."

I tried to resist the urge, but I leaned up then for a firm, biting kiss of his lips, careful to stop before the Hunger might try to claim the moment. Owen didn't resist the kiss, but he didn't encourage it further either, and I wanted him to know he was more to me than his cock.

Maybe Cosmo was right and I needed to speak to Aric. Having the Hunger was all well and good if it secured me the crown, but I knew now it could be used as a weapon against my enemies. Against my own Chosen if wielded by my sister. I needed the upper hand.

And I wanted a measure of revenge.

3.
ARIC

I f the man driving the supply wagon down the rickety road at midnight had any knowledge of nature and its creatures, he would've paused his horses at the sound of the dove call cooing softly through the dark.

Luckily for me and my men, he was ignorant and it was cloudy, so he had no warning but the brief whinny of his horse as we surrounded them on the road.

"Slooow yourself, friend," I said, mainly to the horse, offering it the sugar cubes in my gloved palm, keeping my head down and tilted away from the eyes of the cursing man on the seat.

"Now, now, calm down ya fool," Scrapper cried, jumping on the bench, wobbling a little until the others steadied the wagon. Still, he held his knife steady at the driver's throat as the horses jerked and stomped and a wheel landed in a deep crack in the road, jamming to a sudden and certain stop.

"You'll hang for—" the driver started, but before he could lift up his baton from the floor of the bench, another of my men, Rutherford, had caught his wrists and twisted them behind his back. The driver grunted and huffed, body sagging with resignation, Scrapper careful not to prick him with his knife. "Do you know where this haul is meant to be going?"

I grunted. Of course, I fucking did.

"They'll track your sorry asses down like it's sport with their hounds and their horses," the driver spat.

My men just laughed, hauling boxes of cured meat and wheels of cheese and crates of fruit just near to ripe off the back of the wagon. One reached for a barrel of wine, and I *tsk*'d to draw them away.

"Leave it."

"But, Your—"

"I said leave it, didn't I? Let Sir Hubert piss himself with it," I growled.

Scrapper coughed through the wool surrounding his face. He was dressed in a bundle of layers borrowed from the others, our attempt at disguising his too easily recognized form, and he looked almost childlike to me in the moment. I didn't really know how old Scrapper *was* come to think of it, only that I didn't like to have him on robberies like this where he'd be the most easily caught member of our party.

"Not the horses," the driver said, as I unbuckled the bridles and dropped the reins. I ignored him, and he pressed forward, even against the threat of Scrapper's knife. "Please, if I go back to them with nothing, nothing for all you've taken—"

"You may find the horses about nearby somewhere," I muttered, grimacing down at my own hands. I hated this part. There was always collateral damage, wasn't there? "But you won't be chasing us to the nearest police tonight. Bring him down," I said with a nod to Scrapper.

"We've got it all," Rutherford called.

"Ride on," I answered, and our own court's horses and carts rode away with the haul of the wagon. All but the barrels of wine.

"You don't know what this will cost me," the driver hissed, eyes stinging and watering as Scrapper dragged him down from the bench.

"I do, Marcus of Eventree," I said. "And you'll be repaid. And now, I'm genuinely sorry for this, but it'll be better for you in the long run."

The driver gaped at me and then flinched at the last moment, as my fist snapped up, cracking into his nose. I grunted at the impact and the sharp bolt of pain in my hand as cartilage crunched, and the driver bellowed, stumbling back into Scrapper. I struck once more against his ribs, accepting the punishment of pain in my own body as meager payment for my actions. Scrapper snapped the hilt of his dagger against the other man's temple, and I caught him as he sagged, unconscious.

"Good work," I huffed, dragging the man over to a nearby tree.

Scrapper hummed thoughtfully and I understood his hesitance. The food we'd taken from Sir Hubert would feed many starving bellies around the north, but it might make others' lives worse. This driver, perhaps Sir Hubert's staff. It was a constant balancing act, and too often I felt as though I was on the losing side of the scales. I bound the man loosely to the tree and turned back to the sound of hooves clapping away, Scrapper swatting the horses on their rears.

"They'll turn back to him," Scrapper said.

"It's just to stall," I said with a shrug. "Come on, before any other travelers appear."

I lifted myself into my saddle, keeping an eye on Scrapper as he struggled to do the same, breathless as he settled into his seat. Riding hurt him, bent his joints in uncomfortable directions and left him stiff and aching for too long, but he'd only come tonight on his own insistence.

"There'll be a hot meal back at the bar, and a bed if you want it," I said. The Wing and Rook was a serviceable inn if it had to be. Generally, it was more of a meeting place, occasionally a hideout.

"Are you sure it was a worthy trade?" Scrapper asked. "Distracting the city guards with that rogue of Emory's, just for a little time to catch a wagon of food?"

I frowned, thinking of the man I'd snagged at the festival, the poisoned pin. He'd never admitted to being one of Emory's men, but he sure as hell wasn't mine. The best we'd learned was that he was already wanted in Rumsbrooke for murder in a bar fight. Perhaps Emory had traded the man's cooperation for his own silence, but we had no confession or proof of it.

"He was just another mouth to feed. Better to throw the officials a bone and keep them off our own backs," I said.

We passed the driver's horses on the road, milling nearby, munching away at grass to their hearts' content. I frowned, wondering if they'd move on, or if someone else might come along and steal them before the driver woke up. I reached into my pocket, fingers around a glossy stone I'd found brimming with magic in the river on the way back to Rumsbrooke the night of the festival after the storm. I whispered a charm for safekeeping onto its surface, still marveling that it had the power to hold it at all, and then tossed it to the horses. It ought to be enough to hold them for the night.

"Still think you should've slit his throat for daring to harm Her Loveliness," Scrapper muttered.

"Believe me, I considered it," I answered back darkly. Too many times to count. Perhaps *that* was why I'd passed him onto the city. I was afraid of what I wanted to do to the bastard, all in Bryony's name.

◈

I WASN'T in the habit of considering myself superior for my use of magic, like most magicians. It was a survival skill, not a bragging right, and I was lucky enough to have been able to scrape together my knowledge from a lifetime's worth of study and spying and stealing notes from noble mages.

Still, it seemed foolish for Emory to pride himself on having a thieves' court free of magic.

It also made it dangerously easy to slip past his brutes at the front door of The Yawning Pig. I sported a soft glamour, a recent one I'd devised just in case any of Emory's men were familiar with my old disguises. I was younger looking, with an overly round face and a minor case of boils decorating a patchy blond beard on my jaw. Just plain enough in appearance for me to be ignored by the women Emory kept on hand, and not notable enough to be stared at either.

I was only here for a little light surveillance. It was better to keep the occasional eye on Emory first hand than to trust the rumors that swam upstream to me, even when they came from the likes of Griffin or Scrapper. And I wanted to know if my hunch regarding Bryony's would-be murderer was right or not. If it was, it made our places in the game much clearer.

As King of Thieves, I had to expect threats to my crown. I was nearing fifty. That was bound to make me look vulnerable to a young idiot like Emory. I'd been considering his rivalry as a potential replacement to my own throne. But if he was responsible for any harm to the princess, even unsuccessfully so, that put us squarely as enemies.

I stepped into the Yawning Pig, pausing briefly in the doorway. The Wing and Rook welcomed its share of debauchery. Always from the willing, everyone with one eye on their company's pocket and one hand on their own. We were not saints, my court and I. No one deserved to be stolen from more than a careless thief.

But we didn't *prey* on one another the way they did at the Yawning Pig. I ducked out of the way of two men grappling at one another's throats, a screaming woman seated on a table barely restraining her victorious grin between her cries for someone to break the pair up. Meanwhile, another woman—young, like Bryony—was bent over a table, her cheek scratching the surface as she stared blankly ahead of her as a man rutted against her ass.

I didn't like to deal in flesh, but the few girls who passed through the Wing and Rook in a professional capacity took on their work for the joy of the act until they bored of it or fell in love. Emory seemed to prefer his whores cunning or mentally absent.

I'd nearly made it to the bar where the best gossip would be exchanged between the stalwarts who'd claimed their front row seats at the beginning of the night, when I stopped and made an impulsive dodge to the right, sliding into a booth where a woman was moaning robotically as she rode a man who stared at me in consideration for a moment—was I a rival for the woman, or an observer—before going back to fixing his gaze to her bouncing tits.

In the booth just behind me was the so-called king himself, Emory, not alone but with Bryony's new steward, the bastard Farraque son. The one who'd tried to accuse me at the festival. Interesting. Openly suspicious. Possibly outright conspiracy.

"Yes, well, I never expected the old bastard to show up to the party," Emory grunted, seated just on the other side of the wooden bench as me.

The man across the table from me pulled up the whore's

skirt, glancing at me briefly and letting his eyebrows bounce. Ah, I was meant to be grateful for him revealing her pocked and swat-reddened ass. I nodded to him and pretended to be riveted as I listened to the conversation.

"Her head guard is now looking at me like I'm part of an assassination plot, Em." Farraque's voice was considerably softer, lower. Emory was a bit of a loudmouth as if he always meant for the entire room to hear him speak, even when it was something better to be whispered, but Farraque made me strain to listen. I risked a little bit of magic, fueled by another pebble, to make him out more clearly.

"This would all be a lot less of a bother if you'd started fucking her by now," Emory huffed.

Either Farraque didn't answer or he was simply too quiet, and I clamped down on the bench as I mulled over the words.

"If it were me—"

"I know," Farraque said, and I couldn't tell if that was a note of scoffing or laughter.

"I'd have her screaming and tearing her sheets begging for more," Emory boasted.

I was caught somewhere between wanting to chuckle and getting up off this bench to go and pummel Emory into a pulp. Maybe Farraque too.

So Bryony had a spy in her midst. From *Emory's* court?

"You know while you're here hiding from the other princess bitch, yours is getting ready to host the council? Ah, you didn't. See what cowardice gets you, Danny Boy? Lord Roderick will have plenty to say if you aren't at least *somewhat* attached to her skirts when he arrives tomorrow."

"Fuck."

I grinned, and the man across the table from me grunted, his head falling back. With his eyes off her, the woman's focus drifted until she looked over her shoulder at me and winked.

"You next, love?"

"Just watching," I said, and she shrugged and went back to her work.

"I'll leave first thing in the morning," Farraque said in his rasp.

"Why'd you agree to take the position if you're so reluctant to get the work done?"

"I'm not *reluctant*. You know what the queen's line is supposed to be like. I assumed she'd be the same."

"All women are the same."

I rolled my eyes at that statement and wished Bry—Charlotte—*any* woman for that matter, was with me to hear that idiocy.

"Not this one," Farraque muttered.

"Perhaps you're too much of a gentleman after all, Danny. Throw the girl down to the floor, put your cock in her and—"

"And then get it chopped off by the royal guard? No, thank you, Emory. She's not one of your whores."

"All women are the same," Emory growled.

My hands were ready to burst with flames, itching to grab my blade, to slit Emory's throat and then make quick work of Farraque before he could scurry away. Bryony was smart enough to see through as blatant a carrot dangling in front of her face as Farraque must've been, but that didn't mean he wouldn't get impatient.

Anger was interrupted by the sudden dig of the table into my stomach as the man across from me finally snapped, pushing the whore down and then rutting merrily on top of her with great groans and grunts. I grimaced, and the woman winced, forcing out enthusiastic squeals until he finally ceased.

"Oh, good work, Jimmy," she said, panting. "Very good work."

He stumbled away, barely holding his pants closed, and she sighed.

"Sure you don't want a turn? I'm still wet," she asked, blinking upside down at me.

"No, thank you," I said, winking back at her, jostling the table forward enough to slip out.

"Quit worrying about what Roderick has me doing and worry more about the fact that they caught that man you hired," Farraque grumbled.

"Pft. Martin will be easy, old piece of shit. Anyway, the rules of succession are a great deal simpler in our kingdom. I'll cut his crown off soon enough," Emory growled.

I punched my hands into my pockets and marched for the door. I'd heard enough for one night. Emory could come for my crown if he liked. He had the right. Just as when he did, I would have the right to slit his nasty little throat.

4.
BRYONY

"**W**here have you *been*?" I hissed, hands on my hips. Daniel Farraque sat on his horse above me, windswept with bright cheeks, looking nicely like a hero from one of my novels. "I was in Rumsbrooke."

"On whose orders?"

"Your Highness, I apologize if I was absent when you needed me," Daniel murmured with a bow of his head before sliding out of his saddle.

I scoffed and shook my head. "I haven't *needed* you, and you can stop saying it like that," I said, stepping out of the way before Daniel got it in his head to lunge for me again. "Although if you're in the mood to be needed, my sister, Her Highness, has claimed three of the guards already. I'm not certain if she plans on keeping them, but I'm sure she'd be happy to add you to their number."

I watched with a wrathful kind of glee as Daniel's stare shifted nervously away from mine. It'd been a week since Grandmother and Camellia had stood on the palace steps and greeted me, and while I was growing comfortable with Grandmother's company—especially since she'd started to assist me and Wendell in our slough through the legislations we wanted to remedy—Camellia had made it her mission on the visit to be cumbersome.

When she wasn't seducing the single male staff, she was making erratic and elaborate requests of the kitchen. Two days ago she'd demanded a picnic which very quickly became an orgy, and she'd nearly dragged a married man into the mess of limbs by sheer demand of her magic.

I crossed my arms and stared at Daniel. "I knew it. You *are* hiding from her. I assume it's because she's not your *assigned* princess?"

"She nearly killed an old schoolmate of mine," Daniel said, eyes flashing.

We weren't alone in the stable. I'd come out so that Owen might get to enjoy a little time outdoors again, and he glanced up from where he was crouched by the door, visiting with a few foxes who'd shown up not long before Daniel.

"One of her first Chosen. He was a favorite of hers, so much so that she fucked him nearly to death. Wouldn't let him eat unless it was from her cunt," Daniel snapped, and then his eyes widened and his face paled, body bowing and staying bent. "Forgive me, Your Highness."

I looked to Owen, hands clenching in my skirt, a painful mix of remembering Camellia's hands on him, and my own accidental overuse of the Hunger until his back was red and sore from the sun.

"I see. Oh, just stand, Farraque," I huffed.

He swallowed hard and kept his eyes down as he stood. He was an imposing figure, but he was very careful with himself usually, often vanishing into the background when he wasn't trying to intentionally catch my attention.

"Where is he now?" I asked.

"At home near Highbury. When he grew too ill to perform, she dismissed him. He won't so much as look a woman in the eye now," Daniel added reluctantly.

I released a slow, silent breath while Daniel's eyes were down. "Remain near Cresswell, Thao, or Wendell, and either she'll leave you alone or they will intervene. We've had our own... conflicts with Camellia's appetites while you were away," I said. "But the council are coming today—"

"It's why I returned. And I apologize for neglecting my duties this week."

"Yes, all right, fine." I turned my back to him and moved to Owen, kneeling down and smiling as he nudged the foxes in my direction. They didn't clamor for my attention the way they did with him, but one let me scratch at its chin tolerantly for a few minutes.

"What is the council coming for?" Daniel was still hovering out of the corner of my eye.

"To discuss the allocation of the upcoming quarter's taxes," I said. "And to discuss the land management of potential orchards."

"Do they know about the orchards?"

"Not yet."

"Don't tell them. Their only jurisdiction lies in what the queen's line brings to them to manage."

I looked up just in time to see him turn on his heel and leave the stables in a rush. "I can never tell if he's being helpful or trying to curry favor," I said, landing heavily on the ground and scaring one of the foxes back into Owen's lap, where it stretched up, digging at Owen's pocket which was stuffed full of sugar cubes and grapes.

"Might be both," Owen said. "I believe the story about his friend though."

"So do I. Camellia did send a Chosen home who grew sick. I didn't realize *why* at the time," I said.

Owen pulled his treats from his pocket, handing them to me before rising and dusting himself off. "I'm going to go check his horse since he was in such a rush to leave. Oh don't beg," he said to one of the barking foxes. "She's sweeter than I am, and I know for a fact that she gives good scritches."

I grinned at Owen's wink in my direction as the foxes heaped back onto my lap, little paws begging at my cupped hands. He'd recovered quickly from the moment with Camellia, at least as far as he was willing to share with me. He and Cosmo had stayed close to me for the week until today when Cosmo had begged to take Cresswell and the others so he could go and continue his work on a sculpture I wasn't allowed to see yet.

"Are you nervous?" Owen called to me as I tried to dole treats out fairly and not too quickly, stealing pets when I could.

"Not nervous exactly, but curious. I think Grandmother is on my side, but she will be more diplomatic and willing to negotiate with them than I am."

"Will you follow her lead?"

"I...I think I must? She could still be queen if she hadn't been willing to step aside for my mother. She still *rules* in many ways. I will not be the highest authority in the room, even if she says she will let me direct the discussion."

"He takes good care of you, I can say that much for him," Owen said to Daniel's horse, and I smiled and leaned against the wall behind me, watching him tend the horse, who answered back in that way animals seemed to do around Owen. "Ah, if you say so. I still think he's a snake."

Owen laughed and jumped out of the way of the horse's stomping foot. "All right, all right. I'll trust your judgment then."

"Farraque has a fan in his horse?"

"Very loyal," Owen said, patting the beast's flank. "And not partial to snakes, I think."

"Speaking of, I should probably go get dressed for this meeting full of them," I said with a sigh, tossing the remaining sugar cubes in the air and watching the foxes scurry to catch them before dashing off into the nearby meadow.

⚜

"To be frank, princess, you seem to be misunderstanding the basics of covering the essential needs," Lord Roderick mused, running a finger down the line of our proposed tax allocation.

"I think we just have a different understanding of essential," I answered, staring down at their own offered list of demands. "Why should the people's money go to Sir Edge's estate upkeep?"

"Sir Edge employs over one-third of the farmers in the northern districts, Your Highness," Sir Speares said with a chuckling scoff shared with Lord Roderick.

"Then I assume his profits for the harvest will be rich and he'll be able to afford the repairs himself."

Jonathon Roderick cleared his throat, sitting up higher in his seat and smirking at me. "Princess, you're misinterpreting the...nature of the council's role and our position over the people."

"Gentleman, I doubt very much that many have taken the time to do any interpretation as to your roles and positions, and if they had, the north and much of the kingdom south of here might be in considerably better condition."

"She is impertinent, isn't she, Your Majesty?" Lord Roderick asked, chuckling to my grandmother at my side, his teeth bared in a tight smile.

I tensed in my seat, ready to dive back into the argument, heat spiking in my cheeks at being spoken over, but my grandmother's hand grazed against my skirt under the table.

"Impertinent, Roderick? Be wiser with your tongue. Bryony is ambitious in her goals, but she is also your future queen," my grandmother said, and her severity seemed to have the same effect on the older man as it did on me. "And she's not wrong about that budget. I went over it myself."

None of the men across from us at the long table seemed prepared to argue with my grandmother. At least not outrightly.

"Of course, if there is a good harvest, there would be no need for Sir Edge to take assistance. But farming is a delicate business and—"

"It might be left to the farmers," I said, gaining Lord Roderick's flashing glare before he remembered to correct himself.

Wendell sat quietly to my left, silent through the discussion, occasionally nudging me long enough to catch my attention and direct it towards heads bowed and whispering. He was largely responsible for the budget we had arranged, with my grandmother's help and some from Rebecca Sanders, who sat to the left of him. It was a thorough and careful balance of what the people might be expected to spare, with the absolute civic necessities that needed attention for the winter. Grandmother had arranged a refilling of the northern royal coffers so that we could continue to keep the palace running outside of the people's pockets, but it left the local nobility nearly cut off from financial aid.

"This cannot be a permanent state," Lord Roderick said firmly.

"Kimmery cannot flourish if its citizens are kept pinned beneath a boot of poverty," I snapped back. "What taxes can be taken from empty pockets?"

"Homes, property, possessions, bodies into labor camps and the army," Wendell answered softly.

"It stops now," I said, my eyes fixing from one man to the next.

They weren't *all* glaring back at me. Some looked genuinely shamed, and early in the introductions, I'd heard a man admit that he hadn't bothered coming to a council meeting in over a decade. There was a measure of ignorance to blame in the way things had gone. That and the fact that there hadn't been a will as strong as Lord Roderick's at the table in what I suspected was a very long time.

"Did you call this meeting to negotiate reasonably or to stomp your foot and make demands?" Lord Roderick said, drawing out a few chuckles, several of which sounded nervous.

"This is your second warning, Lord Roderick," my grandmother said lowly. "There won't be a third."

"Your Majesty," he started.

"Don't *cajole* me. Your position, *all* of your positions, are granted to you by the crown so that you might lessen our burden. They were not given to you as reward, but as responsibility," Grandmother said.

"Your nobility are your people too, just remember that in the next quarter when you look at your taxes. There is a correct flow to the kingdom's wealth, and you are perverting it," Roderick said coldly. "You will see the trouble it causes before the winter is up. The people must be kept in their place, just as we must."

"People deserve to eat, to keep their homes. I am not offering them yours," I said.

All down the length of the table, men shuddered and looked aghast. Was that really what they were afraid of? Or was that just some of Roderick's poison?

"So be it, Your Highness," Roderick growled.

❧

"I have concerns, Bryony," Grandmother said, watching the last carriage take its leave down the long road that led to the palace.

"About the decisions made today?" I asked, taking some of her weight as we turned on the steps and moved back inside.

"About their repercussions. There's some truth to Roderick's threats. A network of angered nobility will be a powerful tool against you, especially if all you win is a beaten-down collection of citizens."

I thought of the energy of the festival, of the creativity of the vendors, the wealth of generosity of the cooks, and the wild abandon of the dancing.

"They've been mistreated and there's a lot of work to be done, but I think we've underestimated the common people for too long," I said.

Grandmother hummed. "Rebellion can come from many directions."

I sucked on my own teeth in thought as Grandmother and I made a slow trek for the stairs so I could escort her back to her room. Cresswell was guarding my Chosen in my chamber after dinner, but Camellia had stayed suitably entertained with the collection of men she'd gathered from the staff.

I kept thinking of Daniel's story of his friend, of what I'd seen of the Chosen I'd grown up around and how it compared to my own. I couldn't remember a conversation I'd ever held with a Chosen. They were usually either...occupied, or they seemed simply to be waiting to be used.

"Is it...is it right for us to take Chosen?" I asked.

Grandmother's steps faltered, and she huffed as I held her steady. "Bryony, I am not unimpressed with what you've accomplished, but there are *limits*. You may...may function as you do, but I can assure you that if you have a daughter and she has the Hunger prop—as the rest of us do, she will not be *courting* men patiently as you have done."

"They courted me patiently. And no, I understand the necessity of the Choosing. I am *glad* I had mine. I just wish it were less...mandatory? I...heard a rumor about one of Camellia's Chosen growing..."

"We have all been too fervent with our Chosen a time or two," Grandmother said, voice and body equally stiff before slowly relaxing. "It wasn't always mandatory. That was my mother's doing. The herd of volunteers was thinning, and she was... especially voracious." Grandmother sighed, and her hand patted mine firmly. "You may have a point, but I think I prefer your focus on reforming the nobles rather than the queen's line."

She softened the correction with an amused chuckle, and I sighed and nodded.

"I suppose that means I will have to take her with me when I go back," Grandmother mused with a wicked smile. "And here I thought I might leave her behind."

"I will lend you an extra carriage," I said quickly, and Grandmother chortled.

5.
BRYONY

I tiptoed out of my suite, pausing in the dark hallway as I found Cresswell straightening against the wall across from my door.

"What are you doing out here?" we whispered at the same time.

"Cresswell, when was the last time you were off your shift?" I asked.

He cleared his throat and rolled his shoulders. "I catch breaks here and there."

I wracked my brain, eyeing him from the side as I glanced down the hall. When was the last time I'd been attended by a guard that wasn't Cresswell? Since before the incident with Camellia and Owen at least.

"You're no use to me if you drop from exhaustion," I said softly.

"They leave tomorrow. I have an afternoon shift arranged. What are you doing out of bed?"

I opened my mouth to reprimand him for asking, and then shook my head and sighed instead. He was my guard. Often he seemed to be the only guard who was really interested in protecting me and my Chosen, rather than just standing at the door.

"I'm going to see my sister."

"Is that wise?"

"Likely not, but I'd rather do it on my own than with the others. She'll be less likely to goad me, and I have some words left to say to her."

Cresswell's jaw clenched, a visible tick of muscle lit up by a lamp farther down the hall. "Lock the door behind you. I'm coming with you to stand outside the door."

I glanced behind me at the closed door and tipped my head. "Is there... Am I meant to have a key?"

Cresswell huffed, and then there was a metallic jingle from his pocket as he stepped forward and reached around me to lock the door. He smelled...soft was the only word I could think of to describe it, and it wasn't what I expected from my imposing guard. I wanted to lean in, but thankfully Cresswell stepped back before I made use of the impulse. His hand caught my wrist and pressed the key to my palm before releasing me and nodding in the direction of Camellia's rooms.

I'd arranged her in another wing of the palace, a room that looked down the mountain to the lights of Rumsbrooke. It was one of the rooms that'd been uninhabitable when we arrived, and although I'd never made any direct attempt to repair it or restore the furniture, the magic of the Hunger had seeped into every brick and rug and trinket of the palace so that by the time Camellia and Grandmother arrived, any room was as luxurious as they could hope for.

The door to the suite hung open by a few inches, and there was no guard stationed outside, although Cresswell didn't look surprised by that. Our steps slowed as we approached, and I waited for the usual wet slaps and strained moans that floated around Camellia, but the room was silent.

Cresswell's arm slid out in front of me as I made to step inside, and he raised a finger to his lips before moving ahead, pressing gently on the door and dipping his head inside. He leaned back a moment later and stepped back to the wall facing the door.

"Asleep," he said, shrugging.

Huh, I supposed not even Camellia could keep up her orgiastic habits *all* night and day. Still, it felt especially strange to step into the room and see the tableau before me. Men strewn about haphazardly like clothes dropped carelessly across furniture and floor. Most were still at least partially dressed, pants shoved down to their knees and shirts torn open. One had his ass exposed as he lay face down across the couch. Sam, the most familiar to me of all Camellia's Chosen, lay crookedly in a window frame like an abandoned doll, head pressed to the glass panes.

The air in the room was stale and pungent, and there was a kind of friction that must've been magic, although the edges felt comparatively frayed to the sparkling and fluid sensation I was familiar with.

Sam's head rolled, empty eyes finding me by the door, and I nearly screamed in my surprise, my own hand rising to stifle the sound that never rose. He blinked at me and then turned back to staring out the window. He was naked head to toe, and I could see the prominence of his bones in his body, the way his ribs caught shadows and moonlight, a cage across his chest. He was wasting away, just as Daniel's friend had done, and no one would stop Camellia from running him ragged for her own...

It could not be pleasure. There was no resemblance.

I expected to find Camellia piled in with her new collection of men, but in fact she was alone in the bed. There was only one man, the guard she'd grabbed from outside my door, lying on a bench at the foot of her bed, entirely naked with his arm over his face. He looked almost like a dog resting at his owner's feet, waiting for the first stirrings of morning and the rise of his mistress.

Camellia lay curled around a large pillow, her own strength stark by comparison to Sam's growing fragility. The Hunger must've sustained us in some way it couldn't share with our Chosen because I'd never seen Camellia feasting on anything but men. Her hair was kept shorter than mine, trimmed to her shoulders, and it fanned sweetly over her cheek.

We'd always been sisters, but perhaps never friends. We had the same lessons, but I'd loved learning and Camellia had been frustrated to always be behind me in accomplishments. Had I made attempts to reassure her? To lift her up? I thought so, but at some point my sister's bitterness had become wearying and I'd withdrawn. I sat down on the edge of the bed at her side, watching her steady breath stall, her muscles tensing.

"Fuck off," she muttered without opening her eyes.

"No."

I braced myself, watching the way her body seemed to coil, a predator ready to strike, but then it only loosened languidly, Camellia's lips curling as she stretched and rolled to her back. I felt the stirring, the first fresh taste of magic, and I shook my head.

"Stop. This is our conversation, not theirs. You won't starve for lacking a cock for a few minutes," I said, not making a great effort to keep quiet. By the state of the men in the rooms, I didn't think any would wake until Camellia forced them to.

"But—"

"Camellia, I am going to take the crown one day. I will be queen, and my word will be law in Kimmery."

Camellia's eyes narrowed to slits, lips pressing into a flat line, arms tensing. I saw the moment the discomfort hit her, the urge to cover herself as she lay bare on the bed, glaring up at me.

"Mother is lenient. I will *not* be, and you will have to adapt and become something other than the grasping, selfish creature you are now because I won't let you abuse men, the Hunger, or Kimmery in any way. But if you *ever* attempt to force one of my Chosen again, I won't wait for the crown, Camellia. I don't care what it costs me, I will cut you off from the Hunger—"

"You can't—"

"You don't know what I can do," I said coldly, watching her brow twitch in confusion. "You are *transparent* now, and I will never underestimate you again. I will never trust you. I will always be prepared to pin you down and steal back from you everything you've stolen for yourself."

"Sister," Camellia hissed, sitting up and flicking the sheet over her lap. She forced her eyes to widen in possibly the worst attempt at innocence. "We are *both* of us a long way from a crown. Anything could happen."

A threat for a threat. That was fair.

"Sister," I echoed sweetly. "I know you think that because you mount men like a cat in heat, and that you can suck them dry until they are husks, that you are very powerful. Perhaps you are. But we come from the same line, Camellia," I said, rising. "And we both know I am smarter than you."

Camellia snarled at last, her calm snapping. "You think your

Chosen are so special? They're just cock, Bryony, and everyone knows they prefer fucking each other to coddling you in your prudish bed."

I snorted, and Camellia frowned. So someone was keeping track of Thao and Wendell and reporting back to Camellia? Or there were rumors loose about my Chosen in general. That was fine, I was happy to be underestimated. It would make Camellia easier to manage later.

The man at the foot of the bed was staring up at me now, although I couldn't read his expression upside down. It wasn't hollow like Sam's at least, more wide-eyed probably from hearing the two princesses slashing at one another.

"Men are meant to be used by us," Camellia said, chin lifted. "If they're too weak to serve us, then they can be tossed out like useless trash. You're not noble for treating them like favored pets, you're weak. Your Hunger is weak, just like Grandmother always said it would be. We'll see who wears the crown in the end."

That stung a little, even if it was further proof that Camellia wasn't paying attention this week.

"We will," I said nodding, ready to retreat.

"Speaking of trash, Sam's useless. I'm not bringing him back to the south with me. Perhaps he might be of some use instructing your Chosen," Camellia said, voice steely and bright at the same time.

My back was to her, but I could see her false smile in the mirror and I kept my expression flat. Leave Sam here? The last thing I needed was another man left about the castle in some poor attempt to spy on me, and yet...

I shrugged. "Do what you like with him, he's yours. But don't think I'll take up your cast-offs," I said glancing over my shoulder.

Sam might be left behind to serve Camellia in a new way, but that seemed like a mercy he ought to be granted. I wouldn't touch him, and maybe he'd find some peace away from my sister.

She grinned at me, and I was struck by a sudden pang of sadness as I turned away from her and left the room. I'd read stories of sisterly love, seen maids growing up together in court, seen mothers doting on daughters in visiting dignitaries and nobles. Camellia and I were enemies now, my mother was kind but in an absent fashion, and I'd spent my life till now intimidated by my grandmother.

You have your Chosen, I thought, glancing toward the window to find Sam sitting up and frowning at me, his eyes wide and pale. He'd overheard us then. I nodded once to him, and he remained frozen until I left the room.

Cresswell was a shockingly welcome sight as I stepped into the hall, his body straightening, eyes searching my face. And then the relief of him, the knowledge that he was safety and support all in one package, made my chest sting and clench.

My bottom lip trembled and I swung away, all but running down the hall, comforted by the sound of his footsteps close behind me.

Was this right? Should I have approached her differently? Will there ever be peace between us?

My heart pounded an irregular rhythm as the hall started to blur, my breaths coming quick and short. I paused in a crossway, forgetting what direction I was meant to turn, and the sob came up, ragged and choked to silence.

"Your—" Cresswell faltered, a heavy hand resting on my shoulder. "Bryony?"

He turned me toward him, and I stepped into his chest, hiding my face against his uniform. I refused to make a sound, as if that might disguise the reason for my trembling shoulders and why my fingers dug into the dense wool of his jacket, locking around belts and buckles. His hands landed tremulously on my shoulders, weighing the way I heaved with breath, before smoothing and clasping me tightly against him.

There was a trapped scream shredding my throat, burning for being locked up, and my bones felt as though they were about to break for how tightly my muscles gripped them.

Cresswell scooped me up from the floor, cradling me into his chest and turning us around a corner where the lamps warmed the cool white plaster of the walls. I stayed like that, hiding from myself and the rest of the palace, folded up as small as I could be, until we reached my door, Cresswell jostling me slightly so he could unlock it.

I hadn't realized there was a familiar scent to my rooms until we stepped inside and a delicate floral mixed with Owen and Cosmo's earthier sweetness wrapped around me, my body sagging limply.

My Chosen had filled the empty space I'd left when I'd snuck away, but Wendell stirred as Cresswell stepped into the room.

"Oh! Bryony?"

"Not harmed, but hurting, I think," Cresswell said softly, carrying me to the bed as the others woke. "She went to speak to her sister."

"Royal siblings are poisonous to one another," Thao grumbled.

"Come here, Mistress," Owen said in a sleepy mumble.

Cresswell set me down at the edge of the bed and before I even had a chance to try and move, my men were lifting me up, enfolding me at the heart of the group. Cosmo moved and let Owen take his place.

I hadn't properly cried while held by Cresswell, and now I found myself both too weary and too comforted to manage the act. Wendell brushed his hands over my cheeks as Owen nestled me into the crook of his shoulder, making room for Cosmo to cuddle up on his other side so he could rest a hand just below my ribcage.

"I'll be in the next room, Your Highness," Cresswell said softly.

There was a moment where I thought I might ask or even order him to stay, but it passed quickly as Thao leaned into Wendell's back, his hand cupping my jaw as his lover—*our* lover —kissed my forehead.

"I'm fine, really," I murmured, and Owen hummed almost as if in agreement.

"We'll see the back of them in the morning," Cosmo said.

I WATCHED Camellia's rocking carriage with a mix of anger and amusement, unsure if she thought she was mocking me or simply couldn't help herself.

"I'm grateful," my grandmother said, watching it bounce down the drive, away from the palace.

We stood together at the bottom of the stairs as they loaded my grandmother's things onto the top of the royal carriage. Some of last night's heartbreak lingered in my chest and throat, and I wondered what my grandmother would do if I wrapped her up in one of those tight hugs I'd learned from Owen.

"You could...you could stay a little longer," I said softly.

There was no change for a moment as I gazed up at her, studying the fine lines of her face and soft shades of gray through her hair.

"Mmm, I may return. You know...you know you won't be here forever," Grandmother said, arching an eyebrow. "If you really mean to take the crown, that is."

"I think I might like to keep the old calendar and return south in the spring," I said. I'd been giving it some thought, and if the Hunger could bring life to the land, it made sense that the queen would need to share her time between the regions.

"The spring?" Grandmother's eyebrows rose. "It's not that you can't be spared but...there's some truth to Lord Roderick's words, Bryony. The nobility *are* your people too. You'll have to win their favor before the end."

I nodded, even if soothing some overstuffed egos was the last thing I wanted to worry about.

Cool fingertips touched my chin, and my grandmother drew my gaze back to hers. "You're doing well, and I'm proud to see it," she said, leaning in and pressing her lips to my forehead and whispering, "Even if my lessons did go in one ear and out the other. Perhaps a condemnation of my lessons more than your listening."

I laughed, and Grandmother pulled away, taking the hand of a groomsman who helped her up into the carriage. I stepped back out of the way, catching her eye and nodding as they closed the door.

Cosmo's hand was there waiting for mine as I returned to the stairs. "You make her seem softer," Cosmo said. "And you've become much stronger."

Considering I'd been a useless tragic heap in his arms last night, I thought that was a little overgenerous, but I squeezed his hand in thanks and let him lead me back up the steps to where the others waited.

We were stepping inside when Daniel appeared on the grand stairs, dragging a pale and stumbling Sam at his side.

"Your sister forgot something," Daniel called, face red, looking as though he meant to carry Sam out to the road to catch up with Camellia's carriage.

"That's enough, Mr. Farraque," I said, slipping free from the comfort of my Chosen's company to stand before the two men on the stairs. "Sam is...is a guest here in the palace. Unless you'd prefer we get you a carriage back to your family," I offered, meeting Sam's eyes.

They were an almost milky shade of green, the color sharper for the red rings that surrounded them. He'd been sleepless last night, and it showed in dark circles above the hollow of his cheeks. His hair was a downy white-blond that reminded me of the milkweed by the lake. I could almost picture how he'd been years ago when he'd first joined my sister's Chosen, tall and broad, always wearing a grin and always whispering in Camellia's ear, making her giggle. He'd been almost ten years older than Camellia, but grandmother had said that ensured he had enough experience to please her. He'd aged greatly in the past year and had begun to fade like the words on a piece of parchment left out in the sun.

It occurred to me then that Camellia's cruelty hadn't been a constant state but something that'd grown the longer she'd used the Hunger.

He cleared his throat with a cracked note of disuse and shook his head. "I have no family."

"Then a guest," I said with a nod.

"You're taking on another spy? Isn't one in the palace enough?" Thao balked at my back.

Daniel barely twitched at the implication, but he looked equally troubled by Sam's introduction. I shot Thao a warning look, and he answered with a fold of his arms and a cock of his eyebrow.

"I seriously doubt we are only at two," I said softly, and Thao's lips twitched.

Sam moved down the steps with a perilously shaky gait. He was thin, dressed in pants that barely fit him, and a loose, stained shirt that hung open to his navel.

"I am prepared to serve you in any of your needs, Your Highness," Sam murmured.

I huffed and rolled my eyes, ignoring his offered hand and raising my own to rub at my temples. "I am getting somewhat sick of hearing that," I muttered. I lowered my hands and tipped my head, staring up at him with a twist of my lips. "And to be honest, I don't think you are."

Sam showed no hint of disappointment or offense, just took one step closer. "My hands and mouth—"

"Are very adept, I'm sure, but that's not what I meant," I said, searching that weary gaze for a sign of life, or at least understanding. It flickered, and Sam's hand finally dropped, a vulnerable emptiness making him wilt in front of me. "The palace has a good library, a sporting room, and as far as I can tell, Cook Bertha always has something coming fresh out of the oven. Take a week of leisure at least, and then we'll discuss what you might like to do going forward."

Daniel was frowning, looking between me and Sam, and I waited for him to turn back to me. I caught his eye and widened my own eyes meaningfully. Daniel stiffened in surprise, and he blinked rapidly.

Sam had my instruction, but it was clear he didn't know what to do with it, standing blankly in front of me. Daniel let out a long sigh before moving down to catch the man's elbow. Sam flinched, arm jerking and then quickly going limp, and Daniel shifted to a simple touch.

"Come with me," Daniel said. "We'll catch the remnants of breakfast while the maids air your suite out."

"My suite," Sam repeated, staring at me.

I wanted to shrink back from him, facing the reality of what Camellia had wrought a touch too uncomfortable for me.

Daniel grunted, and Sam's head drooped on his shoulders as he followed the guiding touch down from the stairs and toward the back hall that led to the kitchens.

"Are you sure about that?" Wendell asked.

"Absolutely not," I said, groaning and letting myself fall backward into his chest.

"We'd better have Cresswell put a guard on him at all times. For his own safety as well as our own," Cosmo murmured.

I spun to face them and found the worry tangling each of their faces. "Was I wrong to let him stay? I should've asked how you all felt." I might've been the authority in the palace, but they were right. I felt sorry for Sam, but I didn't *really* know what he was capable of. It was as if Camellia had scooped the man out of the body, and I didn't know what that left behind.

"I think you did right," Owen said, a soft smile growing as he stepped forward, an arm wrapping around my waist and pulling me into his chest. I swooned into the embrace, nibbling and kissing gently on his offered lips.

"I have concerns, but I'm inclined to agree with Owen," Wendell said, leaning in and kissing my shoulder briefly. "Maybe I am too optimistic, but I can't imagine any dangerous goal he might have being able to stand in the face of the sanctuary you just offered him."

"We will plan for the worst," Thao said firmly, touching us both.

"And hope to be rewarded with the best," Cosmo agreed, nodding, and then he released a long breath. "Even with him here, I feel like the palace can breathe again."

"We'd better open all the windows just in case," Wendell mused, before flashing a smile down in my direction. "And I think we ought to take our darling girl up for a very long, restful day in bed. To make up for the sleep she lost last night."

"Restful?" I teased, grinning back at him.

Wendell leaned in, nipping at my bottom lip. "True. Some resting *will* be in order. Perhaps after more important matters."

I squealed and giggled as Owen lifted me from the floor, throwing me over his shoulder, one hand cupped gently on my bottom as he took the stairs two at a time.

6.
ARIC

T he woods had changed in the weeks since I'd traveled up the mountain to the Winter Palace, and the transformation was almost terrifying, too good to be true. There was magic in the trees, every bit as much as the bird song was richer. It called to me, heavier even than the pebbles in the capital or the roses in the garden of the Southern Palace.

Magic had been growing in whispers for the past couple weeks. I'd thought I felt some in the storm the night of the harvest festival, but nothing like this.

I'd never excelled at catching magic right out of the air like some of the better mages claimed to do, but I knew *for certain* that at this moment, I could've waved my hand through the air in the woods and caught threads of power like fishermen hauled their catches out of the sea. The mountain was ripe, and I was tempted to stop and soak it up like a glutton.

But first I needed to speak with my—the princess.

You like her. It was Charlotte's voice in my head—the strongest scrap of the woman I loved still left in my memory was her voice. Dry, always teasing, husky and coaxing until you annoyed her and then brittle as a winter twig.

I do, but—

And I waited for the objections to rise.

But I was the King of Thieves. I had a duty to my court as well as a distinction to maintain. No thief would trust a king who'd taken up a place as a princess's Chosen.

She was too young.

I was younger when you bedded me, Charlotte answered.

"No, you're talking to yourself, fool," I muttered, nudging my horse a little quicker up the road. "And I was a great deal younger at the time too."

A breeze stirred through the trees and carried a feminine laugh with it, my eyes widening. It wasn't *quite* Charlotte's voice just then, but it was close. I needed to be careful. These were no longer the woods I knew. My own penchant for magic was liable to let this new environment play tricks on me.

A better objection than age or our positions was the pattern of our friendship. Bryony was coming into her own, and I might be too strong an influence over her. She needed to stake out her ground for herself, learn how to command and direct. Men like Cosmo and Owen were good for her, would shore her up without trying to steer her.

She likes when you take the lead.

My thoughts were sadistic today, and they conjured up the vision of Bryony laughing in my arms, light and gentle, and flying with me through the dancing crowds at the festival.

I needed to turn back. My head was full of her, and I seemed to be missing my usual restraint. If I went to see her now and she gazed up at me with those great dark eyes of her, lips parted and begging to be kissed...

She had a snake in her court, that was why I was going. Not to let her flirt with me while I soaked it up like the trees in these woods were lapping at the magic on the air, statues thriving quietly on the force that fed them.

I clucked encouragingly to my beast as the road grew steep and we turned the corner. The palace looked bright today in the sunshine, old gray stone almost gone peach in the hazy glow of the day. It was cool out, fall promising a coming shift in the weather, but brilliant and beautiful. I frowned at the palace as I came up to the gate. There were guards stationed there, unfamiliar faces, but they seemed less concerned with my approach than their game of cards.

The last time I'd been here was on a gray day with Griffin, and we'd come up through the woods to the old monolith of a palace. The walls had been cracked, the windows shuttered and blackened with age, the massive steps up to the front door crumpled.

Where's she found the money for this? The labor? I wondered, eyes wincing as sunlight glanced off golden window frames. The palace was not only healed, it was...

It was thick with magic too. One brick from its structure ground down to dust might fuel a lifetime of work for a good magician.

In the face of the beauty of the place, I found dread growing.

Had Bryony hired a mage and I hadn't heard about it? Perhaps Prince Thao had called one up from Mennary?

"Aric!"

I stopped my horse as Owen jogged down the steps of the castle, wearing a wide grin.

"I didn't know you were coming," Owen said, but it was him, so he made the surprise sound especially welcome.

"I didn't know there were renovations being made on the palace," I answered, swinging down from my horse.

"Hm? Oh, those. They weren't really planned. Bryony is busy at the moment, but we can take your horse down to the stables and get him watered and fed while we wait," Owen offered, immediately stepping up and introducing himself softly to Scoundrel, my gelding.

"Would it be rude of me to ask you to handle him so I might explore the palace?" I asked, offering Owen the reins. No one would ever accuse me of missing an opportunity.

He looked up from his murmured conversation, eyebrows rising slightly. "*Inside* the palace?"

Interesting. "Yes, if that's all right." I smiled at him, not too wide. Owen was gentle and often trusting, but not as much of an idiot as he let people sometimes believe.

"That's fine," he said, nodding and turning to leave. "You might bump into Cosmo, but don't bother with Daniel and the other one."

Other one?

I debated mining Owen for another slip of the tongue but it was almost unfair, so instead I hurried up the steps.

Bryony's palace was still poorly staffed, and there were fewer guards stationed about than ever before, but that suited me nicely. What magic I'd sensed from outside now dripped from the walls and blossomed up from the floors inside, as if the new floral tiles might suddenly burst to life as I stepped over them. It was beautiful and it *should've* been eerie, except there was a familiar sweetness to it that made my heart drum.

It can't be.

I didn't *want* it to be true. There were trails of heady sinuous power to follow, many leading up the stairs, but Owen's caution had to do with what I might see outside of the palace. I followed the threads as they twisted together and spun through the halls to the back of the building.

The greenhouse.

The greenhouse had been not only transformed but resurrected. I gaped in horror and awe at lively plants that pulsed with magic, begging me to make use of them, following the vines of ivy up the walls to where they twined around open window panes, delicate fingers pointing to the artfully colored roof that made the space glow.

What has she done? What has she done?

"Martin."

I turned my head, and there was Cresswell. "Stark. Where is she?"

He shrugged and nodded his head behind me, missing some of the cautious formality I expected he used with the others. "In the orchard with a couple of them."

I paced over the mossy tile, even that pounding with life, to the narrow hidden door behind the young hemlock.

Trim me, use me, burn the world with me, it begged.

"Was she...expecting you?" Cresswell asked, and there must've been something in my expression that warned him because he stepped between me and the door as I marched forward.

I tried to wipe it all away and replace it with a soft smirk. "No, but do you really think she'd mind?"

Bryony was terrible at minding her smile around me. Just thinking of it made me ache, made my chest twinge uncomfortably for using the fact. But I needed to know what was happening. This wasn't a normal amount of magic. Not even for the south.

Cresswell huffed and glared at me, but he stepped out of the way and opened the door for me, pointing the way.

He didn't need to.

I could taste it.

It was like the humid and charged flavor of the air before a storm hit, but tinged with violets, and it was pulsing from the orchard down the hill. I traveled there automatically, ignoring Cresswell's murmur at my back.

The orchard was one place that still looked relatively untouched. It was overgrown, the old hanged grooming of the apple trees having given way to new growth that stretched upwards, the grass rich with oxeye daisies and echinacea, but all of it still a kind of wild that seemed honest.

"Ohhh, yes."

Soft and whimpering and sweet, my courage faltered halfway down the hill at the desperate sigh.

Did you expect her to wait for you? Charlotte's voice asked in my head, a little teasing, a little sympathetic.

I swallowed hard and walked slower, heart sinking as they came into view. A sky blue blanket spread over the ground, the trees draped with gauzy netting around them that obscured but couldn't really have been intended to hide them.

Bryony was pressed between the handsome pale ambassador and the golden dark-haired prince, all three of them naked. Her hands combed through Wendell's blond strands, holding his face to her breast as she rocked between them, their hips tightly fastened to hers. I couldn't see Thao's face, it was tucked into her neck on the other side, but his grip on her hips was proprietary, moving her between them in an unmistakable act.

Bryony's high moan made my cock jump as I bit down on my tongue until a metallic bite filled my mouth.

I'd been holding her in some strange place in my head that was more than innocent and less than blatantly sexual, and the balance was broken now. I wanted to duck beneath that netting and drink up her crying pleas for more, force my hand between her and Wendell, and pinch her clit until she screamed and came and begged for my cock next. To pull her out from between them and pin her to the ground and stay buried inside of her, feeling her clutch and gush and cling to me until she was too weak to move.

Wendell's head lifted, and Bryony dove down, fucking his mouth with her kiss and making him groan, making both men buck into her.

I hated them. I hated myself.

Had I really meant to set her on a pedestal out of everyone's reach including my own?

She was exquisite. I knew the moment she would come, saw the tremble and clench of her thighs pinching around Wendell's hips, their fingers tightening on her as her own hands flew away from them.

Her face tilted up to the dappling sun through the trees as she let out a bright cry of anguished relief, body rocking erratically as they fucked her through her finish.

Magic *exploded* in the orchard.

The trees trembled, curled and browning leaves flourishing into fat glossy green fans, a sudden burst of white blossoms appearing and then cascading down to the ground as apples swelled from pebbles into beautiful shining red and green fists.

This was not a master magician at work, manipulating their tools and mining power for technical uses.

This was *creation*. Raw magic at its wildest.

Thao and Wendell moaned, and Bryony's arms embraced them, one draping over Thao's shoulder, as they bucked and stiffened and settled, the three of them so close they might as well have been one strangely beautiful form.

A twig snapped behind me, and the lovers looked up. It was a curious reaction. They didn't look startled, not at first, almost as if they expected to be joined, but when they saw me...

"Oh!" Bryony shrank in their embrace, her eyes wide and the flush in her cheeks growing darker as she turned away, their arms rising to shelter her. I didn't bother to look at them, spinning and finding Cosmo not far behind me, frowning and glaring at me as if it was *me* that interrupted them.

No, you just stared on like a voyeur. That was true. My cock was half hard and my pulse hammered, and even in the moment I couldn't quite decide what I wanted to do—storm away, or run down to the blanket and kiss the shame off Bryony's cheeks.

"Inside, Aric," Cosmo said, dark and inflexible.

Storm away it is then, I thought as I whipped past him, marching back to the palace, ignoring the tremulous whimper from the grass behind me.

7.
BRYONY

"Bryony, wait," Wendell called at my back, his hands just managing to catch me around my waist before I raced up the hill to the palace.

He spun me in his arms, his pants fastened around his hips, hair mused and lips swollen. Thao was shimmying into his own trousers, although he didn't seem to share our haste. I was dressed in a slip, one of Cosmo's shirts, and a skirt I hadn't finished buttoning at my back. I couldn't decide if I wanted to fall back into Wendell's arms and down to the ground or go chasing after Aric to explain myself. My legs were still shaking from my pleasure and the rush of the Hunger, but the ecstasy of the moment had been stolen away the moment I'd seen Aric and his glare focused down on us from the hill.

"You've done *nothing* wrong," Wendell murmured against my scalp. "I don't care if he's too stubborn to see it, that is the truth and the rest will mend."

I sighed and nodded against him, although I didn't really believe it. Aric would be angry, it would be *easier* for him to be angry with me than anything else.

"Are you all right? Do you hurt?" Thao asked, rising and frowning, stepping in close and taking my chin in a gentle grip.

"No! No, I..." I exhaled and shook my head, drawing out the smile I'd been ready to wear just minutes ago. "I feel wonderful."

Wendell smiled at that, kissing me for one brief, deep connection before making room for Thao, who seemed happy to keep supping from my lips until I realized he wouldn't stop. I wrestled myself free, and Thao smiled back at me.

"We'll leave the blanket and finish dressing on our way up

together," Thao said firmly. It wasn't *quite* an order and I bristled slightly, but he was right.

I didn't need to go running after Aric. He wasn't my Chosen, a distinction I wouldn't really make. But it wasn't fair to the moment I'd just shared with Wendell and Thao to make Aric my priority right now.

"Thank you," I said, waiting for them as they picked their shirts up from the ground, shaking off the butterflies and beetles that had come to roost after they were discarded.

"Figures he would come snooping sooner or later," Thao muttered, shrugging into his sleeves. "And you'll notice he wasn't in any rush to turn away?"

"Let's do this later, love," Wendell murmured, frowning at Thao imploringly before resting his hand on my waist and nodding for me to lead the way.

Thao helped me button my skirt on our way up the hill, apparently in no hurry to manage his own shirt. Which was nice actually, and I paused halfway back to the palace to press a kiss over his heart.

"I feel a little hollow now without you both," I said, Wendell stepping in at my back, wrapping us both up in his long arms.

"Mm, you may have us back whenever you please," Thao said, grinning and scratching his teeth softly over the corner of my jaw. "I'm sorry this was interrupted, even at the finish."

I sighed and closed my eyes. My body could still feel them, the wave of push and pull of them both inside me, and my breath caught at the memory, Hunger stirring flirtatiously in my belly.

We'd had a wonderful three days since Camellia and Grandmother left, staying a little closer to the bedroom for our love-making now that we had Daniel *and* Sam roaming the halls. I'd almost forgotten about our ideas for apple orchards until Wendell had offered to walk down with me in the morning, and we'd gotten our idea for a picnic with Thao. Which was less of a picnic and more of a seduction in the grass. I was still hazy on who exactly had done the seducing.

"Well," I said, taking a deep breath and straightening again. "At least it was fruitful."

Thao laughed, loud and cheerful, and Wendell smacked a noisy kiss against my throat.

"I'll tell the staff to go and gather the apples," Thao said as we walked again. "It'll keep me out of your hair and less likely to pick a fight you don't need."

I beamed at him in thanks. It was an odd thing to feel grateful for, but the Thao of weeks ago would've found bickering with Aric an entertaining sport, regardless of the position it left me in.

"Just for that, I will tie you to my bed later and let you lick me clean after Wendell's had his fill," I said, attempting some of Thao's wonderful filthy speech.

He nearly fell right back down the hill in surprise, and I had to race to the door as he growled and lunged to catch me.

Unfortunately, that meant I was giggling as I entered the greenhouse, where Cosmo sat across from Aric, leaning forward and whispering, a frown spread over his face. They both looked to me as I entered, Aric's glower deepening.

"Apologies, Your Highness. I wouldn't have told him—"

I startled as Cresswell stepped forward from the side, his head bowed low.

"It's not your fault. I may have...misled you on the nature of my connection with Aric," I said, eyes sliding to the man in question.

Cresswell didn't correct me, but he also didn't straighten from his humbled position.

So that's another mess you'll have to sort out, I thought, swallowing my sigh as I approached the delicate iron tea table.

"That was the Hunger," Aric said before I could get a word out.

"Yes. I'm sorry I didn't—"

"How long?" I swallowed, and his eyes narrowed, words growling out. "From the start then."

I started to shake my head, but then it wobbled. "No, but nearly."

"You made sure to keep it from me," he challenged, lifting an eyebrow.

"It's not really your business, Aric," Cosmo muttered.

"I didn't want you to be angry with me, and I gave into the cowardly impulse not to tell you," I said, trying to hold myself tall. Aric was slouched in the chair, and even from there, he made me feel small. And yet I *still* wanted to melt into him, to perch myself on that extended thigh and press myself to his chest and take deep whiffs of him, peppering kisses over his throat until he forgave me.

"To be angry with you? For making yourself a fancy little cake of a palace with all the pretty shiny toys a princess could want?" he asked, eyes flicking cruelly over my shoulder to Wendell.

"The palace?" I squawked, jaw dropping. "I—we didn't—I didn't even know what the Hunger could *do*. The palace just happened. It wasn't *all*—"

"You didn't know you were filling the woods with magic? You didn't mean to make that orchard burst with fruit?" Aric snapped, sitting up.

"Well, yes, but—"

"And you didn't think I, a northern mage, might need to know about the sudden flood of power taking place?"

I gaped at Aric, looking to Cosmo and Wendell for help, but they looked as startled as I did. "Is it—have I done wrong?" I asked, my voice shrinking.

Aric's expression fractured then, the anger cracking and revealing something almost like sympathy or perhaps worry.

"Aric, I *am* sorry for not telling you when it should've come up, but the Hunger hasn't changed *me*. It hasn't changed what I want for Kimmery, what kind of leader I want to be," I said, stepping forward slowly as if I were approaching a feral animal.

"Princess, there's enough magic in the trees of the woods that a new mage could take a twig and accidentally blow their own face off in a simple working. You've upset the balance," Aric said softly, making my steps stall.

"Aric, I think we both know she's trying to restore it," Cosmo growled at him.

"Blindly!" Aric answered, standing up like a shot. "Naïveté is charming for a young woman, certainly, but it looks poor on one trying to race into being a queen."

I flinched and resisted the need to spin away, Wendell's hand pressed flat to my back in support.

"What can I do to fix this?" I asked, trying to swallow down the tears in my voice. "We've been *trying* to be careful, to learn what I am capable of."

"I think what you are capable of was made pretty clear in the orchard," Aric growled.

"Aric!" Cosmo roared, standing.

Aric and I both withdrew, his face paling and eyes dropping to the floor as I stumbled back into Wendell's arms.

"I—For—" He looked up, eyes landing on Wendell's arms around my waist, his expression hardening. "Try not to turn the whole north wild with magic for the time being. At least until I know what to do about the changes you've already wrought."

Had he meant making the apples grow, or my act with Wendell and Thao? I couldn't tell, and I didn't want to ask. I generally didn't care who saw me with my Chosen, but that was certainly not the way I would've wanted to be observed by Aric. And whose fault was that, anyway?

"Perhaps before you return, you might send word next time," I said, straightening and glaring back at him. "You've made yourself clear on the matter of being my Chosen. The palace isn't yours to wander."

His gaze flashed on my face, fire in the usually cool gray depths of his eyes. It drew my blush out, but I refused to back down. Aric had intruded on a moment that wasn't his to see. I had lied to him.

And now we were...fractured.

I couldn't breathe under the force of his stare, and I wanted to smash the tension to pieces and fall to his knees and beg for forgiveness, which only made me angrier. I'd apologized for what I'd done wrong already and I couldn't change those choices now.

"Can I have a moment alone with Bryony?" Aric asked, voice rasping.

"No," Cosmo, Wendell, and Cresswell all answered at once.

Aric glowered, but their defense made the painful knot in my chest ease slightly, and I gave Cosmo an imploring glance until he sighed.

"We'll be in the hall," Cosmo said, jerking his head to the others and then grabbing Aric's arm and hissing something in his ear that made the older man's frown deepen.

Wendell kissed the corner of my jaw, catching my eye and reassuring himself that this was what I wanted before moving to the door, but it was Cresswell whose feet dragged the most, until they were finally all outside of the greenhouse.

"The Hunger is not what you think it is," Aric said as I stepped closer, smashing the fantasy I'd been building that he was about to apologize.

"What do you mean?" I asked.

"I... Do you *know* what it's capable of? Really?" Aric asked, the edges of expression turning almost frightening as he loomed.

"Not yet," I admitted. "But some of it."

"Can you control it?"

"Aric! It hasn't been that long that I knew I had it at all—"

"I am not—" He cleared his throat and shook his head, standing up from his chair at last. "You should—You *could* have told me. I am not—ugh!" He covered his face with his hands, interrupting the connection between us before continuing. "I *am* chastising you, yes. I *am* angry. We'll discuss it more later. I need to get back to the city now and see if there's any information that can be found so I—we know—"

"You're being vague where it concerns me, Aric, and I don't like it," I said.

His hands slipped down, jaw hardened and eyes narrowed, and then just as quickly, he sighed and some of the bite was gone from his expression. "Will you forgive me for it, if I don't make you wait as long as you made me?"

He might've meant it as a jest, but it only left me more frustrated.

"Will you forgive me for that, or will you just continue to thrust it in my face at every opportunity?" I snapped.

"Were you *planning* on telling me?" he growled back.

"Yes! I was! But not like *that*."

A flush rose up from his neck and Aric stomped closer, standing so that we were shoulder to shoulder but not facing one another.

"Just try and keep your magic bound up until I get back, before your *enthusiasm* sets Kimmery on fire."

My hands clenched to fists at my side. "Get out, Aric."

But he didn't even give me the satisfaction of waiting for me to finish before he was rushing out of the room.

8.
COSMO

"**B**ut what did he mean by it?" Thao asked, watching Bryony trying to climb the bookshelf in front of her.

Owen's arm twined around her waist, drawing her back. "Point to it, I'll get it down," he said, his thumb digging into her shoulder.

"We don't know," I said to Thao.

"I think he's just jealous because he would've liked to be the one—"

Wendell cleared his throat, head jerking up from the book his nose was buried in to glare at Thao.

"I'm...not inclined to call Aric a liar, but I do think there might be an element of exaggeration to his warnings," I said, watching Bryony.

She had an arm wrapped around her waist and a permanent frown on her face as she pointed to a series of books that Owen stacked in his arms for her.

"And if there isn't, and I really have been upsetting some kind of natural balance?" Bryony asked, glancing at me. "All this time, I've been thinking that the queen's line perverted the power of the Hunger by putting it back into the Chosen, but what if...what if that's what I was *meant* to be doing so that I didn't..."

Didn't set Kimmery on fire.

I'd heard the words Aric had thrown at her before he went running out of the palace like *he* was the one inflamed. In fact, I suspected he probably was, and not just with anger.

"Come here," I called gently to Bryony. I had my own book in front of me, but I was more concerned with my princess. I should've grabbed Aric by the collar and dragged him off to talk some sense into his ear until he was calmed down enough to do Bryony the favor of not leaving her terrified of herself.

"Cos, I can't right now and I don't want—"

"Bryony, come here, or I'll come to you and pin you to the floor and prove to you that your magic isn't *hurting* anyone," I said.

The others went quiet, Bryony's jaw dropping and eyes as wide as saucers as she stared back at me, color rising prettily in her cheeks.

"I'll kiss you until you're bruised," I purred, arching an eyebrow. "Or you can come and look me in the eye and listen."

Essentially, I knew my place. Bryony and I were lovers, and she was generous with her affection and her feelings. I had the dignity to be able to continue my work, and I suspected I had the freedom to come and go from the palace without her if I wanted. But I was *hers*, not just in my heart but also in my body. I was Chosen, and I had no real right to speak to her the way I just had, aside from suspecting she might let me get away with it this once.

That didn't mean the tension in the room was less than knife sharp, or that my heart didn't threaten to beat right out of my chest as she took slow steps toward me.

"Cook says there are enough apples to can and keep through winter for us, and all of Rumsbrooke, and most of the surrounding farming towns," I said softly. "I heard the guards speaking the other day, and the north hasn't seen a harvest like the one coming for well over a century."

I studied her expression, saw the irritation and the caution easing into a wary kind of gratitude the more I spoke.

"The taverns in Rumsbrooke are filled to the beams on the nights they host free dinners, and what coin can be spared is spent on mead so the owners are happy too. You've done so much already, Bryony."

She sighed and sagged, her feet carrying her into my arms as I stood from my chair. "I...aside from the harvest being promising—"

"Stop," I hushed her, tipping her chin up and sealing her lips with a brief kiss. "Aric might be right in some of his concerns, but I think there's more to his anger than concern for magic."

I looked up at the others, trying to communicate the question with a look. Could I take Bryony aside for a few minutes?

I wanted Aric and Bryony to come to some kind of terms on their own. I'd hoped they'd do so by Aric learning to trust Bryony, not just in regards to the kingdom, but when it came to his own feelings, pains. Apparently, that was too much to ask, especially with the obstacle of other men holding some of Bryony's affections.

Owen nodded to me, gesturing back to the cushioned window seats on the far end of the library. The entire vast room had been practically rearranged since our arrival, now brighter with tidy rows of shelves and bouquets of fresh roses held in the golden arms of lovers statues standing like pillars by the windows. I was a little jealous of Bryony's magic when it came down to it, although I'd never mention it to her. She was filling the palace with the kind of whimsical and decadent works of art that might've taken me months to fashion. And she did it overnight, without even noticing.

"Let them read for a few minutes while we speak," I murmured in her ear, nuzzling her temple.

She stiffened, and I mentally cursed Aric, wondering if he'd intentionally put her off our touch with his warning about the Hunger. Easier for him to manage his jealousy if she wasn't letting herself enjoy others.

"All right," Bryony sighed, softening again and leaning into my side as I shepherded her away from our table and over into the sunlight streaming through the window.

She didn't protest as I gathered her into my arms on my lap on the windowsill, resting her cheek over my heart, her skirt spilling over both our legs.

"Aric is jealous, first and foremost," I said.

Bryony only hummed, unsurprised, and I smiled slightly. She wasn't conceited, but I was glad she wasn't totally ignorant of her effect on men. She was beautiful, our princess, but also she was inherently seductive—in her movements, the slant of her gaze, her absolute authority.

"Of me, the others. Of you and the force of the Hunger," I said, making her twitch and look up from my chest.

"You think he's jealous of the magic?" she asked, brow furrowing.

"Absolutely. Aric's not formally trained, and magic is thin here in the north. He's had to struggle to master every inch he's learned, and as far as I know, he's one of the better magicians around. Look at what you've done, Bryony," I said, sweeping a hand around us. "Think of what he saw in the orchard."

Her expression darkened, and she pressed her forehead to my sternum. "I'm trying not to," she mumbled against me.

I hummed in understanding, digging my fingers into the roots of her hair. On that particular topic, I felt slightly worse for Aric. He'd put a barrier up between himself and Bryony, especially where it concerned desire. There was no way seeing her in that ecstatic moment hadn't shattered that wall in his mind.

"Has he...has he ever mentioned his wife?" I asked.

Bryony sat up like a shot, my fingers accidentally pulling on her hair. "He has a wife?" she cried, horror and an ache in her tone that made me sting on her behalf.

"Shh, he's a widower, Bryony," I said, drawing her back to my chest.

"Oh...*oh*."

I smiled at the note of sorrow. Just like that, her own injury transformed into one for his sake.

"Charlotte was the daughter of the King of Thieves before Aric. James was a more traditional thief from what I've heard, less interested in the kingdom as a whole than every man for himself. Charlotte was the idealist, and she found a willing ear in Aric," I said, pausing. "I wanted him to tell you himself but—"

"But he's made of stone," Bryony muttered.

"Mm. So Aric took the crown from Charlotte's father and then added insult to injury by marrying his daughter. Some of the court left as Aric and Charlotte started to make changes to how they wanted to operate. Where they wanted the money coming from. But generally, Aric has been a popular king."

"What happened to Charlotte?" Bryony whispered, wincing.

She had such a capacity for sympathy, empathy even.

"She grew ill about five winters ago when food was very very thin. Aric was running a job when it started, and Charlotte maintained her generosity right until she couldn't get out of bed. When Aric got home, he couldn't find a doctor who would attend her, and he didn't have enough magic to really heal how far into the sickness she'd fallen."

I watched in awe as Bryony's eyes shone, a tear falling for Aric, who'd taken great care to be as scornful as he could before leaving.

"His crown isn't really the only obstacle between us," she said and then shook her head. "Oh, that was selfish to be thinking of my own desires just then."

I didn't bother resisting the urge to lean forward, drawing Bryony to my mouth, kissing her for her own sake, for my gratitude that she was the person she was and that she was in any way mine.

"Aric objected to being Chosen for Charlotte's sake, yes. Probably more her than his position as King of Thieves. I suspect that might've been a temptation. Imagine what he could've gotten away with in your court if you'd never known," I said, cocking an eyebrow. "I'm not telling you about Charlotte to excuse the way he behaved. I could've punched him if he hadn't been in such a rush to leave."

"If there'd been magic in the woods years ago, he could've saved her," Bryony said, frowning and thinking. "I'm still angry with his temper, but I suppose I can understand why the magic is such a shock to him. Do you think it's dangerous?"

I blew out a long breath from pursed lips. "I really don't know. Magic isn't my area of expertise," I said, catching her eye and grinning. "I don't know how seriously I'd take his caution about avoiding feeding the Hunger, though."

Bryony's eyes slid away from mine, her frown turning down even further. "I only know two ways of using it. One hurts my Chosen, and the other is apparently unpredictable."

Fuck you, Aric, I thought wearily.

Bryony looked up and laughed at my expression. "You look like I've taken your toy away!"

I tried to shake it off, but I ended up laughing too. "Ignore that. I'll survive. We all will. Whatever makes you most comfortable. Although, if Aric takes a very long time in returning with some explanation, I may complain."

"Mm, I am not your only company now though, am I?" Bryony asked, pressing a kiss to the corner of my jaw.

Oddly enough, I found myself blushing under her knowing stare.

"I'm not entirely sure how I fit in with them," I said, looking over in the direction of the others, although a bookshelf blocked my view of Wendell and Thao.

"If it ever causes you *any* strife—" Bryony started, and I hushed her words by laying my lips over hers, nibbling on that permanently swollen bottom pout.

"I enjoy them in a similar way to how I enjoy watching Owen with you," I said softly. "The only place I risk my feelings is..." I trailed off, not sure if now was the time to say something, but Bryony's eyes lit up.

"There's no risk, Cosmo. If you can accept that my heart will be shared—"

"Of course," I said, my own heart ready to leap out of my chest and land in her gentle palm.

"Then it's yours in equal measure," Bryony said, smiling.

I couldn't help my grin or the way it threatened to split my face, and my arms twined tightly around Bryony's waist, tugging her firmly against my chest, my head tipping to kiss down her throat.

"Cosmo, I—we still don't know," Bryony breathed, her hands poised on my shoulders, but not managing to push me away.

"Just let me kiss you, hold you, just for a few minutes," I said, nipping at her jaw.

She wouldn't give in to her cravings so quickly. Bryony was too conscientious for that, and Aric had made her skittish of herself for the time being. *Convenient that none of us can have her now that he knows how badly he wants her*, I mused with a huff of breath over her shoulder. She shivered and arched into me, and I kissed my way back up to her jaw, her lips.

A slow and constant seduction it would be then. The fruit would be riper for the picking when Bryony was sure she and Kimmery were safe.

9. BRYONY

Wendell's fists clenched in the pillow, his legs spread wide, framing Thao's back as Wendell gazed into my eyes, a perfect picture of torment as Cosmo bit and licked at his chest. Thao's ass wiggled in the air and his head bobbed, wet sounds of suction timed with Wendell's whimpers.

My lip was at risk of bleeding as I watched them from my chair, the order to *cease* on the tip of my tongue. But that wouldn't be fair, would it? Why should the others not have their pleasure just because I couldn't have mine?

But does it have to be where I watch?

Yes, because they were *my* Chosen. Their pleasure was my pleasure.

Owen groaned, and my eyes flicked to him. He wasn't on the bed with the others, but reclining in a chair that barely fit him, his back to the bed and his fist working quickly over his cock as he stared at me, eyes trailing over every inch of me, always returning between my legs. He could probably see the way I was clenching on nothing, my body desperate for touch. I held myself as still as stone on my chair, afraid that even the smallest shift might send me over. The Hunger was *cavernous* inside of me. I was hollowed out with craving my Chosen.

"Mistress, please. Just a taste," Owen pleaded.

I trembled, wondering if we were pushing too far, testing my limits too much. Would the Hunger take control of my body and satisfy itself if I denied it for much longer?

He whined, his stomach swelling as he twisted his hand over the head of his cock and bucked into his own brutal grip.

"Fuck!" Wendell gasped, and my eyes returned to the three on the bed, tongue lapping over my bruised lip as I watched

Thao's hips flex, his position moved to fit himself inside the other man, the carved muscle of his ass dimpling with his thrusts. But he was blocking the rest of my view.

"Turn, I want to see," I said, the order sharp.

Cosmo laughed and sat up, grinning at me and sliding off the bed as Thao growled but pulled out of Wendell so they could all rearrange themselves.

"Wendell, would you—" I looked to both him and Thao. "Would you suck Cosmo for me?"

My mouth was watering with every passing second. I enjoyed sucking cock for my Chosen. Now I was absolutely *starving* for it, so much so I was sure it wouldn't be safe for me. Just the thought made my cunt feel heavy, my chest rising and falling faster with quick, anxious breaths.

"Gladly," Wendell laughed, playfully reaching for our artist.

"I'll have him moaning and whining around you so hard, your eyes will roll back in your head," Thao added to Cosmo, grinning and tossing his black hair back from his face before settling down with Wendell's thighs over his. Wendell's head leaned back off the edge of the bed, and my hips seemed to rise with Wendell's as they all came together, Cosmo groaning as his cock sank between Wendell's welcoming lips.

"There's just one piece missing," Thao said, his brow furrowed and eyes fighting not to fall shut as he worked himself back into Wendell's ass. He grinned then, and flicked his fingers at the head of Wendell's weeping cock, making Wendell thrash slightly and Cosmo shout. "Who will ride poor Wen?"

My thighs were sticky with arousal, and I thought that I might come whether anyone touched me or not. How on earth was I meant to get to sleep like this?

This was your horrible idea, I reminded myself.

And there was a cold bath waiting for me when it was all over.

"So beautiful," Owen murmured, sweat beading on his brow as the others started to fuck in earnest. "You're so beautiful. Please, Mistress."

I stood from the chair, my robe falling shut and blocking Owen's previous view, but it didn't matter because his eyes were wide and reverent on my face, his hand stroking his cock so fast and rough, I wondered how it didn't hurt. Maybe it did, he did look especially and beautifully tormented as he twisted and bucked in his seat.

I moved to him cautiously, half expecting Owen to leap at me. But he was too good for that. His hand pulled away, fingers flexing and digging into the arm of the chair, his cock still twitching as if there were an invisible hand there doing the work.

"Stay still," I said, holding his gaze.

He nodded quickly, jaw ticking as I moved to the side of his seat. "I won't touch," he breathed.

This wasn't being careful at all, but I wanted to be the one to take Owen over the brink.

"This is mine," I whispered, wrapping my hand around the base of his cock, smiling as it jumped happily against my palm.

"Yes," Owen gasped, nodding.

I worked him more gently than he had himself, but Owen twisted and groaned, eyes on my mouth and hips kicking into my hand as if I was branding him.

"I'll come," he gasped.

"Don't touch," I reminded him, my body pleading with me to *see reason and get fucked*, but Owen only stiffened obediently. I took him in both hands, rolling and massaging his sac as I worked his heavy length until he was painting his own chest with his release as he groaned in my ear. His muscles melted into the chair and threatened to let him slide right out.

"Oh yes, fuck. Fuck, yes," Owen sighed, shuddering as I squeezed the last droplets of cum out of him and swiped them with my fingers, drawing it up to my lips as he watched.

"You really don't want to join?" he asked, but he didn't reach for me.

I absolutely *did* want to, but I shook my head. "Tonight, I only want to watch," I said, before amending with a smile, "Well, and touch a little."

I bent my head to his, and Owen shivered as he stretched, our mouths grazing gently.

"Fucking stars, it's like he's swallowing me whole," Cosmo

groaned, and I twisted, leaning into Owen's shoulder to watch the others.

Wendell's hands were gripping tightly to Cosmo's ass, all but forcing Cosmo to fuck his mouth, and even with the mouthful, I could hear my lovely, quiet Chosen moaning wildly. His own ample cock was wavering and jumping against his stomach as Thao gasped and groaned.

"Yes, exactly like that," Thao hissed, hips slapping against Wendell's ass.

I wanted to touch Wendell too, like I had with Owen, but I didn't trust myself on the bed. It would be too easy to jostle and...

And what? Accidentally find yourself riding cock?

Well, yes.

I didn't need to worry. Wendell's heels pressed into Thao's ass, holding him close, and Thao took the opportunity to fill his hands with Wendell's length, doing some kind of flick with his wrist that made Wendell arch his back nearly a foot off the bed.

Owen's arm circled my waist, but he was careful to remain gentle as I gasped and watched the rest of my Chosen as they seemed to claw and carry one another into oblivion, Thao catching Wendell's spurts against his palm. Cosmo's knees shook, and he held himself up with his palms clutching over Wendell's chest before quickly moving away to let Wendell breathe as Thao stiffened and cried out.

They fell together as a heap on the bed, and I smiled at the way Wendell and Thao drew Cosmo in with them. Cosmo was right that I didn't need to be worried yet, and as if we were sharing the same thought, he glanced up and winked at me.

"You don't look as though that helped," Thao said, smirking at me. "Come here, and we'll make it better."

I shook my head quickly, shrugging away Owen's arms but making sure to gift him with a lingering kiss. "Go to bed without me, I'll be there soon."

Cosmo huffed an irritated sigh, and Owen brushed his hand over my cheek, brow folding with worry.

"You were exquisite," I said to him, looking up at the others so they knew the words were shared with them. "It was exactly what I needed."

For now, at least, until we knew it was safe for me to dive headlong back into the delirious magic of the Hunger and my Chosen.

"I'll wait for you," Owen said, and it was firm enough that I knew not to argue, just gifted him another kiss and then moved for the cool bath waiting for me behind the screen.

I shivered and winced as I dipped my foot into the water.

At least you know your own control, I reminded myself, taking a deep breath and restraining my squeak of discomfort as I slipped into the chilly water.

⚜

MY FINGERNAIL SCRATCHED at the glossy finish of the chair I sat in, poring over the text in my lap. We hadn't found anything specific to the Hunger, but I had been learning a great deal about magic in the past three days as we waited for word from Aric.

Cosmo had urged me that morning to send for Aric, even if I had to use the royal guard itself, but I'd refused.

"You're torturing yourself for nothing," he said.

"I lived many years without indulging the Hunger, I can manage a few more days," I'd answered, ignoring the arch of his eyebrow.

Despite a restful sleep curled up between Owen and Thao, I woke with a pounding headache and a strange combination of gnawing hunger and nausea. Perhaps flaunting my Chosen in front of my Hunger had been a mistake, although I'd enjoyed the show, even if it had left me aching and itchy without my own satisfaction.

I knew I would crack soon, my resolve not to use my Hunger would fail in the face of Cosmo's encouragement or Thao's intentional goading. But at least I'd avoided it for days. That had to count for something.

As long as Aric didn't walk in at the exact moment my resistance *failed*, it couldn't make the situation any worse.

Footsteps padded softly through the aisles of the library

toward my window seat, and I looked up, expecting to see Wendell joining me, or even Owen fresh from the stables or visiting some of his wild pets in the woods.

Instead, I startled at the specter before me.

"Sam!"

He looked more or less the same as he had a week ago when left behind by Camellia. Thin, appearing even taller than he really was for his lack of breadth, hair and skin pale. If there was one thing changed, it might've been that his lips didn't look so chapped and the circles under his eyes were maybe a little less dark.

I hadn't *forgotten* his presence in the palace, but I hadn't seen him until this moment, and I suddenly wished I weren't alone.

He looked similarly startled, and his eyes glanced behind him, a soft clank of metal in the shadow of the library signaling a guard.

"We aren't alone," he said, that crack of disuse still in his voice. I wasn't sure if he was reassuring himself or me.

"Ah, well, don't...mind me," I said, fingering the pages of the book, my legs curling under my lap.

Sam seemed equal parts fragile and unpredictable. I just wasn't sure if I was waiting for an explosion or for him to fall apart on himself.

"Do you want me to—?" He glanced at my skirts as if my sex might drag him under of its own accord.

"No," I said, shaking my head and forcing a smile, before clearing my throat. "I... Sam, you aren't obliged to do anything while you're here. Not on my behalf."

His brow furrowed, the lines deep once they appeared, but he nodded. "That's what Daniel said."

I sighed and nodded. Well, that made one area where Daniel had been helpful. I tipped my head and wondered if it was too soon to ask the question in my head, before deciding to dive forward.

"Do you *want* to be one of my Chosen? I am not taking you on, but if it's—"

"No, I don't," Sam said, eyes widening and shoulders tensing.

My smile came more readily then. "Good, then we're of the same mind where that's concerned."

Sam moved closer, but something seemed to be unraveling in him, a kind of watchfulness that made me equally wary. He leaned against the far side of the window seat, staring at me, but he seemed less tense.

"I would like to have some kind of...something to do here," he said slowly, eyes flicking back and forth across my face to study my response.

"Oh! Well, you may do anything you like," I said, shrugging.

He frowned again. "I...don't remember what I like. But I don't like sitting in my room with nothing to think of, but—"

His words stopped abruptly and his stare went vacant, my chest tightening. I leaned forward, and Sam stiffened, flinching back, making it clear between the two of us who was considered the predator.

"I will talk with Lady Prudence and Mr. Farraque to see what might be useful," I said. "You can try things out, see what suits you."

"Daniel says I'm to do what you say," Sam said, but he was looking down at his own shoes.

I huffed and rolled my eyes. "Well, Daniel does what I say, and I'll tell him to help you find some work you enjoy."

Sam hovered, not really responding, and I realized that I could either go and find Daniel now or I could let Sam watch me read. I considered briefly asking him to help me research, but I wasn't really prepared to trust him that far.

He skittered back as I stood up, and I backed away. "I'll go see him now."

"You were never really like her," Sam said.

I frowned automatically at the thought of Camellia. "No, I wasn't."

"But you do have the Hunger?" Sam asked, frowning.

I sighed and turned away from him, my stomach cramping in response to thoughts of the Hunger. "Unfortunately, yes."

10.
BRYONY

It occurred to me as I searched for him, that I didn't really know where Daniel had set himself up in the palace. Lady Prudence had a lovely suite I'd helped her pick out that overlooked the lake, but as I wandered the halls, I realized I had no idea where Daniel spent his days in the palace.

"Are you lost, Your Highness?"

I glanced behind me and found the young maid, Delilah, watching me from a sitting room doorway, her arms full of logs. It was getting cooler out, the temperature drop slowly finding its way into the palace, and I noticed recently that there was always a fire in my bedroom and sitting room by the time I woke. It wasn't entirely necessary, since I was usually nestled between a pair of human furnaces.

"A bit. Do you know where I might find Mr. Farraque?" I asked, offering her a smile. She shouldn't really have spoken to me, but I wasn't fond of the tradition of overlooking my staff.

"Oh! Yes, I think so. He tried to take a room in the servants' quarters, but we made him take a suite instead. He's in the east wing, just down at the very end of the next left hall," she said, taking three opportunities within her speech to curtsey.

My brows rose. Daniel had wanted a room with the servants?

"Thank you," I said, nodding my head and grinning as she started to bounce away before remembering I was meant to leave first.

I followed her directions into the east wing. I hadn't spent any time in this part of the palace, although Cosmo's studio was just one floor down. The evidence was apparent, some of the palace's new sheen of glamour and magic just a little duller in this wing, as if in all my adventures with my Chosen, we hadn't finished filling the building with the magic of the Hunger.

That's just more proof that Aric's overreacting, Cosmo voiced in my head, but I shook it away. I didn't want to think of Aric, of his anger or his absence. I especially didn't want to think of the clawing, snarling Hunger, or my throbbing headache that made me wince with every echoing step down the tile hallway floors. Rugs would be a great expense, but—

I nearly passed Daniel's door, even though it was hanging open. There was something very nondescript about the hall, so close to the servants' wing that it must've been saved for the less significant members of court. The dark oak door was parted, hanging into the room, and there was a soft shuffle of papers echoing inside. I found myself suddenly shy and aware of being alone, and then I glanced behind me.

I'd ordered Cresswell to take the day off and rest, but there was a glint of armor at the corner of the hall, a guard assigned to stay close but not crowd me.

If I thought of it, I could still remember the grip of Daniel's arm around my waist and the nervous pound of my heart in the moment where I wasn't sure how either of us would respond next. Now in the hall, the memory made my Hunger clench. I grunted out a soft complaint, hand resting against my side.

"Hello?"

Well, shit, I thought, my lips quirking at the realization that I was picking up some of Cosmo and Owen's language.

I stepped up to the door, pushing it further in and making a brief scan of the room—clean, but a little sparse, only one armchair near an unlit fireplace with a bare floor—until I found Daniel to the left, sitting behind a worn desk, another armchair in front it for any guest. He rose quickly, eyes only betraying his surprise for a moment.

"Your Highness, no one told me you needed to see me," he rushed, bowing low. Daniel was usually so impassive that it was reassuring to see him so obviously self-conscious, taking in his own space and starting to move around his desk.

"No, please sit. I am perfectly capable of coming to you," I said, moving to help myself to the spare chair at his desk. "I wanted to speak with you about Sam."

"I am looking for somewhere he might be sent," Daniel said, sinking back into his seat. "I can't decide if a sanatorium will do him any good."

"What? No! I only meant... He spoke to me just now in the library," I said, sitting up.

Daniel stiffened, hands clenching around stray papers on the desk. "He found you?"

"Found me? I wasn't in hiding."

Daniel cleared his throat, smoothing his pages and shaking his head. "I told him to keep away from you."

"That's not really necessary. He only wants an occupation," I said, shrugging and studying the man across from me.

I didn't understand Daniel for all the clues I had to work with. He was reticent, guarded, sometimes so expressionless he blended into the background, in spite of his otherwise imposing presence. But there *were* signs of life in him. His seduction in the training room had been more an act than genuine charm, but there were moments like this one when something appeared to be boiling just under the surface of that blank veneer.

"An occupation?" Daniel asked, words flat but gaze explosive.

"I suppose he doesn't have much to fill his mind that he'd like to dwell on, so it will have to be something that requires focus, but not much strength. Do you know if he's eating?" I asked.

Daniel's jaw worked briefly, short beard twitching with the words he must've been biting off. "I believe Prudence has taken on the role of mothering him, you needn't involve yourself. He shouldn't have bothered you at all."

"He didn't *bother* me," I said, frowning. *Well, maybe a bit.* "Honestly, with your sympathy for your school friend, I expected you to have some to spare for Sam too. We all saw the state he was in."

Daniel scoffed, his eyes falling to the side and his hand cupping his jaw. He had big hands, and I held my breath as my mind conjured an image of those hands spreading my thighs open. The Hunger cramped, and I froze in my seat.

This wasn't me. I didn't *like* Daniel.

"Princess, don't you find it convenient that your sister, your competition to the kingdom's crown, has left her...least mentally stable Chosen dropped in a heap at your feet?" Daniel asked, words rumbling lowly as if he didn't want to be overheard. Not that anyone was likely to overhear. The guard was at the other end of the hall and would only hear if I shouted.

"No more than I find it convenient that the council tried to replace Sir Hubert with *you*," I said, arching an eyebrow at Daniel across his desk.

Those sparks of fire in Daniel ignited at once, his body straightening and those hands I'd been so fascinated with a moment ago splaying across the top of the desk. "Oh, really? Do you want to know what the council wants of me? To *fuck* you. That's it. I report nothing to them, they ask almost nothing of me, they just want one man in your ear and your bed who—"

"Who can try to convince me to be exactly like Camellia! With a mind for nothing but cock and cunt!" I shouted back, rising from my seat. I startled both of us with my language, but of the two of us, it was Daniel who blushed and lowered his gaze.

"Forgive my language—"

"Oh, don't you dare put that gentleman's mask you wear back up," I growled at him, watching him bristle. "I would rather you were rude and honest, than appearing so content to play everyone's pawn. What do you *want*, Daniel?"

He snarled, and the ferocious expression seemed to fit him better than the cool stoicism. "I want to pin your wrists over your head and fuck you until you can't think of what poor *Sam* has to do with himself all day."

"Yes, so you can be the council's mouth in my ear!"

"No!" Daniel roared, rising up and leaning forward, eyes flashing and face just a foot away as we glowered at one another. "Because I can't get the sound of your whines and pleas out of my ears! Because my cock throbs every time you walk into a room until I can't focus on anything but your movements, hoping they turn in my direction. Because I've seen you come on another man's cock, and I know I could make you do the same!"

Oh, dear, whispered some small, shy part of myself at the back of my mind, finally realizing the precarious position I'd placed myself in.

But the Hunger *roared*.

It was as if I wore unseen wings that insisted on taking flight in that moment. I surged across the table, my nails clawing at Daniel's shoulders as I dragged myself to him, my heart already aching for us both. My pulse was one enormous drum beat, slamming steadily from my aching head to my desperate cunt. My teeth claimed his overfull lips, pulling them between my own to suck and worry at the swollen flesh. His breath snagged against my mouth, the shock of my attack leading to a small pause between us.

The Hunger was rising, filling me up in a way that left me a puppet. Or perhaps that was what I would tell myself later when I tried to make sense of the moment and place blame elsewhere.

Daniel took the opportunity presented with both hands, fastening a tight grip around my waist and dragging me across the desk, papers and an inkwell scattering to the floor as he pulled me to him. One arm banded our hips together, the other bracing my back, forcing me into a bow as he arched over me, returning the kiss with a soft snarl.

Magic thrummed and spun like wild vines through me, wrapping itself around my limbs and taking almost total control of my own movements. My head fell back and my lips parted, groaning as Daniel's tongue stroked against mine. He tasted of coffee and salt, and he was solid and warm and *alive* against me. My fingers drove through his hair, holding him to me. We wavered in place, both of us fighting for control, but in the moment, Daniel let me win as I pushed roughly on his shoulder.

The chair clattered backward, and Daniel landed on the floor with a grunt, but I was on him before he could move us, planting myself over his lap and dragging him back to me by his collar. I rocked on top of him, grinding down, feeding the Hunger.

Feeding my own frustrated impulses that I'd ignored. Feeding a petty, private anger with Aric for making me doubt myself, for resisting me.

Daniel was growing hard beneath me, and I pulled away from the battling kiss to gasp for breath, my eyes falling shut and soft whimpers rising as the friction of my movements both satisfied and irritated the itch under my skin.

"You taste sweet. I thought you would," Daniel rasped, one hand encouraging my pace on his lap, the other rising to turn my head so he could suck on my pulse.

"Shut up," I hissed, and I shoved him roughly down, surprised by his laugh and his toothy grin. I glared at him, and he sobered slightly, staring up at me with his hair at odd angles and his collar askew.

"It's all right," he said, grinning again, a surprisingly warm smile. "Take what you need, Your Highness."

I paused, my movements halting as I slid my hand up his throat, fingertips resting on his chin as I stared down at him.

Turn away, Bryony, I pleaded with myself.

To Daniel's credit, he made no attempt to influence me in that moment, holding perfectly still beneath me, gaze growing curious.

I rose up on my knees, and Daniel's gaze shuttered, his smile faltering. My hand lifted from his chin and disappeared beneath my skirt. His eyes widened and then fell shut as his head dropped to the floor with a long groan as I reached for him, cupping his stiff length through the fabric.

Is that an eleven? My breath caught in my throat, and I surrendered to the magic and demand of the Hunger, tearing at the front of Daniel's trousers, reaching inside and taking him clumsily in hand. He bucked beneath me, that beautiful low voice of his broken with moans, hips rising and arm trying to guide me over him. The Hunger was fire in my veins, pinching at my breasts and cunt, squeezing around my throat, and making even the roots of my hair feel sensitive, the weight of the strands pulling at my own scalp.

I closed my own eyes as if I could block out the truth of the scene—what would I tell the others?—and guided the head of him to my opening.

I whimpered as I tried to sink onto him. The Hunger might've been in control, but I was still me and I wasn't really *ready*, wasn't as wholly committed to the moment as I was with my Chosen. Daniel hissed and sat up, arms wrapping around me and mouth latching to my throat, his beard tickling my skin as he sucked and licked and nibbled on the muscle of my throat and shoulder while I bounced on his cock. He was big, thick, and it took me a frustrated moment before I was moving easily on top of him.

"That's it, Your Highness," Daniel rasped, one hand sliding under my skirt to squeeze my upper thigh, pushing me further open.

I cried out, head falling back and eyes gazing unseeing up at the ceiling as he rubbed at my clit, and I began to ride him in earnest.

"Ungh! Yes, yes that's it," he praised

I slapped a hand over his mouth, and Daniel bit my palm playfully, breath huffing. He groaned as I slid further down, grinding and rocking against his lap, shallow movements that kept him buried inside of me. His tongue flicked out, and it was a shocking kind of pleasure that echoed my cunt, making me moan and gasp, bouncing harder, faster. He kept it up, sucking and kissing at my palm, his thumb rolling my clit until I was nothing but movement, purely determined to crest, to reach the finish the Hunger had been craving since the last time I'd come.

I stiffened in his arms, and Daniel took over the work for us both, his arm around my waist hauling and dropping me on his length, hand working at the flesh of my pussy, teasing and touching. My hand slipped over his mouth as I started to shake, and Daniel sucked my fingers between his lips.

Aric's warning was the furthest thing from my mind. Even my own Chosen were distant. Daniel was there in front of me, but it wasn't really about him either. I just needed this horrible pressure that'd been building in me to finally snap, I needed the release.

And then it came, striking me with horror as I realized I had no idea where the magic would go, I pulled my hands off Daniel at the last second and came with a cry and a trembling, toe-curling rush, my eyes slamming shut. I clamped tight around

Daniel's thick cock, felt his breath in my hair, and then the surface of the floor on my back.

Daniel's weight was gentle but his hips were not, crashing into mine as my legs and arms twined around him, my face buried in his throat.

"Oh, Bryony," he growled, his arm around my back tilting me up for the taking until I could feel him *everywhere*, all the way up to my throat. It was punishing and desperate, and I squeezed around him as the Hunger circled, ready for its second course. Daniel's pelvis hit at the perfect angle, his free hand tugging on my hair until my face was turned to his.

For all the rough force of his fucking, the kiss was tender, searching, our breaths finding a rhythm until we were exchanging air. My back slid along the floor, a lace of my dress catching on a rough floorboard and pinching at my waist. I dug my heels against the floor, trying to brace myself against Daniel's driving fucking, my hands reaching out and grasping at the edge of the desk.

"Please," I whispered, although I didn't really know what I was asking for.

Daniel rose up on his knees, his shirt clutched in my fist, back exposed, and he lifted me, working me onto his cock at a new angle that left me limp and breathless.

The next climax came quick and brutal, my body soft and pliant one moment and as tense as a pulled bowstring the next, magic biting at my bones and veins as it burned through me and out into the air. Daniel shuddered and buried himself to the hilt inside me, teeth biting on my jaw as we fell apart together, my body milking his cock for the hot, soft burst inside of me. His arm was so tight around my ribs I could barely breathe, his fist twisted in my hair, and he turned us with a labored grunt, his back against the drawers of the desk with me collapsed against his chest.

His hand in my hair turned gentle at last, soothing carefully down the back of my neck as I trembled through the bright aftershocks. His head turned, lips grazing against my temple, and I flinched away.

The Hunger abated, still a snarl, but satisfied for the moment, and Daniel stilled beneath me.

"You are not Chosen," I breathed, my face tucked against his shoulder like a child hiding in their protector's arms.

But Daniel *wasn't* my protector. He'd made that clear. He'd wanted to fuck me, and ideally, reassure the council of his position. And I...I had just let the Hunger have what it wanted, what I was significantly less sure of, no matter how exquisite it had felt.

I sat up slowly, trying and failing not to feel the shift of him inside me.

There was no fire in the face in front of me now, and no hard exterior either. Daniel was hollowed out. So was I. We were facing one another at our weakest.

"I don't trust you," I said, almost as if it were a decent explanation. "This was a mistake."

"You're blaming me?" Daniel asked.

"No," I said, because I understood the note of fear in his tone. "I'm just saying it shouldn't have happened."

"*Now?* It only just finished," he breathed, scoffing lightly.

I winced as I rose, all too aware of how full I'd been a moment ago.

"Bryony, *wait*," he gasped, lips red and hair rumpled as I stood and stared down at him. His hands reached for my waist until mine batted them away.

"You wanted to fuck me, and now you have," I said, stumbling back and to the side, trying to get the desk between us, for all the good it'd done as a barrier in the first place. I paused and gaped at the windows. They'd been foggy when I entered, rippled with age. Now they were smooth panes in shades of gold and blue, giving the room a peaceful quality that didn't suit the broken moment.

I heard Daniel scrambling behind me, and he stood, tucking his cock away but not bothering to fasten his pants. I'd torn a button off his collar at some point, left a scratch on his shoulder I could see in the corner.

My eyes rose to his and I tried not to flinch at the open confusion, the...*want* still lingering there. It wasn't lust now, and

I suspected he was craving the same thing I was in the moment —some kind of affection to soothe the rough edges of the animal act. Except that I didn't trust Daniel. I didn't like Daniel. And I didn't want to share that with him.

"What do you want now?" I asked.

His lips parted, and nothing came out for several deep breaths until I grew sick of waiting for something I didn't really want to hear and I left the room.

11.
CRESSWELL

I hadn't wrestled with Bryony when she demanded I take a shift off and rest, mainly because I hadn't wanted to explain that I *couldn't* rest in the guard's dormitory when it wasn't where she was.

It wasn't really an appropriate excuse to offer to the crown princess.

So I'd drunk a pint of mead and slept fitfully through half a night and most of a morning before I decided that the princess would just have to forgive me for my vigilance.

"Where is she?" I asked the guard at the door.

"Dunno, library I think."

Except at the library, they said she'd gone to find the steward, and when I'd found Lady Prudence she hadn't known what I was talking about. There was no one stationed in Farraque's wing.

"Where is she? Where is Guard Holloway?" I asked Yorley.

"Saw him follow her out toward the lake," he answered with a glare. "Aren't you meant to be taking a day of rest?"

"Are you saying I don't look rested?" I countered with a cocked brow, not bothering to wait for a response. Let him curse my back. If only Camellia had dragged him back to the south with her too.

I found Holloway picking his teeth under a willow and watched with a frustrated kind of satisfaction as he scrambled to stand.

"She's by the tunnel, said she didn't want to be disturbed by anyone," Holloway rushed out. "See, you can just see her skirts through the grasses."

I ducked to check, Bryony's pale blue skirt glowing through the grass. "Who's with her?"

I didn't want to disturb her with the others, more for the sake of my sanity than her comparative privacy.

"No one," Holloway said, shrugging. "She seemed in a low mood."

That was...odd and a little concerning. Bryony always had one of her men nearby.

"Where are the Chosen?"

"Owen just came in from the woods, the prince and Pope had a late breakfast and went to the library, and the sculptor is working. He came out, but I told him what she said and he went back in."

"You bored?" I asked, itching to go and check Bryony but not wanting tongues left wagging.

"Um..." Holloway was young and fairly unseasoned, but I liked him and he seemed to take his position seriously, unlike most of the others. "No, sir?"

Also, he called me sir.

"I am, I could use a shift," I said, shrugging and watching him sigh. "You can go and grab something from the kitchens, if you like."

He was sweet on the maid, and from what I'd seen out of the corner of my eyes, it was mutual and not moving in a great rush.

"If that's—If that's your order, sir," Holloway said, almost twitching to run back to the palace.

I resisted my grin. "It is."

He took off just shy of racing, and I waited till he was halfway back before ducking out from under the eaves of the willow, taking slow quiet steps in the direction of the tunnel. Bryony was there on the soggy bank of the lake, knees drawn up to her chest and eyes fixed to the water. Her head twitched in my direction, listening to my approach, but she never looked over.

"I asked to be alone."

My steps paused, and I took a deep breath, letting my second nature rise just a touch. Salt on the air. And sex. Not her Chosen, but still a familiar smell. I stamped down on my bear before I could growl, back bunching with tension.

"Did he *hurt* you?" I didn't mean to ask, I understood it wasn't my place, but the words rose up when nothing else would.

Bryony's knees dropped to the side, and her head whipped in my direction, eyes widening and skin pale. I turned my face to the ground, bowing as low as I could as if it could make up for my impertinence, and then stiffened as I heard the trembling breath, rattling wetly from her lips.

No order could've stopped me from marching forward, nothing but the lean of her body away from mine as I ducked down to the ground to try and catch her eyes.

"I don't want to deal with another man right now, Guard Stark," she said, biting down on my title to put me in my place.

I paused and then rolled my head on my shoulders, letting the prickle of my other skin rush up over me. I'd always wondered how the shifting magic worked, but the closest I'd come to an explanation in my own mind was that I stepped out of my man's skin and into another, easier than changing my clothes.

Bryony gasped as I transformed in front of her, but her shoulders drooped, tension bleeding away, and she hiccuped a weary giggle, her hands falling to her lap.

She didn't stop me as I padded closer, even though I was probably five times her size. She didn't stop me from nuzzling at her palms either, not understanding what I could read—the stench of Farraque still clinging to her—only laughing as I huffed and shook my beastly head, sitting back on my haunches.

"No, he didn't hurt me," she said softly, studying me. "I hurt myself by... I'm not sure where it started, really." She released a shaking sigh, and her hand trembled in the air between us until I ducked my head again and butted my ears against her fingers, encouraging her touch.

It was a little like cheating, getting her comfortable with me this way, but I didn't respond to her the way I would've as a man. I was safer for her, in this form. Better able to protect her, soothe her, listen to her confession. The only challenge was restraining my growl where it concerned Daniel Farraque.

"I might've hurt him too, and I haven't decided how I feel about that," she whispered, brow furrowing. She reached out for my paw, and it was strange to be examined this way, to have to sit patiently as she touched the rough pads of my toes, tapping her nail against a claw in absent curiosity.

"I will have to tell the others," she murmured, her breath starting to stutter again.

I grumbled, and she released my paw, scooting in closer and digging her fingers into the fur on my shoulders.

"I'm afraid I will turn into my sister. That the Hunger will never really be fed and I'll constantly be at the mercy of it."

I shifted back and forth, wanting badly to shift back into a man, to scoop Bryony up against my chest. Accidents happen, I wanted to say to her. Everyone makes a mistake. You've only slipped up this once.

And I still wanted to blame Daniel Farraque for it; I was *sure* she was being too generous.

She was sniffling now, little squeaks of tears, and at least as a bear I was more immune to sharing her sorrow. I leaned toward her and let her sink against my massive side, careful not to put too much weight on her or accidentally scratch her. I caught her skirt with a claw, and she took it as invitation to climb over my legs and hide herself in the hunch of my frame. It was an odd feeling, the satisfaction of my man's brain meeting with the accepting but amused bear's perspective.

"I'm not really sure how much of this you understand right now," Bryony hiccuped.

All of it, I thought back at her.

"But I appreciate this. I'm just very tired. And my headache is mostly gone, and somehow that just makes it all a bit worse," Bryony continued. "As if I was being punished for not having sex for days and now I'm rewarded for fucking someone I don't even like."

I grunted, and Bryony went back to crying until the tears began to stutter and she grew heavier against me, and quieter, and eventually I realized she'd fallen asleep.

COSMO STOOD in the veranda doorway, hand over his heart and face sheet white. I could hear his racing pulse from here.

"Damnit, Cresswell, you nearly killed me," Cosmo gasped, yanking open the door.

Bryony was in my arms, face buried in brown fur, limp with exhaustion, and I didn't blame Cosmo for his initial terror.

"What's happened? Is she all right?" he whispered. "She *is* sleeping isn't she?"

I grunted softly and nodded, lumbering awkwardly into the room, Cosmo rushing to protect his art from my overly large form while also keeping his eyes on the girl in my arms. I carried her to the couch on the far end of the room and set her down as carefully as I could, Cosmo joining me to catch her head and shoulders.

"You can't go roaming the halls like that. The guards might be used to Thao, but they won't expect a massive bear in the palace," Cosmo muttered and then looked up at me with narrowed eyes. "You...you *are* Cresswell, aren't you?"

I grinned, and Cosmo flinched and squeezed between me and Bryony, sitting at her side as she started to stir. I finally eased down to all fours, wincing at the scratch of claw on tile, and headed out of the room.

If I ran into a guard, I could shift back in the time it took them to find themselves shocked at the sight of me. And I had someone in particular I wanted to see at the moment. Anyway, I knew where everyone was stationed. I could make it, and as long as I didn't accidentally terrify one of the staff, it would be fine.

There was a small set of stairs leading up to the second story around the corner from Cosmo's studio room, and I was just barely able to squeeze up the narrow flight. The air in the palace was strange with this nose, prickly and full of the smells of humans. The prickling grew sharper the closer I moved to my destination. It must've been Bryony's magic, and just the thought of how it had ended up here, fresh and still soaking into the bricks, made me growl softly.

I found the hall of Daniel Farraque's rooms without incident. Bryony was in the air here, sweet and delicate, snapping with magic. His scent was stronger, thick and woodsy with salt and musk, I bared my teeth and let my paws drag along the floor, listened for the moment when the man in the room heard me coming. His movements paused and his breath stopped, but there was a bitter tang of stress coming from the open door, a tantalizing edge of fear.

I was surprised he didn't move. No man was quiet enough to sneak up on me like this, and it was clear that he was only waiting, listening, heart starting to hammer.

I growled as I reached the door, and Daniel's breath hitched. He was by a set of shelves, his shirt untucked and sleeves rolled up, collar unbuttoned. He wasn't his usual polished self, but his eyes weren't red and puffy like Bryony's either, so I felt justified in the snarl I delivered from the doorway.

"I knew it," he breathed. He held a book in one hand, his perusal interrupted by my intrusion, and the hand lowered, his shoulders dropping as I moved into the room.

He didn't call for the guards, and though I could sense his terror and hear the jerk and whine of his breath in his chest, he didn't move away as I approached.

"I—I didn't... Fuck," Daniel breathed, the blood rushing out of his face as I rose up to my hind legs, towered over him, and snarled down into his face, the hair over his forehead ruffling with my breath. There was white all around his eyes until he squeezed them shut. He flinched and braced himself, speaking again. "I had no intention of upsetting her."

It was a whisper, half thrown to the floor as if he thought the words were useless but wanted to speak them anyway. He wasn't pleading for his life, and he seemed to know *why* I was here.

He thought she'd blame him, my man's brain offered.

I flexed my claws and then shifted back to Cresswell the man, my sword in my grip, raised between us and poised to take Daniel's throat.

"Do it again and I'll rip your throat out, in one form or another," I growled, some of the animal still in my throat.

"I'm not here to hurt her," Daniel hissed, face still turned away but eyes open and on the floor.

"Do you even know why you're here?" I asked, reaching into my coat, pulling out the letter Aric had shared with me, the one that left me sleepless since the night of the festival. I swatted Daniel's cheek with it. "Did you *ask* why you're here? Do you know what your orders will be, or do you just wait to follow them when they come?"

I had the words memorized by now. I dropped the letter to the floor and left the room.

12.
BRYONY

I sat up in the tub, and Wendell lifted a scoop of soapy water up as I closed my eyes, his hand lifting to shield my face as he rinsed my hair. Thao sat by the tub on the tile floor, holding one of my hands, working oil meticulously into every digit, every nail, every crease of skin. Cosmo did the same with my feet as Owen washed me.

In spite of the care, the touch, and the painful amount of love and affection I was feeling for my Chosen in the moment, the Hunger was nowhere to be found. I was beginning to think of my magic as another woman living inside of me, some feminine force that was all appetite until it was time to fess up to wrongdoings. Then suddenly she was happy to slink away and hide while I tried to manage the mess.

"I'm so sorry," I murmured, eyes starting to sting again.

I'd confessed the whole story from Sam's entrance in the library to falling asleep against Cresswell's bear. I'd started over my dinner plate, shifting the food from one spot to the next, unable to stomach the idea of eating. Pretty quickly, the second I'd started to sob out the Hunger taking over during the argument with Daniel, I'd been moved to the bedroom.

"I think we should kill him," Thao said mildly, pausing his massage to frown at a fingernail, picking dirt away and going back to his work as the rest of us gaped at him.

"No," I said.

Thao glanced up, head tilting in curiosity. "He knew better."

"So did I!"

"Stop," Wendell murmured, and I wasn't sure if he was speaking to Thao or to me, but we both settled. "I don't think killing Daniel is the solution for the moment. Bryony, you feel certain he didn't force you?"

"Positive. If anything I might've forced him—"

"No," Cosmo, Thao, and Owen all said at once.

"We all *know* the Hunger is capable of forcing," I said.

"Yes, and you know how it looks, how it feels," Owen murmured, hands stroking my shoulders back into their soft slump as Wendell worked a silky lather through my strands. "Was that what happened?"

I sighed and my eyes shut. "No."

"Now we know something new, which is that it isn't safe for *you* to ignore the Hunger forever," Cosmo said gently. "I'm sorry it cost you. We're not killing Daniel, but you're well within your rights to dismiss him."

I nodded. "I know. I'm considering it."

"How is your head?" Wendell asked as his fingers worked a kind of magic that left my head heavy on my shoulders.

The pound of pain had already subsided, and Wendell's fingers turning circles at the base of my skull ensured it stayed away.

"Aren't you at all angry with me?" I asked, trying not to whine.

"Of course not," Wendell said, kissing my forehead.

"Never," Owen echoed.

"Yes," Thao and Cosmo both said.

Wendell snapped a warning in Mennarian, and Thao shrugged, smiling at me. "I have a jealous nature. If it was Aric, I would understand. I've been warned. But you shared yourself with someone when I wasn't expecting it, and I am... I'm understanding, but yes, a little angry."

'Thank you,' I mouthed to him, and his eyes crinkled at the corner with his hidden smile as he raised the hand he was holding up to lay a kiss on my palm. I turned to Cosmo next and swallowed, trying not to appear as though I was bracing for the worst.

"I think you need to reconcile yourself to the idea that the Hunger is not an affliction you're forced to bear, but part of your *nature*, Bryony," Cosmo said, kneeling down at the end of the tub, his hands wrapped loosely around my ankle. "Aric might know a great deal about magic in the north but that doesn't make him an authority on you or the Hunger."

"Also he is clearly a spiteful, jealous man," Thao added with a toss of his dark hair.

I released a watery sigh, sliding forward in the tub and reaching out for Cosmo. He was ready, soft smile spread over his lips, arms extended as I kneeled and rose, our lips meeting firmly.

"I love you," I whispered.

"I love you, my muse," Cosmo answered, peppering more kisses over my cheeks and forehead before smacking his lips together when he caught some soap on his tongue.

"I wish this tub was big enough for all of us," I said with a frown, turning back to let Wendell rinse the cream out of my hair. "I don't feel right being pampered alone."

"Perhaps the Hunger's magic could fashion a larger tub," Owen suggested.

"Let's worry about that for another time. Both the tub and the shared pampering," Wendell said. "We all need a decent night's sleep together."

I held my breath and ducked beneath the surface of the water, trying to let go of the day's troubles, until my Chosen drew me out again, pulling me into their arms and wrapping me up in a towel.

"No more holding back, from yourself or us," Cosmo said, gentle and firm all at once.

"I promise," I said, rising up to my toes and kissing his chin and then up to his lips, sinking into the kiss.

The Hunger rose as Cosmo's arms wrapped around me, my bare body grazing against his clothed one for a teasing form of friction. I tried not to resent the return of her presence, tried not to think of the fever and fight of those minutes with Daniel, or the sound of his voice, shredded and pleading in my ear.

"Hello, Sam. I hope we're not bothering you," I said.

Sam was difficult to track down in the palace. He had a guard assigned to keep watch of him, but there weren't enough people in the staff to follow the apparently winding trails Sam took through the palace halls. We found him in the western gallery, sitting in a chair, studying an old painting. It was a depiction of one of the warrior matriarchs of the queen's line, probably over half a millennia old. She had golden hair streaming back behind her in a collection of braids, with bared breasts spilling over the frame of a metal corset. Her head was thrown back, eyes wide with ecstatic pleasure as her yellow stallion reared up, cock inflamed. She was holding a spear, and it was thrust through an enemy soldier's heart.

I wrinkled my nose at the image and searched until I found the floral motif.

"Ah, Queen Aster," I said, spotting the weedy purple daisies filling the corners of the painting. "I always imagined her more..." *Not going into battle with her tits out.*

"I think the artist took some liberties," Wendell murmured, blushing a little and glancing at me. "Some resemblance, though."

I might've been imagining the innuendo, thinking of the way I'd ridden his lap this morning, but I bit off my giggle and turned back to Sam.

"Do you like art?" Cosmo asked Sam, moving slowly up to stand in line with the man's chair, but far enough to the side not to startle him.

"No," Sam said.

Cosmo's hands stuffed in his pockets and nodded, shoulders shaking with a laugh as he spun on his heel. "Ah. Studio work might not be for you then."

Sam sat up at that, and I was pleased to find him a little more alert as he stood and faced us. "You have something for me to do?" he asked.

"We've brainstormed a few ideas we wanted to offer," I said, nodding.

Sam had an avian quality to the turns of his head, something that reminded me of Griffin, and I wondered wildly if he had a second nature too. If Kimmerians were keeping it secret, it was more than likely some had ended up as Chosen and...

And kept it secret as Wendell might've done if it hadn't been *me* he and Thao ended up with.

I turned to Wendell and Thao since we already knew Sam wasn't likely to be interested in helping in Cosmo's studio. Which was fine, Cosmo probably didn't want to spend his days training someone when he could be working.

"We're currently researching the north, looking for good places to start more apple orchards. Pears too. Maybe cherries. It's mostly dull work at the moment, studying maps and checking land permits in the Rumsbrooke records, but soon we'll be doing some traveling, talking to men and women who might be interested in the work."

"I'll do whatever you ask me to," Sam said without any enthusiasm in the words, eyes blinking.

"All right, well, that's one option," I said, taking a deep breath and then offering an encouraging smile up at Owen.

"Another is that the Winter Palace doesn't have a game-keeper, and only one groomsman so far, aside from what I can do to help," Owen said.

My eyebrows bounced and I glanced at Wendell, whose lips quirked as he nodded. We'd hired a groomsman at last? It wasn't so surprising to assume that the stewards had taken the initiative at last, without saying so to me. I wasn't meant to be concerned. But I did enjoy knowing the operation of the palace and who helped us day to day.

"If you like animals, I can certainly—"

"I like animals," Sam said, eyes widening, feet scuffing forward.

"Do you? I walk the grounds every day, try to check on the nests and dens, make sure everyone's doing fine," Owen said, shrugging. "It's quiet work, mostly walking. But the animals will learn to trust you if you're patient."

It was obvious how eager Sam was, his whole face had lit up even without a smile, and his eyes were sharp and alert, body buzzing with excitement.

"You have a second nature," Sam said, head tipping.

"Me? Nah, I just like animals," Owen said with a shrug, eyeing Sam back with equal interest.

"Sam...do *you* have a second nature?" I asked softly.

"No!" He stiffened and stared at me, rearing back.

"Oh, I'm sorry," I said, slowing my words and keeping my smile simple. "I didn't mean to shock you. It's just that I know many second natured are...are reluctant to share the information due to the current laws."

"I was until I realized Bryony had no intention of making me register, or anyone else for that matter," Wendell said, eyeing me with the question in his eye.

"Right, it doesn't matter." I laughed lightly and started to turn. "I'm glad you can join Owen in his treks. He's never afraid of wolves, but I worry."

"I used to be," Sam whispered, halting my movement.

My hand pressed to my stomach, and I released a silent breath as Thao stepped in.

"Used to be?"

"I...I can shift, but I can't fly now, so I don't," Sam said.

The cold trickled in, seeping down right to my bones, a frigid warning of what I knew with a sharp horror might come next.

"She broke my wings."

I sucked in a breath, and Sam startled as I faced him again, my eyes wide. "Camellia? She..."

"I can show you," Sam said softly, soft white blond hair catching sunlight with the next tip of his head, making his head glow with white fire.

My mouth hung open. I didn't *want* to see, I thought I'd already learned the worst of Camellia.

Sam didn't wait, or one of my Chosen must've nodded, because I winced in the next second and then gasped as a great snowy white owl screeched in front of us, hopping and trying to beat its wings which hung twisted and tugged, feathers turned in odd directions. Owen landed on his knees, crouching low and stretching his hands out to the owl.

"That's enough. That's enough, Sam, you'll make it worse," Owen said gently, an ache in his words.

Sam reappeared, seated on the floor, arms wrapped around his shoulders, panting hard.

"But his arms are fine?" Owen asked softly, glancing back at us with a furrowed brow.

"It's not the same body," Wendell answered. "One soul, two natures, two forms."

I sank slowly down to the ground, Sam's pale eyes fixed watchfully to my every movement.

"When?" I asked. "When did this happen, Sam?

"A few days after you left for the north. I showed it to her years ago to amuse her, but I... Sometimes I would shift just to... just to rest a little," he said, frowning as my hands rose to cover my mouth. "I started doing it more recently. I didn't think she noticed, and then one day—" He shook his head, over and over, as if he couldn't stop himself.

"Sam, are there others? Does she have others like you? Others she might hurt in this way?" I asked, wanting to reach out, to wrap him up in my arms. He wouldn't appreciate it, and I didn't blame him.

"There's one, but he never told her and...they all saw," he said, nodding toward his shoulder.

So it was unlikely he'd reveal anything now. That was for the best.

"I'm not sure there's anything we can do now," Owen murmured. He'd slid closer to Sam, who didn't seem to care or notice, as if Owen's special touch with animals extended to him too. "It depends on how freshly broken it is in your second form. I don't know how the magic works."

I stood up, moving quickly away, ignoring Sam's flinch. "I know who we can ask," I said, marching for the door.

13.
ARIC

"Y ou're a miserable bastard," Griffin muttered.

"You took the words right out of my mouth," I said.

"Someone should've taken a great many more words out of your mouth, Aric. Spared...quite a few people a fair amount of trouble."

I sighed, grimacing as I lifted the mug to my lips, guzzling the remaining contents before lifting an eyebrow at Otto, my bartender. He raised one back till I glowered at him, and then came to refill my cup. The only person I wish my mouth had spared right now was Bryony, and perhaps myself. I'd been stewing in my own personal punishment for the words I'd thrown at her for days now, trying to make amends in my research. Or just too cowardly to go and apologize.

"You can't afford to be missing the favor of the crown right now. Haven't you been paying attention? Emory is out for your head. Not your court, Aric. He's planning on taking it the old fashioned way."

A King of Thieves was deposed from his seat in only a handful of ways. He could hand over his crown to his heir—a rare manner of the deed, and one that tended to leave courts unimpressed with their new king. Most often, and the way I'd taken the crown myself, a king might be bested in a theft or a fight by their opponent. The old way was the simplest of the three. A challenger killed the old king and took up his crown.

Yes, Emory would like that one.

I'd thought him a young egoist who would grow bored of managing a court of thieves and eventually come to roost when he first appeared. He gave me no trouble, and I'd taken it as a blessing instead of the warning it was. Emory kept his nose clean of my work so that I wouldn't have cause to squash him before he grew more popular. But he'd risen while Charlotte was still alive, and she'd always preferred me merciful.

He'd started to show his colors since Bryony's arrival, whispers turning into warnings. But the attempted stunt at the festival made him an entirely darker creature than I'd predicted. I should've seen his tavern sooner, and I would've known what kind of king he intended on being.

"It's not just my head I'm worried about," I muttered.

"Oh and you're doing such a grand job of being an ally to her while you guzzle down that ale," Griffin snapped back.

You know better, Charlotte's voice murmured. *The crown doesn't rest.*

Which only made me think of Bryony again, and the words I'd thrown in her face, and the fact that she had guards watching her day and night who were loyal to her enemies, and a steward who took orders from someone else and...

"You're on your third night of whatever this is," Otto answered.

"What do I pay you for?" I snarled at him.

"Loyalty," he answered, frown almost invisible through that dense beard of his.

I grunted. Figures. Thieves were mercenaries at heart. Even the ones who ran by the code.

"You should go and—"

"I will," I hissed at Griffin, who glared back at me and reminded me that king or not, she didn't tolerate men baring their teeth at her. I rolled my head on my shoulders, wincing as muscles twinged and bones cracked. "I will. I'll go tomorrow."

"And apologize," Griffin said sternly. "What will you say?"

I laughed at her and shook my head before she could take it the wrong way. "I do know how to make an apology, Griff. I was married to Charlotte. She demanded them and practically composed them for me until I'd mastered my own."

Griff's smile was soft, a rare sight, and she lifted her glass in a brief toast between us.

Truth be told, I *didn't* know what I would say to Bryony. I'd done my digging as I'd promised, found old texts that referred cryptically to the 'source of magic' and the queen's line together, a loose record of when the source became the Hunger. Old magicians were like poets, fashioning words together oddly into metaphor to keep their secrets from one another, but it led to a long line of misinformation trickling down the generations.

And none of that was really at the crux of what needed to be repaired.

I had injured my princess, and I knew it was because I'd meant to injure the part of myself that had developed feelings for her, as if I could break that piece off like a branch of a tree, not realizing until after the wound was there that the feelings went down to my roots too. I had thrown her desires back into her face. I'd treated her as if she were like her sister, as if after all she'd already accomplished, she were a selfish creature.

It wasn't just forgiveness I would be asking for, either. I needed to decide what I really wanted from Bryony, and then learn if it were even still possible after all the shit I'd spouted at her.

"It starts with 'I'm sorry,'" Griff said with uncommon gentleness.

I nodded and stared down at my half-drunk cup before sliding it back across the counter to Otto, who scoffed and poured it into a new cup, topping it off before taking it down the bar as Griffin and I gaped at him.

"Disgusting," Griff said, looking down at her own mug.

"He's always been a little too penny-pinching," I agreed.

The door to the bar banged open at that moment, and I glanced over my shoulder, frowning at the sight of Scrapper dragging himself in with scuffling steps, an eye swollen and bruised, blood blooming on his sleeve.

"Scrap!" I called as he twisted and searched the room until his good eye found mine.

Goody and Robert Jupe jumped up from their table, taking Scrapper's arms over each of their shoulders and helping haul him to me.

"What's happened?"

"I was listening at the Yawning Pig's windows and some of

Emory's men caught me," Scrapper rasped, spitting up some blood.

"Matthew, over here!" Griffin called to Matthew Sloan, a former country doctor who'd lost his practice when it was given away by the council to someone's polished son.

Scrapper nodded in begrudging thanks to Griffin before turning back to me. "He's on his way, Your Majesty. He wants to challenge and he wants to do it here. Tonight. I got away, but they meant for you not to know."

Griffin and I exchanged a long look until Otto interrupted it, slamming an empty bucket down on the counter and catching my eye. "You'd better hack that ale up before it catches up to you while he's got a sword at your throat."

"Aric, you have allies," Griffin murmured.

I glared at the bucket, my hand flexing. They were all right though. I'd drank too much tonight—and the past four nights— to win a fight. I'd not only lowered my guard, I'd left Emory's opportunity a wide hanging gate for him to pass through. I scanned the room, eyes narrowed, all too aware that I was already a little dizzy, and that someone in my court, in my *bar*, had probably been the one to tell Emory I was getting pissed every night.

"If I fly up the mountain, I might get word to them in time," Griffin hissed in my ear.

I nodded. "Yes, go." Emory might take my crown, but I'd rather he didn't take my head off with it. If Griffin could get to the palace... "You'll have to start my apology," I said, pulling a ring from my finger and passing it into Griffin's hand, pressing magic into it until it transformed between our skin. Griffin stared down at the small blossom ring, her lips twitching. "Go to her directly. Guard Stark won't intervene on my behalf unless Bryony orders it."

Because he heard what I said to her, and knows I'm an ass, I added privately.

Griffin nodded, closing her fist around the ring before glancing at Scrapper in his bloodied state. "Try not to die, the both of you. Stall, Aric," Griffin said, arching an eyebrow before rushing for the door.

"Doc, patch up our man," I said, nodding to Scrapper. I turned to the bar and huffed out a sigh before jamming my fingers into my mouth till I started to gag, grabbing the bucket just in time. When I'd finished emptying my stomach, Otto held out a stained and soggy rag and I glared at him.

"I've got a nasty concoction that might help sober you up," he said.

"Do your worst," I answered with a nod, my eyes trailing to the mirror above the bar that reflected the door.

Unless I felt like cheating the code, which Emory would likely do but wasn't my preferred style, I wouldn't be allowed to use any magic. I might get away with some, simply because he was useless at it and no doubt wouldn't spot any attempts by me.

Or you can let him take the crown, accept a rescue before he slits your throat, and go retreat, Charlotte's voice suggested.

Retreat where?

You know where.

It would hurt my court to leave them in the hands of a man like Emory, but someone would rise up, just as they always did. Emory was too selfish to rule so many for long, and I refused to believe he had the power to keep his boots on their throats. Even from the palace, I might orchestrate...

Except I wasn't guaranteed refuge at the palace. I'd made sure of that.

Otto passed me a steaming mug that smelled sick and bitter, making my mouth rush with saliva. I gagged before even taking the first great gulp and then immediately heaved after I swallowed, adding to the mess in the bucket.

"Oh, you *are* a sorry sight, aren't you?"

My hand found the long dagger at my side as I finished spitting and then forced the mug up to my lips, chugging three swallows and glaring fire at Otto. He was a sadist, apparently, as this was the foulest thing I'd ever put to my lips, entirely bitter and burning. But he was *loyal* too, as he'd said, and it wasn't all to do with the coin I paid him. I wiped the back of my mouth with my sleeve and turned to face the pompous peacock in my doorway.

Emory stood wearing his infernal grin, fiery hair tossed to one side, eyes glinting meanly. He had a few bulky figures at his back, and I was glad Griffin had already left for the palace. Emory would cheat, or he would make some kind of spectacle out of this event. He'd brought muscle for a reason.

Scrapper was tucked away with our doctor and a few friends standing guard, and others in my court had moved from their seats, piling together around tables at the edges of the room. No one would rise to defend me. Emory had the right to challenge, and even Otto wouldn't intervene. Some of the familiar faces around the room looked angry on my behalf, wary of Emory, but plenty more looked curious. What would this potential new king change for them? More coin in their pockets?

Yes, if they didn't care where it came from.

"I've been waiting for this day, Martin—" Emory started, stepping forward, stare keen.

I scoffed and mirrored him, yanking an empty table aside to make myself a path. "I'm sorry, were we meant to prepare speeches, or would you rather get to the fight?"

My court laughed, a few cheered with cries of 'yay!' either eager for blood or happy to mock Emory.

His pretty face twisted with annoyance, and we reached for our weapons at the same time.

"No magic," he snarled.

I nodded and then glanced at his brutes. "No extra hands."

Emory grinned like a cat, pushing another table aside, the wood screeching against the floor. "Looking at you, I know I won't need them."

He lunged, snarling, and I grinned as he ran for the attack, dodging around a table and stepping up onto a chair, swiping my blade toward his shoulder just enough to tear his silken sleeve. The chair wobbled beneath me and I landed unsteadily on my feet, jumping backwards as Emory spun to face me again, calming himself.

We took measure of one another for one brief pause. He was an impatient, inelegant fighter, but he was sober and young and I was still unbalanced from drinking, my vision a little blurry, my body wearied from being mistreated for days in a row.

Stall, I reminded myself, painting a grin on my face and sliding a chair between us.

I didn't deserve it if Bryony did send help, but she had an irresistible goodness in her that I'd been craving for weeks now. If I lived through the night, I'd find a way to make my ugly words up to her.

"I'm going to enjoy this," Emory said, tensing and ready to strike.

I believed him.

14.
Bryony

I ate aimlessly at dinner, frowning at my plate, trying not to stare down the table to where Sam sat, similarly listless.

"She comes to hunt tomorrow," Wendell whispered to me, and I nodded. "Nothing will change overnight that hasn't already—"

"Already worsened since it happened weeks ago?" I asked, glancing at Wendell, who wore an equally uncomfortable look on his face even as he leaned in, an arm around my shoulders, and kissed my temple. "I know you're right."

I'd sent for Griffin in the city, but no one had been able to find her, and truth be told, I didn't know what she would or could do. She hadn't *admitted* to having a bird as her second nature, it was more a guess on Aric's part, and she and I weren't really familiar enough with one another for me to ask.

"Your Highness," Cresswell called, his tone strained from the hall. "Your Highness, there is something I think you should see!"

I rose up from my seat, brow furrowing, and moved around the table until I could see the end of the hall that led to the dining room. Cresswell was there, but he wasn't turned toward me, his eyes watching out a window.

It wasn't fully dark out yet, and I ran lightly down the hall until I could look out another window, to the front of the palace.

"Look up," Cresswell called.

There in the sky a small shadow flew, growing larger by the second, a bird in a rapid dive. A hawk!

"Open the doors!" I shouted, running down the hall, hearing Cresswell echo my words to the guards at the front door. "I think she's here," I called back to the diners.

We hadn't given any information to the men we'd sent to

Rumsbrooke, but my heart beat urgently in my chest, steps stumbling slightly as the hawk screeched and Cresswell dove out of the way, a flash of rust-red skipping through the opening of the hall. The sound of flight and a predator's scream echoed around the palace entry, and I reached Cresswell's side as Griffin spun around the high ceiling by the stairs, slowing her flight to a coast before circling down the floor.

She landed on the tile as a woman, her eyes wild and breath coming in short pants.

"You received my summons?" I asked as she jogged for me.

"What? No. Apologies, Your Highness, but he sent me," she said, gasping for air, grabbing my hand and ignoring Cresswell's grunt of objection as she pressed a metal object into my hand. "He's been a miserable, self-sorry fool and he would've given you a proper apology in person, but they're coming for him, princess. They mean to take his crown and his head with it."

I glanced down at the ring in my palm, the twisting delicate vines of gold with preciously perfect leaves cupping the exquisite opal white bryony blossom. And then her words struck me.

I didn't need to ask who, not on either account. I knew who needed me, and I didn't care who it was threatening him.

"Where?" I asked, seeing the worry in her gaze and feeling it amplify to panic in my own heart.

"Wing and Rook. I've told him to stall. I promise you, he's—"

"Bryony!" Cresswell shouted as I jammed the ring onto my middle finger and ran for the door. "Your Highness, wait! Guards!"

But he gave the command a moment too slow.

"There is a man here," I shouted over my shoulder before realizing Griffin was just behind me, quick to match my pace. "A snowy owl. His wings were broken. Can you help?"

Griffin's feet stumbled as her eyes went wide. "What?"

"His name is Sam. It was my sister's doing, and I'm so sorry. You were the only person I could think to ask." I was running for the stables, ignoring the shout of men at my back commanding me to stop. I was the Crown Princess of Kimmery, and Cresswell would just have to learn to catch up.

"I—you'll save, Aric?"

"Yes, of course!" I cried, frowning at the little bite of anger that rose up at his name. "If anyone deserves to throttle him, it's me."

Griffin laughed at that, and the running drum of her feet on gravel ended behind me.

"Shout for the groomsman," Owen hollered behind me.

Yes! Yes, we have one now! And I don't know his name, damnit.

"Groomsman!"

A white-bearded man with tan skin and his shirtsleeves rolled up, stepped out of the barn as I raced closer, his dark eyes going wide.

"I need a bridle and a blanket for my gelding," I said, my own breath coming short. "The others may want saddles."

"It'll take me a minute to get your—"

"No, I don't need a saddle! Just the bridle and the blanket," I snapped.

He stared blankly back at me, and I squinted as I stepped inside, seeing my horse's kit hanging by his stall.

"Nevermind, manage the others," I rushed out, running forward, my fingers clumsy as I fumbled for the latch.

"Your Highness, I should get..." The old man watched as I grabbed the bridle, gentling my motions as I fitted the bit to my horse's mouth and gently fastened the leather straps around his mouth and head. "I'll get you the blanket." I guided my ride out of the stall, and the man met me, slapping a quilted blanket over the horse's back just in time for me to leap up, huffing and ignoring his shocked face as I rearranged my skirts.

I pushed into a canter to leave the barn and then immediately squeezed my thighs around my horse's body, urging him forward, faster, facing the guards and my Chosen who rushed to follow.

"Princess Bryony, you must have *guards*," Cresswell roared.

"Then hurry up!" I answered in a shout, and he had to stumble back to avoid being mowed down.

I was heading right for the gate, which was being pushed shut by three men, when I saw Thao running down the steps, the sheath of an inukat sword in his hand.

"Don't you dare shut that! On the crown's orders," I

screamed to the gate, turning just enough to the front steps for Thao to throw me the sheath. I caught it by its strap, shrugging it around my shoulders, and then leaned down to brace myself against my horse's back, urging him into a gallop as we ran for the hanging gate.

Griffin had said Aric would stall, but how long could he really manage that, especially between Griffin's flight up the mountain and my race back down? Thao and I trained for an hour at a time, an hour and a half at most before we were too exhausted to go on, and that wasn't out and out fighting. Aric had maybe a half hour—three quarters if we were lucky—and some of that was already spent. I dug my heels carefully into my horse, my thighs like iron around his back, holding my seat for both our sakes despite the burn in my muscles.

He might win, I thought hopefully. *He might throw his challenger before I get there.*

He might slip and fail, and I'll be too late, too.

I held my breath and rode, eyeing the sloping mountain road carefully as the sun set behind me.

⚜

"You are a very, very good horse, you know that," I whispered, ignoring the scratch and ache of my legs as my horse trotted insistently through the streets of Rumsbrooke.

I didn't remember the way to the Wing and Rook but my horse seemed to know because every time I asked someone on the street for directions, we were already on the right path.

I gasped as he turned a corner and I recognized the buildings, saw the familiar crow sign hanging at the end of the street.

"I have to give you a lovely name," I said, patting his flank and slowly relaxing on his back as we slowed our approach. My body hurt, my hair was tangled in every direction around my head, my skirt splattered with mud from the road. If the people of Rumsbrooke recognized me with one glance, they second-guessed themselves with the next. I didn't look the part of a princess in spite of my fine gown, and that was probably for the best.

I jumped down from the back of my horse, guiding him to a water stall and tying him to one of the posts. "You kick anyone who tries to steal you, yes?" I said, brightening a little at his whinny before I rushed for the door. All of Owen's conversations were doing our animals good.

This time as I ducked into the tavern, taking the narrow stairs at the left down, my eyes didn't take so long to adjust. It was dark outside and only just a little brighter down here.

I heard the grunts of men, the clash of metal, and the clatter of wood and sighed in relief as I ran down the steps. If they were still fighting, Aric was still alive.

Alive, for now, a cruel voice taunted as I reached the great room and saw the scene. Both men were bleeding, but Aric looked by far the worst of the two, one eye swelling shut, the other red with the blood running down the side of his face. He had a fat lip and his shirt was torn, the arm of the other man around his throat, pinning Aric to his enemy's chest until Aric's face was flush, mouth working as he choked for air. And all around the room, men and women watched without moving. A few looked down to their empty glasses, worry or disappointment on their faces, but no one stood, no one intervened.

The other man, tall and handsome in spite of the cut on his cheek and the sweat on his brow, released Aric, who dropped to the floor with a wheezing gasp.

"The crown is mine!" the red-headed man cried out.

"The king is fallen! Long live King Emory!" the room cried with varying levels of enthusiasm.

"And now, Aric Martin," the man named Emory said, taking a grip of Aric's silver strands before kicking him hard in the back, making Aric wheeze and groan, "I think I'll have your head too, and gladly see the back of you."

The inukat whistled brightly as I drew it out of its sheath. "Absolutely not!"

Aric rasped, but it was only a sound, an acknowledgment, as the rest of the room took one breath and held it.

Emory blinked at me as I moved through fallen and broken tables, my blade raised. He grinned and tilted his head, eyeing me up and down. "I beg your fucking pardon?"

"That man is mine, and I'll take him from you now," I said.

"Is it a challenge?" a familiar voice cried, and Emory and the rest of the room laughed as I searched their faces until I found Scrapper, looking worse for wear, raising one bruised eyebrow at me.

"It is," I said, and the laughter died abruptly.

"No," Aric rasped. "Damnit, Scrap."

"I challenge you," I said, holding Emory's strangely delighted gaze.

"You challenge me?" Emory asked, laughing lightly, glancing down at Aric still held by the sweaty strands of his hair.

"If I win, you turn Aric over with *no* further harm done to him or anyone in this court," I said, thinking of the bruises Scrapper was sporting.

"And if I win, I get to cut off his head and put it where he can watch as I fuck you," Emory said, grinning.

"*No!*" Aric shouted as loud as he could from the floor, but his words were ragged.

I looked Emory over head to toe. He had more damage to his left side, and he was holding a long blade in his right. He must've relied on his offense rather than his defense.

But I would've bet *anything*—even the horrific taunt of his demand—that he hadn't been trained in three forms of fencing and the inukat fighting style. He would be rough and follow no rules, but he was already injured and tired compared to me. And I knew what he saw, what he recognized as he looked at me. A princess, in a pretty dress, near to tears over a man she—

"Deal," I said, and I noted the gasp from our audience and the slight falter of Emory's smile. He hadn't expected me to take that bet, so I needed to seem desperate rather than prepared.

"It's all right, Aric," I said softly, meeting his eyes, letting my own fill up. "I-I won't let anything happen to you."

There was a whine in my voice that I never used outside of when I was with my Chosen, and Aric blinked his one eye rapidly, staring at me. Emory jerked his head at two enormous men who stood against the bar. They hurried forward, gathering a stilled and silent Aric between them.

"You heard the *lady*," Emory said, smirking. "No further harm until after I win."

I gave Emory one single second to seem delighted with himself before I leapt forward, swinging the inukat and whipping it towards his throat. He barely blocked the strike and stumbled back into a table, leaning away with wide eyes as a sudden cheer went up from the room. I hadn't expected to win with one blow. All I'd meant to do was make myself room to move deeper into the circle, passing a table where Aric's own blade lay bloodied at the edge of a chair. I picked it up, and Emory's eyes flicked between my two hands, caution growing.

"That's it, lovey! We'll see who's fucked now!" a woman cried from the audience, and I grinned and waited patiently for Emory to move next.

He was expecting me to strike fast and often because that was what he would've done, and his frown grew as I learned the feel of Aric's dagger in my hand. It was similar to my own, and my left hand wasn't my best, but the two blades would be excellent for distracting Emory.

Footsteps thundered down the stairs, and I waited until Emory's eyes flicked before diving and thrusting, him skirting away with just a knick to his side.

"It's all in hand, gentlemen!" I shouted without turning my eyes away from Emory.

"Don't intervene," I heard Thao hiss. "He doesn't stand a chance."

The next thing I learned about Emory was that he must've been an egoist because those words made him grind his jaw and roar as he ran forward, trying to use force against me. I ducked and spun, and Emory bellowed as I ran the edge of the inukat gently up his spine, just a scratch, but one that bloomed with red on his already sweat-stained shirt.

"You little *whore*," Emory snarled, whipping to face me. "I'm going to leave you bleeding. I'm going to fuck you raw and hard until you can't sit for a week. We'll see what your ass can take too."

I resisted the urge to answer that I knew exactly what my ass could take, but my Chosen laughed, and I thought I even heard Aric choke.

Emory struck again, and I knocked it deftly away before realizing it was only a distraction. He heaved a chair directly for me, and I grunted as it hit me in the stomach and thighs. My hands were busy and my skirt was cumbersome, and Emory expected me to try to avoid the chair, so instead I jumped up, balancing carefully on the edge of its seat and ignoring my own need for air. Thao had taught me that pain was mostly mental, and I didn't have time to indulge. Breath would come, Emory hadn't broken anything and he was startled by my change to his plan, stumbling back as I jumped forward and advanced on him.

"You've got him, Your Loveliness!" Scrapper shouted.

"Get him!"

"Stab 'im in the dick! He don't deserve one!"

"You're not very popular, are you?" I asked, deciding to go ahead and prick that fragile ego once more.

Our blades connected once more between us, my inukat to his long dagger, and I grinned as I tilted my sword toward his face, knowing his could never reach me in the same way. It grazed near a lock of his hair hanging over his forehead, and we both watched as the diamond-sharp edge of the inukat trimmed the lock by a fraction, a little fluff of copper red hair falling to his nose, stealing his focus as I slipped Aric's dagger between us and pressed it to the apple of his throat, hard enough for blood to bead on the tip.

"Challenge completed!" the bartender roared, and the room screamed with a chorus of cheers, but I didn't tear my gaze away from Emory, didn't let him retreat, following him every tiny fraction of flinching, keeping him pinned.

"Cress!" I shouted. "Lock him up!"

It wasn't Cress who came and hauled Emory away, ripping his blade from his hands and dropping it to my feet, but a crowd of the unmoving audience from moments ago, Emory thrashing but not escaping their hold. Figures surrounded me, unfamiliar faces barring Aric out of sight in front of me, and my Chosen unable to break through. Two men reached for me, ignoring my sudden squirms as they bent to their knees and hauled me onto their shoulders.

"Oh! Scrapper! What's happening?" I cried out. "Aric? Aric, are you all right?"

"The king is fallen!" Scrapper cried, squeezing his way through the melee to stand near my feet. "Long live the king."

"The king is fallen! Long live the king!" the room answered.

15.
BRYONY

"**I** don't understand what's happened," I shouted to Scrapper as a raucous celebration kicked up all around me. It made the scene I'd walked in on earlier a funeral by comparison, which was maybe not far from the truth.

Speaking of which, I couldn't find Aric anywhere in this mass. I'd been set back on my feet after the chanting, but I'd completely lost track of any familiar faces but Scrapper's.

"Emory came for Aric's crown. He won it in the *challenge*," Scrapper answered with a crooked shrug, emphasizing the last word in a way that made my skin prickle. "But then *you* came. And you stole it from Emory! Congratulations, Your Loveliness. Your *Majesty*."

I blinked at Scrapper until a woman came up and grabbed both my cheeks, tugging me to her and pressing kisses above each of her thumbs before pulling back and yanking a necklace from around her neck, dropping it to the floor where Emory's knife still remained.

"About fucking time," the woman said, and then she marched away and a man took her place.

He leaned in, about to repeat her performance, and I pressed up a hand between us, making him grin and laugh. "Fair enough, Your Majesty," he said. Then he took the hand, the one on which I wore the ring Aric had sent to me, kissed my knuckles and dropped a coin to the floor.

"I'm the...I'm the king," I said numbly as another man took his place, quick to take my hand, to kiss my knuckles. He dropped a feather to the floor, and it fluttered down slowly, nearly kicked away until I caught it with my skirts. The feather prickled with something that reminded me of Aric's magic.

"Yes," Scrapper said.

"Why am I a king specifically?" I asked, frowning.

"Kimmery already has its queen, Your Loveliness," Scrapper said, shrugging. "The king sits at the other end of the scales. That, and no one's ever bothered to change it."

"Where is *Aric*?" I gasped.

"I'll go and find him for you, Your Majesty." And then he too kissed my hand and dropped something that *looked* like a coin, but I suspected was just a rather nice button.

One by one, the occupants of the room approached me, leaving scratchy kisses on my hand and trinkets at my feet as I tried to catch my breath and sort my thoughts. I came to one conclusion—Scrapper had set me up. He'd been the one who called it a challenge first, making my attempt at rescuing Aric something a great deal more significant.

A hand rested on my shoulder as another woman kissed my cheeks and left an earring at my feet. I glanced behind me and sighed as I found my Chosen at last. Cosmo was closest and most amused, and I glared at his crinkled eyes and twitching lips.

"This isn't funny," I said, lowering my voice as I leaned toward his ear. "I've accidentally made myself King of Thieves."

"Yes, you have. And it looked very deliberate too, from where I watched," Cosmo said. "You taunted Emory and made easy work of him."

Cresswell had taken off the jacket of his uniform, standing in only a pale blue shirt that I decided suited him nicely. He eyed the crowd warily, but he stood less stiffly than Thao, who was tucked safely between Cress and Wendell. I searched for Owen and found him mingling with the crowd, grinning and laughing and drinking a mug of ale. He met my eye and winked, and I relaxed a little further.

"What's the likelihood of this not spreading to the council's ear?" I asked Cresswell.

"We left everyone else at the palace, but this isn't the most trustworthy lot and I don't think you've gone unrecognized," Cresswell said, moving to stand close at my back with Cosmo.

There were stares from around the room, gazes weighing me, and I understood their suspicion. What kind of thieves' court would want a member of the royal family as their leader? If I took my role here seriously, where did that leave my own loyalties to the crown?

"I have to find—Aric!" I gasped as I turned and he was there, appearing as the last man in the room kissed my knuckle and left a coin.

His face was clean, his swollen eye calmed to a well-faded bruise, his lip only bearing a faint cut, and no sign of his other wound. His shirt was still ragged and torn, the only real evidence of the battle he'd just lost, but otherwise he looked healthy, unharmed, beautifully alive. He stood straight, directly in front of me, a hint of a smile on his lips and steel gaze blazing.

"Aric, I can't—" I started, ready to return his crown to him by whatever means necessary.

"Your Majesty," he said, and my words hiccuped on the warm tenor of his voice as he stepped close, closer than any of the others had. "You must," he whispered, so faint I barely heard the words. But I felt the brush of them against my ear, and a warm shiver ran down my spine.

I closed my lips and stared up at him, nodding once and marveling at his rare smile, one I hadn't seen since our dance at the festival. His fingers locked gently around my wrist, raising my hand up between us. He turned over and brought my palm to his lips, kissing the band of the ring he'd gifted me. His lips were slightly damp, as if he'd just licked them, and the kiss drew another shiver right down to my core, soft gray strands of his hair falling over his eyes to tickle against my skin. His mouth skimmed the inside of my fingers up to the heart of my palm and pressed a second kiss that left me liquid and warm.

Aric bent to one knee, keeping a gentle grip on my wrist, fingers teasing over my pulse as I tried to remember to breathe and not simply melt into him.

"Long live the king," he said, and I realized that the whole room must've been holding its breath because he hadn't needed to raise his voice at all.

Cheers went up and bodies rushed into motion all around us, but my Chosen remained at my back as Aric rose slowly to his feet, gaze holding mine.

"I need to speak with you," I said.

Aric nodded and glanced over his shoulder to the bar where the bartender was watching us. Wordlessly, they passed some understanding between them, and the other man nodded.

"We have a new king tonight! Drinks on the house!"

The crowd hurried to the bar, and my breath hitched as Aric pressed in closer, his free arm sliding around my waist.

"Can I have some time with her alone?" Aric asked the men behind me.

"No," Cresswell ground out.

"That's up to her, of course," Cosmo answered, but there was a warning in his voice.

"It's fine," I said to them, resisting the urge to lean into Aric's side. Now that he was safe, I was remembering that I was *angry* with him. And yet...he smelled like incense and ripe fruit and sweat, and I wanted to bury my face against his throat and breathe him in, reassure myself that he was in one piece.

My Chosen parted to make way for us, Wendell squeezing my shoulder in support as Thao glowered at Aric. I expected Aric to turn us back to the bar, leading me to his office, but he ushered me past them toward the entrance of the bar and up the stairs.

"Where are we going?"

"Somewhere properly private," Aric said, his hand squeezing on my waist.

We reached the landing to the exit and then turned a corner I hadn't really made sense of. Something pushed against me, and it took me a moment to realize it was magic and that we were stepping through a barrier Aric had erected to another set of stairs that led up. It was dark, and we'd only taken three steps up when Aric paused.

"Princess... Bryony—" He sounded as though he was strug-gling for air and I reached for him, ready to ask him what was wrong, when his hands found my ribs, gripping tight and pushing me to a wall. His arms twined around me, and I started my ques-tion when his mouth found mine, lips parted and making room for him to clasp and kiss and bite. It was a kiss and a demand. He still tasted a little of blood, and I whimpered as a hand pressed and slid up my spine to cup my head as Aric leaned bodily into me.

"Forgive me," he rasped, and then returned to lick and stroke his tongue against mine. He sucked on my tongue and I gasped, gripping his shoulders. "Forgive me, forgive me, forgive me," he chanted between brutal kisses, hips against my belly, hands molding me against him. He bit my lip, and I whined and arched into him, his breath shuddering out. The kiss settled, and our breath was noisy and ragged in the silent stairwell.

"For which crime?" I asked in a whisper, and Aric huffed, his forehead resting against mine.

"For being an ass from the start," he said, and he dipped his head to graze a kiss over my chin. "For every word that came out of my mouth at the palace." Another kiss landed on the right side of my jaw. "For being a jealous old man." The left side. "For accusing you of misusing your magic. I'm so sorry, for all of it, Bryony."

I huffed, and then the huff became a sniffle, and the sniffle became the start of a sob until Aric leaned back. He was barely visible in the dark space, but I felt his eyes on me.

"Princess?"

"I—I *did* misuse my magic, or it misused me," I choked out, my fingers still digging into his shirt.

Aric was quiet for a beat, and then he scooped me up with his arms around my hips, my feet dangling as he carried me up the stairs.

"Aric, I don't know what the Hunger is, but I don't think I can *avoid* using it without it...making some kind of demand."

He didn't say anything, and I couldn't see his face until he shouldered a door open at the top of the steps. His eyes were on me, face impassive, but my own went immediately to the room we'd just entered. It was large, with a steepled ceiling and enormous wooden beams overhead, tall pillars interrupting the open space. There was a large triangular window ahead of us that overlooked Rumsbrooke, and the room was divided into three sections. A small wood stove with a fire burning inside sat in the far left corner, a table nearby with a half-drunk bottle of wine and a bowl of fruit, and a sink and counter fashioning the area into a kitchen. Closer on the left side and spilling into the center room was more of Aric's collection of magical paraphernalia and a more obvious workspace for experimentation. On the right, against the middle of the low wall, was an enormous wooden bed with short posters and unmade sheets.

"This is your home," I said, studying the details of the space. There was a lamp near the bed, a screened wash space against the far wall, with a low table where bloodied rags had been left behind. I looked up at Aric and studied his face again. "How did you heal?"

"Magic," he said, setting me on my feet. "I gathered some supplies from the woods after..." He frowned and glanced down at the floor. "After I behaved like an idiot at the palace. What do you mean the Hunger makes demands?"

I swallowed hard and gazed back into the room. Aric might've felt sorry for what he'd said, but I wasn't sure he wouldn't have a great deal more to add to it if I told him about Daniel.

"Hm, how about I tell you this then. I think I know what the Hunger is," he said, catching my attention, my eyes growing wide as he tugged my hand and led me to his workspace. Old pages with faded writing littered the table, and Aric lifted one but didn't pass it to me. "I could only find a few places where the queen's line was included, but it seems... Your family has an incredible history of holding the monarchy in Kimmery, princess. Longer than any direct line in any other kingdom. The reason for that seems to do with—"

"The Hunger providing prosperity," I recited.

Aric's head nodded side to side noncommittally. "The Hunger provides..." He frowned, and I realized as he studied the page that he was having a hard time believing whatever he'd discovered. He set the page down on the table and took both my hands in his, thumbs passing back and forth over my skin. "Bryony, I believe the queen's line—the magic you...release—I think you are the *source* of magic in Kimmery."

I blinked at him, my eyes tracing the features of his face as I processed his words. Aric had injured me in our argument, had bruised the trust we'd managed to develop, but I realized with him in front of me that he hadn't managed to quash the feelings I had for him. Aric was, to me, a kind of authority I craved even when I didn't want to, but also a strange source of shelter. When I felt uncertain, doubted myself and my judgment, Aric seemed to be the first person I wanted to turn to for confirmation.

He was an enormous weakness for me, and we either needed to come to terms, or I needed to cut him out of my heart.

"Princess?" Aric murmured, lifting a hand up to my jaw, my face leaning into the touch automatically, strangely soothed by the scratch of calluses on my skin.

"The north went without magic for so long because it went without its queen," I said, and Aric nodded. "We thought my Hunger...that I only felt passion where I also felt affection. That was why it took so long for it to appear."

"There's some mention of an awakening in the texts," Aric said, looking down to the table without pulling away from me. "For most of the queen's line it comes at adulthood, but that might explain your delay... You *thought*?"

"After you left the palace, I tried to do as you said and avoid—"

"Bryony, I shouldn't have—I'm sorry—"

I shook my head and raised my hand, my eyes falling shut. "I tried to resist my Hunger. For several days, I succeeded. I had symptoms of discomfort and pain, and then..." His hand still holding mine tightened its grip. "I made a mistake with a man in the palace I don't trust, don't like. It was...confusing." And pleasurable. And painful too, in a way that didn't have to do with my physical self. "The Hunger won't be ignored."

Aric was quiet for a long time until I met his eyes and sighed at what I found there. Concern, not condemnation. He moved in slowly, and I was stiff as he wrapped himself around me, the gray scruff on his jaw ruffling my hair as he tucked my head beneath his jaw.

"I'm so sorry," he breathed, the words low and terribly slow.

I leaned into his chest, and his arms closed around me.

"I should've come back immediately and groveled. I wanted to find something concrete," he said. "And I was a bit afraid of you tossing me out on my ass as I deserved."

I couldn't really tell him it was all right, or that he was forgiven, because those things wouldn't be entirely true yet, but I did know it *would* be all right, that he would be forgiven. Aric wasn't my only weakness, all my Chosen were, but they were also vital. With time—and knowing him, a great deal of negotiation —I knew he would be a source of strength. For now, I needed him to be a comfort.

I circled his waist with my own arms, felt his sigh stirring my hair, and we remained that way in silence for a peaceful handful of minutes until the evening landed back in my head and I yanked back.

"Oh, Aric! How do I give your crown back? I can't be King of Thieves!"

His eyebrows shot up, and then he grinned. "You have to. I don't want it back, and anyway, no one would take me seriously now. I've been beaten by Emory, and you *trounced* him," he said, smiling fondly. His fingers raised, and he grazed my cheek again. Aric was touching me a *great* deal, wasn't he? "Where did you learn to fight like that?"

I shrugged. "Princess lessons. You can't think anyone will take *me* seriously?"

"Why not? I can guarantee you no one will want to challenge you to a fight. You were masterful."

"I appreciate the flattery, but you're not answering my question," I said with a huff, trying not to blush under his warm stare.

"You earned your crown as King of Thieves—"

"I'm not a thief!"

"—and while you can gift the role to someone else, it will make them look vulnerable. You're better off holding the title and appointing someone in the court to help you run things here in Rumsbrooke for the everyday. Emory was working for the council, you know. Why not have a thieves' court operating for your own purposes for a time?" Aric leaned on the table, but he didn't give up his grip on my waist, pulling me in a little to stand between his feet.

"You really don't want to be king anymore?" I asked, frowning.

"I knew my time was coming. I'd even started looking

forward to it this past year," he said calmly. He looked so easy, and I couldn't recall ever seeing him this way or us ever communicating so openly. "I was just stalling on pointing toward a successor who could've stolen it from me."

"Well, I appoint you to run things for me," I said.

He frowned then. "Mmm, no that won't do. We're a clever court, and they'll see right through that or think I'm puppeting you."

"Aric," I growled. "I don't know *how* to run a thieves' court."

"You need someone strong, someone who knows the rules and the history but won't be married to them, to try and mold you into old kings."

"Quit pretending you haven't already thought of someone for me," I scoffed, and Aric's grin flickered to life.

"You have allies," he said.

I frowned and stared at him, thinking. "Scrapper's not right, is he?"

"No, but he'll be a faithful spy for you. Probably better than he was for me because you're prettier."

Quit flirting with me! I wanted to shout, except that I was enjoying the sudden shift between us and thinking over and over the kiss in the stairwell, the grip and bite of him.

"Griffin," I said instead.

Aric pretended to consider this, even though Griffin was the only other thief I knew. "She's not well liked, but that just means she won't have friends she tries to influence you for. She's fierce, the men know not to crack jokes behind her back and the women respect her. She's just lawful enough to suit you, but still a rogue at heart."

"You're very amusing when you try to act like you haven't been steering me in that direction," I said.

"I think quickly. I was certainly *not* expecting you to take on Emory," he growled, brow arching. "I thought you'd send Stark to save my neck."

"I would've had to argue with him that you were worth saving, and I didn't think I had the time," I said.

"You were probably right," Aric said, nodding. His lips curved up. "Have I said thank you yet?"

"You've absolutely let it slip your mind," I said, crossing my arms over my chest.

His grip on my hips tightened and he pulled me in, fitting us together so I had to tip my head back to look up into his face. "Thank you, princess," he purred, and I waited just a beat too long for his face to lower to mine before I realized he was waiting for something.

"What will you do now?"

"Hmm, I could just manage the bar, although Otto doesn't like it when I'm underfoot too much..." Aric pretended to think again as I held my breath. "I suppose, if you wanted the help, I could continue doing research on your magic, maybe even teach you ways to control it as you release."

My eyes widened at that. "Do you think so? How...how exactly would you do that?"

Because we both knew perfectly well *how* and *when* I released the magic.

Aric sobered and stared back at me. There were faint strands of the revelry from the bar beneath us rising through the floorboards, but we were alone, in the relative quiet, waiting for something to fall into place between us.

"Do you still choose me?" Aric asked, brow furrowing and words careful, just shy of worried. "After all that I said and the ways I hurt you, do you still...?"

Did I still want Aric?

"You are, and always have been, my Chosen," I said softly, holding his gray gaze.

And when his hand rose to circle the back of my neck, our bodies colliding, my arms circling his shoulders as our lips met in a frenzy of begging and demanding, the Hunger purred smugly in my chest.

16.
BRYONY

Aric groaned as I sucked on his bottom lip, my fingers raking through coarse strands of his hair, his own palm gripping my ass and holding me tight to his hips.

"Please," I managed as I pulled away for a breath, but Aric wanted his revenge for my teasing.

He straightened from the table, his arm circling my hip and lifting me from the floor, his teeth dragging over my lips before his tongue plunged between them. My knees lifted, squeezing around Aric's waist, my skirt taut between us. My back met the door we'd shut behind us, and Aric pinned me there, my hips wedged between his and the wood surface. He nuzzled down against my jaw and I stretched my neck, trying to guide him to my pulse where I was especially sensitive. His hands shifted to my thighs, tugging my skirt up and out of the way. I whimpered as he bit my throat, and the chafe of horseback riding without my saddle met the coarse fabric of his pants.

"What do you need, princess?" Aric rasped, nipping and sucking on my skin.

"You. I want to claim you," I breathed, the words coming without thought.

He chuckled. "Claim me? Is that how it works with the others? I will be different, you know that."

My head thunked against the door, and I blinked at him, trying to clear away the haze. "You will be mine, Aric. I won't share." He frowned at that, and an amendment occurred to me. "Outside of Charlotte, that is."

His eyes narrowed and his head tipped. "Cosmo?" I nodded, and he sighed. "I love her."

I relaxed, and his hands slid under my thighs to help support me. "I know," I said, leaning and kissing his lips. He answered the touch softly, sipping lightly, licking the flavor of us both from my mouth.

"I will have to be in Rumsbrooke sometimes. This is still my home. And my priority will always be—"

"Aric, I'm not asking you to *obey* me, and I'm not trying to conquer you," I said gently, kissing his chin. "Your priority will be to our people, as mine is, and your perspective from these streets is why I need you in my court."

"And what piece of you will I own, hm?" he asked, pressing in, grinding against me as he sucked on my earlobe. "Will you obey *me*?"

I sucked a breath and moaned as his kisses on my throat grew rough and claiming. "You will have to share," I breathed, trying to rock against him even as he held me firmly to the door. "My body and heart, at least. You may have...some obedience."

"Some? Very well. Hold onto the ledge, princess," he said, humming as I raised my hands above my head until I found the top of the door jamb and gripped it. "Good girl. You want this now? While the others wait downstairs?"

I thought of my Chosen in the bar below. Not one of them would be surprised by some reconciliation between Aric and I, not even Thao who had admitted he was already begrudgingly prepared for this inevitable union. Maybe it would be better to wait, to speak to them first or to settle my place as King of Thieves, but I had Aric now and I was terrified of letting him slip through my fingers.

"Will you...will you come back to the palace with us tonight? After everything?" I asked.

"Mm, yes," Aric sucked on the muscle of my shoulder and then released it with an audible *pop*! "I can spare a few days away at a time. You'll have to come and go more often too now. Would you rather wait until you have your pretty bed?"

I sighed. I had all the confirmation I needed. Aric wasn't talking about fucking me now and seeing me later. I squeezed my legs around his hips and smiled at his grunt, hissing at the burn of my thighs and the press of him against my core.

"I want you now, with everyone downstairs," I said, rocking

against him, smiling at the way his eyes hooded and darkened, a predator's stare.

Aric growled, his fingers digging into my flesh under the drape of my skirt. "If you're too loud, they'll hear you," he said, and then his mouth took mine in a ferocious, claiming kiss. He braced me with one arm under my hips, his free hand fitting between us, two fingers sliding up and down over the lips of my sex, dipping into my opening. "Mm, nice and wet, princess."

I moaned, ignoring his warning about my volume—which seemed more like an invitation anyway—and Aric laughed, a warm and happy sound, sliding his fingers into me and grunting as I squeezed on them.

"You can tease me later, Aric. I want your cock inside me," I gasped.

"Hunger?" he asked, voice tight as he twisted his touch inside me.

I blinked and realized that *no*, it wasn't the Hunger. My magic was there, present, certainly, but it wasn't driving me. We were of like minds, the Hunger and I. Aric was ours, and he needed to be tasted.

"*I* want you," I said, nuzzling him, scratching my cheek on the scruff of his jaw.

He huffed as I nipped along his jaw, stretching until my arms pulled. His hand pulled free of me and jostled between us, and I decided that I'd only promised him *some* obedience. I dropped to my feet, ignoring his growl of protest, and spun us in place, putting his back to the door before dropping to my knees.

"Bryony," he growled, but his hands didn't stop me as I pushed them away, finishing the work of unbuttoning his pants and pulling them down his hips enough for his cock to bob free. He was only starting to get hard but he jumped against my palm as I gripped him, and the door rattled as Aric's head fell back.

"I'll be good in a minute," I said, taking his cock in hand, working his shaft gently.

"Fuck," Aric breathed. "Fuck, your breath even..."

My breath was rushing over the head of his cock. He wasn't especially large, like Wendell or Owen, which made my plan more manageable. I looked up just in time for Aric's head to fall back forward, his eyes wide as he watched me lean in and suck on the head of him. He tasted clean and a little soapy, and he was the loud one as I licked him from tip to base, feeling him grow and stiffen with every tiny touch, until his pulse was thrumming against my palm. I sucked him hard on the next pass, flicking my tongue back and forth on the underside of the head, bitter fluid seeping quickly to my tongue.

"Enough!" Aric groaned. "I swear it hadn't felt that long till you took me in hand. Stand *up*, Bryony!"

I'd thrust him to the back of my throat, made his cock twitch in my mouth when he gave the command, and I pulled free grinning. He was properly hard now, his smile flashing even as he growled and grabbed my arm.

He dragged me to the closest flat surface as I giggled, spinning me away from him and then forcing me to bend over his work table, my breasts smashed and my nose full of the smell of parchment and ink.

"You're a bit of a brat, but I suppose I knew that already," Aric muttered at my back, and I gasped as he threw my skirt up over my back, exposing my ass to the air.

I screeched as his palm cracked against my cheek, but I didn't have a chance to be outraged as he leaned in, grinding against my ass, his cock wiggling between my cheeks.

"That was for not following orders. Grab the edge of the table. Good girl," he purred as I squeezed my hands around the edge of the table. "This is for how well you suck cock."

He didn't hesitate, pressing the head of his cock to my weeping cunt and then driving in. I shouted wordlessly, bouncing back into him, spreading my heels on the floor until I could feel his sac brush against my clit. Aric's moan was ragged and soft, his hips nudging gently against my ass as if he was testing his own depth inside of me. He seemed exactly right in the moment, full but easy, gliding smoothly out as he retreated.

Aric slammed back in and we both cried out, his balls slapping against my clit.

"Aric, yes!" I cried. I heard the huff of his laugh, and it made me grin. He liked the idea of everyone downstairs hearing me cry out his name, of knowing what he was doing to me, their old king and their new king joined in a debaucherous union.

He fucked me roughly, his body slapping into mine, the legs of the table squeaking in time to my cries, my own hips following the steady rhythm, rising up to meet him, my cheek falling to the top of the table as I moaned.

Crack! I gasped, a silent scream in my chest as heat burned on my left ass cheek with another smack of his hand.

"That was for barging into a sword fight on my behalf and taking that horrible bet," Aric growled, his hands pinching around my hips.

The warmth of the slap bled into my cunt and I moaned his name, head rolling back and forth over some old piece of spell work on a page.

Aric moved one hand to push on my spine as the other raised me to my toes, changing his angle inside me, taking him deeper and making him grunt with every thrust.

"Aric, yes! Yes, please! Please, Aric!"

He laughed again without stopping, his balls drumming against my clit with every thrust.

"Wicked girl," he breathed. "Darling. If he had hurt you—"

"Hush," I whimpered, squeezing my eyes shut, wobbling on my toes, hands sliding over papers as my blood began to rush and pound in my veins.

Crack!

"Ahhhric!"

Thump, thump, squeak, went the table legs.

"That's for making me half hard while I was bleeding, just at the sight of you with my blade in your hand," Aric groaned, his rhythm starting to stutter.

"Aric! Aric, I'm going to—"

"Don't you dare come!"

Except Aric's voice, gravelly and breathless and gasping from the force of our fucking, was too much of a catalyst for my pleasure, his notes a kind of caress on my sex. I came with a bright scream, unnecessarily noisy and breaking into giggles as magic pounded through me and then out on a whine, making the building shudder and groan, and a great guffaw rise from downstairs.

I sobbed as Aric pulled out of me at the peak of my climax, making me clasp and gush around nothing, my legs trembling.

He yanked me up from the table, papers fluttering away, and tossed me into his arms before carrying me toward the bed.

"If you'd wanted to make me last longer, you shouldn't have been so good," I said, glaring at him.

Aric grinned and snorted, a boyish expression on his face, before tossing me unceremoniously into the center of the bed. I bounced with an *oof,* and he followed on his hands and knees.

"Hands in the pillows, and if you disobey me again I'll fuck my hand instead of you," he growled.

My hands shot into the pillows and I nestled back, bending my knees and spreading myself wide for his viewing. The bed smelled of him, dense and sweet and smoky, and I wanted to close my eyes and sink into the comfort of the sensation, but the view of Aric before me was too good to ignore. He rose up to his knees, cock jutting up proudly, slightly curved and shining with my arousal. His eyes drank me in hungrily, and my sex clenched at the promise in his stare.

"You look..."

"Like your wicked brat?" I asked, and Aric grinned, his hands sliding up the insides of my thighs, gentling over the reddened marks from my race here.

"I was going to say divine, like some sexual deity waiting to be given physical devotion."

"Oh, well, I like that too," I murmured, blushing. Aric brushed his knuckle over the red mark, brow furrowing. "I rode here without a saddle is all."

"Does it hurt?"

"Stings a little, nothing serious."

His palm covered the spot, and there was a warm prickling before he drew away, the mark vanished. "Might as well do something useful with all the magic you've put buzzing through the air. Speaking of..." he said, leaning in and resting over me. The prickling signal of his magic covered me from my shoulders down, and I gasped and shuddered before suddenly finding myself bare.

"Don't worry," Aric said, as I gaped at my own naked body. "Your dress is just there."

I looked over to where he nodded to the screen, my dress draped over it. I sighed, and Aric's hands slid up my naked sides to my arms, all the way to my wrists. He lifted them, and I reached for the headboard before feeling silk slither around my wrists, the tell-tale prickle and Aric's grin telling me everything.

"Excuse me if I don't trust you to behave again," Aric said, grinning and nipping at my chin before leaning back. "These bruises..."

"From the chair Emory threw," I said as Aric frowned at a few dark splotches on my ribs, his hands stroking there to heal those marks too.

He sighed and surveyed his work as I squirmed and looked up, examining the ties holding my wrists above my head. They were pretty, gold and red swirling with charcoal and pink, just scarves but ones I'd never seen before.

"Are you quite done?" I asked, looking back at Aric. He was still fully dressed, although dissembled, and he surveyed me with a satisfied smile.

"Nearly," he said, pulling his collar up at the back, shrugging his shirt off over his head and tossing it to the floor. "You look very pretty like this but I think, as my princess and my king, you need some ornamentation."

He laid down on his belly, the hairs of his stomach tickling against my sex as Aric nuzzled into my breasts. I whined and pulled on the ties of my hands as Aric sucked at the tip of my breast. The prickle of magic was sharper then, forming to a pinch, and I gasped as Aric's tongue swirled over my skin, leaving something cold and metallic behind. He pulled away to reveal a metal and enamel bryony blossom identical to the one on my ring, now pinching the tip of my breast.

"Aric!" I gasped, but I was arching into the ache of the clamp as Aric left cool wet kisses across my chest. Kisses that transformed into a golden chain, leading from the clamp.

My eyes fell shut, and I moaned as his mouth covered my

neglected breast, breath and tongue hot and wet, until the prickles sharpened and the cool metallic pinch took over. Aric pulled away, and we both stared at his handiwork, Aric's finger reaching out to tug gently on the chain, drawing on the pressure of the jewelry on my breasts.

"How—Where on earth did you learn this?" I moaned, my hips bucking into air, my cunt aching to be filled again, something about the constant pressure of the clamps leaving me desperate.

"Mm, you make so much magic it's practically a matter of imagination," Aric murmured. He left the chain on my chest and worked himself out of his pants, one hand reaching to pump his cock back into its stand. "Would you mind one more decoration?" he asked.

My eyes widened. "But...where will it go?"

"Hmmm, on me, for now," he said, but there was a terrible secret in his grin.

"Fine," I said, but the magic prickled over my shoulder. I couldn't see anything at first, but I felt the cold slither.

"Don't be frightened," Aric said gently, his hands petting my freshly healed thighs. "It's only magic."

I held my breath and stiffened at the first wiggle of gold out of the corner of my eye, a scream in my throat at the sight of the snake swirling over my skin, toward my breast. It was undeniably beautiful, its movements sinuous and life-like, while its appearance was like perfectly crafted jewelry or a mechanical marvel. It was only as thick as one of my fingers, and only long enough to wrap around my wrist maybe twice. My study of it as it moved distracted me from Aric, and as the delicate jeweled head of the snake nudged against the blossom biting at my nipple, I moaned and Aric sank back inside of me.

"It's been a long time since I've had sex and I don't want this to end too quickly, so this will help," Aric said, his breath thin as he lifted my hips to meet his, sinking in deeper from this position, the curved head of him stroking beautifully inside of me.

I was about to ask how it would help when the snake slithered quickly over my belly to where Aric and I were joined, curling itself around the base of his cock and tightening. It moved until the jeweled head, with glittering emerald eyes, tapped and nestled against my clit, nudging back and forth over the sensitive nerve.

"Ohhh, I think you're mad," I groaned, twisting on the bed. Just moving made the bryony blossom jostle and tug, and I whined.

"Do you like it?" Aric laughed.

"I *love* it."

He leaned forward, bracing himself up with a hand on either side of my shoulders, hair hanging down in his eyes as his smile softened and his weight sank gently into me. He was tall enough that he could keep his chest off mine and still lean his head down to peck and sip at my lips. My breath was fast, embarrassing weak sounds falling quickly from my lips as the blossoms on my breasts shifted with every catch of air and the toy against my pussy squirmed and stroked me as a finger might.

"Aric, please, move," I gasped, trying to ride him from below but not finding the right way to move with my hands tied above my head.

"Oh trust me, darling, I will. First though, we need to discuss this matter of you tossing magic everywhere," Aric rasped, although he rewarded me with a few testing nudges. The snake slithered against my sex, remaining even as he pulled away, and I gasped as he balanced on one hand to flick lightly at a blossom.

"Now?! Really, Aric just *fuck* me," I cried, thrashing a little and pulling at the silk around my wrists.

"Shh, don't pull. Yes, now. This time as the magic rises, I want you to contain it," Aric said, his thrusts growing just a fraction deeper, his kisses on my lips and chin nibbling.

"I—what?" I moaned as Aric kicked my heels farther apart, stretching the inside of my thighs and making him sink more fully into me, his hips just rolling in a fascinating figure eight that all but made my eyes cross.

"Don't let the magic out. Hold it in. It will feel like pressure I think, but there's no reason why it won't work." Aric pulled out fully then, and I cried out, my hips rising as the snake pulled away. Had he known I was edging closer and denied me my finish? "Are you paying attention?"

"Yes, yes, hold the magic in. Aric, *please*. Oh!"

Aric's head ducked down, kneeling on the bed, and he caught the chain between my breasts with his teeth, tugging up roughly and making me shout.

"I haven't enough hands to do everything I want," Aric rasped. "Next time, Owen or Pianetta will have to help. Do they share you too?"

I moaned and shuddered, nodding as he lined himself up again and sank in.

"Beautiful," he said, watching his cock's descent into my weeping core. "You'll do as I ask?"

"Yes, *please*," I said, nearly in tears.

Aric took my mouth in a deep kiss, his tongue stroking in time with his sudden thrust as I whimpered and sighed into him, my heels sliding in his sheets. His bed was firmer than mine, and it gave me nowhere to go as he pounded into me, not that I wanted to be anywhere else, the bed creaking and bouncing beneath us. The blossoms pinching on my breasts tugged and ached, echoing down to my cunt with every motion. Aric groaned into the kiss, slowing his pace down as I started to clutch and flutter around him, the snake's head urgent on my clit, flicking back and forth.

"I'm going to—Aric, I don't know if I can!" I cried out as the edge loomed closer, magic pounding through me, tickling my skin, waiting and ready to race out.

Aric slowed further, his slide in and out of me like deep breaths, grinding into me with every connection. "You can. Like holding your breath, Bryony."

My body strained, my chest tight, and I squeezed my eyes shut. Aric grunted as I clamped down around him, waiting to fall. He was right. I could hold the magic in, but it seemed to keep me dangling at the edge of my orgasm, balanced on a knife tip waiting to topple. I whined, the sensation a painful bite of pleasure, my skin feeling ready to burst.

"That's it. Breathe through it, darling," Aric murmured, kissing my jaw, my cheeks, my throat as I trembled beneath him. "They aren't the same. You can fall and contain the magic at the same time, just find the edge between the two."

I didn't believe it existed, and my lungs grew tight, like I might never take a breath until I gave up on Aric's idea. He reached up, soothing his hand into my hair, and I don't know if he worked some magic of his own, but I felt a snag in my chest and imagined sliding in, fitting myself in the space between. The orgasm ran through me like honey, slow and shuddering, my neck arching so I could press my face into Aric, biting down on his shoulder to bury my groan of relief. It was my first orgasm without magic, less stunning but equally sweet. I was more aware of us this way, of the fit of him inside me and the way our stomachs brushed together, the grunt of feeling from him as I squeezed around his length.

"Good girl, princess," Aric rasped, starting to rock again. "You have it?"

The magic burned in me, somewhat resentfully, and I waited until the sting started to ease before sagging back into the pillows.

"I have it. You didn't say it would hurt," I said, pouting just a bit for effect, but softening as I saw the worry in his gaze, his hips stalling. "I'm fine. Mostly teasing."

"Mmm." He ducked, brow furrowed with thought, but kiss gentle and probing. "Could you do it again?" He nudged into me, bucking lightly, and I gasped, nodding. "Do you want me to untie you? I'd like to watch you ride me, get to play with those pretty little tits of yours."

I squirmed, panting, immediately eager for more. The Hunger was too, the fire of holding onto my magic turning pleasant and stimulating, pooling at my core. Aric laughed and shifted, untying the silks by hand.

"Did you use all the magic on these?" I asked, shimmying a little and moaning at the feel of the blossoms. How far could my magic go, I wondered? Was one orgasm only enough for a few of these magical toys?

"No, I let some take care of the building. Probably caught the attention of a few of the tricksters downstairs too. I...I overreacted before," Aric said, drawing my hands down to my belly, massaging them gently. He raised one and kissed my wrist, gazing at me through the fall of his hair. "Magic will be good for the north. *You* are good for the north. For me."

I sat up, sliding onto Aric's lap, immediately beginning my ride and watching his pupils grow wide, his mouth parting on a moan he tried to contain.

"I haven't quite forgiven you for some of what you said," I whispered, watching his reaction.

Aric struggled to keep his eyes open, his hands gripping my ass to help me bounce. "Don't. It doesn't deserve forgiveness. Just allow me to be better."

I nodded and bent. It was my turn now to control the kiss, to control Aric. I squeezed my thighs around him as if he were my horse, turning him on the bed and pressing him down into the sheets, my pace growing hurried, my ride long and rapid.

"Oh fuck. You might kill me," Aric groaned, but he watched me take his cock, eyes fixed to the spot in that way men seemed so fascinated by. I preferred to watch their faces. Seeing Aric's face grow flushed and tangled with pleasure, his tongue wetting his lip as sweat dewed on his brow, gave me a feeling like falling from a great height, all weightlessness and rushing.

The snake grew languid, and I wondered which of us was in control. I wanted to come with Aric, and I wanted to make him wait and ache for it. I seemed to be managing that so far. I took his hand from my ass and lifted it to my chest, catching his attention as I hooked his fingers into the chain.

"I think I suddenly understand why men wait their lives to be Chosen," Aric grunted, breathless. His heels braced against the bed as he began to buck to meet me, toying and twisting the chain around his fingers to create a slow but insistent pull.

I was loud, using his name more than I might've normally, just because I could hear the cheers from below when I did, saw Aric's face light up with a kind of egotistical joy that was rare and beautiful on him.

"Bryony," he begged, and it was a satisfaction deeper than orgasm.

"Yes," I moaned, my pleasure rising.

Aric said magic was almost a matter of imagination, and it was *my* magic. If he could master it, surely so could I? I called to the snake, and Aric yelped as it began to pulse over my clit until we were both frenzied and clumsy. I called again and it started to slither over my hip, unwinding from around Aric's cock. He pulled once, a little too hard, on the chain, and then shook his fingers free, returning his hand to my hip to force me on the hilt of his cock, over and over, our bodies beating rough like beasts.

I'd forgotten my instructions about keeping the magic in, more intent on crashing with Aric. His body arched, head thrown back, bellow thunderous, and my hands clawed on his chest as I came apart, threads of magic rushing through me with the crystalline, ecstatic edges of the orgasm. The magic twined around us, tying me and Aric together on the mattress until our pleasure fused. Aric's hands slid up to my back, pulling me down to his chest as I thrummed and shook.

"I forgot," I rasped, still squeezing and whimpering.

"Shh." His chest heaved with breath, and I winced as he nudged one of the blossoms. "Mmph, here."

The snake had worked some magic of its own, or responded to mine, elongating enough to wrap around my waist, transforming into an ouroboros, biting its own tail just above my belly button.

"This will sting and ache," Aric said softly, rolling me onto my back before unlatching one of the blossoms from my breast. I stiffened at the pound of pain, and then Aric ducked down, sucking it into his mouth, laving and soothing it until the feeling dulled and I sighed.

"You won't be able to hold the magic every time anyway," he said, and then repeated the process on the other breast, leaving me limp and stunned in his arms as he lifted his head and smiled down at me. "It was only practice. We'll try again plenty more."

It was a promise of sorts, as were the kisses Aric covered my chest and throat and jaw with, slow strong presses that made me drowsy, until drowsiness turned directly into sleep.

17.
COSMO

I gave them a little more time, even after the bar glasses quit jostling on the wall and Bryony was done with her performative shouts. I wasn't sure what I expected to walk in on —probably more fucking, with less volume—but I was gratified by what I found instead.

Aric held a sleeping Bryony in his arms, a sheet draped over their hips, her chest pressed to his. He didn't look up as I knocked and entered, too busy studying the young woman with her head leaning back against his arm.

"Are they getting impatient?" he asked.

"No, but I think they'll start trickling out soon," I said.

Aric nodded and looked up. I wondered if he knew how soft he looked as he watched her, or if there would ever be a day where that ease wouldn't vanish when he turned away.

"She should speak with them. Remind them of their loyalty to her. Rumors will get out either way, but it might staunch the flow."

I nodded and shrugged. Aric knew his people better than I, and he would guide Bryony gently until this strange turn of events sorted into something better.

"You didn't plan this did you?" I asked, frowning.

Aric didn't bother looking offended or surprised, but I believed the slow shock that took over his face as he shook his head. "Believe me, I thought I'd considered every scenario, but I certainly hadn't planned for this one. I haven't planned for her at all," he added under his breath, the words awed.

I sighed and sank against the door jamb. I wanted to fight with Aric, remind him of every instance where he'd made an ass of himself and hadn't deserved her. But Bryony wanted this man, and he at least looked like he had the good sense to see his fortune now.

"I won't err again," he said.

"Good." I wanted to move for the bed, but Aric hadn't ever shared a woman and I wasn't sure how likely to be possessive he might end up. Bryony would set him straight if he was.

"Grab her dress, I'll wake her," Aric said, nodding back behind him.

Perhaps cooperative then.

I went ahead and listened in as I crossed the room, passing the bed and hearing Aric rumble sweetly to our princess.

"I'm sorry to wake you."

"Mm, no, I should go downstairs. You'll come?"

"Of course. I'll hang back. You need to address your people. But I ride back with you tonight, remember?" he said, and I heard the catch of relief in her sigh. "Come here."

The kiss was breathy, and I glanced over my shoulder to catch the reverent hold of her face in his hands, smiling at the pair of them.

The linens rustled and the floorboards creaked, and I grinned as Bryony wrapped her arms around my waist briefly, pressing her cheek to my back before letting me turn, her dress in my hands.

"Thank you for being patient," she said.

I waggled my eyebrows at her. "Yes, well, patience has good profit, doesn't it?" I teased, laughing at her blush and Aric's snort as he wandered around, searching for his discarded clothing.

"Oh, Aric, put on a new shirt, honestly," Bryony said, turning and letting me help dress her.

"This? It's my favorite," Aric said, holding up his black shirt, still slightly shredded from his fight. But he shook it out, a jolly twist of his lips as it settled, restored and solid again.

"All that griping over magic and you seem awfully keen to use it," Bryony muttered, sliding her arms into her sleeves.

Aric laughed, a little embarrassed but not enough to keep him from using another burst of magic to sort the disarray of his desk into a tidy display again. "Yes, I'm very adaptable," he said, and then he strode up, a pair of blossom earrings in his hand and a golden chain twisted around his wrist. I watched the pair of them in interest as Bryony flushed at the sight of the earrings, but she arched her neck to let him pin them to her ears.

"Where's the snake?" Aric asked, smirking.

"Under my sleeve," Bryony said, going a little breathy.

"Wear it around your neck," Aric said, a gentle command.

Bryony blew out an exasperated breath, and I jumped as the golden armband I'd seen twisted around her left arm slithered up out of her sleeve and over her shoulder, a jeweled snake that twined itself around her throat.

"What on earth?" I gasped, its green eyes glinting at me.

"Yes, Aric thinks he's very clever," Bryony huffed.

Aric grinned and caught her waist, pulling her against his chest and pressing a firm kiss to her lips with a smack of emphasis. "I am very clever. I'll go down now. Give you a minute." He nodded once to me and kissed Bryony's jaw once more before retreating, heading out the door and thunking down the stairs.

"Cosmo," Bryony said slowly, turning to face me and looking a little nervous, her lips twisting.

I leaned in, kissing her forehead and then ducking down for another from her lips, smiling as she sighed. "Are you happy?"

"Yes, and he *is* sorry and I'm not quite forgiving him yet, but—"

"But he is your Chosen," I said, cupping her neck and taking another kiss. "You don't need my permission. I knew Aric would regret his words. If he fucks up again, he'll have more to answer to."

Bryony laughed and nodded, relaxing at last and then stiffening a moment later, eyes going wide. "Did he say I'd have to make a speech?"

I grinned and found her hand, leading her reluctantly to the door. "The court downstairs likely knows you are the princess. You just need to reassure them that you can be the King of Thieves *and* the Princess of Kimmery."

"But *can* I?" Bryony murmured, pausing at the top of the steps and staring down into the darkness below.

"Aric's led this court to stealing from the rich and spreading the wealth amongst the needy. Is it possible you might find you have a common enemy?"

"I won't be able to juggle this forever," she said.

"No, not forever," I agreed, stroking my thumb over the back of her hand.

"But it *could* come in handy for the time being," she said slowly, eyes taking on a wicked glint. It was good that Aric had gone down ahead of us. If he'd seen that look in her eyes, I think he would've dragged her back to his bed.

I would never say so to anyone, but that look reminded me a little of Aric's late wife, Charlotte, when she cooked up a new idea and wanted to trick Aric into thinking it was his. The two women were vastly different, from wildly different worlds and tackling their obstacles in very different ways, but it wasn't too surprising Aric had found himself in love with them both. He had good taste at least.

"Ready?" I asked.

Bryony took in a great breath and drew her shoulders back, nodding. "Ready."

The bar was congratulating Aric on his good fortune of not being dead when we arrived, but Bryony stole the focus easily, striking and strange in her rumpled gown, hair mussed and cheeks glowing from sex. A few chuckles rose up from some of the men, and Aric shot glares in their direction, realizing the slight error made from his and Bryony's coupling.

The laughter settled quickly though. Bryony was small, and she was pretty, but there was a heaviness about her when she stepped in front of a room of people and held their attention.

"I think we all know that my rise as king was unexpected," Bryony said, drawing stirs of conversation. "I understand some of you may question my right to the role. And I welcome your challenge," she said, cocking an eyebrow and looking in the direction the laughter came from.

"Ye'd wet yerself trying!" Scrapper shouted from the back, and this time the laughter was appreciative, Bryony smiling playfully.

"You know who I am," she said, and the room quieted. "But here, with you, I am your *king* and your king only. I want you to thrive, every bit as much as I want Kimmery to thrive. The farmers, your neighbors, the soldiers. The magicians and shifters hiding their talent, their second natures!"

The room held its breath as she paused, their eyes going wide, lips parted, waiting desperately for her promise.

"I refuse to turn a blind eye on men who steal from those weaker than them, less able to defend themselves, with less means," Bryony said, voice darkening, a warning going out with the first tease of potential. "The council has this country pinned under laws and taxes that suck its people dry without delivering the benefits they're intended for. Turn your gazes on them. Find your hands in *their* pockets, not each other's."

"And where will all our thieving go, eh?" a voice called out from the crowd. "Up to your fine palace?"

"My palace needs no finishing, thank you very much," Bryony replied, some of the prim princess leaking out between the cracks of the roguish young woman, and it drew out appreciative and amused chuckles. "Your king needs no further wealth, she only needs your loyalty and your *secrecy*. Only your oath that the harm you do lands on the shoulders who bear the weight of tearing Kimmery down!"

"Aye!" the voices of the room cried out, mugs raised and sloshing in her direction, rowdy cheers and howls lifting.

From behind her, I could see the slow shift of her shoulders with her sigh, the room content with what she'd offered. I stepped up to her side as they turned in to one another, conversations rising noisily.

"Drink some with them, make them forget you wear that fine gown," I said in her ear, and Bryony nodded, turning and catching a quick kiss from my lips before diving into the crowd. I found Cresswell and my fellow Chosen at a table by the wall. Cresswell stood with my nod, moving after Bryony to keep her safe, as I walked over to join the others.

"So I take it we are stuck with the rogue?" Thao asked as I sat down next to him.

"Where's Owen?"

"Taking care of the horses. Or having a chat with them," Wendell said with a laugh. His cheeks were flushed, and it looked as though he'd refilled his ale again. He and Thao had run down the mountain as tigers, so at least I didn't have to worry about them managing their seats for the ride back up.

"Yes, Aric is returning as Chosen," I said to Thao, raising my eyebrow, challenging him to speak against it.

He only grinned at me and raised his hands in surrender. "I'm not about to object. It was bound to happen. Who could resist her?"

I turned back to the room, searching the crowd until I found her accompanied by Scrapper and Cresswell, being introduced to the thieves' court.

"She'll want every damned one of them at her coronation," I said fondly as she beamed at a deadly looking beast of a man who glowered at her, his scarred cheeks blushing.

"We still have to ensure that happens," Wendell said quietly. "This is certainly a risk."

"It might pay off," Thao said, surprising us both. "What? It's true. If this court is loyal, it can do work against the council Bryony would never get away with openly."

"And if it goes well, she'll build loyalty with the kind of citizens who don't usually think fondly on the monarchy," I said, watching Bryony giggle with a pair of pickpocketing fortune tellers, the snake around her throat winking at me in the light.

❧

ARIC RODE WITH BRYONY, his own horse following obediently behind his master as Aric held a sleeping Bryony against his chest, wrapped in his coat with him. We were nearly back to the castle, and the moon was high, the night turning sharp and cold.

Two tigers walked calmly on either side of my own horse, and an enormous dark bear shifted through the trees, warning away the predators of the woods. Owen rode along next to Aric, and I could see his breath in the air, big white puffs like smoke.

"Here it comes," Aric whispered, and together we all looked up to the sky.

They looked like stars at first, the first fat white flakes of winter coming down. Bryony stirred with Aric's nudges, and I smiled at her gasp as she looked up in time for snow to kiss her cheeks.

"But the harvests—" she said.

"Will be safe. The snow won't make it down the mountain," Owen promised.

"This will be their first warning before the frosts start," Aric said, and I watched with minor fascination to see the way he pressed his face into her jaw, taking the same deep breaths of her that Bryony took of the crisp air.

I'd seen Aric with Charlotte, and he'd always been affectionate, flirtatious. Where some men bemoaned their wives, made jokes of them, Aric had celebrated Charlotte. It'd been years since she died and I'd never seen them in their younger years, so I didn't know if this was the same, but it was good to see him being soft and sweet, for Bryony's sake but also for his. Maybe he *had* been ready to let go of his crown, maybe the change would be a relief for him.

"I'm not sure you'll like it very much," Bryony said as we reached the palace gates. Aric huffed, but she continued. "It's all very clean. We have proper lighting too, so you'll be able to see more than a few feet in front of your face."

"Oh, har har," Aric grunted.

Cresswell emerged from the woods in his human form, startling the guards who were opening the gate with his sudden appearance. He led the way to the palace steps, and the doors opened, Griffin and Daniel appearing from inside.

"What do we tell him?" I asked, frowning at Daniel.

"Nothing," Bryony said.

Aric glanced over his shoulder at me, a dark expression slanting in my direction. I wasn't sure, but I got the impression Bryony had given him some idea of what had happened between herself and our inconvenient spy. I nodded, and Aric turned his glare to the door as the groomsman came running up the path for our horses.

"You can help him tend them tomorrow. Tonight, you come to bed with the rest of us," Bryony said to Owen before he could object.

"Aric, good to see you," Griffin said mildly, moving slowly down the steps.

Aric slid down from Bryony's horse, lifting Bryony down after him before turning to the other woman, a hand extended. "Thank you for your flight," he said, sober and soft.

Griffin shifted uncomfortably as she shook his hand, and I fought my smile. Bryony dove in next, wrapping her arms around the older woman.

"Thank you!"

"Of course, Your Highness," Griffin said, face twisted awkwardly, a begging glance turned in Aric's grinning direction.

"Your *Majesty* now," I whispered as I headed up the stairs.

"What?!"

"Save it for the morning," I heard Aric answer.

"I—all right, fine. I have...some things I'd like to discuss with you as well, Your..."

"Bryony, please."

I met Daniel at the top of the stairs. "You didn't need to wait up."

Daniel ignored my glare, studying the others. "Everyone is safe?"

I blinked and frowned at him. He didn't sound...surprised, but relieved. Genuinely so. I looked over my shoulder, and his eyes were on Bryony, flicking to Aric and back again.

"Yes, perfectly," I said.

"Good." The word was under his breath.

Can we turn him? I wondered. Was it worth it, was it safe? Could Daniel be made loyal to Bryony, and if so what would it accomplish? More importantly though, what did Daniel need from Bryony to make that change, because I didn't think he deserved to even remain here.

"There are baths being arranged already and some cold dinners sent up. They can be ignored, but I thought... I'll leave you," he said, nodding and ducking his head, retreating back into the shadows of the palace.

Wendell's sleeve brushed against mine as he joined me in the doorway and our eyes met, equally suspicious and uncertain.

"It will wait," I said, and he nodded.

"Come share the suite with Thao and I," Wendell answered as we stepped inside. His smile was almost shy, blond hair hanging over one eye.

A warm arm circled my back, spice in the air and silky black hair falling over my shoulder as Thao rested his head there. "Yes, it will give her some space with him and Owen for a night before we all start negotiations over her time."

"You don't mind?" I asked. I enjoyed Thao and Wendell, enjoyed touching them or simply watching, but the connection was still fairly superficial. Outstanding sex, but always a bit for Bryony's sake.

"I like to sleep between you both," Thao said, lifting his head and gifting me with a shining, playful smile. The selfish prince, but not really.

"He likes more than that between us," Wendell laughed. "Come on, we'll walk her up with the others and then give them space. I haven't sorted out the geometry of the five us in bed with her yet, but we'll let Aric see how he likes Owen's snoring."

"It's not that loud!" Owen called from the back.

"I mistook you for Wendell's tiger!" Thao shot back.

Bryony's laugh drew out my grin, and I spun away from the others, grabbing for her as she reached me, letting me wrap her up in my arms.

Aric followed behind her, his eyes on the palace interior, some of the giddy softness from the ride up the mountain moving into awareness, of the wealth and magic of the place, and the difference between it and the home he'd just left. Bryony wanted what was best for Kimmery, wanted the common people to thrive and have good tables and be healthy. But she would always be royal. She would always have *more*, live richer.

If Aric was really going to accept he was Chosen, he would have to accept that now he would have more too.

18.
BRYONY

"Tell me what Sam is doing here."

I stood on a balcony in the northwest wing of the palace, overlooking the woods where Owen and Sam were setting out to check on some of Owen's favorite residents. Griffin stood at my side, arms across her chest, vivid red hair plaited down her back. The world was frosted this morning, trees trimmed delicately in white that everyone said would vanish by afternoon.

"Do you mean my intentions or his?" I asked her.

"He told me about your sister as if it...as if I shouldn't be appalled. He wouldn't show me the owl or let me near him, but he spoke like none of it mattered. Are you going to make him Chosen?"

"No!"

I shouted too loud, startling a handful of birds out of the nearest tree and making Aric pass by the balcony window, his eyebrow raised in question. I'd found a suite for him to use for magical study, and I suspected he wanted it simply to have a bit of his own space he could control too, which was fine. I shook my head at him, and he slipped away again.

"Absolutely not. I don't think that would be right for him at all," I said.

"Just checking," Griffin said, and I was surprised to find she looked a little embarrassed. But her arms loosened from around herself, and she braced herself against the edge of the balcony. "I agree. What are your intentions then, and what do you mean by his?"

"I am offering him a place that is not with my sister. He says he doesn't have any family, but I don't know if that's true. The others...are concerned that my sister left him here to—to spy on me, or perhaps even hurt me. I don't know."

"His fear of her is sincere," Griffin said.

"*My* fear of Camellia is sincere. I knew she was self-interested and impulsive and...I knew she was spiteful. But I didn't know she possessed this much cruelty. "

"What will you do about her?"

I closed my eyes and lifted my face, ignoring everything but the bite of cold and the sting of sunlight just starting to crest over the roof of the palace.

"If I have the crown, Camellia will not have Chosen. She will have to pay for the crimes against the ones she's been given," I whispered.

A hand settled gently on my shoulder, and I appreciated that Griffin didn't agree, didn't speak at all. Thinking of Camellia, of what she'd done and what that meant for the future between us, created a dull ache in my head and heart, a pressure that left me struggling to catch my breath.

"If your sister gave Sam orders to follow, I don't think it will take much for you to give him reason to ignore them, if you haven't already."

I nodded. "Camellia would have a difficult time imagining not getting her way. She always forgets that she's not alone in possessing desires and hopes." I blew out a breath and shook my head, opening my eyes and glancing at Griffin. "Do you think his wings can be fixed?"

"I know of a fox that got injured in a trap, was able to pull themself out, and shift back to their human form. But they only waited a few hours to get help, and the paw was mostly ruined from the start anyway. I won't really know what state he's in until he shows me," Griffin said. "Owen mentioned having some experience tending an injured barn owl, so if the injury is still young, then maybe."

But don't hold out hope. Those were the words missing.

"He brightened up when I talked about flying. I thought it would bother him, but he seemed happier," Griffin said. "May I come back and speak with him when I come to hunt?"

"Of course! Actually, about that, um, your position," I said, bouncing nervously and shifting to face her.

Griffin stiffened, a wary animal as I hesitated.

"So I am King of Thieves now, apparently," I whispered.

Griffin grinned, eyebrows rising. "So I heard."

"And I need you to run the court for me," I said.

Griffin blinked, and I realized as she stared at me that she had a pretty ring of amber in the green of her eyes. "Sorry, what? I thought you said something stupid."

"Griffin!" Aric snapped in warning from inside, but I just snorted out a laugh.

"There's no one else I can ask, if you think about it," I said, a little sheepishly. "Not that you'd be my last choice, of course!"

"I *should* be! The thieves' court hates me!"

"They don't really! At least, the women don't. I did test your name out a bit last night as I was meeting everyone. And as far as I can tell, the men who hate you...well, you had good reason to make them do so," I said shrugging.

"Princess—"

"I'll be Bryony, or your king for now," I reminded her, and watched her swallow nervously. "But listen, it can't be Aric—"

"My ass it can't be—"

"And Scrapper's better off as my spy and..."

Griffin stared at me again, hip cocked and arms back over her chest. "And you don't know anyone else," she said flatly, eyes narrowing.

"I don't *trust* anyone else," I corrected, waggling my eyebrows and winning a laugh from her. "I know it's a lot to ask of you, hunting, Sam, now this."

Griffin sighed and leaned forward on her elbows, her head drooping down, braid slipping over her shoulder. "I...I know of some people we could trust to help in the woods. Trying to help Sam is what I want, it's not a favor for you..."

"I need you on this, Griffin," I said quietly.

She was silent and still as I held my breath and waited. Aric was in the room behind us, moving furniture around, flipping through pages of books we'd been sifting through, probably listening in.

"You do," Griffin said at last, straightening and meeting my eyes briefly before glancing to the open doors. She leaned in and lowered her voice. "You need more than thieves too. If you're going to be the people's princess, you'll have to include us all."

There was the faintest emphasis on the word 'us,' and my eyes widened. Did she mean...shifters? I nodded slowly, and she mirrored me.

"It might take time, but you already have a good beginning," she said, smiling slightly. "I will help you, be your representative."

There was double meaning to all of it, and I bit my lip, studying her face with the same interest she studied mine. Aric wasn't watching us, and I pointed to the doorway frowning and mouthing, 'He doesn't know?'

Griffin shook her head. "We're better at keeping secrets than thieves," she whispered. "They're boastful. We're frightened."

I caught my breath and nodded slowly. "Then I want to help," I murmured back.

She relaxed and straightened, looking down over the balcony to the quiet of the woods. "I thought as much. I'll return to Rumsbrooke. The other courts will need to hear of your taking the crown from Emory and Aric."

"Emory *and* Aric?" I asked.

"Mmm, didn't he tell you?" Griffin asked, raising her voice and turning it to the open doors. "The old man let Emory build his own court, thought it would keep him complacent. You have two unruly packs of rogues to win over. You got a start on one last night. I think the other will be harder to please. You've given me a horrible load of work—"

"And she'll be sure to remind you of it at every turn," Aric said, appearing in the doorway. "Go on and get started, won't you."

"Watch your tone, I'm your superior now," Griffin tossed, arching an eyebrow.

Aric looked to me, frowning, and I smirked. I didn't really know if that was completely true, but I liked the disgruntled expression on his face and decided he could stand to leave it there.

"I take my leave, *Your Majesty*," Griffin purred to me, delivering a bow Wendell would've been proud of before flashing into a hawk and taking to the air with a bright scream.

"I suppose I earned that, but she didn't have to enjoy it so much," Aric muttered, squinting at the sky until Griffin was too far off to see. "Come here."

The bid was full of warmth and promise, my skin already prickling to be touched. I didn't know what time we'd made it back to the palace, but even with dozing on the trip back, we'd woken early enough that my eyelids were already drooping with the desire to dip back into bed. Preferably with Aric and Owen and all the others too.

I shook my head, and his head tilted, lips curling up until I spoke. "I want to talk with you."

"That doesn't sound like as much fun as what I had in mind," he growled gently, a second attempt. When it failed too, he sighed and nodded. "At least come inside, your cheeks are pink with cold, and there's a fire and tea waiting."

I followed Aric into the room, checking what had already begun to change. The space suited him, half paneled walls and tall bookshelves, dark stained wood with black and green vine-covered wallpaper. I wasn't sure how much of it my magic was responsible for, but the room was in good shape when we found it in our search.

Aric was kneeling in front of a heavy wood and black marble table, pouring tea for us both. There was a large empty chair available on one side and a low couch on the other, and I settled for the latter. I wanted a conversation, but also the connection of having Aric close. He looked stiff and somber in front of me as I took my seat, more like the Aric I was familiar with than the one I'd spent the night with.

"I'm afraid you're going to change your mind," I said softly, watching every tiny shift in the man in front of me.

It was a quick transformation, a frown of confusion with a sudden open shock, the teacup rattling as he dropped it to its saucer and rose up, sliding close on the couch and hunching to meet my eyes.

"You didn't want to be Chosen, and there were times where I

thought...I thought you might want *me*, but never...all of this," I said.

Aric's hands were rough against my own, and I pressed my lips together, trying not to remember their possessive grip on my hip that left the faintest marks on my skin this morning.

"You were relieved I was alive last night, and now you remember you're angry," he said.

I looked down to his hands, running the tip of my thumb over a scar that ran across the tops of his fingers. "It's more than that, Aric. You're here now, but you still don't have to be and I... I'm afraid you won't stay. Owen, Thao, and Wendell all...wanted to be here from the start, and with Cosmo I know when and how it changed."

"Look up, please."

I lifted my chin and tried to smooth my face as I met Aric's gaze. He was calm, somehow seeming to frown and smile at the same time, eyes running back and forth across my face, reading me like words on a page.

"I am yours, Bryony," he said softly, lips finally curving up at my small gasp. "Somewhere between you running into the Wing and Rook and blurting out your mad plans, to the night of the festival...dancing with you but also seeing joy on people's faces that I hadn't seen for years. Hope." He swallowed hard and frowned again. "Is that... It might not be romantic enough to fall in love with you for your care of Kimmery."

I grinned at him and shook my head. "No, I think I like it better. I know how much it means to you, I can weigh it."

Aric nodded, one hand pulling free to cup my chin, lifting it for a gentler version of our kisses from the night before. "What keeps me here is wanting you safe, wanting to help you carry burdens," he said, pressing a kiss to each of my cheeks and then another to my jaw. "Wanting to make magic with you. To tease you and see you smile and make sure you get to dance."

I sighed and leaned into him, and Aric wrapped his arms around me, pulling me up to his lap, tucking my head against his shoulder.

"You should be angry," he whispered. "My words to you

resulted in..." He stiffened and continued, and I heard the hard swallow in his throat. "You don't have to keep that man here."

"Mm, wait," I said, wiggling and sitting up, bracing my hands on Aric's shoulders. "Yes, I denied my Hunger because of what you said, and yes that created a desire for a man I don't trust when I didn't think that was possible. But it's...not simple enough to place the blame on your shoulders. And it doesn't belong on his either."

Aric's head tilted, and I knew he was reading me again, as easily as Cosmo sometimes did. "You enjoyed it?"

"Physically, yes," I said, blushing, but Aric remained impassive and it made it easier to continue. "Emotionally...I was upset with myself. I think that moment created an opportunity for Daniel and I to...to become lovers the way I am with the others. But it would've meant that he had achieved what the council asked him to, and I would wonder where his loyalty really lay from then on. I pushed that opportunity away."

"Do you want him?" Aric asked.

"I want to understand him. Know for certain that he's against me or with me. I don't think *he* knows," I said. "Is that foolish? To make an opening for someone I can't really trust to not betray me?"

"You want to think of him in terms of strategy?" Aric asked, and I nodded. "Then no, I don't think that's foolish. If you succeed, he's potentially a useful tool in the game. But if you don't know his loyalty, you have to treat him as such."

I frowned, and Aric reached up, pushing strands of hair back behind my ears.

"And if I think of him in terms of...of just as a man?" I asked.

"Be honest with him. Lay out his choices. Make any boundaries of information and trust clear," Aric said. "Sex complicates emotions, Bryony."

"Sex usually only comes *with* emotions for me, but yes, I've learned that," I said, playing with Aric's collar and thinking through the discussion. "You'll support me?"

"Always," Aric said immediately, and then he blinked and grinned at me. "Well, within reason. I'll challenge you too, you know that?"

"In private," I said, holding his gaze. "Never in front of the council. You know I listen to you, what your opinion means to me. But these men want to puppet me, and I can't ever look as though I'm someone else's mouthpiece."

Aric nodded once. "In private, I promise."

I sighed and softened back into his chest, curling my legs up on his lap and smiling as his arms circled me.

"What more needs done today?" he asked.

I blinked and let my heavy eyes fall shut. "I'm not really sure. Wendell would know."

"You need rest," Aric murmured, turning his head and pressing a kiss to my forehead. "You saved a man's life last night."

I huffed a laugh and melted as Aric turned us on the couch, draping me over his chest.

"Tea will grow cold," I mumbled into his shirt.

"I'll heat it up when you wake."

"How?"

"Magic, princess," Aric whispered. "And then we'll make some more."

19.
WENDELL

hree-hundred seeds to the West Hambach hills. Five-hundred to Indiva for the northern fallow fields.

I scribbled the notes down and paused, frowning. The Indiva seeds would need to be sent soon. Who knew what Bryony's magic had done to those fields, and there was a decent chance they wouldn't even be fallow. Easier to plant the trees now that way.

The seeds would be sent with some of Bertha Umber's samples of pastries our dinners had been blessed with, hoping to inspire local bakeries. There was just the matter of growing the trees *quickly* without too much suspicion.

My scratching paused at the sound of footsteps in the library and I glanced up, dropping the pen altogether at the sight of Aric. He was staring up at the painting on the ceiling with appalled amusement. He was dressed casually, only dark pants and a loose white shirt that either didn't have very many useful buttons, or he just didn't care to use them.

"Did she do this?" he asked aloud, and I hadn't realized he noticed me until he glanced in my direction.

"We think she just uncovered it. Some of it has changed a little, more wildlife and flowers than when we first saw it," I said.

"Hm...can't say for sure those helped," Aric mumbled before shrugging and shaking his head.

"We haven't mentioned them to her. Her power spooks her more often than not," I said, watching Aric's reaction.

He flinched and nodded. "I don't want that for her, and I'll work to improve it," he said.

"Good. We all...we all have some measure of influence over her, but yours is different, more immediate." His expression turned grave, and in spite of my remaining ire, I tried to soften my words. "We all knew you'd be a bit of a favorite when you finally came around."

Aric huffed but his lips twitched, expression brightening. "Have you seen her?"

"No, I assumed she was with you." And that was why he looked so disheveled.

He shook his head and smiled, moving toward the table. "She bounced out of bed early this morning. I thought I'd enjoy research all day, but instead I find myself wandering about, missing her."

I relaxed back into my chair, nodding, relieved Aric was willing to be that open with me. If he was with me, he'd be even more so with Bryony and she deserved that from him. "She feels like a slave to the Hunger sometimes, and worries about using it to force us, but sometimes I wonder if *we* aren't the ones using the Hunger to catch her attention."

I fought my grin as Aric looked down at his own open shirt and grunted, frowning again.

"You're working though," he said, glancing at my papers.

"Planning the apple orchards we're starting through the north," I said, showing him the paper. He skimmed the list, and his eyes looked up over the page to me.

"How much do you know about apples?"

"I... Not very much, why?"

"Because apple seeds are unpredictable. They don't necessarily grow the same tree they fell from, and not all apples are very good to eat."

I frowned back at him and shook my head. "The palace orchard..."

"Was likely transplanted one tree at a time," Aric said, watching my face fall. "Sour and bitter apples make cider, but that won't feed the nation."

"Fuck," I muttered.

"How long do you have before you send the seeds?" he asked.

"Days. I suppose more if we delay, but it's getting late to start planning."

"If you grow the saplings with more control, they'll have a

better chance planted in the spring. Let me see if I can't write a charm for them? We can use Bryony's magic to grow them, can't we?"

"Yes! Yes, I think so," I said grinning. "You think it could be done? It's a great amount of seeds."

"Bryony makes a great amount of magic," Aric murmured. "I noticed. I know a few others in the area who I'm sure have started to as well. If I can fashion the right charm to guarantee good seeds, I can get help casting it."

"Thank you, Aric," I said, and he shrugged. "No, I mean...I understand your initial suspicion but thank you for being willing to see her for who she really is. For being on her side."

Aric didn't look bashful, not really. He was probably too stoic or stubborn for that, but his gaze shied away as he nodded. "I'll go find her."

I glanced up to the near wall to check the clock and smiled. "Actually, I think I know where she might be."

❧

ARIC GAPED as Bryony charged at Thao, blade drawn, expression ferocious, our lovers clashing together in a furious and brutal kind of joy. Thao's leg raised, ready to wrap around Bryony's and pull her down, but she hadn't missed the movement and her body created a beautiful arch as she butted her hip against his, knocking him off balance and making him scramble to roll back to safety.

"Emory didn't stand a fucking chance, did he?" Aric asked, grin growing wide. "We have ourselves a warrior queen in the making."

Next to me, Cosmo's pencil could barely keep up with his attempts to sketch quick vignettes of motion between Bryony and Thao.

"Are you going to sculpt them?" I asked him.

"Mm. But I think Thao might be replaced by the rogue."

"A making of a King of Thieves," Aric said from my other side. "It'd be a good title. Bryony would put it in the royal gallery."

She likely would too, in spite of her reticence to be sculpted thus far.

"He's a surprisingly good sport, considering this started off as him training her," Owen remarked. He sat on the floor at the sidelines of the training room, three kittens climbing over him.

"I think he's given up on trying to keep her an inukat purist and is more focused on trying to keep up with her," I said, shrugging. "Bryony's sabre fencing makes her a more aggressive opponent, and it challenges the way he's used to fighting."

Sure enough, with a few more twists and jumping steps, Bryony was at Thao's back, her blade turned flat against his throat in a quick tap of victory. Thao sagged and grumbled, but I caught the pride in his struggling smile. He liked being bested by her. I couldn't blame him, especially as I laughed and watched Bryony bouncing on the tips of her toes. She circled him, crowing happily, and Thao was ready to catch her as she leapt at him, biting roughly at his lips, making him stumble as she wrapped her legs around his hips.

A throat cleared in the doorway, and I frowned as I looked over and found not Cresswell, but Daniel.

"What did you need, Farraque?" I asked quickly, seeing Bryony sliding free of Thao's embrace from the corner of my eyes.

Daniel ignored me in favor of watching them. "Have another in you?" he asked, tense but calm.

"I'm done for the—" Bryony started.

"Not you, Your Highness," Daniel said, bowing to her and rising with a faint smile on his lips. "I already know you can easily best me."

Bryony shifted closer to Thao, almost like she was blocking him, but Thao just stood straighter and grinned.

"I'd gladly duel you."

I frowned and crossed my arms over my chest, flicking my gaze between my lover and the spy. At my side, Cosmo slid his sketchbook to the floor and leaned forward, elbows on his knees. Aric was sitting up straight, his gaze on Bryony, his hand clenching on his own thigh as if he was restraining himself from calling her over. Smart man.

"What's your weapon?" Thao asked.

"Mm, I fence, but I like the look of that," Daniel said, eyeing the inukat sword.

I shook my head at Thao. He was too fucking prideful and he'd underestimate Daniel, whom we didn't really understand.

"Bryony's blade is made for her, it'll be too light for you," Thao said with a slight sneer at Daniel's large frame. I nearly sighed with relief, but then Thao continued. "You may use mine, and I'll balance accordingly with hers."

"Thao," I snapped.

Thao raised an eyebrow back at me. He'd tried to teach me inukat when I lived in Mennary, but sword-fighting had only ever been something I'd suffered through for schooling. I didn't have any skill, and I completely lacked the taste for it. Still, the lessons had been time alone with him, and I'd been happy enough to pay attention. Bryony's blade suited her quick movements and stayed flexible for her, but it would lack the strength to match Thao's own style and technique. Thao would be giving Daniel a clear advantage in the weapon.

Bryony exchanged a silent conversation with Thao before passing over her inukat sword, ignoring Daniel's approach as she moved quickly to us on the side of the room. She slid onto Aric's lap, but her hand found mine, squeezing tightly. I wasn't sure if it was meant as reassurance or mutual support, but I held on regardless.

"You've been watching us," Thao said, holding out his own blade to Daniel who rolled his sleeves up over his elbows, revealing brawny muscled arms.

Daniel nodded, unashamed. "I know the ceremony, the stances."

"Very well. You may fight like Bryony, who refuses to follow the rules," Thao said, winking in her direction.

She growled under her breath, settling as Aric kissed her shoulder.

"He'll win," Cosmo breathed to me.

"Someone's going to end up bleeding," I whispered back.

If Daniel was terrible, it might be all right. Thao would enjoy beating him without being vicious about it, probably. But if

Daniel gained any measure of ground in the duel, I was afraid Thao might channel his jealousy and anger over Bryony a little too sharply. If Daniel was *surprisingly* good... I didn't trust him or what he'd do, but I trusted Aric and Bryony, who both sat poised to strike if necessary.

"*In oshka*," Thao said, voice calming and turning low and soft as he settled into the deep, spread crouched pose, feet far from one another but body balanced to the back instead of front like with fencing.

Daniel mimicked him, and I frowned as he held Thao's sword in an almost familiar way. He looked comfortable with an inukat, not clumsy. Either he'd used one before, or he was *extremely* good at observation.

"*Ett amink*," Thao said, the start of the match.

Neither moved, which was customary, and Bryony held her breath at my side. Thao liked to wait for his opponent to move, as patience was a big part of the inukat fighting philosophy, but I could see his brow furrow as he watched Daniel, who seemed equally happy to remain in stasis.

Daniel was not like Bryony. He wouldn't attack aggressively, wouldn't make it easier for Thao to respond, to observe. He withheld himself from the fight, and I could tell Bryony wanted to jump out of her seat and make them get on with it. Finally, Daniel was in motion, moving swiftly but not with Bryony's same grace, aiming for Thao's right, a harder side to defend in inukat and a good starting move.

Thao responded easily, expression sharp and expectant as he moved into a new position, turning rather than retreating. Fencing was forward and backward motion, a narrow playing field. Inukat gave endless room for the opponents, provided they remained orbiting one another, neither ever running off field or creating more than the allowed open space between them.

Daniel circled in the opposite direction, and I realized that any observation he'd made, it had been to follow *Thao's* style of fighting, not Bryony's. It was smart. They were similar builds, Daniel a little stockier and broader, Thao a bit taller. Thao used patience, but Daniel had plenty of that. Thao liked contrary movements, but those worked better against a traditional opponent.

"What do you see?" Cosmo asked.

"They're..." I frowned, my eyes tracking Thao carefully as he tested Daniel with a soft attack. "They're well matched in this. Thao is much smoother. Daniel might've been practicing, but he's never actually fought this way before. It's..." I hesitated and then lowered my voice, tipping my head to Cosmo. "Daniel would make a good training partner for him. Challenge him differently than Bryony."

I wondered how he would look against Bryony during sabre fencing too.

"He's very adaptable," Cosmo said, nodding once.

"It's what makes him unreliable," Aric whispered.

"Shh." Bryony shifted on Aric's lap, leaning forward and watching the men avidly.

Daniel attacked next, and this time he mixed in some of Bryony's energy, although he was clumsier with it and Thao was quick to answer. The blades crashed, and Thao snarled as he pushed into Daniel, Bryony's lighter balanced sword taking more effort from him in the push.

"Twist," Bryony hissed under her breath, but I wasn't sure who she was directing.

Daniel stumbled back, spinning away as far as he could without surrendering the match, brow tangled as he evaluated his next options.

"This is..." Cosmo hesitated, lips twitching.

I fought my own smile. "Yes," I agreed.

Watching Thao and Daniel *was* stimulating. Sexually, yes. Thao was exquisite, already shining with sweat from his sparring with Bryony, triumphant when he gained ground against Daniel. Daniel too was pleasant to watch. Handsome and animal. It wasn't just that though. Thao *was* the better fighter, and there was a kind of satisfaction in seeing him pushing Daniel back, slapping the outside of his thigh with the flat of the blade. It wasn't worth anything in inukat the way it would be in fencing, more of a warning taunt than a point for either side.

Daniel had cut in where he didn't belong, claiming a moment

with Bryony that was *ours*. We were her Chosen, not him. I wasn't a fighter, but I'd considered tracking Daniel down and throwing a punch to his stupid beautiful swollen mouth when Bryony had told us what happened. Watching Thao beat him in sword fighting was better.

It didn't happen quickly. Daniel was good, and he was learning with every minute. But with Thao's style of fighting, he was unpolished still, and outmatched. The longer it went on, the more I wondered if Thao was dragging it out. Bryony was twitchy next to me, occasionally huffing and shaking her head.

"Enough," she whispered, her fingers digging into Aric's thighs as she perched, ready to fly off his lap at any moment.

Anger was bleeding into Thao's expression, the jealousy he'd admitted to days ago manifesting in rougher attacks to a rapidly faltering Daniel. I wasn't sure what I really wanted. For Thao to win, of course, but did I want Daniel injured out of revenge? Cosmo leaned forward too, eyes worried as he watched the men.

"Quit toying with him!" Bryony called out, frowning, but there was a wicked glint of excitement in her eyes too, her chest heaving.

"He's earned it," Thao answered, laughing roughly, leaping suddenly forward and making Daniel duck and stumble away.

There were only two ways for an inukat match to end. Either an opponent surrendered by moving too far away from the orbit of fight, or one delivered a blow that if not restrained would be fatal.

Daniel refused to surrender, and I was beginning to worry whether Thao would show restraint or if he'd just injure Daniel for real.

Daniel huffed and straightened, struggling to catch his breath as he settled into another defensive position. He was just *letting* Thao attack him, over and over. Thao seemed to realize it at the same moment I did, his eyes narrowing and attack drawing back. Bryony was vibrating in anticipation, Aric's hand massaging the back of her neck in an attempt to soothe.

"You knew better," Thao hissed.

Daniel swallowed, nostrils flaring and eyes flicking briefly to Bryony. "I'm not going to apologize to *you*," Daniel said.

Thao growled and attacked, swinging and feigning a direct blow before twisting on the heel of his foot, rotating the blade as Daniel dodged forward. Thao caught him from the side, moving like a dancer, the blade cutting directly through the air, right to Daniel's throat—

And just barely kissing the skin there. It was a scratch, and Thao retreated immediately, not even drawing blood.

"I won't withdraw a second time, so I don't recommend challenging me again," Thao said softly.

Daniel's shoulders sagged, his inukat lowered unceremoniously as he wavered slightly in place. There was sweat running down the back of his shirt and on his temple, and he looked more relieved than anything else, nodding lightly.

Bryony stood, and for a moment I thought she looked angry as she gazed at Thao.

"Out, Daniel," she said softly.

Daniel passed Thao his sword back and turned away from us, heading directly for the door.

"Am I not allowed to defend you?" Thao asked after Daniel walked out.

"Put those aside," Bryony murmured, and I fought my smile as I suddenly understood the intensity in her expression, the predatory sharpness her features had taken.

Thao set the blades on a shelf, his eyes watching her warily. They'd need to be properly cared for, and I imagined it drove Thao a little mad to leave it to later when his training demanded immediate respect for the weapon. His instincts were demanding immediate obedience to our mistress instead.

Bryony prowled forward, and Thao took cautious steps closer.

"You don't fight like that with me," she said softly.

Thao raised an eyebrow. "I don't want to *hurt* you."

"Mmm...you should try," she said, and then she grinned and leapt, her fingers digging into Thao's hair, legs twining around his waist. She threw the weight of her body, and Thao grunted as it pulled him to the floor, his own smile stretching as he rolled them and pushed Bryony's back to the floor, their mouths connecting fiercely.

"She *should* learn to wrestle," Owen mused as one of the kittens elected to leave us to our new occupation, racing from the room.

Aric stood from his own seat, and I wondered if he would leave until he settled on his knees, watching Bryony gain the ground in the battle, tearing Thao's pants open and biting his neck as she flipped them on the mats again.

"You're going to have to contain it this time," Aric said, smiling and watching as Thao crouched up, taking ravenous licks and bites of Bryony's throat as he pulled her shirt up over her head.

"Fine," Bryony gasped, rocking over Thao's lap and glancing at Aric with hooded eyes. "You can talk me through it—"

"She *loves* when we talk," Thao laughed. "Don't you, greedy girl?"

"But you'll have to wait till I've finished with the others for your turn," Bryony said, moaning and stilling as Thao managed to squeeze his fingers inside of her fencing trousers, wiggling them inside of her and making her squirm for more.

Aric laughed, and Cosmo and I jumped up from our seats, eager to help Thao strip Bryony out of her clothes. The sooner she was done with him, the sooner we'd get her in our arms too.

20.
BRYONY

"Do you mind his snoring?" I whispered to Aric.

My bed met my expectations, fitting us all comfortably together, although with Thao, Wendell, and Cosmo on one side, it left Aric between Owen and I. The two men had room to themselves, but Owen's face was turned to Aric's ear, and I could tell my newest lover hadn't fallen asleep yet.

"It's a price I'm willing to pay," Aric whispered back, squeezing the hand I held over his chest. "If I'm back after dinner, would you mind if I went to Rumsbrooke tomorrow?"

"I wondered how long that'd last," I said, and Aric immediately began to turn, curling in closer, unable to pull me out of Thao's cuddling grip. "No, it's all right. I figured you'd want to go back sooner rather than later. Yes—"

"Only for the day," Aric murmured, pressing his lips to my forehead. "To check on the bar, see that Emory is still in hand until we can think of how to put him in a prison properly. And I have some books I'd like to bring back with me so I can get started on the seedling spells."

The seedling spells. That was the reason I was positively buzzing with magic, feeling like at any second I might begin to glow or burst vines and blossoms of my own.

"You could come with me. The court won't be turning over their taxes for a few more days, but it wouldn't hurt for you to be seen before then, as long as we're careful."

I smiled, rubbing my cheek over Aric's chest, his free hand digging into my hair to sift through curls. It was tricky to fit us all together, especially with the way we seemed equally eager to be touching in our sleep. I often woke up to dead limbs, or caught an elbow to the side.

"We need a faster way to communicate between there and here. Or at least more regular. But yes, I'll come. Griffin might come up to see Sam that way."

"Griffin will be grateful for any escape, I think," Aric murmured.

I opened my mouth to tell him what she'd said to me on the balcony, the hints of a shifter community that might back me if I could deliver better rights and liberties to them. She'd intended it at as a secret, and even if I trusted Aric—and everyone else in this bed—the only way I could prove I would be a trustworthy queen to them was by not testing that trust. I wondered briefly if Cresswell knew anything of it, and wished I could ask.

"Sleep, darling," Aric breathed. "We'll leave after breakfast."

"Not before? We can start earlier, I don't mind."

Aric was quiet for a beat, and then he huffed a little, chest rumbling with a restrained chuckle. "The palace is infecting me already. I don't want to miss Bertha's chocolate and coffee she sends up."

I grinned at that, nipping Aric's chest and then settling down to fall asleep. I would be sure to send Cook Umber my thanks.

❧

ARIC ROLLED his eyes at me the next morning over the breakfast spread as he poured coffee from the pitcher into his cup of dense chocolate.

"Will I be in the way if I come too?" Cosmo asked us. "I'd like to go buy some new pigments and catch up with a few friends."

"Of course," I said and then tipped my head. "Will you need a carriage for pigments, or—"

"We'll take a carriage," Aric said, shrugging as I arched a brow. "I'll need it for the books and a good stock of my tools. We can leave it at Rebecca Sanders' and ride to the Wing and Rook on horseback. You can't wear that though," he said, eyeing my dress.

"Why not?" I asked, glancing down at my gown. It was vivid red and low cut, the fabric airy and flowing. It didn't look like any of my other dresses, and I was fairly certain my magic had fashioned it at some point.

"Because you look..." Aric struggled, brow furrowing, and I thought I knew what he was going to say until what came up was, "Very distracting. You'll attract too much attention."

"She'll attract attention if you put her in a potato sack, Aric, she's stunning," Cosmo said.

"From whom?" I asked, grinning.

"From me," Aric grumbled.

I started to laugh, but the sound stalled in my throat as Daniel stepped into the room, our eyes connecting. The few words he'd spoken yesterday ran through my head. *I'm not going to apologize to you*, he'd said to Thao. Did that mean that he felt he owed me one?

I thought I might owe him one too, but I wasn't sure what that would mean for either of us.

Before Daniel could make up his mind about whether he was staying or going, the doors opened again, Cresswell appearing with Griffin in tow, both of them rushing past Daniel to the table.

"I need to speak with..." Griffin frowned, her eyes flicking between Aric and I before settling on me. "You, Bryony."

I stood from the table, and Aric hurried to do the same, Griffin moving to the far end of the room. She paused in the corner, opening her mouth to speak but I shook my head. Cosmo and I had found a secret passage on this side of the room weeks ago when we were...fucking about the palace, basically. I leaned into it, pressing the knot of molding shaped like a grape bundle, and then looked over my shoulder to find Cresswell just behind me.

"Oh, good, you better come too," I said, taking his arm and pulling him into the small compartment room that led to a narrow hall that ran a circuit through the heart of the first floor. It was dark as the door closed, and Aric's fingers circled my wrist briefly, a little fizzle of energy running through me before candles on the wall lit up, casting orange shadows over us. I stared at him, a little surprised he could just pick magic off me in that way, and his thumb stroked over the back of my wrist before releasing me.

"What is it, Griffin? I have Aric safe and sound this time," I said, enjoying Aric's amused scowl.

"Emory, he escaped. One of the men we had guarding him is dead and the other is missing. I'm assuming he had more support in Aric's court than we realized," Griffin said, frowning and pacing the space. "It happened sometime in the night, after midnight, and we found the body at dawn. He could be nearly anywhere."

"Who can we actually trust?" Aric asked gruffly.

"Even if *you* could trust them, that doesn't mean Bryony can now, Aric," Griffin hissed. "And it's not your head wearing the crown anymore! Who do you think he's after?"

"I didn't have any trouble the last time," I started, but the thieves spoke over me.

"You think I don't know the position this puts her in? I never intended for her to *challenge* him. You were supposed to send the *guard*—"

"You should've found someone before now!" Griffin shouted back.

"I found *you*! I just needed to buy time to prepare you for it!"

"If the two of you would please shut up, none of this is doing us any good," I snapped. Aric and Griffin caught their breath and turned away from one another, shooting me equally exasperated looks as if I were meant to sympathize. "Emory will need to be found. Aric and I were already going to Rumsbrooke. We can start questioning—"

"You're not leaving the palace," Aric said quickly.

My jaw dropped as I stared at him. "I'm what? Aric that's *my* court now."

"I know. I know it is," Aric said nodding and stepping forward, hands out and raised to placate. "But King of Thieves isn't your *only* duty, and if Emory is a greater or vaster threat than we anticipated, if he has more support than I thought, it puts you in equally great danger."

"I can fight—"

"You fought Emory in an outright challenge, in front of many witnesses, Your Majesty," Griffin continued, softer. "He was abiding by a set of rules, loose ones, I'll admit, but still. He wasn't allowed to sneak up on you. Wasn't allowed to have help from anyone."

"Your Highness, I agree with them. You are more than a King of Thieves. Emory is either looking for outright escape or revenge. You shouldn't be the one to track him down, you should be the one who makes the order once he's been apprehended," Cresswell said, stepping up to join the others in front of me.

Aric was tense, prepared to argue with me and not give an inch, and I knew it wouldn't matter that I was his king, and he was my Chosen. He would never submit to an order from me like the others would, not if he thought he was doing what was best for me.

"You're making me remain here," I said, flatly, staring back at Aric.

"I'm pleading with you to," he said softly, taking one step forward and holding his hand out, waiting for mine.

Oh, sneaky. He was too smart.

I sighed and slid my hand over his, closing my eyes as Aric's fingers clasped tight around my own, and he bowed to kiss the back of my hand.

"I want to be sent for the moment you find him. Cresswell is right. I will be the one to give his punishment. His and anyone who helped him. Publicly. I can't be the preciously guarded object to these men, Aric," I said.

"I understand," he whispered.

I wanted to kick his shin just to make him glare and fight me. I didn't like that he already knew to manage me by appealing to my feelings for him, my own impulse to soothe his worry.

"Cresswell, go and inform the guards to be on the watch," I said. "Griffin, I'd like a moment—"

I didn't need to finish the words, Griffin was hurrying for the door. "I'll wait for you outside Aric."

Alone in the small room, Aric stood straight again, wary and stiff, ready to fight with me.

"I don't care which of you is really in charge, I need you to look like you're obeying Griffin's commands," I said.

Aric sighed, his hands catching my waist and drawing me to his chest. "Agreed. I'll be there to assist her."

"He could've ridden far away from Rumsbrooke by now," I murmured, my arms circling Aric's shoulders.

"Yes, but someone will know. It'll be better to catch him sooner than give him time to infect another city, or decide he doesn't feel like hiding and have him come back when we aren't expecting him."

"You think he wants my crown?"

"I think he doesn't want you to have a head to wear it on," Aric whispered, ducking his own head and dressing kisses over my shoulder. "I like this dress, for the record."

"Yes, I gathered," I said, trying not to smile as Aric pushed one sleeve off my shoulder, trying to kiss his way down to my breast. "Stop it. You know you don't have time for that... What are you trying to do? Work the Hunger up and then pawn me off on one of the others to distract me?"

Aric straightened, grinning. "Don't be absurd, you're far too clever for that to work," he said, and I scoffed and shook my head, starting to pull away. He held my waist and pulled me back into his chest, my head falling back to stare up at him. "Don't worry, I'll be back."

"After dinner," I said as Aric's head dipped, nose tracing against mine, lips threatening a kiss goodbye.

"Breakfast tomorrow," he coaxed. "If we haven't found him before tonight, we'll get our best information then with the drinkers."

"Fine," I sighed, and Aric sucked on my bottom lip until I pulled away. "But you have to send word, at least."

"You'll hear from me by nightfall," Aric said with a nod. "I like your guard, keep him close. And the others."

I nodded, and Aric waved his hand, the candles flicking out with little whiffs of smoke as he pressed my back to the door, kissing me deeply. I dug my fingers into Aric's back, trying to set aside my frustration for the moment just to enjoy the kiss. I didn't like being left behind, especially not when it was 'for my protection.' But the others were right. I wasn't going to draw answers out of skittish thieves, if I could convince them to talk to me at all.

"Be careful," I breathed.

"Did you know, the only reason I attended the Choosing at all was to steal from the castle," Aric whispered roughly.

"What?! Aric," I laughed, beating lightly on his back. "What did you steal?"

"The greatest treasure the crown had to offer," he said, his grin against my chin as I grew impatient and pinched him for my answer. He nipped me, and then kissed my pulse. "You, princess."

My breath caught, and Aric righted the shoulder of my dress, pulling the door open and tugging me back out into the light of the dining room where the others waited impatiently.

"I love you," I said, jogging to keep up with him, my hands tight around his.

Aric looked at me, lifting my knuckles to his lips but didn't answer. Silly stoic man. I'd make him shout it, chant it, after he returned.

My feet stopped, my hands sliding free, holding Aric's gaze as he stepped away, winking before swinging around to face Griffin where she hovered in the doorway.

"Well? Let's go, Griff. Can't waste time," Aric teased, marching past her.

She growled after him, and I hid my wringing hands behind my back as Aric looked over his shoulder at me, worry twining through my chest as he vanished down the hall.

21.
BRYONY

"Your Highness."

"Bryony," I corrected in a snap.

"She needs to move when she's anxious, she can't help it," Cosmo murmured to Cresswell.

"That may be, but it would be better if she were moving in a more...stationary way," Cresswell muttered back. "Bryony, please. If I could convince you to return to your rooms where it would be easier to guard you."

"Fine, fine," I said, turning quickly around a corner to take my pacing right back to my rooms.

I'd sparred with Thao. I'd tried sitting for Cosmo and failed terribly. Owen had wanted to take me horseback riding, but Cresswell refused.

Behind me, someone jogged along the tile to catch up with me, and I expected Owen or Wendell until that warm dense smell of Cresswell reached my nose. My steps slowed and my eyes lifted to his clear green ones.

"I don't mean to be difficult," I said, reaching for his arm and delivering a tenuous smile as he pressed my hand to the crook of his elbow.

"You aren't being—I understand," he said. "Is it worry for Aric, or frustration of being cooped up?"

"Both."

"You like being more hands-on," he said, more to himself, and I looked up in time to catch him blushing. "With problems, I mean. You try and solve them yourself."

"I suppose so. It just seems to me that my family has made a habit of delegating without bothering to check the results, and that's left others suffering," I said. "Also, and no one say this to Aric, but the last time he went up against Emory—"

"He was off his game," Cosmo said, joining me on the other side, his arm around my waist. "Don't worry about Aric. He has more allies than Emory, regardless of Emory managing to escape. It's a different playing field entirely. Outside of the challenge, he'll be able to use his magic too. Come on, we can play chess. Or read to you. Or..." He arched a brow, fixing a teasing smile over his lips.

I shook my head. "Sorry, I just—"

"Or you can pace a hole in the floor," Cosmo said gently, pressing a kiss to my forehead. "Whatever you need."

"I'm sorry to pull you away from your work."

He shrugged. "I'm not sure I could focus when I knew you were worried. I'll sketch while we wait."

We reached the doors of my suite and Cresswell's fingers squeezed over mine, holding my touch in place as he glanced over the two guards stationed outside.

"Stanley, I'd like you to stay with me. Walsh, grab Putnam and scout the perimeter."

"Scout for what exactly?" the older of the two guards questioned.

"Anyone but court or staff," Cresswell answered in a clipped tone. "I'll hold your station for you. Send Yorley and...Brummer around as well."

"Are we expecting a siege?" Walsh pressed, eyes narrowing.

Cresswell stiffened and stood taller, ready to speak, but I couldn't resist interrupting. "Do you often question orders from your superior, Guard Walsh?"

"I—No, Your Highness," the man said, bowing, eyes moving skittishly between Cresswell and I.

"I'm relieved to hear it, but I'd prefer to see the evidence."

"Yes, Your Highness." He bowed and hurried out of our way, and Cresswell fought a smile.

"I'll be just out here," he said.

"I'd rather you come inside with the rest of us," I said, smiling up at Cresswell, who turned an even darker shade of flushed than before.

"I..."

"Do you often question orders from your superiors?" Cosmo asked, nudging me with his hip as he pushed the door open and waggled his eyebrows at Cresswell.

"Stanley—"

"I'll be fine out here, sir," Stanley said, bowing.

"See, he'll be fine," I said, tugging Cresswell into the sitting room with me.

"I..." Cresswell stalled again, his eyes wide with something almost like panic, twisting as Thao closed the door behind us.

"Did you doubt the rest of us to keep you safe?" Thao asked me, smiling and moving for the window seat, Wendell following him so they could restart their paused game of chess.

"Of course not, but Cresswell calms me," I said.

Owen and Cosmo exchanged a quick smile before Cosmo moved to the desk, where he'd left a sketchbook open.

"I'll just...go and have a nap in the other room," Owen said, heading for the bed, flashing a smile at me over his shoulder.

"Close the door, I can't concentrate with your trumpeting," Thao muttered.

"Har har," Owen answered, passing Thao and ruffling the other man's hair. "Maybe I want Wendell to win."

"Thank you, O," Wendell said, the two of them beaming with conspiracy at Thao's teasing scowl.

"I calm you?" Cresswell asked, following almost obediently as I moved to sit on the couch, placing myself in the middle and nodding my head for him to sit at my side.

"Of course you do," I said.

It was true. Cresswell was becoming a bit of a rock for me to cling to when the winds began to buffer and blow around me, whether it was my sister or Daniel, or now this with Emory. And I did lean as Cresswell sat down at my side, fitting into the narrow space I'd given him.

"I take it I don't calm you," I said softly as I found him rigid and frozen at my side. He eased a fraction at the joke, his left arm stretching over the back of the couch, gripping the frame like he was afraid he might touch me.

"Your Highness—"

"Bryony!"

He sucked in a deep breath, brow furrowing, and I twisted to face him. It gave him a little more room away from me but my left my knees pressed to his thigh, his extraordinary warmth seeping through our clothes into me.

Cresswell shifted, leaning toward me, head lowered and gaze holding to mine. "Princess, I am at your disposal, of course, but..."

"But you're exempt from being Chosen," I said, echoing the words he'd said to Camellia.

Cresswell's eyebrows jumped. "I—yes. Yes, and I'm a shifter."

I nodded and shrugged, glancing toward the window. "Thao and Wendell are shifters too, of course. Are you registered?"

"I am. I was a ward of Kimmery. There was no...there was no hiding it," he said.

Our voices were growing softer, and it hadn't escaped me that the rest of my Chosen had given us this space, busying them-selves elsewhere. If Owen were really falling asleep, we'd all have heard it by now.

"I want to do away with the registration of shifters," I said, and realized I only mentioned it to try and appeal to Cresswell.

This had been coming on slowly since the festival, hadn't it, this slow-simmering attraction to my guard? Cresswell had been at my side since I'd arrived in the north, making a road for me on untraveled ground, glaring over my shoulder at every threat.

His head turned to the door, a puzzled frown digging over his forehead like he was trying to sort out why he was inside the room rather guarding from the hall. I reached for his hand, marveling at the size of his palm, turning it over in mine and studying the strength of his fingers as they twitched at my exploration.

"I would give my life for you, Bryony."

My heart stuttered in my chest and my chin lifted, lips parted. He looked as though I'd wrenched the words from them, torn them from his lips, and he took a great gasp of breath. Wendell and Thao bickered companionably, and Cosmo's pencil scratched quickly, our conversation for our ears only, the rest of the room carrying on without us.

"I'd rather it didn't come to that," I said, blinking foolishly back at him.

The left side of his mouth hitched, but the rest of him looked sorrowful. "You don't have enough people you can trust, not really."

"I trust you," I said.

He nodded. "As you should. I am your guard, body and soul. I will never let any harm come to you *provided you don't run out of the palace without warning*," he added, cocking an eyebrow.

My fingers were fiddling absently with his as I thought over his words, scanning his face. "You don't want to be Chosen," I whispered.

I held my breath as his head dipped, resisted the urge to close my eyes as his forehead pressed to mine.

"More than almost anything," he said, breath brushing my cheeks, my lips, a kiss but not quite. He leaned back and blinked heavily. "But not as much as I want to keep you safe. And I'm not sure I can do that properly from..."

"My bed," I said slowly, feeling a pressure behind my eyes and a delicate but persistent shredding in my chest.

He swallowed hard, his entire body flinching and his hands gripping onto mine as he nodded. "I need my focus to be outside of you, to be sure nothing ever touches you, and I...I know my place, Bryony. This isn't it."

This wasn't the same pain as when Aric had refused me over and over, even when we'd fought in the greenhouse. Aric's cuts were quick and sharp. This was an endless weight pressing down on my heart. Cresswell knew me, cared for me, *wanted* me. He wasn't denying his feelings for me, he was denying us the use of them.

Before I could think of the right words to persuade Cresswell to change his mind, he leaned forward, kissing my brow with a faint pass of his lips, and then rising. My hands clutched his, trying to hang on as demands and pleas ran through my thoughts.

"Cress—"

"I'll be outside with Stanley," he rumbled. His hands flexed and shook mine loose as he pulled away, moving quickly for the door.

I watched his back, the noble strength, shoulders squared and head held high, until he disappeared through the door. There were no words between Thao and Wendell, no scratch of Cosmo's pencil over paper, no sweet racket of Owen sleeping. Just the sound of my uneven breaths.

"Fool," Thao hissed.

My shoulders slumped.

"Bryony," Cosmo started gently, but I shook my head.

"Don't," I whispered, words choked without any air in my lungs.

My empty hands fell to my skirt, fisting in the fabric. I stood and headed for the bedroom, wishing Owen might pretend to remain asleep as I hid under the covers. But he rolled over as I approached, eyeing the empty area behind me and then spreading his arms. I puffed a wet sigh and swallowed down the burning lump in my throat as I crawled onto the bed, sliding into his embrace.

I squeezed my eyes shut, face pressed to Owen's shoulder as footsteps approached. The bed dipped at my back and it could only be Wendell—he was the only one tall enough to tuck his chin over the top of my head and his feet beneath mine.

"That was just one conversation," he murmured. "Think of how long it took for you to tame Thao." Someone, Thao probably, snorted from off the side of the bed.

"And you only just got Aric to cooperate," Cosmo said from the foot of the bed, trying for teasing.

I just grimaced. "Are you telling me to bully Cresswell for wanting to do his job more than..."

More than he wanted to bed me? Except that wasn't what these men were to me. I sighed and rolled, turning my face into Wendell's throat next, he and Owen making steady work of soothing me with their hands, Owen's fingers going to the buttons down the back of my dress. The Hunger barely raised its head.

"I think what we're saying is that this isn't a decision Cresswell will make once," Wendell said gently, leaning back to find my eyes with his sky blue ones. "Over and over, every day, at every moment, he will have to decide to resist his own feelings for you."

I whimpered, and Owen kissed the back of my neck.

"Mistress, no man could do that. There will come a time where he will realize it only hurts you both," Owen said.

I fiddled with Wendell's collar. "What if he's right? What if we're safer with him on the outside?"

"He's a very good guard, and very loyal, but I don't care if we have to search the whole world, surely *someone* else could manage the job? And it's not as though you are without protection within your own Chosen," Thao said, leaning against the headboard and reaching over to comb stray tendrils of hair away from my face, and then away from Wendell's. "I would rip anyone's throat out who dared to try and harm you."

Wendell hummed with agreement, and Cosmo climbed onto the bed, pulling my feet into his lap.

"I'm not a fighter, but I'd stand in the way of anyone who tried to hurt you, little muse," Cosmo murmured, expression uncommonly grave.

My heart thumped anxiously, and I shook my head. "Don't say that, come here."

Owen made room for Cosmo at my back, and Thao slid down at Wendell's, arms stretching around me and sliding under my hips until I hovered in a tangled cradle of a hug.

"Aric will return shortly, Cresswell will relent soon. By spring, Kimmery will have the beginning of orchards and rich farmland. We will mend the roads and moderate the taxes and wrangle the laws from the fists of the council to make them fair," Wendell said, decorating kisses across my face until my eyelids fell shut.

"I said we might go south in the spring," I murmured. "Although I will miss the north if we do."

"We'll go south, and you'll win the hearts of the people there too," Cosmo said. "You'll show the queen the depth of your Hunger and the good it can do."

"We'll host my family at the castle and create an even

stronger treaty of alliance," Thao said. "My mother is a liberal, she'll like you."

"All will be well, Mistress," Owen soothed.

I sighed and softened in their arms, dozing to the murmur of their voices.

22.
BRYONY

The evening was gray, the sky misting over the mountain, something that wasn't quite snow or frost but clung to every surface and glittered dully. It ran like tears over the glass panes of the windows in the greenhouse where I sat and fussed over notes for a letter to my grandmother. There was a great deal I couldn't tell her now, but I did want to find a way to mention claiming Aric as my Chosen, if only to goad and gloat. I'd already received two letters from her since her departure, and while they were mostly news of her discussions with the Southern Council, there was a friendliness to the exchange that brightened my mood.

I wasn't sure if it was a storm or just the evening, but the room grew darker every minute until even the pretty lanterns Delilah had lit for me weren't enough to see by. Cresswell was at the door, his back to me, the pair of us trying to ignore one another in a painful way. My Chosen were right, I thought. Eventually, Cresswell would change his mind, decide that he could love me up close and not just at a distance to protect me. I would help him reach that decision, but for now I was giving it a little time.

"Is it time for dinner?" I asked his back.

"I believe so, Your Highness," Cresswell answered without turning.

I grimaced but didn't correct his formality. He'd fumbled around my title as if it felt as clumsy and uncomfortable on his tongue as it did on my ears.

Wendell was reading with me, but Thao and Owen had gone with Cosmo to his studio for something a little more active than sitting and waiting for someone to bring news on whether or not Emory had been retrieved.

I stood, and Wendell followed suit, moving to my side as I closed my notebook around the letter and slid it into my pocket. Cresswell turned from his stationed place just in time to watch my eyes fall shut and head tip back as Wendell dressed my throat in faint kisses. It wasn't an intentional taunt, Wendell was just excellent at providing touch when I hadn't even realized I needed the comfort, but I could see the tension on Cresswell's face when my eyes opened again and he was still watching.

What else would he watch, standing like stone and refusing to touch?

Wendell's arm circled my waist, and he guided me gently forward to the hall, Cresswell keeping a cautious width of room between us, when a flurry of movement bounced and echoed off the tile. It was often difficult to place sound and where it came from within the palace, but the sound was urgent. I ignored Cresswell's lead toward the direction of the dining room and headed for a connecting hall just in time to see Owen passing on the other end at the front of the palace. He looked hasty, shoulders hunched forward, legs moving at a quickening jog.

"Owen!"

"The horses," he called automatically without looking back. "The stables, something's wrong!"

"Bryony," Cresswell said, but this time he didn't wait in the hopes that I would listen, hurrying back to my side with Wendell as I started after Owen.

We didn't like to waste candles and oil keeping the whole palace lit, and the hallway seemed impossibly long in the dark. Even the windows at the front of the palace were full of shadows, night falling with a great and sudden cloud of darkness.

"Is it the storm brewing?" Wendell asked, but there was no answer for him. We reached the spot I'd seen Owen running down just in time to watch him vanish out of the front of the palace.

"Bryony, you stay at my side," Cresswell bit out, his hand clamping on my shoulder as we hurried after Owen. But he didn't try and tell me to stay put at least.

"He just took off," Cosmo called from behind us. "He got stiff and pale, and then started running."

The horses, I thought, wondering, not for the first time, about Owen and his connection to animals.

The rain was growing heavy, sloppy almost, just at the edge of turning into snow, and there was no sign of Owen as we reached the open door, or the guards normally stationed there. Water pooled on the tile floor, and Daniel was escorting Lady Prudence down the stairs as we all piled around the doors.

"Well, what's tonight's commotion then?" Lady Prudence asked, fairly cheerful as Daniel left her side to join us.

"Could it be...magic to lure Owen out?" Wendell asked, frowning.

I didn't know and I didn't really care, charging out into the storm, wincing at the immediate lash of cold wind and icy slush that struck my skin and soaked into my dress. Cresswell remained fixed to my side as I hurried down the steps, his hand finding mine, grip warm and as solid as an anchor. To the left and down the slope, the gate of the palace was closed, and I thought I could see guards sheltering there. And to the right...

It took a moment to see through the thick mess of rain.

"Smoke," Cresswell said. "Get back inside."

But he didn't let go when I ran forward with him, ignoring his command, hearing the shouts of the others at my back.

"What could be on fire in this downpour?" I shouted. But I already knew the answer.

The horses. *The stables*.

"Owen!" I screamed, feet slipping in the slush on the gravel briefly, Cresswell's hand like iron holding me up and steady.

"That smell," Cresswell said, bowing his head to me. "Oil, or accelerant. A lot of it too."

Which explained why the stables were burning in the middle of a vicious storm. The flames licking the structure of the building looked weak at first, lapping lightly up the walls, until we were close enough to see through the open doors. Inside was an inferno.

"Owen," I breathed, my heart feeling still and cold in my chest. "Owen!"

This time Cresswell held me back, arm wrapping around my waist, my feet tangling in the sodden hem of my dress, our clothes sticking together as ice ran down my collar and between my breasts.

"Look," Cresswell said, pointing to the ground in front of the stable.

A body, on the ground. I gagged and my knees crumpled, and Cresswell herded me closer. Smoke rushed off the surface of the stables, billowing up into the air and clinging to the branches of the trees overhead.

"The groomsman," Cresswell said.

There were men shouting, shadows moving around the edge of the building, and my eyes flicked to one I thought might've been Owen, frame large but graceful.

Cresswell and I reached the body and he knelt down, but it was clear by the dark stain on the stone around him and the wide stillness of his eyes that the older man was dead.

"Emory is here," I said, voice low. Cresswell didn't move, and I wasn't sure he'd even heard me. I looked up again and knew the perfect shape of the body standing at the mouth of the stables, broad shoulders and tapered waist, face staring in at the blaze.

"I've got to go in."

I yanked free of Cresswell's loosened grip, crying out Owen's name at the same time Cresswell shouted mine. Owen pulled the wet fabric of his shirt up over his nose and ran inside the stables as I chased after him, stalling at the sudden scorch of warmth that stole my breath as I got close.

I had magic, but I didn't know what it would do. Could it make the flames stronger, strong enough to beat back the rain and burn through Owen? Or could I smother the fire? It was too much of a risk.

An arm banded around my waist, and I thrashed until I realized it was only Cresswell catching up with me.

"What do we do?" I gasped.

"Stars above, Bryony, you stay *outside*—" Cresswell snapped, voice furious and hard.

"But—"

"I'll drag Owen out, even if I have to knock him unconscious."

I sagged and stared up at Cresswell, the fire bright on his skin, catching in the glassy shade of his eyes, warming soft freckles over his forehead. I paused, but only for a moment which was less time than we really had, and nodded.

"You stay here, and you hold this," Cresswell said, passing a belt into my hand. A dagger belt, one with a heavier hilt and blade than my own. I nodded again, wincing away from a sudden burst of heat, reaching for Cresswell at the last second and failing to reach him, my fingers sliding through the water evaporating off of us both.

You've just watched two men you love run into a fire, and you haven't done a fucking thing about it, I thought, wanting to run after Cresswell too, feeling the call to follow pounding in my veins, making me sway with the beat of the rain on my back.

It was stupid not to pay attention. The fire was an obvious distraction.

And Emory was quick.

I gasped as a hand clasped over my mouth, an arm so tight around my ribs it made them ache. I kicked and twisted as I was dragged back, away from the glow of the fire in the stables, into the shadow of the woods. There were figures running for us, but their eyes were on the flames, not me.

I pulled Cresswell's dagger from the hilt just in time to be thrown to the ground. The blade dug into the earth as I landed, lodging into the dense root of a tree and sticking there. I yanked once, twice, and then gave up, scrambling away and onto my back just as Emory dove down. He had a knife, a small one, and a rich collection of bruises around his face, one hand bandaged in a way that made it clear he was missing a few fingers. I ripped the skirt of my dress, the pretty red one Aric had appreciated, as I struggled to stand, every inch of me stiff with cold, sore with being thrown.

"Don't shout for them," Emory hissed, as I opened my mouth.

I eyed the dagger in the tree root briefly, and then Emory's own clumsy grip around his knife. It was in his left hand this time, when he'd fought me with his right. That was good for me, his usual hand being injured. It would make his fighting weaker and give me a place to target to distract him. I skirted back at his approach, my hands behind me to try and avoid cornering myself against a tree trunk.

"You really are just one fucking problem after another, aren't you?" Emory breathed. His nose was crooked now, hair matted and greasy from his time in a cell. "You won't fuck the men you're meant to. You set about playing queen before you've even been granted the crown. Then you take *my crown*!" He stiffened, breath ragged, and I wondered if his ribs were injured too.

I had no weapon, but Emory was a mess.

You have magic, idiot, I thought, and when Emory lunged for me, I ducked and slid across the ground, grabbing up a handful of leaves. He paused, straightening, and laughed at the mess of dead leaves and twigs in my grip. Behind him, at the stables, something groaned and croaked ominously, and a horse went careening out of the fire, tail alight.

"Princess, this is a pity, because I was really looking forward to fucking you. Really making it hurt too, just because no one else would ever dare, would they? But I'm not sure we have the time," Emory said, prowling closer.

It took a moment, the Hunger so far out of reach, my own body so numb, but I kept myself safely out of Emory's grasp, trying to edge my way back to the others as I channeled magic into my fist.

My focus was split. The fire. *Owen*. Emory in front of me, and I knew right away whatever I was fashioning wasn't an elegant dagger. But it was cold and hard in my grip, and my fingers fisted gratefully around it. If nothing else, it was something to channel my panic and energy into.

"Cat got your tongue, princess?" Emory asked, gritting his teeth and frowning at me.

He wanted me scared. He probably wanted me pleading with him. When I didn't answer, he lunged, and I ignored the stab of his knife swinging for me as I thrust my fist at his stomach. We both hit our marks, but his was at my right shoulder and mine was in his belly, up under his ribs. I wasn't holding a knife but a half wreath of blades, their ragged edges shaped like leaves.

I gasped and released a strangled scream as his knife struck bone, but Emory gagged, eyes bugging wide as he staggered back in shock, a flood of blood running down his stomach into the torn fabric of his shirt.

The blood of my own wound was somehow welcomingly warm by comparison to the oozing chill of the rain soaking into me, and I ignored the throb, the drum of pain that ran down my arm.

"I'm going to kill you," Emory breathed, calming slightly, the understanding in his snarled expression that in doing so, I'd no doubt return the favor.

He lunged again, and I braced myself for the searing pain, the clash and thunder of contact when he struck.

I was torn away, a strong arm pulling back around my shoulders, spinning me out of the way, a hot hand cupped over the wound in my shoulder.

Daniel Farraque stood at my side, holding me to his chest, sword pointed at Emory.

"No," he said, the word rising out of him in a long growl.

Emory wavered, eyes as wide as their swollen bruises would allow, the sword digging directly into the mark I'd left myself just days ago. And then he dropped to the ground with a groan.

"Danny Boy. You fucking bastard," Emory breathed, and then he chuckled and growled at his own joke, arm banding around his wounded stomach, shoulders heaving as he winced with every breath.

"Bryony!"

My name was roared from near the stables on a sweetly familiar tongue, and I softened against Daniel who kept his blade pointed at Emory on the ground.

"She's here! Safe. I have Emory," Daniel answered with a shout of his own.

Aric came galloping on horseback, my Chosen running after him. Except—

"Owen," I moaned. "Cresswell."

"They're out of the fire," Daniel murmured. "The smoke will have done some damage, but they're fine."

Then I really did crumple. Aric was quick to leap off his horse, sliding through the muck on the ground to catch me.

"She's bleeding, right shoulder," Daniel said, looking down at his own dark and glossy hand covered in my blood.

Aric didn't ask questions, just took my hand in his and pressed it over the wound. I gasped, the force of magic applied to the wound every bit as painful and shocking as it had been to be stabbed.

"Shhh, it'll pass, princess," Aric murmured, his eyes focused on his work. "Stars above, Bryony, what is that?"

I glanced down at my fist, still wrapped tightly around the wreath of leaf blades and shook my head. "I needed a weapon."

Aric's mouth was warm on my forehead, my cheeks, my mouth briefly, although I wobbled as I tried to chase the touch. "Let it go now. I have you."

My grip was stiff and eased slowly, and I realized that whatever I'd fashioned, I'd done so around my fingers, like a dangerous collection of rings fused together, refusing to be stolen from me.

Aric peeled our fingers off my shoulder and pushed my gown aside, wiping away my blood to see that my skin was whole again, although it looked like there might've been a mark left behind. He frowned and then carefully eased my new weapon off my other hand, passing it to a stunned Cosmo.

"Good girl," Aric murmured, kissing me again and then lifting me into his arms.

"Thao, Wen, escort Farraque as he takes this scum down to the dungeons."

Thao and Wendell didn't ask any questions, just transformed into their tigers as Daniel slid the sword in the sheath hanging over his shoulder, watching as Thao prowled around Emory's trembling form. I didn't know if the man was shaking because of cold or bleeding or Thao, but I reached my hand out in his direction.

Emory let out a garbled scream as I thrust magic in his direction, not caring if I did as tidy or thorough a job of healing him as Aric had done with me.

"Bryony?" Cosmo gasped.

"We need to question him," I said, my lips numb with cold, my body shivering, and rage burning through me hotter than any fire ever could.

23.
DANIEL

A great orange tiger, Thao, I reminded myself, lay in front of the locked cell we'd thrown Emory into hours ago. Emory was collapsed in the corner, head hanging down until his chin sat on his chest. I didn't know if he was sleeping or dead or ill, and I wasn't sure I particularly cared.

I was returning after a hot bath and a plate of food I barely knew what to do with, my head too full of the recent events.

I knew what the council wanted. What Emory had full permission from Jonathon Roderick to do with Bryony. I was here in the palace on their behalf. I was meant to be their ally.

I'd stopped Emory from killing her, or more likely doing more damage. Bryony held her own, even unprepared. If she hadn't *healed* him, a shocking revelation of her power, I suspected he'd probably already be dead.

I flinched as Thao stood, the tiger vanishing in lieu of the man. He shuddered, and water dripped off of him, still there from before his transformation.

"The cell is warded by Aric's magic. You can't let him out," Thao said, glaring at me.

I didn't bother objecting, only nodded. "Cresswell and Stanley Piper are coming shortly," I said.

"Good." Thao groaned and rolled his shoulders, eyes still narrowed at me. "I'm going to the others... Thank you for preventing him from harming her any further," he said, and hurried to leave the small room of the cellar.

I sagged against the wall, eyes on Emory, thoughts on the princess tucked away in her suite, no doubt surrounded by the comforting figures of her Chosen. Had she healed Owen too? How much was she capable of?

A chuckle from the shadow of the cell sounded and I stiffened, glancing over as Emory groaned and lifted his head from his chest, neck cracking as he stretched it.

"You get your hero's fuck in?" he asked. "She finally spread those witch's legs for you after that clever stunt? Fuck, Dan, I did you a favor didn't I?"

Emory was a wreck, and I suspected he not only knew it, but that it was a deeper scar on his pride to be dirty and bruised and broken than it was to be locked up.

"You should've run," I said.

"Let me out and I still can," Emory answered just as quickly.

We stared at one another, Emory barely visible in the shadows, me lit up by the torch fastened at the wall. I could guess what he was thinking, but he could probably see it written all over my face.

"You don't want to. What is it, Danny Boy? Hoping with me tied up, you'll get to slide into position at last, make Roderick happy and daddy proud?"

I stayed silent, poised against the wall, watching as Emory scooted forward into the light. He looked like one of the madmen they found in Rumsbrooke's gutters in the winter.

"Roderick was never counting on you," Emory hissed. "The council always knew it was going to come down to getting rid of the girl. To come down to *me*. There's a spare heir. This bitch'll never make it to the throne."

I blinked, my body remaining placid but for the way my fingers scratched at the rough stone wall behind me, wanting to tear open the cell, to beat Emory down to little useless scraps.

"No, you just want her, don't you? Just want that pretty little cunt to look at you and not see the waste of space you are. Our father would've better spent his seed into a bucket than your mother, Danny Boy," Emory said, laughing a little, although the sound was wet and ragged.

I stiffened and stared at Emory. Emory without a last name. Emory who never fucking bothered using mine. Who'd sought me out on a night of revelry with my few friends from school. Who'd dragged me into his filthy world and begged for me to bring Jonathon, to create a line of communication.

"Your mother was a maid, mine was a whore," he said, flat and toneless. I stared at him, my chest a vise around my heart, my stomach churning. There wasn't much of a resemblance between us. I looked like my mother's side of the family.

Maybe there *was* some of my father in Emory though. Some of that elegance I lacked. And maybe his beauty came from his mother.

And maybe he was just a liar trying to weasel his way out of the cell I'd helped put him in and he didn't have a clue who his father was.

"Let me out, brother," Emory whispered. "Find a way. You can keep your hero cock in her."

Footsteps were approaching and Emory's voice lowered with every echo.

It might be true, his claim. It might not be. Family was beginning to mean a great deal less to me than it had just weeks ago.

Cresswell Stark entered the room, arms crossed over his chest, breathing a little roughly from the smoke he'd inhaled earlier. He glanced at me briefly, eyes narrowing.

"He said the council was always planning to have him assassinate her." Emory snarled from the cell, but I ignored him and continued, "I never heard the words directly, but the night of the festival he implied he was behind the attempt against her. I was told to blame any mishaps on Aric's court, but I assumed they meant thieving not—"

"You fucking snake!" Emory growled, staggering up from the corner.

"Who is they?"

"Emory, Jonathon Roderick. I doubt Jon was the only one aware," I said.

Cresswell grunted as Emory hurled poisonous insults in my direction, a dark, wheezing laughing cracking through the words.

"We'll question him."

I nodded, heading for the doorway, trying to feel the burn of Emory's anger at my back.

"You think your neck won't fit in a noose too, Dan?!" Emory bellowed.

I was positive it would, and entirely unsure if spilling my guts to Cresswell, to *anyone*, would save me from that fate.

My steps scuttled as a shadow overtook me in the narrow stairwell, and I pressed myself to the wall as Aric Martin appeared and stalled in his own path.

"Ah. Farraque."

"Guard Stark is waiting for you," I said.

"Mm. I...Bryony wants to speak with you. I think she's gone to your rooms," he said.

I stiffened, and my head shot up to stare at the older man. His stare was scrutinizing and more aware than I was comfortable with. Bryony was...

The bite of her nails in my cheek as she covered my mouth, the desperate grip and slide of her on my cock.

Aric only stared back at me, eyes narrowed, less suspicious than the others but clearly trying to read me.

"Is she...all right?"

Aric huffed and started to pass me. "She's angry and she's armed. Tread gently."

I swallowed hard and nodded, but he was already gone. She had to know Emory and I had some acquaintance, he'd made that plain enough in his taunts. I grimaced at the thought of what that ornamental and monstrous weapon she'd fashioned might feel like at my throat. But if I wasn't going to run out of the palace and seek safety, then my next smartest move would be to make sure the princess wasn't waiting on me and growing impatient.

I moved through the staff corridors up through the back of the palace toward my rooms. It was the fastest route and also the one least likely to leave me running into any of the Chosen.

They could be there waiting with her. They wouldn't want to leave you alone with her again.

I'd barely slept since I'd taken that selfish, impulsive leap to let Bryony conquer me. Partly because I couldn't get every agonizing, exquisite second of the fucking out of my head. And partly because if she wasn't going to claim me as Chosen, the next logical assumption was that she'd either cut my balls off, toss me out of the palace, or both.

She'd kept her word in avoiding me, ignoring what happened, but aside from the tension in everyone's stare, there'd been no real change. I hated the stalemate.

"Daniel."

I stalled as the pale figure stepped out of a doorway, Sam looking everywhere in the hallway but at me.

"Get back to sleep, Sam," I said, frowning, my body urging me to go to Bryony as fast as I could, even if it meant she slit my throat when I got there.

"Are the horses all right?"

"Most of them. Men are seeing to them now."

"And the princess?"

I chewed on my own tongue, trying to check my impatience. "She's waiting to speak to me now."

"It wasn't me."

I blinked, head cocking, frowning as Sam started to retreat into his room. "What wasn't you?"

"The fire," he said softly.

My hands clenched to fists at my side, suspicion warring with the obvious answer. "We know that, Sam."

He sighed and then the door shut, my eyes glaring at it for a beat before the urge to see the princess outweighed my curiosity in the strange man.

I stopped in the doorway of my office. Even prepared for her to be here, waiting on me, she seemed like a vision at first. I'd taken the first chance to clean up and dry off, but Bryony stood in that crimson red gown, fabric now shredded up the leg and over one shoulder. She was dry as far as I could tell, but her hair was tangled and there was still blood staining one hand.

She spun, and I stepped back briefly at the blazing stare that met mine. This was a new version of the petite and playful princess I'd grown accustomed to. Oh, she could stand like a queen and stare down her nose at us all, taunt the council with her authority. But the woman in front of me was ferocious, pale, and stealing all the light from the room to dress her skin. If she'd snarled and growled, I would've bared my throat like prey.

I took three steps forward, aware that a new beast had claimed this territory and I was now an interloper.

"I didn't know he was coming here," I said.

"What did they tell you?"

I wanted to lie prostrate on the floor at her feet. Bryony wasn't a woman at all, she was some kind of creature, wilder and more dangerous than any of the two-natured. More potent. If she felt any Hunger in the moment, I suspected it was for blood rather than sex.

"To take the steward position, to let you claim me."

"Let me?" she asked, brow arching. Her words were long and articulated with sharp edges, each syllable a warning.

"They knew you exhibited the Hunger. I thought they wanted me to listen in, to share what I saw, but they were only ever interested if I was fucking you yet."

"And when you did?"

I shook my head, holding that eerily vibrant green stare. "I didn't tell them."

That startled her, just a little, her eyes blinking briefly. "Why?"

"Because that was...that was for me." I frowned and glanced down at my feet, nearly flinching as she strode to the middle of the room with quick long steps.

"Come here."

I moved closer, aware that she had to tip her chin up to look at me and still feeling as though I were the smaller of the pair of us.

"Tell me of Emory."

I said it all with a compounding and heavy relief, offering more than she rightly needed to judge me. From scrambling for connections with legitimate sons as peers in school, to Emory's quick cultivation of a friendship and subsequent boost into Roderick's circles. The quick call for me to take this appointment as her steward, the meeting at the Yawning Pig, the night of the festival.

"You knew none of Emory's plans?"

"Not unless they wanted me involved in them," I said, jaw ticking. I didn't expect her to believe me, I sounded like I was trying to dig my way into her favor. But all I had was the truth, even if the information was a weak offering.

"He's your friend," she said, and some of the smooth steeliness of her expression faded, revealing a hint of the woman I recognized beneath.

I gaped, puzzled at the word. "He's...something." Emory was as close as I'd come to a friend in life, as was Jonathon. But I was aware they both might have been poorly applied to the word.

"Why did you intervene?"

"He was going to hurt you," I said, frowning. Of all the questions she'd asked, I thought that one had the most obvious answer.

"And if I kill him?"

Not '*If he's put to death.*' If *I* kill him.

"Would you wish to intervene then too?" she asked, head cocking. There was a scratch on her throat that hadn't been healed yet, and I wanted to cover it with my hand, feel her pulse under my palm and reassure myself that this was *my* princess and not some mystical predator from the woods.

"No," I said. I frowned and then shook my head. "Yes. I would wish to, but I wouldn't."

Emory was an ass, and his ambitions had always been assisted by a violence I'd found distasteful. But there was some laughter, and some rare moments of feeling understood by someone mixed in with my memories of him. I hadn't lied thus far with Bryony, and I didn't want to start, even for as small a one that would be.

"What do you want, Daniel?" she said, a little ragged sigh in her voice, an echo of the question she'd left me with before.

And just as it had before, my head spun at the words. Since when did I have *options*, damnit, and why hadn't anyone ever prepared me to make a choice? Bryony frowned at me and started to draw back, and there was one small, crystalline fragment of understanding that I could grab onto.

"You."

At last, Bryony appeared in earnest, with an irritated puff of breath and a roll of her eyes. I sank to my knees and risked the integrity of my hands by reaching them out to take hers.

"I am not asking to be Chosen, or steward, or even trusted. I am not the council's man. You can have my neck in a noose, or you can use me against Emory, Roderick, any of them."

"What do you *want*?"

"Your mouth on mine!" I stared up in the wake of the words bursting out at me. She was frowning down at me, which felt more right somehow than being above her. "I *want* to be yours. In every way, but I know that—"

Her hand pulled free of mine and dug into my hair, and my words froze, eyes falling shut as she pulled me forward. My face pressed to her stomach and I groaned at the scent of her, still full of violets but mixed with sweat and the damp richness of the woods and the smoke of the fire. Her fingers combed steadily through my strands, gently tugging at my roots, fingernails scratching at my scalp.

My arms rose slowly, circling her hips and squeezing around her. She was quiet, and I had a sudden moment of disorientation, feeling small and young, soothed. Then she pulled on the back of my neck, and I leaned into the touch, shivering as she scratched through my beard.

"What if I asked you to be my spy? To try and keep the council as far from knowing any details as you could for me?"

"Then that's what I'd do," I said, shrugging.

She frowned, and I thought I'd answered wrong, until she slowly sank down in front of me, the pair of us kneeling on the carpet together again. "And what if I never wanted you to contact Roderick again? That I'd be forever suspicious of you. That you would always be on the fringes, kept at arm's length?"

I blinked, studying the sinking weight in my stomach at her words.

"I would still be yours," I said, slightly disgusted with myself for knowing it was *true*.

She sighed, and I couldn't resist the impulse to lean into her hand as she rubbed against my skull under my ear. "Daniel, why?"

My blinks were getting lazy as if I were a cat being lulled into a good nap, and it took me a moment to sort my way through the drowsy, lustful feeling that grew to the truth. It was there again, unpleasant and clear.

"You are the only person in my life who has offered me a choice. And it will be you, every time."

Bryony whimpered and leaned forward, pressing her forehead firmly against mine. She smelled of blood and flowers and earth, and I couldn't decide if I wanted to press myself into her or scoop her up into my arms for safekeeping.

I barely noticed the kiss at first, the gentle nudging of her nose against mine, the pass of breath over my lips. There was no Hunger this time, this was entirely the young woman in front of me experimenting with a simple touch. It was easier than I expected to hold still and let her continue the exploration with little presses of her mouth to mine, enfolding my upper lip between both of hers.

My hands were still on her waist and they flexed impulsively. She hummed as I pressed back, catching a brief taste of her on my tongue before she pulled gently away.

"Then you are mine now," she murmured, frowning at me and smoothing my hair back from my forehead. "I hope neither of us comes to regret it."

24.
BRYONY

"Do you really think this is a wise decision?" Cosmo whispered, crowded close to my side on the bed as I sat against Owen's hip, my knees pressed to my chest and my hand rubbing circles over his back. He was wheezing raggedly in his sleep, and he kept waking himself with bouts of coughing. Aric had helped me use my magic to heal him, but it was thin after the events of the night and had only done about half of the work.

"Bryony, do you *trust* him?"

"No, not really," I said softly.

"Then...why? Do you have feelings for him?"

I lifted my chin and glanced tiredly at Cosmo before glancing toward the door. Daniel might've been in the sitting room. I wasn't sure actually. He might've gone back to his own suite after escorting me to mine.

"Some."

Cosmo's expression twisted, but when I let my legs slide to the side and I leaned toward him, he was ready, wrapping his arms around my shoulder and burying his face in my hair. Thao and Wendell had gone back out to help keep an eye on what was left of the stables. The rain had abated, and now it was just a matter of making sure the wind didn't manage to start the fire back up.

"Bryony, this isn't... You don't have to do this," Cosmo said.

"I know." I'd told my Chosen my plans regarding Daniel before going to speak to the other man, but I understood why Cosmo remained wary.

"What if this is just what he wants?" Cosmo breathed.

I smiled to myself briefly, knowing this was exactly what

Daniel wanted, which was somehow less than I'd expected him to ask for. It was almost frightening how little he asked for, really expected, because it left me feeling tender for him.

"It is. And it's what the council wants too. It's just a matter of knowing if the two are related," I said, resisting the impulse to snap at Cosmo. There was some jagged anxiety left in me that I couldn't shake, and it was a steady battle not to lash out at Cosmo or anyone else.

"And you think they're not."

I shrugged and leaned back. "I'm not asking you to trust him, or to relax around him."

"Bryony, you're not asking at all," Cosmo murmured, but he smiled as he said it, softening the chastisement of the words. "And you don't have to. I love you. I just don't want you to...hurt yourself for the sake of political leverage."

I blinked and then sighed and shook my head. "It's more than that. He's..." I pressed my hand over my chest and then up to where I'd already healed from Emory's stab wound. I wished it was me left healing and Owen who was perfectly fine. "He's like a craving. Not as clear as I have for you and the others, or even as persistent as Aric. I want to claim him because I want to be sure no one else can? It's too soon, but also Daniel is..."

"Inevitable," Cosmo said, frowning. "Then it will be up to the rest of us to watch him carefully. If you're going to claim him, you'll have to do so fully and that includes your heart, Bryony."

Owen groaned and then rolled over, shifting to sit up and clearing his throat with a few rattling coughs as I jumped from the bed to bring him warm water and honey, grateful to have a task that allowed me to move again.

"We'll protect you," Owen rasped.

Cosmo shared a small smile with me. Owen was more trusting than I was.

"Just help me give him a reason to be true to his word," I said, leaning in and pressing my lips to Owen's forehead. "Thao will be jealous, Wendell watchful. But my Chosen are more than individuals, I think."

"Mm. You mean befriend him?" Cosmo asked.

"I don't mind Daniel and his horse—" Owen cut off, breath

catching in his chest and lips turning down with sorrow. "Oh, Bryony. Sweetheart." I blinked at him, and he shook his head. "Your gelding. He didn't make it out in time."

My hands fisted in my skirt at the reminder, its own separate pain and a vicious reminder of how close I'd been to losing *Owen*.

"I know. I'm so sorry, Owen. You did everything—too much even," I said. My hands were greedy for his skin, wanting to hold onto him, keep touching just so I could be sure he was here with me, but my hands were still full of that angry tension and I was afraid I would hurt him.

The door creaked open, and Cosmo smiled at the entrance.

"Ah, good. You're looking better," Aric greeted. "Now, why can't I say the same for my princess?"

I rolled my eyes and ducked my head, but Cosmo grinned and gave me up. "She's refused to stop playing nurse. The bath is cold."

"Then I will warm it," Aric said.

I braved a look over my shoulder, pressing my lips together and trying to stay firm under Aric's glower. "I'm fine."

"Owen will be too, princess. You need a warm bath and a good sleep."

"Aric—"

"I'm building the fire up. You can pull the screen back and watch how well Cos and I care for your hero, but I'm putting you in that bath, and I think I'll have you drink some kind of poisonous brew of Bertha's too," Aric said, striding forward.

I stiffened, well aware that Aric was not above tossing me over his shoulder in this case.

"He means a soothing tea," Cosmo murmured. "I think."

"Please, Mistress. And then come to bed," Owen croaked. His eyes were wide, and he'd grown increasingly pitiful over the past minute, playing into Aric's commands. "I'll sleep better with you at my side."

"Oh, honestly," I huffed, standing up and wincing as I tried to reach back for the buttons of my dress.

"No, let me," Aric said, hurrying. "Your muscles will still need some mending, in spite of the magic. Just as Owen's lungs need to clear."

I sagged, but I didn't fight as Aric started to undo my dress, while Cosmo helped Owen with the drink. Owen had been in and out of sleep since we'd gotten him back inside the palace, and I hadn't had the chance to do more than ask how he was feeling for most of the night. Now the questions that had been pushed away in the flurry of panic rose up again.

"You heard them," I said. "The horses."

Aric's fingers paused and then picked up again, one hand soothing up and down my spine as he exposed it. "You're too chilled still," he muttered.

I was busy watching Owen, who met my eyes and shrugged weakly. "Not...not heard. I felt them. Only when they were alarmed. And then when they were in pain," he said, words aching either from the smoke or his own depth of feeling for the horses.

"Owen...have you always been *feeling* the animals you care for?" I asked.

It was like I'd found a puzzle piece that didn't match but fit perfectly inside a design I'd thought was already finished.

Owen didn't look bothered by my question, just gave it the same careful thought he would with anything I asked of him. "Yeah, I suppose so. It's there if you look at them. You learn to match the feeling with the ways they move and the sounds they make."

Aric's touch had stopped entirely, his own warmth keeping me from shivering in the open room. Cosmo stared at Owen, and I suspected his thoughts were turning the same way mine had started to as I saw Owen running down the hall before anyone in the palace knew of the fire.

"But you weren't looking at them," Cosmo breathed.

"Yeah, but those were big feelings. From all of them," Owen said, frowning as if that ought to be obvious.

"Fucking stars above," Aric whispered, and then he began to laugh, a warm chuckle.

I turned to look at him, peeling off my dress and smiling that Owen managed to hold Aric's attention better than my bare skin did. "Have you heard of something like this?" I asked.

"I don't... No, I don't think so," Aric said, almost gleeful.

"Owen. have you always known what animals are feeling, or only since you've started having sex with Bryony?"

I gasped, clapping my hands over my mouth, but Owen shook his head.

"I've just always gotten along with animals that way."

Aric tugged me to his side and soothed his hand down the back of my head as I sagged with relief. "You, bath," he said, kissing the top of my head and then shepherding me to the tub. He hummed and touched the water before I even offered to fix the temperature, which was good because I was feeling especially drained at the moment.

I climbed into the tub, groaning as the warmth seeped into my chilled muscles, while Aric pushed back the screen so I could see the bed.

"Have you not told anyone else about your gift?" Aric asked Owen, sitting on the edge of the tub. I wondered what it would take to get one of them to join me, and then decided I would rather move quickly and get into the bed so I could share it with all of them.

"My gift?" Owen asked, shuffling to sit up.

Aric huffed, and Cosmo fought his smile as he dug his fingers through his dark curls. "With animals."

"Mm, my family. Groomsmen in the army, I suppose," Owen said.

I leaned forward and tugged on the hem of Aric's shirt, whispering, "Don't laugh. If he's always had the ability, he might not have ever needed to question why."

Aric glanced down at me and then scooped up warm water and poured it over my head, making me splutter. But it felt good and washed away some of the smoke clinging to me, and Aric grinned as I wiped the water out of my eyes.

"Will you mind much if I ask you a million questions, Owen?" Aric asked, and I resisted the impulse to splash his back.

"'Course not," Owen said.

"I think you have a form of magic, although not one I've ever encountered before," Aric said.

Owen nodded and shrugged. "If you say so."

Aric peppered Owen with simple questions as I washed, and

Cosmo stepped out of the room briefly to call for tea. Owen could tell the difference between a shifter and a real animal, but he could also tell the difference between the two-natured and the rest of us.

"That was one of the few things I did learn. Not to say so," Owen said, gravely. "I accidentally got a man registered when I asked what else he was. He was working the fields with my dad and I. It got back to the magistrate, and my dad wouldn't take me back. We found a new town to help in."

"Mm, yes, I suppose the council would've been glad to use you to sniff out others," Aric said, moving slowly to the bed to continue his questions.

Cosmo returned with a tray of tea, taking it to Owen's side and then bringing me a cup. It smelled like mint and lavender, and there was a little ring of lemon floating on top.

"I feel foolish for not noticing it sooner," Cosmo said, and I nodded. "And I think I might be starting to feel a bit plain amidst all these tigers and mages and...Owen. Perhaps that will be something I commiserate with Daniel on."

I sighed and turned in the water to look at Cosmo, sipping on my tea. "I will be careful."

Cosmo smiled sadly and pushed damp strands of hair off my cheeks. "Let us be careful for you. If you're going to let yourself care for him, you should do it fully."

I caught Cosmo's hand and gripped it tightly in mine. "Do you know, I think of you as my compass? Sometimes, everything seems to be spinning madly around me, and then you appear and I know immediately where I am and what direction to point toward."

Cosmo stilled and blinked down at me before leaning in, ignoring the fact that he soaked the cuffs of his sleeves as he took me by my neck, drawing me fiercely forward for a firm kiss. "Thank you," he said roughly.

"I think that's what I needed to say to you," I answered.

He pecked my lips again. "Say it after I finish washing and braiding your hair. It's time to rest."

I sighed and sat up, drinking the rest of the tea as Cosmo dug his strong sculptor's hands into the long locks of my hair, sudsing and rinsing them and the rest of me. Aric brought a towel, and the two of them took their time in drying me, or tormenting me, I wasn't entirely sure of their aim.

"I want Wen and Thao back in bed," I said. "And I need to know what Emory said."

"You will, tomorrow," Aric said.

"Aric."

"Princess."

I opened my mouth to argue my case but instead ended up in a massive yawn that left my jaw aching.

"Mm. That's what I thought," Aric muttered as the door to the bedroom opened and Thao and Wendell appeared.

"Where are the horses?" Owen asked.

"They're being looked after in the western ballroom," Wendell said. His cheeks were sooty, and he peeled quickly out of his own clothes, moving for the tub.

"It's the oddest looking stable I've ever seen, and I'm not sure the room will recover from the smell. But we only lost two horses," Thao said, following Wendell.

I wanted to go to them, but the subject of the horses was sure to be difficult for Owen. He wasn't just good with animals or a lover of them, he'd *felt* their pain. I slid under the sheets to his side, soothed by the warmth of his skin as I pressed my cheek to his chest.

"Emory can hang for all I care," Owen muttered, wrapping his arms around me.

I looked to Aric, and the grave expression in his gaze hardened as it met mine. Emory likely would hang. What frightened me was that he probably wouldn't be the last.

25.
BRYONY

I woke early, my eyelids protesting how little rest they'd been given as I peeled them open. The bed was warm, full of bodies nestled comfortably together, even Aric who had sprawled in his slumber, slapping a leg over Owen's.

I shifted in the bed, and Wendell's arm slid from my waist as he rolled with a huff, sharing Cosmo with Thao on the far end of the bed.

"Mistress," Owen whispered.

"It's all right," I answered, bending my head to kiss his forehead. "I'll be back. There's just something I need to do."

"It's barely dawn," Owen said. It was rare for him to not be purely agreeable with me, and he frowned as he reached up, tracing a curve underneath one of my eyes. "It's not just rest you need, is it?"

I forced my smile, trying to keep it gentle. "I'll be fine, really."

Owen's gaze flicked back and forth over mine. He didn't believe the lie, I was sure. Was only weighing it against his trust in me. He nodded somberly, and his own hand slid away from my hip, letting me sneak carefully out of the end of the bed.

He was right. I needed a handful more hours of sleep, to be sure, but it wasn't the real symptom plaguing me. The Hunger was never really sated for long, but ever since the woods the night before, it had begun to change. Last night, I'd been restless and irritable, but this morning was so much worse. I didn't want to be touched, I wanted to raze my nails through someone's skin, rip them apart. I was ravenous, but it was anger fueling me, not desire. My body panged with the craving, bones grinding and aching inside of me.

I dressed quickly in a skirt and one of Wendell's sweaters, rolling the cuffs up several times. Owen watched me from the bed as the others slept, nodding goodbye as I left the room.

Cresswell was there in the sitting room, sitting up in a chair with his eyes shut and legs stretched and crossed at the ankle.

That was just yesterday, I thought, remembering the feel of him so close, even as he was pulling away from me, refusing our connection.

He stirred as I stepped closer, an accidental smile on his lips that quickly faded as he sat up. "Bryony."

"I want to speak with him."

Cresswell's mouth hung open for a moment before understanding finally sobered him. "Aric and I learned everything—"

"I don't have any questions for him, Cress. I want to speak with him. I can find my own way down there," I said, heading for the door.

He scrambled behind me, hurrying to open the door for me and to follow me into the hall. "I suppose I'm meant to be grateful you're even telling me," he grumbled, and then he cleared his throat. He straightened out of the corner of my eye, obviously remembering that he was trying to play the part of the obedient and duty-minded guard, rather than my friend.

"I'll leave that up to you, but I appreciate the chaperone," I said. I opened my mouth to say more, to ask the favor that I was ashamed to even need. *Can you make sure I don't tear his cell open and finish what I started last night?* "Can you brief me?"

"He admitted to collaborating with the council, that he had orders to arrange your assassination at the festival. Apparently, his coming here was a personal grudge."

Good. That meant the council probably didn't know he was here.

"Is there anyone who can corroborate the story about the festival?" I asked.

"The man hired by Emory, I suppose. He hasn't spoken, surprisingly, but then again you didn't—" Cresswell cut himself off abruptly.

"I didn't slice him open with a wreath of blades," I suggested.

A warm hand settled on my shoulder. "You did what you had

to do. He's being kept in the cells in the city, I can communicate with them."

I nodded and sighed slowly. Even Cresswell's reassuring touch made the Hunger prowl angrily, and I shrugged it off before I lost control of myself. He stiffened, and his hands folded behind his back.

"I want you and Aric to question Emory again, ask him for names, anyone who might've known the connection between Emory and the council," I said.

"Why? If Emory himself admits to it?"

"It needs to be done today," I said.

"Bryony," Cresswell breathed, but we were reaching the steps down to the dungeon now and he stopped me, taking the lead.

I touched my hand against the cool wall as we moved down the stairs. Some of the Winter Palace's cracks and disrepair were still evident down here. It was damp and cold, although the torches were eerily ornate, clawed hands reaching out from blossoming bursts in the stone. That certainly looked like my magic.

We arrived at the cell, and my eyes flicked directly to the crumpled heap of the man in the corner before glancing to the guard Cresswell greeted. He was younger, probably close to my own age, and I knew he was one that Cresswell preferred to assign to me over many of the others in the palace.

"You were right. Walsh came by twice last night, offering to take over," the guard said.

"Thank you, Stanley," Cresswell answered quietly. "Wait in the hall, if you don't mind."

Stanley nodded, bowing to me as he passed.

"There are troubles with a guard?" I asked Cresswell.

"Nothing I haven't been managing. But yes. Walsh is for the council. Some of the others are for the crown but—"

"But of the two, the crown is infinitely preferable," I said, nodding.

"I've made sure you're only ever protected with men I trust implicitly," Cresswell said.

My heart panged, and for a moment, the rage of the Hunger abated. I'd kept my gaze on the form of Emory as he pretended to ignore us, but I glanced to Cresswell briefly, smiling. "Of course you have. Clean house. Get rid of Walsh and any others. I'm sick of pretending we aren't in the middle of a battle."

Cresswell was quiet, and then he nodded deeply. "Gladly, Your Highness."

Emory coughed, or laughed, and he shifted in his corner, lifting his face. His hands were tucked protectively against his chest, and the new feral part of me wondered what exactly Aric and Cresswell had put him through, and how much more he could take.

"Battle, princess? You think you're prepared for battle?" Emory taunted, his words warped by his split lip and a catch in his voice like he couldn't take a full breath. "You couldn't even finish me off. You're not supposed to heal the enemy, you stupid cunt."

Cresswell growled, and I lifted a hand, stilling him before he moved in front of me. "You're not getting a second mercy, Emory," Cresswell warned, and then added to me, "We think he has some internal damage too. He'll be dead soon."

"Can he make it back to Rumsbrooke?" I asked.

"Rumsbrooke?" Cresswell asked.

Emory began that rattling pained laugh again as if I thought I were taking him back there for safekeeping.

"Tonight. I'm calling my court together," I said, and Emory's laugh stopped abruptly. I could barely make out his eyes, they were too swollen, but I held his stare and let him see the truth in mine. "I will make it clear, as King of Thieves, what happens when I am threatened by traitors and men too weak to steal my crown."

"You bitch—"

"You pathetic, rancorous, greedy fool," I snapped back, stepping up to the grate of the cell. "You had every opportunity to be even remotely useful to the world, to your peers, and you chose horribly every time. You are the root of your own destruction. I am the axe."

I sucked a breath as Emory lunged forward, his own strangled yell evidence of how little he could do against me in the condition he was in, let alone the cell. I watched him fall to the floor and groan, back heaving as he tried to right himself.

"I don't know that it would've gone differently, but you've dug your grave by coming here. At the very least, you've done me the favor of not feeling sorry for you," I said.

I stepped back and turned to Cresswell, relieved as his eyes met mine squarely.

"An execution? I'll take care of him myself," he said, shoulders squared and chin high.

"No. I'm not doing this as princess, but as King of Thieves. It has to be my own hand. Send a man down to Rumsbrooke and tell Griffin to call the court together tonight," I said, heading for the door.

Cresswell followed quickly, and we passed the young guard, Stanley, on his way back to watch Emory.

"Your Highness—Bryony wait," Cresswell hissed, reaching for my elbow.

I yanked it away from his hand and glared at him over my shoulder, trying to smooth my expression when he reared back. I pointed up the stairs, and Cresswell relaxed and nodded, following me up and waiting to speak whatever was on his mind until we were out of earshot.

"Bryony, you can't do this yourself," Cresswell murmured as we moved together into an empty hall.

"I absolutely can," I said, standing as straight and tall as I could after a night of sleeplessness and anger and worry all boiling together.

Cresswell frowned and looked around before catching my waist in his hands and pulling me into a room that must've been someone's study at one point. His touch was scorching, or my skin rebelled at his grasp, and I pulled free.

"No, listen to me. This is different than you defending yourself last night," Cresswell said, keeping his voice low, even as we were alone. "Emory's no threat to you right now. Not the way he was last night."

"Cresswell—"

"I know you can do it, physically, but I'm telling you—"

"It *must* be done."

"Don't do this to yourself!" Cresswell growled. "It's not a satisfying act, Bryony!"

The day was cloudy, and the grounds outside the narrow window were coated in a layer of what was either fog or smoke, or some combination of the two. The room was gray and cold, small enough that there wasn't really anywhere for me to turn or pull away to.

"Bryony, please."

"I have to do it myself, in front of them, or there will be a constant line of men trying to find a way to sneak in and finish what Emory couldn't," I said. My arms wrapped around my waist as Cresswell stepped forward again, hands stretched out to clasp me. I resisted his touch, every word passing between us making the beast of rage inside of me rise up, grow impatient and harder to contain.

"You should never have—"

"But I did. I am King of Thieves, and I don't intend to step down until I know that the position has been of some use. This has to be done. I have to do it. No one else."

"But—"

"I want to!" I shouted, a growl in my throat.

My hands struck out in fists at Cresswell's chest, forcing him back a step, his eyes wide with shock. I shuddered and turned to the window, covering my face. I released a long breath, trying to rein in the thick and jagged energy burning through me. I needed it for tonight, more than this argument with Cresswell.

"Very well," Cresswell said softly. It wasn't a placating tone, more resigned or restrained.

"Send a man to Rumsbrooke," I said.

"Yes, Your Highness."

He left me in the room, alone with myself and trapped with the brutal animal still prowling inside of me.

⁂

"Why aren't you saying anything? You're the only one of us she'll listen to," Thao snarled at Aric.

If telling Cresswell of my intention to execute Emory publicly and by my own hand had gone poorly, it was nothing to telling my Chosen. The only two who had yet to give a thorough objection were Aric and Daniel.

I stared at Daniel now. We'd already discussed this, my intent to kill Emory, but I wondered if he changed his mind in the face of what was hypothetical now becoming true. But he met my gaze fully, with less of his old calculation and this time with more awareness...or understanding. He nodded at me, grave but accepting. He was still mine, in whatever small way I'd claimed him so far.

Aric cleared his throat, and I looked at him next. He sat by the hemlock in the greenhouse, where we'd gathered for a lunch no one was interested in after I'd made my announcement. His head shook slowly back and forth, skin pale and eyes wide on his own lap.

"Because I'm afraid she's right," Aric said.

"Aric!" Cosmo's pacing turned fevered again, up and down the aisle of the greenhouse, always stopping just short of reaching me.

"Emory's in poor shape now, and we have him secure here, but either one of his allies will act next or seek to retrieve him," Aric said.

"The law would see him hanged regardless," Wendell said.

"The law would. But it would be as if Bryony took what was due to her as Princess of Kimmery, not King of Thieves," Aric whispered. He frowned, brow tangling, and finally looked up at me. "I wish I'd never gotten you caught up in my mess."

I stood cautiously up from my chair, crossing to Aric's, waiting to know if I was still blazing with anger or if I was calm enough to soothe him. Aric didn't wait, an arm snagging around my hips and drawing me to his side.

"Our troubles were entangled from the start," I said, turning his chin up to stare down at him. "Emory's plans against you were always part of the council's against me. I wouldn't trade this decision for your life, even if I'd known on the night of the challenge what would happen."

Aric nodded, but there was still sorrow in his gaze until I bent and kissed him, his eyes closing and his hands coming up to turn my head just so. My chest burned and ached, and I pulled away before he was satisfied.

"Couldn't one of us kill him for her?" Owen asked gently, shocking the rest of us. But he looked serious, hard and angry even, which I couldn't remember ever seeing on him before.

"Not without Bryony appearing like a weak and coddled leader," Aric said.

"You really feel prepared to do this?" Thao asked, sagging back in his chair with the sense of the inevitable.

I opened my mouth to tell them of the fire in my heart, the fact that the Hunger for their touch had been replaced with one for tearing Emory open. An execution seemed too easy for this bloodthirsty feeling, but it was the necessary step. And I hoped when it was done, I would be myself again. Otherwise, I was afraid of what I'd become and what kind of queen it might make me.

"I do," I said instead.

☙❦❧

THERE WAS an old warehouse in Rumsbrooke once used for making beautiful handmade wood furniture. The owner had died and the son, who'd made friends in the dubious circles of the city, had let his father's business dwindle away as he made his own profits in the underbelly.

"He ended up as king, very briefly, and the warehouse was left for court business," Aric said, his voice in my ear as we rode together through the streets of Rumsbrooke toward the western fringe of the city. "By all accounts, he was as lousy at managing thieves as he was at business."

I hummed, my eyes on the shadowy alleyways we passed, on the figures who moved in the same direction as us, eyeing me with understanding. We were like a subtle and solemn parade toward the vast black building pressed up against the city wall.

"You have me worried, princess," Aric whispered in my ear.

"You don't need to be. I'm determined to see this through," I said.

Horse hooves clapped quietly at our back. I would've preferred to ride alone, rather than with Aric tucked around me, but I'd lost my horse in the fire, and I didn't want to ride in the carriage we'd stuffed Emory into with Cresswell and Thao. Daniel remained at the palace after some discussion, concerned that one of Emory's men might be in our audience and recognize him.

Aric sighed, one hand leaving the reins to draw my hair aside so he could kiss my shoulder. "That's what worries me."

I swallowed hard and turned my head to the side to catch Aric's eye. "Did you prefer the sweet, ignorant girl?"

He frowned at me and shook his head. "It's always been your strength that made it impossible for me to stop thinking of you. It's your warmth I'm searching for now. But I think we'd better wait until this is done to find it again." He pressed his lips to my temple, and I grabbed his free hand and gave it a desperate squeeze.

If anyone was going to put me to rights again, it would be my Chosen. Just not until this was over with.

We reached the warehouse and Aric swung down first, hesitating in front of me before stepping back and letting me manage my way down on my own, a little tick of irritation in his cheek. Aric liked to play the rogue, but I knew he was as much a gentleman as Wendell in some ways, and it satisfied him and Cosmo both to nurture me.

"I'll keep to the fringes," he said. "By now, everyone knows what I am to you, but—"

"But in this court, you are only my mage and my lover," I said.

Aric's eyes heated and he pulled me to him suddenly, slanting his mouth over mine, taking rough, biting kisses from my lips as I held myself still, the wild anger in my chest buzzing and clawing behind my ribs. He pulled away with a slightly pained expression and headed directly for the door as Griffin appeared and approached.

"Cosmo," I called, before he could follow Aric in.

Cosmo stopped and turned to me, face guarded and body stiff. He took slow steps closer, appearing as though at any moment he might turn heel and run from me, or from the warehouse.

"If this is too much—"

"Of course it's too much," he hissed as he reached me. "Isn't it?"

"I don't know. I am..."

"You're numb," Cosmo accused, frowning and studying me.

"I wish," I muttered. I huffed and rolled my head on my stiff shoulders, eyeing him carefully. "Will this change how you feel about me?"

Cosmo's jaw clenched, and he looked down the street we approached on. The trail of thieves was thinning now. They were all waiting inside for me.

"It changes how I see you. But I don't know that it changes how I feel," Cosmo said.

I wanted to reach for him the way Aric had with me, but I was too afraid of myself. Cosmo lifted my hand from my side and raised my palm to his mouth, kissing the flat of my fingers and meeting my eyes.

"I can't say that I don't understand why this is happening. I just wish it weren't," Cosmo said, then he folded my hand over his and kissed my knuckles.

He'd soothed himself in the process more than he had me, but I squeezed his fingers before he left, letting Griffin take his place at my side.

"Are you all..." She trailed off as Cresswell and Thao passed us, carrying a weakly thrashing Emory between them, his feet trying to dig into the ground but only skidding and dragging along. Griffin's eyebrows rose and she turned back to me. "A show of force?"

I nodded, finding my tongue heavy and dull in my mouth.

"Good. I have a man or two I can trust to—"

"No. I will do it," I said, wishing I sounded stronger. I was certain, I was uncomfortably prepared, but my voice was just over a whisper.

Griffin took an assessing glance over me before nodding once. "Good. I will be at your side. If you hesitate, falter, even trip, I will join you."

She reached her hand out between us and I shook it, both of our grips tight. If there was one person who could commit this act with me, it might be Griffin. She was my right hand in the court, and we were both women under scrutiny and burdened with these men's doubt.

Still, I would manage it myself.

"Here," Owen said, taking the bag he'd carried off his shoulder, pulling the flap open.

The Hunger, the new and violent version of my magic, gnawed on my lungs and crawled through my ribs as I reached inside. There was magic left on my weapon, the strange half wreath of dagger-sharp leaves, and I'd used it earlier to fashion the piece into something new. Moonlight struck the leaves, their edges dulled by a remaining trace of blood, and I raised the piece up to my head, settling it carefully into my hair with the combs I added. A crown for a king. I'd dressed to avoid attention, borrowing a maid's skirt and one of Cosmo's shirts, but I wanted to remind the crowd waiting for me of both of my identities.

"A warrior queen," Wendell murmured, his smile shy and a little injured looking.

"Come and find me when you are done, Mistress," Owen said, tilting his head to try and catch my eye.

I nodded absently, and they stood at either side of me as we walked toward the doors, both of their hands touching my back briefly until we crossed the threshold and they moved into the crowd.

The warehouse had an odd collection of furniture—old crates stacked high, and beautifully crafted tables and chairs gone crooked after being abandoned. The room was full but not crowded, and for the first time I got a sense of exactly how large this community was.

"Is this all of them?" I asked Griffin.

We were heading for a platform built of crates, and Thao and Cresswell waited there, Emory kneeling between them, their hands both keeping him upright and holding him in place.

"It's more than just Rumsbrooke," she answered. "There's some small courts here too, a few country folk. I think it's anyone who might've had time to hear word of you calling the meeting and still make it in time."

That was both good news and bad. It meant I would be making a dark impression on a larger group of people and hopefully avoiding more attempts like Emory's in the future, but also that word of my rise as king had already spread too far.

My Chosen stood close to the platform, ready to intervene if needed. Aric had men at his back as he promised to, one of whom was the bartender from the Wing and Rook. They were there as another line of defense, and he nodded to me as I caught his eye.

Voices stirred through the massive room as Griffin and I approached, echoing around the rafters, birds and bats shuffling in their nests.

"Do I need to address the visiting courts?" I whispered to Griffin.

"Not for the sake of politeness, but they weren't really invited. My guess is they won't expect you to notice, so if you want to call them out on it, it'll make you look sharp."

I nodded and took one tall step up with effort to rise to the platform, keeping my eye on the audience rather than the man crumpled between my guard and my Chosen. Thao looked surprisingly well suited to the thieves' court. His sleeves were rolled up to expose the dark tattoos covering one arm, and he'd tied his hair back, a few dark strands falling loose. His inukat hung over one shoulder, and he kept his face set and firm as I approached, rather than full of the sympathy and worry that the rest of my Chosen wore. We knew our roles, Thao and I. I'd learned mine from my grandmother perhaps, how to be hard and immoveable. I wonder if she craved the liberty to falter the way I now did.

I stepped in front of Emory to the edge of the platform, close enough for Cosmo or Owen to reach out and touch my skirt, but I kept my gaze over their heads, staring out and studying the faces looking back at me until the impatient conversation grew stale and quiet with curiosity. Men and women—mostly men—watched me. I'd won a few friends the night I'd grabbed the crown, and they were there in the mix, but the overwhelming number of eyes looking back at me were suspicious, wary, or outright hateful. Tonight would either tame them or stir up new animosity.

"It appears I called my court together and have received unexpected guests as well," I said, just loud enough to carry into rafters and bounce to those who hovered at the back, watching from the shadows. A few chuckles rose up, more nervous stirring.

"It also appears that in spite of my position as your king, and the undeniable claim I have on the crown, there are those of you who would seek to help unseat me," I called out more clearly over the stirring. I stepped to the side and gestured back at Emory. "For the man who lost his own crown by *my* challenge!"

A few supporters cried out in the mix. Another man shouted, "Worry about your own crown, sweetheart, and leave us ours!" He received an almost equal amount of cheering. But the majority of the men and women remained watching me, eyes narrowed, waiting to see what I would do.

"If anyone else doubts my right to rule, my ability to *serve* you all and your interests, or my strength," I said, stepping slowly and deliberately along the edge of the platform. "Then you may have my crown, but only by my own hand."

A puzzled silence followed, and I marched back to stand behind Emory between Cress and Thao.

"Just as Emory will now have my crown," I said, reaching up to my hair and gently taking out the wreath of leaves as frowning faces watched on.

I wrapped my fist into the wreath, ignored the dull bite of the combs against my palm. My other hand took a mean grip of Emory's hair, and he laughed uncomfortably, voice wet and eyes bloodshot as I yanked roughly, exposing his throat to my audience.

"You won't," he said, grinning at me. Someone had knocked two teeth loose, and his nose was crooked now. I almost felt sorry for him.

Aric. Owen. The stable. My life. My right *to rule.*

"I will," I said softly.

I nodded, and Cresswell and Thao stepped back. Emory tried

to pull away, but either he wasn't strong enough or he really didn't see it in me—the starving creature made of rage and fire.

And in truth, there was a moment where I wondered if I would change my mind. Griffin was on my right, Cress and Thao my left. Any one of them would've done it for me, gladly.

I raised the crown of blades in my hand and someone beyond the platform gasped one small 'oh' before it came down in an arc, snarling and biting and dragging through Emory's throat, chewing from one side to the other. There was a spray, little bright flecks of red dressing over his chin, but I watched his eyes and the genuine surprise there as warmth rushed over my hand. He jerked in my grip, and finally it flickered, a little second of horror.

And then he began to fade.

26.
OWEN

I kept my eyes on her, my mistress. Cosmo groaned and turned away, and Aric made a soft grunt of pain, but I only watched her.

Her fist held Emory up beyond the last second he was able to do so himself, and his greasy strands slid slowly out of her fingers a few beats later. She looked up from the body at her feet; her hand, crown, and wrist coated in red that dripped to the wooden boards. She looked over the heads of us all, a little lost I thought, but also cold and firm, enough to fool those who didn't know her better.

Those who didn't know her sweetness and gentleness, the ache it caused her when she thought she'd hurt me. And the anger that rose in her when she knew others were hurting.

"I think we will understand each other better now," Bryony said, clear and flat. "I will be a true king to you, a fair one. Never a weak one. Don't test me again."

"Long live the king!" someone cried from the back.

Aric sighed and nodded, waiting for a few voices to start to echo the refrain before picking it up himself.

"Long live the king," I said. *And stars protect my mistress*, I added to myself, watching her abandon the body and move to the edge of the platform, away from us waiting for her in the audience.

Cresswell followed her, as did Griffin, and Thao came forward to join us.

"She did well," he said softly as voices raised and bodies began to mill about around us.

Aric stood tall, staring out over heads, and I followed his gaze, seeing Bryony move aimlessly through the crowd, nodding and greeting people. Everyone gave her a healthy amount of room, and I wondered if it had to do with her still holding that bloodied crown in her hand.

"I'll go and—"

"No, let me," I said, putting a hand on Aric's shoulder. He frowned and looked me over. "Cresswell and I both served in the army. We know a little of what this feels like. Let me go and speak to her."

I kept my eyes on Bryony via Cresswell, saw the moment she came to a standstill at the heart of the warehouse. Cresswell dipped, speaking in her ear, and then a moment later they both veered quickly for the door. I didn't wait for Aric's answer, following the path toward the door, weaving my way carefully around the bright conversation of thieves and rogues and con-artists.

I reached the door and paused, taking a deep lungful of clean night air, letting it dilute the notes of copper and bile clinging to my nose. Footsteps clapped away from the warehouse, running toward the wall of the city. Cresswell followed at a slower pace, and I jogged to catch up with his back just in time to catch the sounds of retching.

"She should've let us do it for her," Cresswell said under his breath as we walked together to the crouching bundle of our princess, her hands braced against the wall and body knotted in on itself.

"She's strong. He was her enemy more than the men I fought on battlefields were mine," I answered. "But I wish she hadn't needed to. Let me."

Cresswell stopped, shoulders tense and eyes fixed to Bryony's heaving back. "I'll make sure no one comes out to see."

I moved slowly to Bryony. The crown was discarded on the ground, away from the mess she spat into the wide gutter bordering the city. She pushed off the wall and fell back on her ass, her palms bracing herself on the brick, head tipping back and face lifted to the open sky.

"I will be fine in a moment," she rasped, twitching at the sound of my approach.

I knelt down a few feet away from her and waited for her

head to turn, eyes to slowly focus on me. "I wore myself hoarse throwing up every time I walked off the field," I said.

Bryony blinked. She looked a little drugged, not tired, but hollowed out. "I can't imagine you killing men."

"I don't remember if I did," I said, shrugging. "It was madness. I mostly tried not to get killed. But I remember faces. I don't know if I killed those men or someone else did, but I remember them. Just as you'll remember his."

Bryony's face crumpled briefly, eyes sparkling with sudden tears, and I slid across the mucky bricks of the city to wrap her shuddering body in my arms. She held her sobs in, shaking and biting off her moans behind clenched teeth. I buried my nose in her hair, took deep breaths, releasing them slowly, waiting to see if she would unwind or let my rhythm settle her.

"I had to," she squeezed out, the words grinding between her lips.

"Yes," I said, even though there wasn't a true answer. Not when it came to killing a man. No one ever *had* to kill someone. Bryony had made a choice and gone through with it, and I would never second-guess her.

"I thought I would feel better," she murmured, more to herself than to me.

I kissed the crown of her head. "You will." I looked back to the warehouse, where a group of men were carrying the body out through the doors to a cart, to dispose of it away from any watchful eyes. "For now, we'll go back inside."

Bryony hummed and let me help her up from the ground. She held her bloodied hand away from her and I ducked, tucking the crown back into my bag and fastening it securely shut. We didn't want someone snatching it, and who knew with thieves.

Cresswell joined us, blocking Bryony from the eyes of the men, and reached out with a dark cloth in his hand. Bryony grabbed it and began to rub her skin roughly, blood staining the cloth and flaking away to the ground.

"What am I supposed to say to these people?" Bryony said, breath catching as she began to scratch at her own skin.

"Nothing," Cresswell said.

I caught her hand in both of mine, hiding the remaining

stains from her eyes. "Go in, and wait for them to come to you. If they have any sense, they'll keep to themselves."

⚜

For the most part, the court did give Bryony room, and this time her Chosen stayed close at hand. Aside from Aric, we might not be thieves but we were *hers*, and we were going to stand at her side.

"Well, lass. You certainly make an impression on a man."

For the most part they avoided us, but there were a handful of minor kings in attendance and they each took their turn examining the newest member of their rank.

Bryony's smile was somehow hard and coy at the same time. "I hope from here on out it is the right impression. Clearly, some were left confused."

The king before us, a weathered old man who was only as tall as Bryony and twice as wide, leaned back with his laugh. He'd gone directly to Aric, who was quick to defer to Bryony and Griffin, and both eyed the man like they were just waiting for him to make one more slight against them.

"I'd like to say we'll have learned our lesson, but we're a surprisingly thick-headed lot for being so deft in other areas," he said, grinning. Aric had introduced the old man as Gullet, which seemed like a nickname, but he'd never bothered correcting it.

"But for myself, I won't take many reminders," Gullet said, leaning into Bryony, just enough to lower his voice but not so close that she bristled. "My wife is my own brains when it comes to court, and I find my work better for it."

"You've certainly improved your cons since you married," Aric said, a note of warning in his voice.

Gullet grinned and nodded agreeably, holding his stare to Bryony. "Kings of our kind aren't inclined to alliance, Your Majesty. But if I might speak for a moment as your...citizen, then I would just say that your time in the north has done my people good. My court and my neighbors. You have my favor if you ever need it."

"And he'll have one in return," Griffin said immediately.

Gullet shrugged, raising his hands in a boyish shrug. "Naturally."

Bryony eyed him quietly, so removed from the woman I knew well that even I wasn't sure what she was thinking of the man before her. Then she put her still blood marked hand between them, outstretched for his taking.

"I will consider us on good terms, Your Majesty," she said.

Gullet's happy expression faltered at the sight of her hand, her reminder served. He sobered and took her hand, shaking it slowly, revealing the depth of the man beneath with a brief bow to her.

He left shortly after, managing to scrounge up another joke between him and Aric before making his exit.

"That's the last of them," Aric said, his hand automatically reaching to cup her waist as if he'd been waiting all night to do so. "Let's get to the horses."

"You don't want to stay in Rumsbrooke for the night? Manage business?" Bryony asked as we moved as a group for the door.

Aric stalled and then shook his head. "No. I really don't."

"Otto is already at Wing and Rook, and Scrapper has set up camp at the Yawning Pig until we find someone to manage it. I'll shoo the last of them out of here and come by tomorrow or the day after," Griffin said.

"Yawning Pig?" Bryony asked.

"It was Emory's bar. It's the court's now," Aric said as we broke outside. "Do you want the carriage?"

"Stars, no," Bryony muttered, flinching. "I'll ride with Owen."

"You will?" I asked, fighting my smile. It seemed foolish to be so pleased, especially since Bryony was still not herself, but the thought of holding her on the ride back to the palace was a pleasant one.

She forced a smile for me and followed me to my horse, Echo, pausing and letting me lift her into the saddle before following her up.

"I'm sorry you had to do such an ugly thing tonight," I said as I settled in behind her.

"I don't want to think about it," she said softly as the rest of her Chosen climbed into their own saddles and Cresswell and Thao readied the carriage.

"I know," I said, taking the reins. Echo was nervous beneath me, the horses still stressed from the events of the night before. I soothed my hand over his flank and clucked gently, letting him choose his own pace.

"But I will think of it, won't I?" Bryony whispered.

My heart sank in my chest, and I thought of the faces that came and went in my mind, so often and so disjointed, I wasn't even sure if they were true memories at this point.

"Yes," I said, kissing her temple and absorbing her shudder in the circle of my arms.

27.
BRYONY

"**A**re you sure about this?"

I stiffened under the blankets, curled in on myself, cramps wracking through my muscles and tearing at my stomach. Owen? What was he doing in my bedroom? He'd said he wanted to spend the day with his horses.

"Not entirely," Aric answered. "Wait here."

I held my breath, the shuffle of footsteps whispering over the carpet on the way to the bed. I wasn't entirely sure what time it was, only that Aric, Wendell, and Thao had left the bed first to organize the seeds, Cosmo after, and then Owen to check on the horses. And then I had simply...remained in the bed, my teeth clenched and my fingernails biting into the heels of my palms, my body tightening with every passing second.

I'd done what I needed to. I killed Emory. And instead of the horrible weight and drag and terror in my chest passing, it only seemed to grow. I wasn't even sure if I was capable of getting out of the bed now, and I tensed as the mattress dipped behind my back.

"Princess, what's going on?"

I shivered and rolled, a small agonized whimper escaping my aching jaw.

Aric pulled the covers back, silhouetted by sunlight that made me hiss, blindingly bright. My eyes watered, and I twisted my neck until my muscles burned, burying my face in the mattress.

"Fuck. What is this? Hunger?" Aric asked.

"No, it's...different," I managed.

His hand settled on my back, and my skin trembled as if it were trying to crawl away from the touch. There was a spark of magic that made me squeak with pain, and Aric gasped and yanked his hand back. A moment later, the pain faded, just a little fraction.

"It's the Hunger," Aric bit out.

I shook my head and faced him again, blinking against the strain of light until a broad body appeared and pulled the curtains shut. "It's not. It's like anger, but worse," I said, even as my lungs tried to strangle the words.

"That may be, but your body is catching my magic like a fish hook," Aric said, shifting closer but not trying to touch me again. "You haven't touched any of us, have you?"

"There were bigger issues to deal with than me *fucking* you," I snapped.

"You seem to be forgetting that you are different, Bryony! You have Chosen now, your Hunger is awake. If it makes demands, you must meet them," Aric said.

"And if its demand is for blood?" I cried, my body starting to jerk with rising sobs.

Aric sighed and reached a hand up to brush his hair away from his face. "I see. All right, we'll sort this out, princess. So you have an appetite for violence, probably from the sudden threat of Emory?"

Aric made it sound so logical as if I were only one of Owen's creatures but with a strange and explicit diet.

"Aric," I whined.

"You can't cure hunger by starving it, Bryony," Aric said, softening. "Let me help. Or rather... How do you feel when you see Owen? Or I can track one of the others down?"

I folded my lips between my teeth and looked up over Aric's shoulder to where Owen stood by the door, worry clear in his gaze. I groaned as my body seized and seemed to lift me from the bed, a battle waging in my bones as I fought the urge to lunge for Owen where he stood. I knew what would happen too when I caught him, and Owen had already had to suffer demands from the Hunger too often. It didn't seem quite fair to put him through it again after Camellia, especially not when I was so... outside of myself, as I had been with Daniel.

"I'm afraid I'll hurt him," I breathed.

"Mistress, you could never," Owen gasped, frowning and stepping forward before pausing at Aric's raised hand.

"Why not you?" I asked Aric, frowning.

"I noticed it last night as you slept. It's like you're eating magic up. I'm not sure how that will turn out for me," Aric said, shrugging. "You didn't answer me though. How does it feel when you look at him?"

I groaned and wrapped my arms around my legs. "Like I want to run a sword through everyone and everything between us."

"Oh, Mistress," Owen said softly, sympathy and sweetness all perfectly mixed on his face.

Aric smirked and reached out to me, before stopping himself, his fingers clenching. "I've been doing some reading on the Hunger in the library, Bryony. I think this will help. Your power is reacting defensively, protectively even. We just need to remind it you are safe, that those you care for are safe, make it docile again. Quit biting your lip like that, you'll make yourself bleed."

I forced out a long breath and looked at Owen again. He was so strong. He'd been through so much already with me, and he took every inch of it in stride. Maybe I did want to touch him, I just wasn't sure if it was passion or violence or both. Cosmo and Wendell would try to soothe me, Thao would antagonize me into a temper, but Owen would ride the moment out with me for good or ill.

I stretched my hand out to him, and Aric sighed and slipped off the bed, making room for Owen who came to my side readily. His hand was giant in mine, and I tugged him closer, the scrabbling beast inside me climbing up to claw and bite and *claim* him. Mine. My Chosen, my *love*.

Owen was quick, gripping tighter to my hand and pushing it far back behind my head into the pillows. I groaned and twisted as he bowed over me, my free fist rising to grasp at his chest. It too was caught in his grip and then pressed to the bed, stretching me so that I couldn't arch up.

Owen's face hovered over mine as I tried to hold in the growl of frustration scratching my throat. His eyes flicked back and forth over my face, lips turned down as he studied me.

"Are you sure?" he asked. "I don't want to hurt her either."

Instead of the animal inside me roaring at being captured, I knew the moment it began to settle, still scratching, but patient.

"You would never," I rasped to Owen.

Aric remained by the edge of the bed, watching us and then looking back to Owen. "Kiss her."

Owen's smiles were so full, so shining, it genuinely left me breathless to see it appear now, even as he held me pinned to the bed. He ducked, catching my bottom lip between his teeth, biting gently and sucking the mark. The growl I'd been holding back slipped out, and I squirmed, digging my heels into the bed and trying to break free of his unforgiving grip on my hands. I fought my way into the kiss, struggling beneath him.

"Watch it, she's—" Aric started, but it was too late.

I slid my left leg across Owen's lap and then hooked it around his back, yanking him closer. Owen laughed, our teeth clashing as he fell forward, and then I twisted my wrist free in his distrac-tion, flipping us on the bed. *Mine.*

The beast was free, my fingers digging into his shirt, twisting and pulling until threads began to rip and buttons popped. I bit at Owen's lips, sucked on his tongue, dragged my kiss down his jaw, gripping the flesh of his neck between my teeth. He caught a wrist again, and I cried out as he twisted one of my arms behind my back, the other left fisted in his open shirt.

"All right?" Owen asked

I panted and gazed down at him, my arm held firmly behind me, Owen's lips swollen and wet, a fresh red mark on his throat from my bite. And he just looked...careful and happy, chest heaving and smile stretching while I squirmed and tried to free myself as I nodded.

"Do you want him to touch you?" Aric asked.

I was in my nightgown, knees straddled on either side of Owen's hips, and his free hand slid between us, knuckles grazing up and down the insides of my thighs. I wanted to fight, I wanted to scratch my nails down Owen's chest, watch him surrender beneath me. I wanted to bite his throat and mark him as mine so that no one would ever dare touch him, harm him again. I gritted my teeth and nodded, playing along with Aric's game, aware of him watching from behind me.

"Get her off quick, see if it helps," Aric said.

"I don't mind your claws," Owen said, stretching up and kissing the corner of my jaw, nuzzling against me and laughing as I bit his earlobe and sucked on the spot. "But I think Aric is right, and feeling this way has you unhappy."

"I don't mind your claws either," I said, surprised by the admission. "Or your strong grip."

Owen grinned. "Yes, Mistress, I remember how pretty you sound as you obey me."

And then he reached between my legs, grazing a feather-light touch over the lips of my sex, spreading them and finding my clit with his thumb.

Damnit. Aric was right. The relief was minor, but immediate, as if whatever ferocious power had me in its grip eased just enough to let me breathe again. I moaned, and my head fell to Owen's shoulder as his touch swirled, the soft threads of pleasure a balm against the anger boiling in my chest.

"That's it, Mistress," Owen murmured as I squirmed closer to his hand, grinding myself into his touch and trying to find a way to force those thick fingers inside of me.

"Fuck me," I breathed, biting the tendon of his neck and making him grunt.

With my right arm twisted behind my back, my left made a clumsy effort to finish opening Owen's shirt, my scratches gentled as he distracted me by plunging one finger into my cunt, pumping quickly.

"Oh!"

Owen's head turned, his lips and tongue on my temple, my cheek, then down to my mouth as I arched my neck to meet him in the kiss. I let him lead this time, too focused on the building warmth in my core and my own appreciation of his broad chest.

Owen fit a second finger into me, crooking them forward and moving quickly over my clit until I stiffened and waited for the inevitable crash.

"That's it, I can feel you trying to take more of my fingers already."

"Owen!" I whimpered, pressing my face into his shoulder, clamping my teeth around the muscle as I started to shudder.

"Grab her other hand," Aric said, and I gave it up willingly as my orgasm rushed slowly through me, taking the pinch in my heart with it.

I shuddered as Owen moved my wrists behind my back and then gasped with the first cool slither over my skin, my own grin growing as Aric's golden snake present wrapped around my wrists, holding them in place.

I twisted my hands as it finished coiling, finding the snake moved with me but refused to let up its grip.

"Too tight?" Aric asked as I looked over my shoulder at him.

He was moving back to an armchair by the window, and I could see the small smile of delight he was trying to hide. I wanted to tease Aric for never asking permission first, but I was too happy to find that the thrill in my chest outweighed the lingering scorching, snarling feeling.

"Is this really for Owen's protection, or do you just like the look of it?" I asked instead, sitting up.

Aric barked a laugh but took his time in studying me before answering. "If it were only for aesthetics, who could blame me?"

I scoffed and caught Owen glancing between us, his glossy fingers resting beautifully on his full bottom lip.

"Hello," I said, smiling.

Owen leaned in, nuzzling my cheek with his nose. "Hello. You look like you're feeling better already."

"Let me watch you clean those."

Aric laughed in the background, but Owen held my gaze until I pulled it away to watch him slide his two fingers between his lips, taking care to make a noisy sucking sound. I hummed as his tongue peeked between them, and then they pulled free with a *pop*!

I spread my knees farther apart and watched Owen's eyes darken as I rocked gently over his lap, his cock half-hard and growing stiffer.

"I thought I was losing you," he said softly, frown returning, damp fingers coming up to stroke my cheeks.

I bit my lip and sighed as his hands reached down to caress up my thighs and over my sex. "I thought you were too. Thank you for coming to find me again."

Owen beamed at me. "Always." I gasped as he gripped my hips and tossed me back on the bed.

"Careful with her arms," Aric said.

Owen didn't leave me on my back but turned me to face the headboard, pushing my sheer nightgown up over my ass, bundling it under my bound wrists. "Stay like that," he said roughly, and the command prickled uncomfortably against the remaining anger, but also made me clench on nothing with want.

"Did you notice that you held the magic in on your own this time?" Aric asked.

I huffed, resting my forehead on the bed, aware of his gaze from the window, of Owen's rustling behind me as he stripped out of his clothes. "Does this really have to be a teaching moment, Aric?"

He laughed, and I could see his legs stretching out ahead of him, crossing at his ankles.

"You're really going to just sit and watch?" Owen asked.

"Until I know she's recovered," Aric said. "Another orgasm and the burst of magic should do it."

"Another good squeeze on my cock should too," Owen said brightly, hands settling gently at my hips and soothing up and down my legs. He scooted closer, and I lifted my face on a small gasp with the first nudge of his cock between my legs. It hadn't been that long, had it? The past few days had seemed to stretch on and on.

"Support her shoulders," Aric said.

"Please ignore him," I huffed, looking back at Owen over my shoulder. "If he wants to set the rules, he can get involved."

Aric huffed and Owen grinned, my mouth falling open as I gazed back at him. He was so beautiful, his chest heaving with anticipation. I had the sudden urge to just turn and *lean* into him, to find a way of touching every bit of him all at once.

He bent forward and kissed my hands where they tangled together, then both of my elbows, making me squirm with the ticklish sensation, and finally the center of my back. His cock dragged back and forth against my sex, and then he repeated the path as his hands moved up from my hips, one grasping my waist and the other a hanging breast.

He hummed and rocked against me, teasing my sensitive flesh with the dull friction of him just *rocking* against me until I grew wet again.

"Please," I murmured. "Please fuck me."

My hair was falling loose over my shoulders, swinging with the gentle rhythm of Owen as he mimicked sex without doing it properly. I moaned and arched into the touch on my breasts as Owen gripped tight, painful even, and then he released me. I whimpered and shivered, my body searching for that touch. It returned a moment later, fingers tangling into my hair, pulling it back from my face with a rough grip that left me bowed.

"Ah, yes!"

"I don't mind sharing you, Mistress, but I know I'll never have enough of you," Owen moaned.

Up and down he dragged against me, impossibly patient despite the painful catch of his voice.

"Even if we were the only two people in the world and I could fill every second of my day with you."

My heart clenched and my stomach cramped, but at last it was a familiar feeling, my Hunger begging for the man with the ragged tear in his voice. "Owen," I breathed, leaning back until his hips kissed my ass. "Please, I want you."

He let out a shuddering breath, fingers tightening in my hair until my scalp ached, his hand on my waist shifting to line himself up at my opening. He pushed in slowly and smoothly until my body resisted him, and then started to pull out again. My mouth fell open on a silent cry. It'd barely been a couple days since I'd had my Chosen under me, in me, surrounding me, but it was as if I really had been starving.

Aric will be so annoying if he knows he was right, I thought, and then promptly the thought left as Owen thrust in again.

"Fuck," he gasped, wrapping an arm around my waist, leaning in and being careful not to put my arms in a trapped position as he began to fuck me.

It was slow and steady, Owen working his way in so gradually, it was more like he was taunting me with the pace. I tried to push back, but every time I did, his hand twisted in my hair, pulling me into an arch, a shivery path running down from his grip to my cunt. I whined as he settled fully inside me, my eyes turning to where Aric watched, quiet but absolutely in tune with my every sound, flinch, shudder. His hands gripped firmly to the arms of the chair, one heel digging into the carpet like he was holding himself back from joining us.

My smile stretched as I shouted with Owen's first earnest buck, our skin slapping together. "Yes!"

Owen was all gasps and groans as I squeezed around him, his pace quickening, the snap of his hips rough against my ass, the tugs on my hair as rhythmic as his thrusts. I was pinned firmly in place with my hands behind my back, and I let my eyes fall shut, finding an unexpected relief at being unable to reciprocate, to do anything but *take* him. The week had been dark and full of pressure, and the deed I'd committed the night before...

I whimpered and my eyes flashed open at the first hint of a memory. Aric rose from his chair and prowled to the bed.

"That's it, princess. That's better, isn't it?" he purred, his eyes finding mine with an intensity that demanded I hold his gaze.

Gratitude replaced anger, relief replaced fear, and when Aric reached out to drag the tear off my cheek, the spark of magic between us was a kiss.

"Do you want the clamps?" he asked.

"I want you," I gasped, the words broken on a squeak as Owen beat inside of me. "I want both of you."

Aric climbed onto the bed, and Owen let me press my face to Aric's stomach, his own hand gripping onto the back of my neck instead. Aric smoothed my hair back as I nuzzled against the crotch of his pants. He laughed and leaned away, undressing from the waist down, gasping and groaning as my mouth sought out his cock immediately, lapping at the head of him where a little pre-cum was gathered. I couldn't touch, but Aric wasn't overwhelming the way Owen or Wendell were, and he seemed content to let me lap and lick, sucking on him to the rhythm of Owen's more insistent fucking. I moaned around Aric, shook with the pound of Owen, and still I wished another of my Chosen was here to touch me where I burned.

Or I did, until Owen's hand on my waist slid over my belly and down to my clit. Aric's hands soothed over my back, my shoulders, and down to my breasts as I was swallowed under the drumming, building, pulse of pleasure, my mouth on him as messy and coordinated as Owen was turning inside of me.

There was a tremble, and I pulled off Aric with a gasp, my balance and strength failing as the wave of magic and ecstasy swallowed me under. I tried at the last moment to hold some of it in, but Aric only hushed me, my head resting against his hip, his hands brushing down my sides as I trembled. Warm fluttering aftershocks followed with Owen's faltering movements at my back, his fingers squeezing as he stiffened and groaned, grinding against my ass.

The pain was gone, and all that remained was Hunger. It might've been the first time it was a real comfort to feel again, and I giggled at the notion.

"There's my princess," Aric murmured, sliding his hands under my shoulders as the snake loosened around my wrists and twined up my arm to wrap around my throat. "Better?"

Owen's hands softened and his arms circled my waist, pulling me down to the bed with him, resting me against his chest as we caught our breath.

I kissed his arm, and he shivered as I traced my fingers over the muscles, smiling at Aric.

"Better. I still want more."

Aric was kneeling on the bed, pulling his shirt off over his head, and he grinned at that, his pants hanging open and pushed halfway down his thighs, cock erect and beading fluid at the tip.

"Well, I should hope so. Hold her down, Owen," Aric said.

Owen huffed and then shifted out from under me, catching my pleasure loosened arms and pulling them back over my head.

"Are you really so afraid I'll bite or scratch you?" I asked Aric.

"Of course not. I just like to have you at my mercy," Aric said, grinning wolfishly. He stood from the bed and kicked his pants off as I laughed.

"You just like to show off with your toys and little plans," I said.

"For that, princess, I'm going to make you beg for mercy," Aric growled, and then he grabbed my ankles and tugged me into a stretch between them, pushing my legs as wide as they would go and diving down to feast on me as I screamed with the joy of the game.

OWEN'S MOUTH traced damp patterns over my shoulders as Aric bounced me on his cock, his hips rising to meet mine in the fall.

"Fuck, fuck, come on, princess, once more," Aric growled. "With me, Bryony."

Aric groaned, fingers squeezing on my hips to hold me still as he came. Owen tugged on my hair, and I came with a shudder and a moan as if they were wringing the orgasm out of me like I had nothing left to give.

But that was never really true, was it?

Aric hissed as I continued to move, and Owen's arm wrapped around my waist, pulling me off him and dragging me back down to the bed, rolling me onto his chest, ready for my next insistent wave.

"It's all right, we can take a break," I said, even as I squirmed against him, lifting my chest toward his lips to encourage him. My skin was red and scratched from stubbled chins, my legs actually sore from riding Aric. And still there was a persistent, painful hollow sensation inside of me.

Owen huffed and bit gently on my nipple, glancing up at me with a wrinkle of laughter in the corner of his eyes as I twitched and gasped.

"You say that like you think I've had enough of you."

I relaxed under his stare, and then we both stiffened as the door opened. Cosmo appeared, stained with charcoal and plaster, frowning in surprise at the three of us, and suddenly I knew exactly what I wanted, or rather, what that anxious animal in me needed at this exact moment.

I scrambled out from under Owen, leaping from the bed as Cosmo chuckled at the sight of us. His eyes widened as I ran for him, and when I collided with his chest, he let me tackle him to the floor. My hands took his face in a fierce grip, pulling his mouth to mine.

My Chosen. Mine. Safe. I needed the others too.

I whimpered into the rough, clumsy kiss, and my arms twined around his neck, holding him tightly.

"Aha," Aric said from the bed, still winded.

Fabric shifted and footsteps approached as I nibbled on Cosmo's jaw and he arranged me on his lap. When the steps grew closer, my head turned and I growled in warning, frowning at Aric. He just smiled placidly back at me.

"I said your magic was reacting protectively, didn't I?" Aric said. "We need to work on your instincts."

"I'm not an experiment," I snapped, cuddling closer to Cosmo. Aric cocked an eyebrow, and I sighed and forced myself to settle. "Fine. You were right."

"Do you want to be alone?" Owen offered.

I shook my head, and then Cosmo lifted me effortlessly from the floor, holding me carefully as I attacked his shirt, trying to reach more skin. "I want you, all of you. I want Wendell and Thao too."

Cosmo kissed my shoulder as he deposited me back on the bed, settled between Owen's thighs. "Lay back with her, hold her gently."

I sighed, my hands itching for Cosmo as Owen drew me back against his chest, shifting us back toward the headboard. Cosmo undressed, watching me with a smile.

"Do you forgive me?" I whispered.

"Oh, little muse. Yes. I only hurt for you." Cosmo crawled forward as Owen's fingers drew over my skin, circling around my overly sensitive nipples and back up to my collarbone.

"I'll call for the others, and then I'm getting a bath and doing some magic," Aric said, winking at me. "You two have it from here."

Cosmo and Owen made twin grunts of agreement, and Cosmo pulled my hips forward, hooking my knees as he lined himself at my entrance.

"Aric!"

He stopped and turned, grinning as Cosmo slowly slid himself into me, letting me feel every little stretch and point of connection as I shuddered and my eyes almost fell shut.

"Thank you," I said, trying to hold onto one last little bit of sanity to meet Aric's eyes.

"Always, princess."

I slid one hand back to clutch at Owen, and the other reached for Cosmo, drawing him down in a deep kiss, reassuring myself that we were all whole and safe and together.

28.
BRYONY

"As long as Bryony has her mother's—"

"Really Grandmother's—" I corrected.

Wendell nodded. "As long as she has the crown's support, she does technically wield more power than the council. It should be the queen making these decrees, or the dowager queen on her behalf."

"I can guarantee you that Roderick isn't the only councilman looking to unseat her," Daniel said, leaning against the arm of the couch I was sitting on. "I'm sure he's working with Lord Thomlinson in the south."

He was close enough for me to feel the warmth of his hip against my shoulder, but I could sense his hesitancy still. He was the only one of us not sitting, and while everyone was behaving themselves—even Thao—it was clear Daniel was nervous about being part of our number. I was a little nervous about him being part of it too, regardless of how determined I was to include him in our discussions. He needed to feel a part of my Chosen, a part of *me*, if this was going to work. That meant I needed to make the choice to trust him with my plans.

"I know more of the Southern Council than the Northern," Wendell said slowly. "I can make some inquiries with old acquaintances."

I turned to look up at Daniel. "The man you knew, Camellia's Chosen she...mistreated," I said for want of a better word. "Was he nobility?"

Daniel's eyebrows jumped and he nodded. "Southern family too, the Binghams. That's a thread that might be easily picked at."

Wendell's eyes were wide, lips parted. "I'd heard the son had troubles, but it makes sense it was hushed if it were related to the crown. Yes, I think I know of some families who might be reached out to in that case."

"You want to build up ill-feeling toward Camellia?" Aric asked.

"I want the council to think seriously about her as a potential queen," I said carefully. And maybe I needed to know if there was anyone willing to speak out against her if it came down to it.

"The council may not want the queen to be popular. It distracts from public opinion of the council if the queen's line can still be blamed for failures to the people," Daniel said.

The others all looked at my new not-quite Chosen, and I tried to gauge their responses to him. Aric was obviously willing to get along with Daniel, and I wasn't sure if that was because he was accustomed to a spy being useful, or because it made him feel a little less guilty about our fight and everything it led to if Daniel was accepted by me. Owen was, of course, welcoming. Even Wendell seemed to value Daniel's opinion in the political discussion, which meant Thao remained docile.

Which just left Cosmo.

I reached for him at my side, sliding my fingers over his where his hand rested on his lap, leaning into his shoulder. He hadn't looked thrilled when Daniel walked into our morning meal to join our discussion. He didn't look thrilled now either, but his expression was smooth and he turned his head to kiss my forehead. It felt automatic, somehow, and I studied his face and the way his eyes slid away from mine.

"Tell me what you're thinking," I said.

Cosmo's eyebrows rose. "Me? Bryony, I'm not sure I'm of much value in a political discussion."

"I didn't ask what you were thinking of politically," I said.

Our private conversation drew the others' attention, and Cosmo shifted uncomfortably. "I'm just...struggling to keep up, I think." He chewed on the inside of his own mouth as we all waited quietly, and then huffed out a breath, his hand rising to rub over his forehead. "An awful lot has happened in less than two weeks. You ran off to save Aric, became the King of Thieves.

And then we were attacked and you bring him, Daniel, into the fold. And you- you—"

"Killed a man right in front of you," I said, staring at Cosmo. Had he been thinking of this all as I'd tackled him to the floor and made him fuck me? Had I ignored that tension in favor of relieving my own?

His mouth squeezed shut, and his eyes widened as he gazed back at me.

"I haven't reconciled myself to it yet, either," I said.

"You seem to be managing," Cosmo bit out.

"Now, wait—" Aric started, but he stopped as I raised my hand.

"I'm sorry," Cosmo breathed, eyes falling shut. "I'm trying, I really—"

"Shh. Stop." I pulled my hand from his and rose up to my knees on the couch, taking Cosmo by the shoulders and pressing my lips to his forehead. "I can't change what happened with Emory, no matter how much I hated the act. And I won't change my decision regarding Daniel. He is mine. It's what I want. Outside of any strategy," I said, looking over my shoulder to Daniel, who gripped tightly to the back of the couch as he listened. "Regardless of anything that's taken place previously. I don't need you to agree with me every step of the way and I know that outside of us, *all* of us, you are my Chosen. But Cosmo, I promise, when we are alone that I want to be yours. And if that means knowing that you are unhappy with me—"

"Bryony, no."

"Or with something I have done. Or you have lost your muse to the woman who wants to be queen," I said, seeing the flinch that said more than his refusal could. "Then I will gladly bear those burdens."

Cosmo's scratched and calloused artist's hands smoothed up the side of my cheek, and I leaned into the touch. "Bryony. Little muse. I think you have more than enough burdens as it is."

"But I have so many hands to help carry them. You are all my Chosen and my council. The only ones I really trust right now. I think this has to be an exchange of support if I'm going to love you properly," I said.

Cosmo sighed and drew me in for one of his deep and endless kisses until I was falling into his chest. He bundled me closer, sipping on my lips, a quiet kind of apology for his indifferent mood this morning.

"I don't doubt your decisions; I just worry about the toll they take," Cosmo murmured. "But you're right. We bear them with you. Farraque, quit standing around like you're about to be told off and just come sit down like the rest of us."

Cosmo had made room on the couch by pulling me into his lap, and Daniel filled it quickly, his broad body squishing me wonderfully between them.

"I love you," Cosmo whispered in my ear, kissing my lobe and relaxing beneath me.

I spared one more second to press my lips to the dimple on his chin before turning to the others. "Do we have enough time to get apple trees in the ground still? Winter feels like it's around the corner."

"No, but we'll be ready at the very start of spring. Holes are being dug now to plant with the start of the thaw, and we've found several places for the seedlings to grow in the meantime," Wendell said, turning to Aric.

"I've sorted out a spell to ensure we grow enough fruit trees, and I have a surprise for you, princess," Aric said. "It can wait if you're very comfortable piled in on that couch that looks like it's not sure if it can bear all of you."

Owen was on Cosmo's other side, and he shifted, creating a worrisome groan from the furniture.

"Show me my surprise," I said, and Thao was quick to pull me to my feet so we could watch the awkward jostling of the men trying to unwedge themselves from the cushions.

THERE WERE STILL horses in a ballroom, although the new stable construction was coming along nicely according to Lady Pru and Daniel. Now too, there was an apple tree nursery in Aric's office.

"It took a few tries," he said carelessly, turning me away from where I was examining a young sapling growing out of a hand-painted porcelain vase.

"There was no time to wait for pots?" I asked.

Aric's lips twitched, and I rolled my eyes. He was just ornery.

"You've mastered a charm to ensure what kind of apple tree grows from the seeds?" Wendell asked.

"I have, and I've already passed it on to a few mages. There won't be perfect accuracy, but a cider farm here and there won't hurt," Aric said with a shrug. "But that isn't the surprise. Come out to the balcony."

His hand squeezed around mine and he seemed almost giddy, his steps bouncing a little as he hurried me to the balcony, throwing the doors open and letting a rush of frigid air in. Thao cursed at my back, and he huddled between Cosmo and Wendell as we all made our way out to the balcony where a great heap of earth had been piled up.

"When on earth did you do this?" I asked, frowning at the dirt.

"He bullied the guards into helping," Cosmo murmured in my ear.

"Never mind that. Here is your present, Bryony," Aric said, taking the hand he held in his own and turning it palm up, pulling a small black seed from his pocket and pressing it to my palm.

"The ground is coated in this horrible white ice, what is she going to do with a seed?" Thao muttered.

But I kept my eyes on Aric's silver ones, wondering what the mischief dancing there might mean.

"You saved your magic, didn't you?" Aric asked.

I nodded. After Aric's lesson with Owen, I'd reunited with all my Chosen, and I was now brimming with magic.

"A tree on the balcony?" I asked, arching an eyebrow.

Aric grinned, his wolfish smile coaxing me up to my toes, but he only granted me a brief kiss. "Go on. Plant it. Make it grow."

I walked carefully up the dirt pile to the peak at the center, and knelt. There was already a layer of snow dusting the earth and I brushed it away, creating a hollow to nest the seed in, then covering it again. I usually let Aric manage my magic for me, only really drawing on it to create curious whims or in desperate moments like the one with Emory. I settled my palms over the earth and closed my eyes, ignoring the sprinkle of snow on my cheeks as I tried to conjure warm thoughts.

"It's freezing," Thao whispered, and was quickly hushed from several directions.

The magic left me eagerly, my palms heating like I had them turned up to the sun, but for a moment there seemed to be no change, my nose wrinkling. Aric's fingers grazed against the back of my neck.

"It's working. Give it a minute."

And just as he offered the words, the ground beneath my palms began to tremble. I opened my eyes just in time to see the first green sprout curl upwards from the earth. Aric crouched at my back, cupping my neck with one hand and helping direct my magic, a little shine of light gleaming down on the rapidly unfurling sprout as it stretched and strengthened and began to sprout leaves. I kept my spot on the cold ground, feeling the wriggle of roots under my fingers as Aric seemed to command the tree taller.

"Do you feel a strain?" he asked.

"Not yet," I said, grinning and breathless as I watched an apple tree grow in rapid motion, branches swelling and sprouting new tendrils.

"Be ready to catch the apples. We'll put this one in hibernation for the winter before we're done. Now, as much as you can spare, princess," Aric said as the others hurried closer.

My eyes were up, watching a tree stretch and spread and sprout above me as I held my breath and poured the well of magic I'd stored up from the night before into the roots. I lifted one hand and wrapped it around the trunk, until it grew too thick for me to close my fingers. This was more than one year's growth, the magic feeding the tree close to maturity, a few bright green leaves falling to make way for darker fatter versions.

There was a collective gasp with the first sudden burst of pink and green blossoms, the air full of the scent of lemons and violets. I withheld a whimper when a moment later the petals cascaded down, catching on the cold gust of winter wind, one resting against the sleeve of my gown just long enough for me to see the creamy center and the threads of gold. And then I saw the first swell of yellow-green fruit and I watched, rapt, as a fresh apple grew before my nose until it weighed down the still tender branch. The yellow spread and deepened to a bright gold, giving way around the top to a soft blush of peach that striped softly around the sides.

Cosmo was laughing, quick to catch an armful of apples as they started to ripen and drop from the branches. I released my magic, feeling the sudden hollow of Hunger I'd made by spending so much at once, and spread my skirt out to catch more fruit, grinning as it thumped into my lap. Aric caught one in his palm and knelt, offering it to my lips.

"Try it," he said, a warm smile on his lips as his eyes watched me.

I leaned forward, taking a bite and feeling the satisfying crunch of the dense fruit first, and then the sudden shock of tart flavor, quickly gentled by a delicate sweetness. My eyes widened as I chewed, and Aric grinned.

"What's it called?" I asked as the others tried their own apples, happy and surprised hums rising up around us.

"The Princess Apple."

I choked on my next bite, and my cheeks warmed.

"Oh, I like that," Owen said as he chewed.

"I'm not sure I do," I said through a laugh.

Aric leaned in and pressed a kiss to my forehead. "Inventor's choice," he said.

My Hunger and heart were in a warm harmony at that, and I tipped my chin up for a proper kiss. "It's a very good present, if an impractical place to plant a tree."

"It's my favorite kind of apple, so I'll be glad to have it so handy," Aric said.

"It's very tart," Thao said, taking a thoughtful bite.

Aric's answering smile was wicked, and I pointed at him in warning. "I'm feeling very fond of you at the moment, and I think you should consider your next words carefully," I said.

Daniel huffed, swallowing his laugh but not managing to

restrain his smile. "Let me take these down to Cook Umber. They'd make pretty candied tarts."

"We should send some down to Rumsbrooke too," Wendell offered. "They'd go nicely with the wild pigs and pheasant Griffin was taking."

Owen started gathering the apples in his arms. "I'll help Dan while the rest of you get our mistress inside. She looks like she needs warming up," he said, winking at me.

I hesitated over inviting Daniel to join us when they were done, but I hesitated too long, Aric letting the apples in my skirt roll gently to the ground as he scooped me up in his arms and carried me back inside, my Chosen quick on his heels.

"You spent a great deal of magic on that," Aric growled softly. "We'll make sure you're not wanting."

"Not in any way," Cosmo added, grinning at me over Aric's shoulder.

29.
BRYONY

"There are hundreds of ways that law and leadership can take shape in a country, and I've been doing my best to get to the root of Kimmery's," Wendell said, pacing in front of me. "History isn't usually preserved as well when it comes to those who lose the throne, but I have discovered the queen's line wasn't *always* the monarchy in Kimmery."

I blinked, clearing the fog in my mind that had been previously occupied by thoughts of how handsome Wendell looked with his collar undone and his sleeves rolled up. His hair was growing a little long, and it was mussed from his fingers running through it as he flipped through pages. I pushed aside the book I'd been doing a poor job of reading—as passionate as I was about Kimmery, I found I preferred having Wendell and Aric and the others explaining legislation to me, rather than digging through circuitous language myself—and sat up in my seat.

"Our reign was interrupted?" I asked.

Wendell raised a finger, balancing the book in one palm. "No! In fact, the first record of a queen as the royal leader is nearly a thousand years old. Queen Euphorbia. She was a warlord. War lady? She conquered Kimmery's king, Ygris III I think, in battle, literally taking his soldiers from him and convincing them to fight for her."

I raised an eyebrow. "Convinced them *how*?"

"Mm, it doesn't say." Wendell shrugged, and we shared a look. "I think it's reasonable to say—"

"The Hunger," we concluded together.

I blew out a long breath and sank back in the chair. I'd found Wendell an office of his own. He was my Chosen, but he was also my most capable diplomat, just as Aric was my personal mage.

Plus a nice cozy study was much easier to heat in winter than the entire library.

"Where did she come from?" I asked.

"That's what I haven't learned yet, but she added a good deal of the mountain territories to Kimmery, so that's my best guess so far," Wendell said, coming to lean against his desk and giving me a lovely long angle of man to gaze at. "What's interesting is that she didn't just kill the king and take his throne. She killed him, and then married his son."

"Easiest way to be sure the family line wouldn't try to resurrect itself," I said, shrugging.

Wendell's lips quirked. "That was my thought. They had a daughter, and then Queen Euphorbia married five more men and her first husband died. The book takes special note to mention natural causes."

"Oh." I frowned, thinking of the way Camellia could wear a man down to nothing with her Hunger. Was that a natural cause?

"There's been no interruption since, although there was a heavier history of war for a number of centuries. Kingdoms testing the queen's line's strength."

"All of this still leaves the council as a bit of a new addition," I said.

Wendell nodded. "The family names remain nearly identical throughout the history of the council. What I can't quite determine is whether or not its invention was the reigning queen's idea or the council's."

"The *idea* of the council doesn't sound terrible," I admitted. I often thought of my Chosen as my own council now. They were indispensable to me in every way, including my political role.

"True. And there were always advisors," Wendell said, flipping through pages, his brow furrowing as his ankles crossed. He sucked his teeth as he thought, and I tried to focus on the subject of ruling and not the purse of his lips. "The problem with Kimmery's council is that it only represents a small fraction of Kimmery's people. You know, in Noren, the people are able to elect representatives for themselves. They even break it up, smaller regions than simply north and south. It might potentially weaken your rule—"

"If it were fairer to the public of Kimmery, I would rather be the one to facilitate my own position's failure, than leave everything in the hands of the council as it currently stands," I said.

"The idea alone would win you favor to start with. Noren's king resisted at every step and would have had a revolution if it wasn't for his son stepping forward and smoothing communication. They're more figureheads now, but we if we approached this from the right angle... You'll need allies in the aristocracy. There's no way around it, I think. And we'll have to be quick now because..."

I lost the thread of Wendell's speech as I drank in the flush rising in his cheeks and the excited fidget of his feet as he rattled off ideas for new shifts in Kimmery's government. His sunny blue eyes lit up, and all at once I found myself on my feet, pressing myself up the long line of him, pinning him to the edge of the desk as I reached up for his face and dragged it down to mine.

Wendell made a soft sound of surprise, and then the book dropped to the floor with a careless thunk as his arms circled my waist and he leaned into the kiss, licking at my lips and gasping as I sucked on his tongue. He groaned and his hands gripped me tighter, my body arching into his taller frame as we kissed endlessly, until we were both catching our breath even as we tried to take more.

"I find your mind very stimulating," I breathed, Wendell's lashes fluttering against mine.

"Oh, really? Should I tell you my feelings on the rise of the social democracy in Samp-mph!"

I braced a knee on the edge of the desk and then jumped up, forcing Wendell back and down into the mess of papers covering the surface. He laughed and groaned as I pinned him down, settling myself onto his lap and tearing at his buttons.

"I thought you were joking! Thao says I drone," Wendell said, grinning and pulling my skirts out of the way.

"It comes undone on the side," I breathed, pushing Wendell's shirt open. His skin was growing lighter now that summer was over, and I leaned down and pressed my face to his collarbone, biting gently and taking a deep breath of the airy clean smell of him. I rocked on his lap and smiled as his groan vibrated against my cheek.

"Do you want to find the others?" Wendell asked, voice ragged.

I paused in my gentle feast of his flesh on the way to nibble on his nipple and then sat up, finding his dizzy expression. "Do *you* want to find the others?"

Had it ever been just Wendell and I? Things had been a little mad since...well, since we'd gotten back from the festival. Things were finally slowing down, hours returning to our routine where we could focus on the minute details of my rulership. Hours I got to spend getting to know Wendell more deeply in all his curiosity and open-mindedness and thirst for understanding. And now I thirsted for him.

His smile softened and he leaned up on one elbow, reaching his other hand up to brush at my cheek. "If I have the chance to keep you to myself, I absolutely want to."

I smiled down at him and twisted, raising my arm. "Undo the button."

He did, and then pushed my hands away as he unwrapped the plum-colored dress from around me as if I were a present. His eyes turned a deeper shade of blue as I shrugged the sleeves down my arms and let the dress fall to the floor with a soft liquid rush of fabric, hurrying to pull my slip off over my head. I reached down for the laces of my stockings and garter, and Wendell stopped my hands again, his smile growing feline and hungry.

"Leave those. You look gift wrapped," he said, words throaty and dark as he snapped a tie against my thigh.

I raised myself up on my knees, helping Wendell with his waistband, reaching immediately for his cock as he bounced beneath me, shoving his pants down his thighs. Wendell's golden chest heaved as I teased my fingertips up and down his length, his head falling back with a long groan as my other hand cupped his sac in a way I'd observed from Thao and Cosmo.

"I'm not as—as good at saying wicked things as—"

"I don't need you to be like anyone else," I said, bending forward and pressing a kiss to his warm chest. As much as I loved the almost poetic filth of Thao's speeches during sex, I liked Wendell's quiet intensity just as much.

His hands squeezed my thighs, guiding me down, joining my hands in a tangle as he pressed his length against my sex, encouraging me to rub myself on him as he grew hard. His fingers slid between us to stroke insistently at my clit, and he grinned up at me as I started to whimper and grow impatient.

"I want you to get me nice and slick for you," Wendell said, cheeks blushing. "And then I'm going to bend you over the desk. Or the armchair, what do you think?"

He was fully hard, pressed between his stomach and my sliding pussy as I rocked on top of him. Wendell was probably my most patient Chosen, and anytime he was involved he always made sure I came before anyone even fucked me. I considered testing that patience now, teasing him as much as he did with me, and then decided it'd be easier and faster if I just played along.

I glanced down at the papers on the desk and then back over my shoulder at the tall armchair and its deep cushions.

"Better not ruin the paperwork," I said, gasping as Wendell swirled his fingertip directly against my clit and hunched beneath me to suck on my breasts.

I slid my fingers into those silky blond locks and let out a high, breathy moan. Wendell was quick and observant. He pinched at my clit gently and I came with a bright cry, a soft and surprising flash of giddy heat and magic bubbling through me. I drew back on the magic before it could do something ridiculous with the room and then squeaked as Wendell sat up, lifting me from the desk with so little effort.

Three steps to the chair and he set me on my feet, cupping my face for one deep kiss, tongue laving against mine, and then another as I tried to climb back into his arms. His cock was smearing pre-cum against my belly and my own thighs were already a little glossy and damp. Wendell pulled away with a hum, and for a moment I wished Cosmo and Thao were here to appreciate our beautifully rumpled diplomat. Then he turned me around and swatted my rear.

"Knees on one arm, hands on the other," he said, with surprising directness.

I blinked at the chair in front of me and imagined the precarious balance of the position he was suggesting, but then he nudged me forward. He held my thighs steady as I climbed into place, my palms landing on the other arm with a smack. The chair wobbled, and Wendell released one of my legs to hold the back of the chair.

"If you let me break my nose—"

"I would never. I'm very partial to your nose. No, keep your thighs closed like that," Wendell said as I started to shift my thighs apart.

Which was good because the arm wasn't really wide enough for him to fit between my legs.

"Hold still, just like that," he murmured, the hair on the inside of his legs tickling my feet. The sticky head of his cock nudged against my ass, and my eyes widened as he pulled my cheeks apart, adjusting himself until he was pressing against the opening of my cunt.

"Oh stars," I hissed as he started to push in. I was swollen from my orgasm, and with my thighs pressed together I felt even tighter as Wendell pushed in.

"Yesss. Push back, love," Wendell murmured.

I sank back, forcing Wendell into me, and we both groaned at the tight pressure of him inside of me, of me sucking him down into my core.

"Can you ride me like this?" he gasped.

I absolutely could and I did it eagerly, starting with small movements to be sure Wendell could keep the chair and me from toppling over. When it held steady, I grew more insistent, my ass bouncing against his hips as they kicked gently into me. It was a dull kind of pleasure, intense but also shallow for me without any stimulation to my clit, but Wendell made the most delicious sounds in response, and I grinned and grew rough as his fingers dug into my ass.

"Fuck. Fuck you're so tight," he hissed. "Oh, *shiiiit*."

Wendell grew quiet and obscene, his words barely audible over the sound of our skin slapping. I tucked my smile against my shoulder and peered out of the corner of my eyes. His gaze was focused on my ass as it bounced, attention rapt, fingers clenching roughly over my cheeks.

"So fucking pretty," he murmured, and I giggled, interrupting his stare. Wendell blushed and then held my eyes as his hand lifted briefly and then came down with a *crack*!

"Oh!" My elbows folded, and Wendell groaned, sinking deeper into my channel as my back arched.

"I watched your ass the other night as Aric did that," Wendell ground out.

Slowing my pace of riding his cock, I moved my hands down to the cushions, bending my body forward, our breath stuttering as Wendell leaned into me, his cock so deep I thought I could feel the weight of it in my heartbeat.

"Do it again," I offered.

This time Wendell watched my flesh bounce as he spanked me, and I buried my squeal in my hands, nearly forcing him out of my cunt with the clench. Wendell groaned and then braced a foot on the edge of the chair, taking a new angle and a sudden control. I howled into the cushion as he bucked into me eagerly, the chair trembling with the force of his thrusts and a new pounding tension building in me. I wiggled my fingers between my thighs, barely managing to brush at the lips of my sex, but the gentle tickle against my clit paired the with booming feeling of Wendell inside of me was enough. With the next sharp slap against my ass, I came with a muffled scream, my teeth around my fist and a bright flash behind my eyes. Wendell grew frantic and uneven inside me until his hips stuttered and his weight leaned into me as he coated my core with warmth.

I stiffened at the sound of the light clap from the door, but Wendell only huffed, leaning forward to wrap his arms around me. He maneuvered us with a careful slide, holding me against his chest as he fell into the seat, one leg draped over the arm I'd braced my hands on, the other resting against the floor. When I peeked, Thao and Cosmo were closing the door behind them, twin hungry grins on their faces.

"I was a little rough with her. Be gentle to start," Wendell said, and then he reached down and coaxed my legs open, spreading me wide with my legs hooked outside his, displaying me for their eyes as our mixed release slipped out of me.

Cosmo reached us first, hip checking Thao out of the way and sinking to his knees in front of me with a bright smile, watching as Wendell's cock softened and slid out of me.

"Ready, little muse?" Cosmo asked, stroking his hands on the inside of my thighs.

I sighed and reached back, clasping Wendell's hands in mine as Thao surveyed the three of us and settled to his knees behind Cosmo, making plans of his own no doubt. Thao was never very patient.

"Always," I said, and my eyes fell shut with the kiss of Cosmo's mouth on me.

30.
BRYONY

My hands twisted in my skirt, Cosmo's hand soothing up and down my back as we watched Griffin hover anxiously around Sam and Owen.

"You don't have to do this, you know." Griffin's voice was low, her head bent to Sam's.

Sam looked...well, he looked rightfully nervous and pale, but also more present than I was used to seeing him. If he was improving, I hoped what he and Owen were about to attempt wouldn't set him back again.

"I know I don't. But even if I never fly again, I miss my owl," Sam said, turning those giant pale eyes up at her.

I bit my lip, unsure whom I agreed with in this situation and knowing it wasn't my place to intervene in any way.

"We're just going to get a better idea of the condition," Owen said to them both. "Sam, you can shift back at any time if you're uncomfortable. I'll talk you through everything. If we can reset the wing, Aric and Bryony are ready to help with healing."

"Unless you'd rather I go," I added quickly from the other side of the room. I was hovering by the door to Sam's rooms with Cosmo and Aric at my side and Cresswell waiting in the hall. My guard and I hadn't come to terms with our conversation about our feelings yet, and I couldn't explain the way I ached with *missing* him when he was never very far from my side.

Sam blinked at me, still wary, still probably waiting for me to transform into my sister, but he shook his head.

"We may have to come closer if you need magic," Aric warned gently.

Griffin shifted slightly in front of Sam, blocking him protectively, and I suspected she didn't even realize the movement. She knew better than to think I would ever harm Sam. I wondered what she'd do if I pointed out her instincts around the man. Probably tell me to fuck off. But Sam was probably handsome, in a strange sort of way, and he was a shifter...

None of your business, I reminded myself.

"Do what you need to," Sam said, straightening and nodding at us both, although his eyes shied away from mine quickly.

"I'll shift first," Griffin said gently.

I wasn't sure what her hawk would be able to do to help, but she transformed with a waver in the air, and then there was a well-sized red and brown hawk sitting calmly on the carpet.

"Take your time," Owen offered Sam. "There's no rush. I'm going to take a good hold of you, but only to keep from jostling you. Just try to keep your human mind present."

Sam nodded and he rolled his shoulders, almost like he was reassuring himself that he still could. And then a moment later a beautiful white owl with crooked wings was screaming and bouncing anxiously on the floor. Griffin's hawk screeched, and Owen dropped quickly to his knees, his hand dodging away just before the owl's head swiveled and snapped.

There was a risky negotiation that I gritted my teeth through, resisting the urge to turn away as Owen made several attempts at reaching for Sam until Griffin butted her head against the downy white and gray chest feathers. The birds calmed, even as Sam let out an uncomfortable screech as Owen examined the shoulder of the wing.

"I don't think it's a clean break, but it is fresh," Owen said. "I can reposition it, and magic should help heal it cleanly."

"Bryony supplies the power but it will all work through me," Aric offered the owl, a confused grimace on his expression as it hooted and screamed, the sound bouncing around the simple room.

"I don't understand shifters the way I do animals, but I think we better try it. He's not pecking my arm off at least," Owen said.

I followed at Aric's back, his hand in mine so he could channel my store of magic, and I hid myself at his back for Sam's comfort.

"There's going to be a fight," Owen whispered. "Focus on the pain first and the healing second."

Aric nodded, and together we kneeled. Griffin shot me a sharp and familiar look out of one bright yellow eye, warning me from coming closer, or just being her usual wary self.

"Ready," Aric said.

I winced at the crunch, my head turning away at the owl's scream, and I pressed my magic into the air, feeling the prickle of it in Aric's hand, the almost sizzling sound of it in the air, cloaking around the wing. The bird's screams settled first, although it still fought against Owen who held the wing in place.

"Nearly done I think," Aric said in a thin breath, his focus on the magic. "Yes. Yes, that's good, it feels strong."

Owen released the wing and it flapped easily, Griffin's cry celebratory.

"Sam, do you want to take a break or—" Owen's lips curled up as the owl hopped gingerly around, the difference in the wings painfully clear now.

"I'm fine," I said before Aric could ask, nodding eagerly. "Let's help."

The next wing went smoother, Sam's guarantee of a good wing better medicine against the pain than any magic might be. He cried out but held still, and Aric was quick and focused, only the slightest sensation of draining dragging on me by the time we were done. It was fine. I was more than well stocked with magic and the means to make more. Sam could have any he needed.

"Done," Aric said with a sigh.

Owen released Sam and then the owl screamed, wings spreading wide and beating roughly. He jumped and called again, rising into the air.

"What's wrong?" Aric shouted over the sounds of the bird screeches, Griffin joining Sam in solidarity.

Owen scrambled back out of the way of Sam's massive white wings. "I dunno. He should be okay?"

I knew.

I jumped up from behind Aric and ran for the window, wrestling back Sam's curtains and unlatching it quickly, the sound of the predator birds loud at my back. I threw the windows open and dived out of the way with a gasp, vivid blue and white eyes meeting mine briefly before Sam paused once on the windowsill and then dove out to the cold winter air. Griffin followed him with a happy screech, and I twisted, watching Sam vanish in the snowy scenery, the only clue of him was the red and brown hawk following his tail.

My breath hitched, a pang in my chest that I held tightly in place until Owen reached my back, his arms wrapping tightly around me.

"I'm glad that worked," Owen said, resting his chin on the top of my head.

I blinked quickly through the anxious tears in my eyes and gathered an easier breath, squeezing Owen's arms around my chest. "Me too. Thank you, my love."

Owen kissed my ear, Aric and Cosmo joining us on either side of me, the four of us watching from the window the slow spiral of the red hawk and the white owl over the lake.

⁂

IT WASN'T until after my Chosen and I had taken our dinner together that we saw Griffin and Sam again, and I wasn't expecting it to be with such grave expressions on both their faces.

"What is it?" I asked, rising from the couch in front of the grand fire, Wendell's fingers remaining tangled with mine, the book he'd been reading still perched on his knee.

Cresswell followed them into the cozy room on the ground floor, his eyes meeting mine briefly before rising to stare over me. Thao had Cosmo draped over him like a blanket on the couch opposite me, and Aric was asleep in one of the armchairs. Even Daniel was with us, chatting with Owen about the horses, or the woods most likely.

"What's happened?" I asked, looking to Griffin, watching the nervous way she shifted closer to Sam, ready to protect him from me. I was starting to get a little offended by it if I was honest.

"I have something to confess," Sam said, his voice soft.

The room hushed, Cosmo quick to sit up, both him and Thao twisting to face Sam at the door. At my back, Owen and Daniel approached, their vast shadows rising like guards at my back.

"I'm happy to hear anything you have to tell me, Sam," I answered gently.

"Keep calm, please," Griffin said, but it was directed to the men around me this time.

Aric stirred in his chair, perhaps sensing the tension of the room, just as Sam spoke.

"My mistress left me here with instructions to kill you."

Aric leapt up, rumpled and startled, and Cresswell shot forward from the door.

"No!" I cried out before anyone could grab Sam up, unintentionally causing the man to flinch in response. I hurried past him and Griffin, resting my hands on Cresswell's chest to halt him in place, his gaze blazing at the back of Sam's head. "Cress, calm down. I'm fine. We knew this was a possibility."

"I won't do it," Sam said, and there was a flatness to his tone that left the others staring at him watchfully.

"Cress," I whispered, sighing with him as his chest deflated under my touch, his cool stare falling to me. "I'm fine."

"What were her instructions?" Aric growled out.

"It isn't his fault," Griffin snapped.

"Of course it isn't," I rushed to say, releasing Cresswell slowly and stepping back. Even Wendell was standing now too, all my Chosen on alert to protect me. It was touching. A bit thrilling too, but it was making Sam tremble.

I returned to the heart of my men, running soothing touches over their arms as I passed them, and then took my seat on the couch again.

"Sam, I don't believe you would hurt me. Not if you didn't need to," I said. "Just as I vow never to harm you."

Wendell sat first, then Cosmo with a huff as he yanked Thao's arm down to follow him.

"She didn't tell me how, only that I should if I could," Sam said. He frowned and admitted vaguely, "I might have if you'd... I thought of killing her sometimes too."

I winced but nodded and then glared at a bristling Aric, who ignored my warning and moved to my side, clamping a hand on my shoulder and angling himself toward me in his seat.

"This is a confession, not an attempt," I said gently.

Aric only shrugged.

"I don't want to kill you. I don't want to...to be your Chosen, but I won't hurt you. Any of you," Sam said, and he looked to Griffin to include her in his statement. "Please don't make me leave here. I like the woods. I can fly again."

"You will not be my Chosen," I said, catching his eye. "And you may remain here in the Winter Palace, Sam."

"Bryony—" Cresswell started.

"Sam, I extend you a promise of *safety*," I said, for the other's sake more than his. "And please, if there is anything else I or my Chosen should know about Camellia, don't be afraid to tell us."

"Now that I'm gone, she'll wear down Igor next. Then probably William," Sam said. "She doesn't go anywhere without one of us. Not even after she started meeting with council members. She won't fuck the older ones, but there's a couple she lets have their turn. She told me it was for diplomacy, but I don't think she really cares."

"Names," Wendell said, gripping tight to my hand. "Sam, can you give us names?"

I let out a slow breath, my mind spinning as Sam hummed and produced a few names. Camellia had wanted me dead, or was at least willing to see if it could be managed. My sister. My *monster* of a sister.

"Look at me, princess," Aric said, quiet and private.

I turned to him, but I didn't really see him, not until he leaned in close, pressing his lips to my brow.

"We won't let her win, darling girl," Aric said.

I nodded, but it ran around and around in my brain. What would it take to defeat Camellia? Was I prepared for the cost?

I HESITATED AT THE DOOR, bouncing on the balls of my feet and eyeing the length of the hall. Cresswell was on his break, and

Piper did his duty from a longer distance, which made it only *slightly* less embarrassing that I was hovering outside of Daniel's door.

At the sound of footsteps approaching from inside, I knocked quickly before he could find me standing dumbly outside. The door opened and Daniel blinked at me.

"Are you busy?" I asked.

"I... No? Well, I'm taking letters down. I was going to let you read them first," he said, holding up a small collection of unsealed letters.

"Read them?"

"Yes? I thought you might like to know what I was telling the council and my father."

A sick weight sank in my stomach as Daniel and I stared at one another. He was right, actually. I probably did need to know, but it didn't sit comfortably with me that I was presuming a relationship with a man while treating him like a suspect. Not that the relationship was more than a kiss at the moment.

"It can wait," I said. "Would you like to go riding with me? Owen thinks the horses are getting cabin fever. I can't tell if he thinks that's an actual illness or not."

Daniel's lips quirked, and I wanted to poke my fingers into those secret dimples in the corners that he hid so carefully with his beard.

"A ride sounds good. Will you be warm enough?"

I glanced down at my heavy wool gown and the tight velvet jacket, and then raised my hand, conjuring a little magical warmth on my fingertips. "I'll be fine."

Daniel caught my hand in his, his eyebrows lifting at the heat of my touch and then he paused, his thumb brushing over the back of my hand. I watched, swallowing hard, as he raised my hand to his lips, the full swell of his kiss pressing softly over my knuckles. His eyes fell shut and then before I could think of anything to say, he twisted my wrist and repeated the kiss against the heel of my palm. It was a seduction, but it seemed like a selfish one, his nose nuzzling just over the spot where I dabbed perfume that morning like he was recalling the scent.

"Sorry," he said, lowering my hand as his eyes opened, warmth rising to his cheeks. "Let me...grab my coat."

I stood in a stunned silence as he retreated back into his rooms, my Hunger purring in my chest. She knew as well as I did the promise of pleasure Daniel presented, but the soft fluttering in my belly from his kiss was new. And welcome.

"Do you want the letters now?" he called from inside.

I bit my lip and weighed between trust and common sense. "Let's give them to Wendell and Aric," I said. *I don't want to read your mail, I just want to believe in you*, I thought.

Daniel didn't look the least bit bothered, returning to where I waited in the hall, dressed in a handsome navy jacket with silver buttons. "All right. Ready."

Piper was at the corner of the hall, his eyes directed down as we passed, Daniel's hand resting against my waist.

"The stables should be complete soon," Daniel said. "The workers are ahead of schedule."

I hummed, chewing on the inside of my lip, antsy at the mild conversation. I'd claimed Daniel, and yet things still felt so undecided between us. Stilted even.

"I hope they aren't putting themselves at risk in this cold weather. I don't mind the horses being in the palace, and I think it's put Owen at ease since the fire."

Daniel huffed a little and I frowned, turning to stare at him, but it wasn't a mean kind of laughter I found on his face.

"I like your unconventional court," he explained, and then his gaze softened. "I like the way you take so much care with your Chosen. And your staff. Lady Pru has been relying on the charity of old family friends for years, and I..."

He fell into silence and swallowed hard as we descended the stairs.

"I never saw very much of the Chosen who lived in the castle, but I don't know that any were given offices or studios, that's true," I said, and Daniel nodded eagerly, picking up the dropped strand of conversation.

Owen waited for us in the ballroom-turned-stable, two horses saddled with heavy blankets for warmth over their sides.

"One of the laborers brought Crescent up from the country

for you to try," Owen said, presenting me a young black horse with a shocking white face and blue eyes, a black mane braided down the horses neck and a white crescent moon on its chest. "He's young, a little spirited, and his face spooked some potential buyers, I think."

"Hello, Crescent," I greeted, taking the apple from where Owen hid it for me and offering it up to the nervously shifting horse. The white markings on his face did look almost like a ghostly skull, and I imagined meeting this horse on a dark road with a dark rider on its back. The vision made me smile, as did the soft chuffing breath against my palm as Crescent took the bribe and let me stroke his neck.

I looked up at Owen who smiled at me. "He likes you. I think he'll test you on your ride. If you give him freedom, you might win his loyalty but you'll have to keep up with his energy. If you rein him in—"

"No, I don't think so," I said immediately, meeting Crescent's eerily beautiful gaze. "We will cooperate with one another. I don't mind a race now and then."

Owen nodded and leaned in, kissing my temple. "I thought you'd get along."

My heart panged. For the horse I'd lost, but mainly for Owen who'd understood it better than I, who had loved the creature for its own sake and for mine.

Daniel's horse was huge in comparison to Crescent, one with an elegant copper-brown coat and who looked closer to a draft horse than a riding horse. But Daniel had a build that suited the animal's size, and I tried not to feel too much like a dwarf as I took my seat on Crescent's saddle, while Owen went to open the garden doors for our exit. Daniel had to hunch through the doorway, and I grinned as I followed him out, Crescent already eager to move into a trot. When we cleared the doorway, I gave him leave, and he was quick to take the lead over Daniel's steadier ride.

"Mm, we are similar then," I whispered to the horse, allowing him to choose a route toward the woods.

"Do you prefer the north or the south?" Daniel asked, moving just behind and to the right of me.

"I miss the south, the view of the sea, but I think I prefer the freedom I have here in the north. Have you been to the south?"

"I went to school with the noble sons at Gilding's just along the coast from the capital, but I didn't get out much. I...also prefer the freedom I have here," he said quietly.

I looked back and found his eyes on me, warmth rushing to my cheeks in spite of the cold winter weather.

"What of your father's estate? If you are Chosen, it might be passed on to someone else."

"My father never signed anything to make me his heir. I was groomed for it after his wife died. It was a possibility used to keep me in line, I suppose," Daniel said, frowning and looking out at the woods.

"But it was a possibility you wanted."

"To be a wealthy duke rather than a laborer? Or a country lawyer if I'd been a better student? Yes, I wanted it," Daniel said sharply, and then he grimaced at me. "It was hard not to. I had the steward position after school and I enjoyed the work, but the taunt of more was not without its temptations."

"I'm not judging you," I offered softly, focusing on the stillness of the scenery and Crescent's cheerful snuffling and exploration.

"I am," Daniel answered.

Our horses moved away from one another, traveling aimlessly through the woods with nudges of encouragement, the silence filling the moment to an almost stifling degree.

Daniel stopped and waited for me to ride slowly in a circle to face him. "I'm not Owen. I'm not...inclined to be satisfied with my surroundings, no matter what they are. I came here thinking of what I might have when I was done, rather than questioning the actual cause for being here. I grew too used to being told what to do and unable to know the reasons why."

"And what if the council's plan had worked and I'd taken you directly to my bed?" I asked.

"Knowing what I did of your sister, I had assurances that I'd be given a reprieve from the duty at some point," Daniel said solemnly, the pair of us staring at one another.

A reprieve from having to fuck me. It wasn't funny. Especially not in the context of Camellia; just the thought of her made me ache with worry. But in terms of Daniel and I? I snorted, and he huffed out a laugh, shaking his head.

"I'm glad to be wrong. About all of it," he said, smiling.

I took in a long slow breath, studying Daniel fully, the glint in his gaze, the breadth of him, the secrecy in his smile. As a man, he was certainly growing on me.

"We're nearly to the road. Ride down to Rumsbrooke with me?" I asked. "I want to visit the baker."

Daniel's eyes crinkled. "As if he wouldn't bring all his supply directly to the palace for you."

"It's the rolls," I said, turning Crescent and encouraging him into a trot again. "I like them fresh and sticky."

I grinned at the sound of Daniel's rough, startled laughter, and the heavy beat of his horse's hooves behind me.

31.
BRYONY

I caution you against any sense of comfort or success, dear granddaughter. What little cooperation I gain in the south is quickly turned awry again. Your mother stands with me as long as no one else is able to catch her ear. Lord Thomlinson is planning to travel north with a few peers at the end of this month, and I suspect the council is at work.

You were right. They have too much leniency. I've enclosed a note from your mother expressing her full faith in your decisions. Find the council and use it if necessary.

You have my full faith too.

In most things.

- Dowager Queen Violet

I smiled at the letter in my lap, even though the majority of it left my stomach in knots. We'd had nearly three peaceful weeks. The apple trees were growing, the land rights for the orchards were secured, the money from the first month of taxes had been reserved for public use, and Aric had started secret work with his mage contacts on repairing the roads so nothing might interrupt doctors or food supplies to the northern territory.

I suspect the council is at work.

Now, with just a few lines, the peace I'd been enjoying transformed into a well-disguised trap.

Thao slid into the seat at my side, the greenhouse still fresh and lush as sunlight melted the snow on the windows and beat warmth into the room even as it remained frigid outside. I leaned automatically into Thao's side. He sought out the warmest rooms to spend his time in, but he maintained that he was constantly cold and had taken to ordering hand-knitted sweaters from local wives in Rumsbrooke and the surrounding farms, and the effect was deliciously cozy. I dug my fingers into the weave of the cables on his sleeve and he caught the letter in my hand.

"Mm, Wendell is on his way," Thao said, frowning at my grandmother's delicate script.

"It isn't good news, but I suppose it's what we've been expecting," I said, burrowing closer.

Thao's arm pulled free, and I started to pout until he wrapped it around my shoulders, letting me nuzzle into his collar. "If I'd realized the effect sheep's wool had on you, I would've altered my wardrobe sooner," Thao said.

"I can't decide if it's sweaters I prefer, or *you* in sweaters," I teased.

Thao growled, an imitation of his tiger, and I laughed. It was definitely the addition of Thao. He made the wool smell less like grass and hay and more like a very nice morning in bed, not unlike the one he'd given me earlier when he'd declared he'd be having his breakfast before the rest of us.

Thao's free hand slid down to my bottom, his head turning for our mouths to meet, just as the greenhouse doors opened.

"Griffin is here, Your Highness."

Thao glared over my head as I winced at my title on Cress-well's lips. I shifted in my seat to find him standing stiffly in the doorway, Griffin rushing in.

"I'd offer to let you continue, but this really can't wait," she snapped.

I sat up, Thao let his arm drape over the back of the loveseat, and Griffin dropped into the chair across from us at the table. "I think we both know you wouldn't be shy of interrupting and that I wouldn't ask you to. What's wrong?"

"It's the council," Griffin said, gaze blazing.

I looked at the letter in Thao's hand and then back to Griffin. Our brief reprieve was officially over. "Do you know what their plan is?"

"Barely, but I know it's about the two-natured," Griffin said. "You heard?"

"Only the Dowager Queen's suspicion that they were gathering together here in the north. Who did you hear from?"

Griffin's jaw clenched and she breathed slowly through her nose. "I can't tell you that."

Thao stiffened and looked between us. "I can leave, if it's—"

"No. It's not you. I'm sorry, Bryony, but it's not my place to say who I heard this from."

Another shifter then. I opened my mouth to remind her that I wanted nothing but equality and peace of mind for shifters and then shut it again. I didn't *need* to know, and Griffin did trust me. That was why she was here.

"The council is gathering for a vote. It's not unanimous, and it's bad enough that they're trying to keep it under wraps until the vote has passed. That's all I know," Griffin said.

"Do you know when? Or where?" I asked.

She frowned and shook her head, huffing and sweeping her hair back from her face with one hand. "They didn't say, probably because they didn't want me storming in," she bit out, eyes rolling up to the ceiling. "I got word this morning, and it could be tonight or tomorrow or next week."

"Actually, no. I think I have a clue. Grandmother's letter just arrived and in it she said Lord Thomlinson and his peers were preparing for the end of the month. I know that's this week really, but—"

"Lord Thomlinson," Griffin said slowly. "You're right. I can put eyes out to find the carriages."

"I will go, Griffin," I said quickly, seeing her gaze go distant. She glared at me and I shook my head. "I mean it. I will go and I will put a stop to it, I promise you that. If your ally needs to remain a secret, what better way to be sure of that than me going on my grandmother's information, rather than you on your source's?"

"This is about more than me. This isn't their decision to make, Bryony."

"No, and I know it isn't mine either, and I'm sorry the shifters can't represent themselves in this matter." I leaned forward and reached for the other woman's hand, catching it my tight grip before she could pull away. "Griffin, they won't persuade me, they won't reason with me. They won't even force me. I will *stop* them. Whatever it is."

"She won't be alone," Thao added from my side. "I can put the weight of the Mennarian trade deals into the discussion. My family hates the legislation against your shifters. And Wendell can hunt down any precedent that might be made from Kimmerian laws."

Our argument was working, and I slid my free hand into Thao's, squeezing gratefully. Griffin's anger was faltering to acceptance.

"Owen can sense shifters?" Griffin asked.

I blinked, confused by the turn of the conversation, and then nodded.

"Take him with you," she said, holding my stare. "It... He may be useful too."

Suddenly, I understood where Griffin's information was coming from and why it hadn't been *more* helpful.

"I've been researching the council members with Wendell. There are men whose loyalty is to the crown, and others whose loyalty is to their merchant vessels that trade with Mennary," I said. "If it goes to a vote, it won't be unanimous and I will ensure it doesn't pass."

Griffin's shoulders gradually eased. "We've had enough, Your Highness. If this passes, whatever it is—"

"It won't," I said.

"If it *does*, the shifters of Kimmery won't accept it. And we won't remain peaceful."

Griffin meant the words as a warning. I took them as a promise.

"I will stand with you," I said, my chin lifting.

Finally, Griffin squeezed back, a hard glint in her eyes and the faintest smile on her lips.

❦

"THE QUEEN'S note of support for you will be enough for Gareth Cleaves," Wendell said, pacing back and forth in front of the fireplace of my sitting room. "His family has always been crown loyalists. I imagine Lord Thomlinson is only bringing his allies with him, but we can make an argument that any vote can't be counted without the others."

"Here are the names of the men who rely on my family's permission to trade," Thao said, adding four more names to our list of potential allies that we had spread across the low table.

My Chosen were gathered together, Daniel included, and Cresswell stationed himself by the door, so potently present in my mind even as he remained silent.

"Why am I coming again?" Owen asked. "Not that I mind going with you, of course."

I bit my lip and shuffled on my knees to face Owen, who sat on the couch in my sitting room. I had a feeling he wouldn't like what I was about to say, and I hoped he'd forgive me for the plan.

"I think there might be an unregistered shifter on the council. At least, that was the impression Griffin gave me. If you can spot them—"

"Oh, Bryony," Owen said softly, the heartache in his eyes.

"Owen, I know, and believe me, I don't want to point to them across a room and shout it. I won't. But if there were an opportunity to speak to them alone, it may make an enormous difference to an entire mass of shifters who have no voice of their own," I said.

Owen sighed and studied me. It was rare for Owen to express anything but agreement with me, and I didn't want to disrespect his opinion when he gave it.

"You won't expose them?" he asked.

No. But I might threaten to. "I may not even need to know who they are. If there are votes against the measure, theirs might join the number," I said.

"All right. I'll come," Owen said, and he leaned forward to meet me in a soft kiss. I held his face to mine when he started to pull away, taking one soft kiss after another until his lips twitched with his smile.

"I'll be there if you need any additional magic," Aric said.

"No," Thao, Wendell, and I all said at once.

Aric stiffened in the tall armchair he'd been reclining in and narrowed his eyes at us.

"You are my Chosen," I said.

"But you're still a rogue, aren't you?" Thao finished for me, and I was surprised that he managed not to sound antagonistic with the question.

"Well, of course, but—" Aric started.

"Bryony must present herself as an authority and as...well, morally superior," Wendell said with a wince and shrug.

Aric glared at him and then at me, and my jaw clenched, waiting for his argument. Instead, he grinned. "Princess, do I sully your reputation?"

I arched an eyebrow. "You sully something, I'm sure."

Aric laughed and rolled his eyes. "You're sure, though? I could disguise myself, stay out with the carriage."

"I have plenty of magic and a measure of control," I said with a shrug. "Stay here and keep an eye on the rest of my matters. Now, we just need to figure out where they're meeting."

"I may have an answer to that."

The room as a whole turned to stare at Daniel in his seat to my left. He stiffened under our gaze until his eyes landed on mine. I had an itch to go to him, to block the others out of his sight to help him relax, but I resisted, leaning against Owen's legs.

"I received a letter from my father in exchange for the one I sent him. He said he's receiving guests. He doesn't have a seat on the council, or he refused the one he was offered, but we already know he's Roderick's ally," Daniel said.

"Having the meeting in a presumed unbiased location seems likely," Wendell mused, frowning. "And Danser Hall is more central. Well away from the attention of Rumsbrooke."

"There's a village nearby with a meeting hall too, if Roderick and Thomlinson wanted to appear less social."

"The Farraque estate would be private though. And it does sound as though the council is trying to keep this under wraps," Aric said.

"Will you come?" I asked Daniel as the others discussed the odds of the location.

Would he come with me to his father's estate, and stand as my ally?

"The council will cut ties with me," he answered back, just as softly.

I opened my mouth to say that the time for subterfuge was over, but what came out was, "I would rather they know you were mine."

Daniel's expression sharpened, his focus on my face so intense it drew out a blush. "Yes, I'll come."

Thao cleared his throat and I startled, finding his smirk aimed in my direction. But that wasn't all. Cresswell's eyes flicked between me and Daniel, brow furrowed and lips turned down. I waited for him to look back at me, but it was only for a second, the worry on his face vanishing behind a stone mask once more.

"If we are right about who is in attendance, we remain outnumbered by at least five," Wendell said, joining me on the floor by the table, reading over the list of names once more. "It will come down to you, Bryony. You must convince them. Or overpower them."

32.
BRYONY

Crescent was at a steady canter beneath me, Owen and his chestnut stallion close behind, Cresswell looking back over his shoulder to reassure himself that he had the lead. A black raven had arrived at the window of the breakfast room this morning, pecking at the glass before transforming into an unfamiliar man with a message from Griffin.

The bird shifters were watching Danser Hall and its surrounding roads. Carriages were on their way.

We'd left immediately.

Two more guards followed us with the carriage, carrying Daniel, Wendell, and Thao, while Cosmo and Aric remained at the palace, or more likely they'd snuck off to Rumsbrooke together. That was fine, I planned to have this matter dealt with as quickly as I could, and to return to the palace by nightfall.

My breath fogged the air in front of me. The snow was thin on the roads and fields south of the mountains, but in another week or two winter would lie like a heavy blanket over the rest of the north. I wanted to be enjoying warm fires and hot tea and Thao in sweaters—any of my Chosen in sweaters, for that matter—but first the council would have to be dealt with, yet again.

And again and again and again, until you have the crown, I thought. Or until my mother and grandmother might be persuaded to look at the kingdom differently and take back more of the responsibility of care for our people's well being.

"Nearly there," Cresswell called over his shoulder.

Crescent wanted to shoot forward to the front, the tense restraint of holding back expressed loudly through his stomping hooves and the occasional push in speed as he dared Cresswell's own ride to slow down. I relaxed and leaned into his motion, letting him take the lead as we reached the gate of the Farraque estate.

Danser Hall was beautiful, the avenue lined with pine and oak trees, a deep pond following the curving road on the right side, a vast and tidy garden of hedges and hibernating rosebushes on the left. And a wide and elegantly ornate nobleman's hall ahead of us, made of softly brown brick and glittering with tall windows. There was carefully manicured ivy trimming the wings, held in check just enough to compliment the natural beauty of the grounds.

This was what had been dangled in front of Daniel's nose his entire life like a carrot for a mule. It was also what he was willing to give up in his loyalty to me. I had a minor moment of doubt as I took it all in. Was it right for me to turn him away from his father, from the council's support, just for a place as my Chosen? I had more respect for him than they did, but he would always be one of many with me, when here he might someday have sole ownership of his entire domain.

It's his decision to make. You gave him the choice, now let him use it.

Crescent resisted my pull on the reins for a moment, before relenting and slowing down to a trot, allowing Cresswell and Owen to catch up with me. Black and glossy carriages with family crests painted carefully on the doors lined the drive as we approached the house.

"How far behind the meeting do you think we are?" Owen asked.

"Not long," I answered, eyeing the broad wingspan of an eagle passing over the roof of Danser Hall. "Wendell said there would probably be a meal and wine before the vote, or at least enough time for Roderick and Thomlinson to try and grease palms and secure the response they were hoping for. I'm hoping we're arriving while they're gathered and talking, so there's no time for them to notice our approach."

And it looked as though we were in luck. While a servant opened the front doors of the hall and a pair of groomsmen came around from the rear of the building, all three of them looked puzzled by our arrival.

"Let me announce you," Cresswell said without waiting for

my answer as he pushed ahead, his horse skidding to a stop at the front steps, peppering the staff with pebbles from the drive.

"He seems cold," Owen whispered to me.

"He is either angry with me or..." I shook my head and huffed.

"Or himself," Owen finished, a sympathetic smile on his face.

Wendell and Thao had made an effort to polish Owen up for this occasion, ordering him a new suit and tall brown riding boots. The man at my side was familiar, but also somehow comical, like a watered-down and stiff version of the Owen I loved. He'd already undone the elaborate knot Wendell had tied at his throat, and I had a feeling he'd be unbuttoned and rugged before we made it home again.

"The crown princess?" the servant was whispering as we approached, wide eyes darting between me and Cresswell.

"Her Royal Highness herself, here to speak with the council."

"The-the council?" the old man stuttered, flicking a nervous gaze back at the doors. "N-no, this is a- a family party."

"Is it now? A family party of all the noble families of Kimmery?" I asked, pulling Crescent to a stop and smiling as his ears flicked irritably. "Am I not included?"

"Will you bar the doors to Her Highness?" Cresswell asked, a hand reaching down to his sword.

That seemed a bit like overkill, and I rested my hand on his elbow without thinking, a brief exchange of amusement passing between us before we remembered our own discomfort with one another.

"Lennox."

The skittish servant looked more terrified by the bark of his name from the door than he had when I'd spoken to him directly, and my eyes traveled to the man standing there, immediately aware of who was staring back at me. Edgar Farraque, Duke of Banesdale.

He both did and did not resemble his son. Edgar's hair was black as ink to Daniel's fawn color, and he appeared to be even taller. But there was a strength and ferocity to him that I recognized as the passion Daniel usually kept bound up. Behind us, at a distance, the sound of our party's carriage rattled on the avenue.

"Your Highness," Edgar Farraque said, his voice more velvet than his son's, and more full of courtly flourish. He bowed low at the top of the steps and then took the path down to us, Lennox scurrying backward out of his master's way.

I had no doubt that I was windswept from the ride, and the hem of my skirt was mud-splattered, but I was also well aware of the deference due to me and I stood proudly with my chin high at his approach, raising my hand for him to take when he was close. His hands were smooth and a little clammy as they wrapped around mine. Up close, I could see that the color of his hair touched his scalp too, and he smelled a little of boot polish. There were lines beneath the powder on his face—age refusing to hide and leaving him strangely distorted for the attempt—and enough cologne to make my throat tickle.

His kiss to my knuckles was nearly illicit, too wet and too lingering, and I wrinkled my nose and pulled away when he took too long in doing so.

"What an honor," he murmured to me, dipping his head again. "And a pleasant surprise, I'm sure."

"I understand there is a gathering of councilmen here today, Your Grace," I said.

Edgar's smile reminded me of a snake's, flat and curling uncomfortably at the corners. "A gathering of friends, really. But yes, many councilmen are in attendance." His eyes scanned over my shoulder at the approach of the carriage. "Ah. There are more of you."

"A number of my Chosen accompany me today, and my head guard, Cresswell Stark," I said, stepping away from the man and giving in to the urge to retreat to Owen's side, taking a deep relieving breath of him.

It was obvious the moment Edgar Farraque spotted his son descending from the carriage. His face went white beneath the powder, the smile vanishing and cold blue eyes narrowing. "Daniel." The word was clenched.

I kept my eyes on Edgar as Daniel's boots crunched over the

pebbles until he reached my side. He delivered a shallow bow to his father. "Your Grace."

Edgar took one brief glance at Wendell and Thao and then gestured for the door. "Please, allow me to show you to the others."

So little was said between them, and it somehow left my spine prickling with tension. Daniel offered me his arm in full view of his father, and I curved my hand into his elbow, squeezing there briefly. Both men were stony and guarded in front of one another, and there was nothing I could do to relieve my Chosen but that minor touch.

Danser Hall was as elegant inside as its exterior, restrained and simple, its appearance austere and ancient, with tall creamy marble pillars and polished stone archways leading from one room to the next. The floor was new, decoratively angled tile in shades of black and navy, and our footsteps echoed ominously in the austere space.

I wondered how much time Daniel had really spent inside the hall, or if it had always been kept carefully out of his reach. I wanted to ask, but I was too aware of the tight shoulders of the duke just in front of us as he led us quickly through the halls. There were portraits on the walls, and both Daniel and I slowed as we passed one. Where there'd been little resemblance between Edgar and Daniel, the woman in the portrait was clearly related to my Chosen in some fashion, right down to the perfectly plump bow lips.

And then the doors at the end of the hall opened and the steady thrum of male voices reached my ears, faltering as Edgar stepped inside.

"Her Royal Highness, Princess Bryony, deigns to visit," Edgar said, with just an edge of sarcasm.

"What?!" one voice squawked that I thought sounded a little like Sir Speares, and then the rest of the room fell into a hush.

The room was vast, a dining area of some kind meant for large parties, and full to the brim with more councilmen than I'd ever seen together thus far. Certainly more than had been on the list that Wendell and the rest of us had prepared. For a moment, I simply followed the slow guiding arm of Daniel as I took them all in. There were a few like Jonathon Roderick, who looked younger—around Wendell's mid-thirties—but the majority were old, gray and white the most common hair colors.

The air was thick with cigar smoke, and most men had a glass of amber liquid at hand. If I hadn't known better, it *would've* seemed like a gentleman's gathering. Like they all might put on wool coats in a minute and go out together for a hunt. Unfortunately, I had a feeling the hunt was taking place right here in the comfort of the warm room.

"Your Highness, you catch us off guard," a familiar dry and dark tone greeted.

Lord Roderick stood up from his seat first, the mass of men in the room following suit quickly, a collective bow delivered at an almost eerily uniform pace.

"But perhaps that was your intention," Roderick said upon rising, lips curving with the imitation of a smile.

"Is it not my right, Lord Roderick, to call upon the noble families of my kingdom? To call upon my councilmen?" I asked.

"Your mother's kingdom," said a man to Lord Roderick's left.

Lord Roderick was tall and lean and had the look of a predator. This man who spoke was almost as tall, but three times as wide, with a flushed red face and swollen jowls. I knew immediately he must be from the south for how well fed he seemed to be, how richly he dressed, and he almost did look familiar, like he might've passed through the castle once or twice.

"Lord Thomlinson," I said, pleased when he looked a little startled by my guess as he nodded deeply in acknowledgment. "Yes, my mother is Kimmery's queen, and I am her daughter. Do you believe she makes the distinction so strongly? That she does not wish for her heir to take an interest in the affairs of state? As you appear to wish I would not."

"Not at all, Your Highness, I merely—"

Roderick cut Thomlinson's blustering off with a sideways glance and a quick clearing of his throat.

"You are, of course, welcome in your interest, Your Highness. You've arrived at a—"

"Gathering of friends, so the duke told me," I said, forcing the same smile on that Roderick wore and watching as his faltered. "It must be very convenient for the council to all be so friendly and able to visit one another. I am very happy for you all. However, I think we are all well aware, and I include myself in this, that this is not a social meeting."

The room was quiet, the smoke still and hovering as though all the men collectively held their breath. One man, very elderly and stooped, wobbled in place and held on to the back of his chair like a crutch.

"Please, sit. My Chosen and I will join you, and you may continue to speak as friends," I said gently.

I took two steps toward the table, and a man was quick to offer up his chair. "Sir Weston, Your Highness," he murmured to me.

"Thank you, Sir Weston." A loyalist by Wendell's reckoning.

One by one, the men returned warily to their seats, most of them looking to Roderick and Thomlinson for guidance. The hush remained heavy in the room, but the smoke dissipated as one of the younger men moved to crack a window.

"Pope," another greeted Wendell softly behind me. "Good to finally see you at one of these...in spite of, well..."

Owen took the seat he was offered on my right, his lips brushing my ear as he sat down. "Red waistcoat, across and five down from you."

He'd found one.

"A couple others too."

My eyes widened briefly and then I regained control of myself. Three shifters here on the council? That meant it wasn't really more prevalent amongst commoners than nobles.

"Someone send for tea," a man called.

"Better make it coffee," another muttered, pushing his glass and cigar away.

"I believe I interrupted your conversation, Lord Roderick," I said to the head of the table, my eyes snagging on his steely gaze. "Please resume it."

Jonathon Roderick appeared from the corner of the room, bending to whisper in his father's ear, but the older man grimaced and pushed his son away.

"A conversation which was not, perhaps, suitable for ears such as yours," Lord Roderick said, lips smirking.

"Why should a matter of the rights of men not be suitable for our princess's ears, Nathaniel?" Sir Weston asked, having remained near my chair with his arms crossed.

I couldn't have hid my triumph even if I tried, but it was Weston that Roderick glared at, and the room fell into a deeper hush.

"Shifters are not *men*, they are beasts in men's clothes," Roderick growled, and I was too startled by the murmurs of agreement and the nods of many men in the room to be properly appalled at his words.

"I think you forget that not all of Kimmery shares your views," Sir Weston said at my back.

Lord Thomlinson laughed low and relaxed into his seat, continuing to sip his drink and let his cigar smoke billow gently toward my nose. "And you forget, Weston, that the *majority* of the council does share it."

"I do not, Lord Thomlinson," I said, biting around the words and baring my teeth at the man. "In fact, I happen to be especially fond of shifters, as I am of their rights, and indeed the rights of all the people of Kimmery. What is proposed?"

Lord Thomlinson's confidence faltered, and Lord Roderick looked to him with a nervous apprehension. "Surely His Highness, the prince, understands I mean no slight against himself or his family," Lord Thomlinson said, suddenly realizing who else was in the room with me, his eyes flicking toward Thao. "It is an entirely different kind of thing."

"Gentlemen, what is proposed?" I snapped.

The room was quiet and it wasn't Sir Weston who spoke up, but one of the younger men, the one who'd gotten up and opened the window. "There is a party of the council who proposes that registered shifters and their kin be moved into monitored work camps, rather than being allowed to live freely."

Beneath the table, Owen's foot pressed gently on top of mine. Here was one of the three.

"Your name?" I asked.

He hesitated with a bow. He'd appeared plain at first, but

there was something striking about him—perhaps not handsome, but something that held the gaze. "Jack McCallum, Viscount of Cambell, Your Highness."

"Your Highness, as it stands now, shifters are permitted to live freely, disperse, unlawfully procreate with decent people and create more of their kind, or go into hiding. They should be contained!" One fiery declaration was made from an older man near the young viscount.

"Live freely?" I asked sharply, my hands forming claws against my lap. "As I understand it, the council has already ensured that shifters must identify and be registered, must only serve in particularly exhausting and labor intensive positions, are subjected to particular taxes, denied the majority of public care, and are excluded from many potential privileges that their fellow Kimmerians look forward to!"

"Your Highness—" Lord Roderick started.

"No!" I stood up suddenly, glaring back at the man, meeting the fire in his stare with my own. "What you *propose*, Lord Roderick, is an abomination of law. Of a kingdom's duty to its citizens."

"We seek to guard Kimmery's citizens against those who may be a threat!" Lord Thomlinson barked, his face turning deeply red. "You are a girl, not a queen."

"I am a princess! I am of the queen's line. I wield the magic of the Hunger, and I will take the throne," I answered back, every word clapping around the room, making the men sit back in their seats. And some of it was with offense, yes, I could see that. I hoped what I read in the others was respect as I imagined it would be. I hoped there was *some* decency left on this council, or at least a little fear.

"You fear the two-natured. Why? Because they are *more* than you?" I asked, frowning at the men. "To be sure, you have now in this room with you three spectacular specimens," I said, and with that statement, I caught the stiffening of the third man in hiding, but it wasn't them I spoke of. It was Thao and Wendell who approached my side with confidence and then transformed themselves, making men on either side of me race away with great gasps and one horrified screech. Owen pushed his seat back to give Wendell room to rub against my side, his great white head leaning into my waist.

"Is it their claws?" I asked, raising a hand and smiling as Wendell's great paw rested gently on my palm, his claws flexing carefully. "Their incredible strength?" Thao rose up, his own claws clacking against the wood table which groaned beneath his weight. "They are majestic, these men, in their second-natures. They are ferocious. They could certainly eviscerate you in one leap, one bite." Wendell licked his jaw and showed off his fangs to the room of trembling men.

Behind me, there was a soft whisper and then a great huff and a stifled growl, before two massive brown and padded paws rested on my shoulders, Cresswell standing twice as tall as me at my back, his fur brushing against my skirt.

"My guard has never been more capable of killing my enemies than he is now," I said, holding Lord Roderick's hateful gaze. "But these supposed beasts you see before you? They are still men. I no more fear them now than I do when they stand handsome at my side in their gentleman's clothes. And if I, a small young woman, have no fear of them, why gentlemen, should you?

"You use their strength for your gain while trying to tear it from their own grasp. You forget that Kimmery's blessing has always been its magic, for as long as the queen's line has ruled. It is not just the two-nature who set us apart. We have powerful mages. Many of our people bear gifts we barely know of yet. This should be a matter of celebration, not legislation," I said, barely catching Owen's eye and smiling.

The young viscount had his hand over his mouth, but I could see his gently shaking shoulders. The man in the red waistcoat had wide and reverent eyes fastened to me. The one who'd stiffened when I spoke stared mournfully down at his wrinkled and spotted hands, but he nodded slowly to himself.

"A very witty argument, Your Highness, to be sure," Lord Roderick said drolly. "But the council is not a *circus*, nor should matters of Kimmery's legislation be. You are our princess, but not our *queen*, who puts her faith in us. You have no real say in this room."

"She is to inherit, Roderick," Weston breathed, even as he remained shrunk away from Thao's swatting tail. It really was absurd that these grown men should be more afraid of Thao and Wendell than my own grandmother was, I thought.

"She has not *yet*," Roderick snapped back.

It didn't matter. I dropped Wendell's paw and he restored himself to a man as I reached into the deep pocket of my skirt.

"I didn't know your family had shifter blood, Pope," Sir Speares said, sneering.

Thao stood again too, sweeping elegant black hair from his face. "Ambassador Pope's second-nature is my gift to him," Thao said. "My family takes our privileged forms with the utmost respect and deference to our ability. It is a blessing to our bodies and to our people. We have long frowned upon Kimmery's treatment of this blessing, however it varies from ours, and I will write to my family to seriously consider their alliances, if Kimmery should treat our kind with such exceptional disrespect."

Lord Thomlinson stiffened at this, his eyes widening and flicking about the table as men shifted uncomfortably.

"If it is the faith of your queen you seek, I have it here in this letter," I said, lifting my mother's note into the air, watching with an incomplete satisfaction as Roderick's jaw ticked. I knew as well as he did that my mother's faith was easily won, that she might just have easily promised Thomlinson her support. But the other man looked gravely back at Roderick, and at least for the moment I had won.

Sir Weston stepped forward, eyeing Cresswell with a hard swallow, but he took the letter from my fingers and read it to the room.

"...My darling and wise daughter will know best how to serve our good kingdom, as she is a true embodiment of our great queen's line..."

The note was effusive in its praise, and Owen turned his face to mine, beaming at me as if the words were some perfect gold mark, impossible to refute. I buried the shame that wanted to rise to my cheeks. I knew the truth. My mother was liberal with her confidence in me, but a little empty too. She reminded the council that I was good, and would know best, but she didn't assert herself against them. Still, it was working in some places, the shift palpable as men began to confer with their friends and peers, as Thomlinson and Roderick looked uneasy in their authority.

"It seems you seek to make the council defunct, Your Highness," Lord Thomlinson said, which was a clever kind of cut against me, as it made the men rustle anxiously.

"Not at all. I seek to remind the council that its duty is to be a reflection of the will of the queen's line and what is best for the people of Kimmery. *All* the people of Kimmery," I said. "And I sincerely believe that if the people were given a voice in this matter, their opinions would not reflect your own."

A couple of nobles scoffed, but for the most part, I had the council's attention.

"And how can you be sure?" Lord Roderick asked, glaring at me.

"I cannot. Put your proposal to a vote here today, and if it passes, take it to the people next," I said.

"Give the people a *vote*?" one man squawked, but Sir Weston was quick to jump in.

"Yes, just as many of us have suggested for several years now!"

"A vote it is then. Here, now, between the council members," Lord Thomlinson barked, glaring at the men at the table as he wobbled and pulled himself upright. "And if it passes, we shall discuss how best to implement your commoner's vote."

"We have a system, ready and drafted," Wendell said at my side. "It will be easily managed."

Thomlinson glared back at my Chosen with a sneer, but it was Roderick's face that simultaneously left me sure that we had, somehow, both won and stirred up a great deal of grief for ourselves. He looked defeated, and he gave me the deepest, most loathsome, most openly vicious stare, so much so that it drew a growl out of Cresswell who was still a bear at my back.

"Perhaps Your Highness will give us leave to take our vote in private and away from the intimidation of your *beast*," Roderick spat out.

I bristled for Cresswell's sake, but nodded to the men. "I will give the council, who has the responsibility of using their best and most ethical judgment, the privacy for the vote."

Roderick puffed and fumed, but said no more as I turned with my Chosen and headed for the door. Behind me, silent this whole time, Daniel remained in the background, gaze blazing on me. I hadn't really taken the time to feel proud of this performance, but it seemed suddenly impossible not to under his stare, like he was lit up from within and it was shining on me too now. I smiled shyly at him and he held the door open for me, for Cresswell who transformed back to my gleaming guard, and for my other Chosen, Owen's hand squeezing around mine.

"You are beautifully terrifying," Daniel whispered in my ear. "Have I mentioned that before?"

It was an odd compliment, but it made me flush and bump my shoulder against his arm as the door swung shut behind us.

"I think you have their vote, Bryony," Wendell said.

"I have your cooperation to thank for that," I said, looking at the five of them and smiling as the voices raised in the closed room behind us.

"You improvise well," Thao said with a nod. "Our second-natures was a clever touch. Did you have it planned?"

"No, I would've told you, of course. And you didn't *have* to shift," I rushed out.

Thao only smiled and stepped closer, his hair brushing my shoulder as he kissed the curve of my neck. "It was my pleasure. The smell of their fear was exhilarating."

"It was only a shame I couldn't let the bear out more," Cresswell said, and at last he gifted me with his warm, brilliant smile.

And then there were footsteps clapping on the tile closer, and Daniel stiffened at my side at his father's approach. Edgar Farraque hadn't been in the room with us, but I was certain he must've heard every word in some way. There was no other reason for him to look so furious with his son.

"Daniel," he bit out, his hands clenched at his side.

Cresswell shifted in front of me, but I pushed him back slightly, shaking my head and touching Daniel's arm, silently asking him what he needed as he looked at me.

"Daniel!"

Daniel swallowed, eyes on mine, and then lifted my hand to his arm. He needed support, and it was his. I moved with him at his side, holding my gaze to his face, watching the way he held his head high as he approached his father.

"What are you *thinking*, coming here like this? For this cause?" Edgar hissed, glancing briefly at me and stiffening. "Excuse me, Your Highness, but—"

"I attend my princess," Daniel said, and I tried to focus on the friction between the two men rather than the delicious rasp of Daniel's voice. "My mistress. Where she wishes me to."

"You take your new role as steward perhaps a little too seriously," Edgar huffed. "It is not your place to appear here like this. To use our...connection in such a way."

I tried to stay calm, but my hand clenched around Daniel's arm rather than use it to reach out and *smack* this man across the face. Daniel's head began to bow, his shoulders tight, and then he paused, relaxed, and held the older man's gaze, saying nothing.

"Daniel. You risk everything. You realize this? You risk it *all*. You break with the council, you humiliate me? You will leave everything you might have ever gained, here behind you, and it will *never* be yours, do you understand?" Edgar asked, ignoring me, his princess, completely in favor of snarling at his son. His son who had been promised nothing, only ever shown the possibility of it.

Daniel was quiet, and I expected to see the struggle on his face. There was a wince of his eyes, yes, but also a faint smile on his lips.

"No. Today, I will leave here with all that has ever, truly, been given to me," Daniel said softly.

I frowned at him, puzzling through it, until Daniel's hand lifted and covered mine on his arm, squeezed over the back of my hand gently.

Oh.

His head turned to me, and my heart soared, entirely away from this fussy pristine manor and solely alone with the man at my side, just for a moment. Daniel meant me, and all I had only barely begun to offer him.

"Daniel," Edgar snarled, reaching out.

I raised my hand and there was magic on my palm, totally unformed but still strong enough to make Edgar Farraque choke and pull his hand away just as quick as it had started to lash out.

"My Chosen makes his own mind clear in this matter, Duke Farraque," I said.

Daniel hummed, his eyes crinkling in the corners as he raised my hand to his lips and kissed my knuckles. "Indeed. I know what I want."

Which left me unreasonably flushed and wishing I could squirm with pleasure in this hallway in front of this horrible man. Thankfully, we were all interrupted against whatever might have come next when the door to the meeting room opened.

Sir Weston was there, as was Lord McCallum, the viscount. "The proposal fails, Your Highness. Twenty-nine votes against, twenty-six for."

My heart stuttered as Wendell clapped and Owen whooped until Thao yanked on his arm, grinning and shaking his head gently.

So *close*, I thought mournfully.

But a victory all the same.

33.
BRYONY

I wanted to leave immediately. Edgar Farraque's rage was barely restrained at my back, and many of the men who were leaving the failed vote seemed equally vexed. But Wendell gave me one significant look, and I swallowed my discomfort and began to mingle. I had a duty to greet the men who were eager to assure me that they stood with my statements —they were primarily younger, and I suspected that some of them only had interest in holding their seats. And also one to soothe the egos of the men who glared at me and my Chosen, as much as I was able to do so.

I acted grateful. I acted docile in some cases, serene in others. I was haughty and stern where I needed to be.

And I Hungered through every second of it, my eyes tracking Daniel's movement, his own still holding that happy laugh, always sure to keep himself in my sights as if he knew exactly what I waited for. What I wanted.

Owen's hand cupped my waist, and Cresswell remained close at my back. I craved them too, any touch really, but the clear tug was in Daniel's direction. He was an unfinished end that needed tying in. My Chosen who needed to be claimed in earnest. As Wendell worked the older conservatives toward our cause, and Thao reminded the trade-inclined nobles of who their allies were, I watched with a predator's stare as Jonathon Roderick approached Daniel.

"I must tell you, I'm gratified to know that a member of the royal family feels so strongly in favor of the two-natured," the young viscount, Lord McCallum, said, bowing over my hand.

"Of course," I said absently as Jonathon's head bent to Daniel's ear. Daniel flinched and frowned, his jaw ticking shut, and he answered Jonathon with a shrug and a shake of his head, lips pressed in a hard line. "I'd like to believe I'd have felt the same regardless, but I cannot stand to think of the people I hold so dear to me being treated the way Kimmery has been treating its two-natured citizens."

At my back a warm palm brushed against my spine, retreating quickly, some secret note from Cress that made my heart pang as I watched Daniel try to leave Jonathon's side only to be caught against the wall. Daniel was broader and taller than Jonathon Roderick, but I was beginning to realize there was a kind of timidness he hadn't conquered yet, a restraint that had been beaten into him.

"Indeed, Your Highness. A two-natured friend is good to have on your side," Lord McCallum said.

He caught my attention at that and I met his eyes at last, a deep brown color that held warmth. *He means Griffin, I think.* Or perhaps that I had won the friendship of shifters at large with this stand against the council.

I spared the viscount a smile as he bowed briefly. "So is a determined princess," I said, and he laughed. "If you'll excuse me, Lord McCallum, I think it's time for my Chosen and I to take our leave."

He stepped back, and Cresswell followed me to Daniel, Owen breaking off to gather the others.

"...I don't know what you think you're doing, but at the very least you can dig into Emory's disappearance," Jonathon was hissing as I reached them.

"Emory's never been reliable, and he only aligned with you where he thought it would serve him," Daniel answered, his eyes holding mine over Jonathon's shoulder.

"As did you, I'm sure," Jonathon spat.

Daniel smirked as I withheld my laugh. "That may be true. It hasn't worked out exactly as I planned, but perhaps I did get the better end of the deal."

"Oh, perhaps?" I answered back, arching an eyebrow. Daniel grinned and Jonathon whipped around, schooling his fierce expression as he faced me. "Excuse me, sir, but you stand between a woman of the queen's line and her Chosen."

Daniel's dimples flashed as Jonathon stumbled back, glaring at him. "Of course, Your Highness. Always a pleasure seeing you again."

I didn't bother hiding my scoff, but I grabbed Daniel's hand, drinking in his deep sigh as he moved away from the wall. We left Jonathon Roderick, the rest of the council, and his horrible father behind in the hall as we headed for the doors.

"Ride back in the carriage with me," Daniel murmured at my side, his eyes focused ahead but his cheeks full of a smile he kept trying to hold back. I would make it break free.

I bit my lip and looked behind me for the others, stumbling slightly when I got a good look at Cresswell and his grave and shuttered expression. His eyes were focused over my head, but his face was pale and it looked as though someone had struck or stabbed him. As if I had. Had he known before now what was growing between Daniel and I?

Guilt churned in my stomach, but when he glanced down at me, hollow and cool, that turmoil hardened. Cresswell knew how I felt about him. I was of the queen's line and I had taken Chosen before him, and Daniel didn't change those bonds, and they didn't change what was frozen between Cresswell and I. Only Cresswell could fix that now.

Wendell, Thao, and Owen met us on the steps of Danser Hall as the carriage pulled up, and Thao eyed the way I was pressed to Daniel's side with narrow eyes and a thin smirk. He'd admitted to his jealousy over Daniel when the Hunger had thrown us together, and I wondered now if it wasn't just Cresswell who resented my newest Chosen.

"I'd like to ride back in the carriage with you," I said to Thao and Wendell, glancing at Owen. "Crescent won't mind riding back alone, do you think?"

Owen laughed at that and shook his head, heading for his horse, while Thao and Wendell exchanged a slow smile.

"I'd rather like to stretch my legs," Wendell said.

"Mm, yes, it was nice to shift but too stifling to be expected to behave. You two take the carriage, we'll run along," Thao said, winking at me.

My breath caught, and I pulled free of Daniel to run to Thao, clutching at his collar and pulling him down for a fierce, pressing kiss.

"Ah, well in that case I want one too," Wendell teased, and I pulled away laughing, twisting in Thao's arms to let our lover kiss me more gently. Wendell sucked briefly on my bottom lip and then leaned in to whisper in my ear. "Enjoy him. Enjoy the ride."

I blushed as they pulled away, shifting into their feline forms and jogging ahead down the road. Owen snatched me up next, kissing my forehead and cheeks and chin and nose until he pressed his mouth over my giggles and kissed me till my breath ran out.

"You did good princessly work today," Owen said, grinning and pulling away. "Take a reward."

Another blessing from my first and sweetest Chosen, I blushed and nodded as Owen moved to seat himself on his stallion. Daniel was waiting by the door to the carriage, and I stepped forward to join him when a soft touch on my elbow made me pause.

Cresswell stood at my side, studying Daniel at the carriage with a deep frown on his face that turned to worry as he met my gaze.

"Bryony, are you certain about him?" Cresswell asked.

I was glad he asked me now, and not a week ago. I was glad I could tip my chin up and smile at him and say, "I am."

Daniel had never really acted *against* me, he'd only been placed in my court with the intention to distract me. And in spite of our duels and arguments and the ugly way we'd come together the first time, I had somehow won Daniel's loyalty. He had mine now too. But that wasn't all Cresswell needed to know.

"I'm certain about you too, Cress," I said softly.

His fingers on my arm squeezed briefly, and his breath stuttered, eyes widening. And then he closed himself off from me, the pain as sharp as it had been in my sitting room, cutting through me as his shock was shadowed under a stern acceptance.

"You have my loyalty and my vow, Your Highness," Cresswell answered, dropping his hand away from me.

I squeezed my lips shut around the bitter thoughts swirling in my head and hurried down the steps, aware of Daniel's keen stare, and Owen's, and hell, probably even some of the men still in Danser Hall. I stepped into the carriage, sighing at its cool darkness against the heat of embarrassment and rejection in my cheeks, and then slid to the far side as the carriage rocked and Daniel joined me. I pulled the curtain shut and then twisted, pressing myself into the man at my side as the door clicked shut behind him.

Daniel stiffened briefly, and then his arm wrapped around my shoulder, pulling me closer with one hand and tugging his own curtain shut with the other.

"Are you all right?"

"Fine. Wrung out," I admitted, tipping my head back and finding my face against Daniel's throat, the prickle of his beard catching in my hair. I inhaled a long gulp of him, finding an intriguing combination of smells there, sharp and warm and dark. His skin broke out in goosebumps as I released my sigh, and I wet my lips, just barely flicking my tongue against his throat and smiling at the hard swallow that followed.

"Are you all right?" I echoed, reaching up and sliding my hand into his jacket to rest my palm over his heart as the carriage jerked forward and began to pull away from Danser Hall.

"Me? I am...liberated is I think the term for it," Daniel murmured, his own hand coming up to cover mine.

"Do you think you'll have regrets?" I asked, frowning and thinking of his father's words. Daniel had answered them valiantly, but to give up a lifelong dream of being the independent owner of such an estate seemed like the kind of thing someone might second-guess.

"Not as many as I think Roderick and the duke will have," Daniel said, although his laugh sounded a little ragged.

I sat up, and his arms squeezed around my waist, holding me to his side and making me smile as I studied him. There were little flecks of gray at Daniel's temples, and I reached up to brush my fingertips against them now, watching the way his eyelids grew heavy at the simple touch. I'd noticed it the night Emory had tried to kill me when I'd staked my claim on Daniel in his rooms. This man craved touch, soaked it up with a desperate relief that reminded me of the Hunger. He leaned into it now, his heart pounding under my palm on his chest as I dug my fingers into his hair.

I realized in that moment that with most of my Chosen, I received a kind of care. Owen offered pure affection, Cosmo emotional strength, Wendell and Thao their political guidance, and Aric seemed to tame me and my magic. Daniel might've been of some use against the council, but that had nothing to do with this craving I had for him. It was the opposite, really. What drew me to Daniel was his obvious *need*, not for sex but for care, and for belonging, for someone to say 'you are part of me.'

"Will you have regrets?" Daniel asked, wincing.

"No," I said immediately, smiling at the small gasp he admitted.

"Not even... Something passed between you and Stark," Daniel said, his heavy focus studying me carefully. It'd seemed aggressive when he first arrived at the Winter Palace, but I suspected now he was just used to trying to find truths from a community of people who thought it was easier to lie to him.

"Cresswell feels he does me more good as my head guard than one of my Chosen," I said, shrugging. "You don't need to worry about that."

Daniel frowned and laughed a little, a small huff. "Why not both? Wendell is your advisor, I am your steward, Owen is practically your groundskeeper."

I wrinkled my nose at that, but I couldn't argue. "I can't ask you all not to have your own lives. As long as you're satisfied with the—Oh, Daniel, do you even like being the steward?" I asked, stiffening in his arms.

"I do, actually," he said, leaning in and hesitating for a moment before bravely closing the gap and skimming his lips over mine. "I like to be busy. And despite my best efforts, Lady Pru is impossible not to get along with. I enjoy working with her."

I beamed and brushed my nose against his again. "Oh, good."

"Your Highness—"

"Bryony."

"Mm, Bryony," he said very slowly, batting long lashes at me.

"I'm sorry your guard hasn't come to his senses yet. But I'm very grateful to be alone with you on this carriage ride."

"What you said to your father—"

"I meant it," Daniel whispered, leaning in again and grazing his mouth against mine.

"I know," I said, clutching my hand over his heart, squirming my hips closer to his as the Hunger stirred restlessly in my chest.

"Bryony—"

I should've let him speak. There was probably more to say between us, more to settle, but with every little press of those swollen lips of his to mine, I needed more. I seized it then, holding his face with my free hand, my body arching to his as I sucked on his lips and he answered in kind.

After Daniel and I had sex weeks ago, I'd spent a fair amount of effort *not* thinking about every little detail of the experience. The size of Daniel's hands as they spanned my waist, the deep flavor of him on my tongue, the way my hips stretched as I settled over his lap. He dragged me there now, our mouths fused in an endless kiss, my fingers digging into his shirt and through his hair. Daniel groaned as he pulled me against his groin, the top of my head just brushing against the roof of the carriage, bumping against it as he bucked a little.

I broke away with a giggle, my hand on his chest going to the roof and Daniel gaping at me and then flushing as he glanced up.

"Sorry."

"Don't be," I said, bending and nipping at his mouth again. Those lips were sinful and pillowy like Cook Umber's best cakes.

"Tell me what you want," we both said at once, grinning at one another.

"Go on," I urged, swiveling my hips over his, smiling at the heavy blink of his eyes and his soft shudder. I stroked my hand through his hair and down the back of his neck, reaching my thumb around to press over his pulse. His pupils widened, and I squeezed experimentally, shocked at the way his chest heaved raggedly.

"I...I want this to last," Daniel said, his expression pained as he held me firmly against him. "I don't want to rush. I want to feel you around me until neither of us can bear it any longer."

Well. My lips hung open at that declaration, and Daniel's eyes fixed there, one hand reaching up to stroke over my bottom lip. I nipped at his fingertips and then sucked his index and middle finger into my mouth, humming as he bucked again, his head dropping back with a groan.

"I want you to be stripped bare," Daniel gasped. "I wanted to tear you out of that dress, you know? To feel you close. I want to feel your skin on mine, everywhere. Should we...should we wait until we get back to the palace? I only wanted to be near you."

"Only that?" I teased after pulling off his fingers and reaching behind me to fumble with the laces of my dress.

Daniel looked up, his cheeks flushed and a shy smile on his lips. "I just mean—"

"I don't want to wait. There'll be plenty of time for the bed too," I said with a shrug as the dress loosened around me. "I need you now."

Daniel's hands scrunched the fabric at my waist, keeping me from pulling it off over my head, his eyes laughing again. "So matter of fact."

I rolled my hips again, sighing at the scratch of his pants on the inside of my thighs, the girth and grind of his arousal against my sex. "If you object..."

Daniel huffed and then I was surrounded in silk, laughing as he wrestled my dress off of me. His eagerness stuttered to a halt as he exposed me. The carriage was dim, but there was enough light bleeding through the curtains for him to really see me.

"Fuck," he said plainly, eyes swinging up and down and caressing against every inch of my skin before narrowing down between my thighs, lips licking. "That's the prettiest little cunt I've ever seen in my life."

I choked slightly and then squawked as Daniel lifted me and spun me around, sinking to his knees on the wobbling floor of the carriage.

"Daniel—I—Oh!"

There was no preamble, no teasing or promises, just two massive hands cupping my ass and lifting it from the seat of the carriage to Daniel's voracious mouth. His tongue lapped in a long stroke that covered areas I wasn't sure had ever been tasted before, or at least not with that level of attention, and then those perfect fat lips of his wrapped around my clit. I let out an obscene groan and crumpled into the seat, my fingers digging into Daniel's hair and heels driving him closer for a moment until I remembered I still had my *shoes* on. Daniel's nose was nuzzling against my clit and his tongue was burrowing into my sex and I had my fucking shoes on and he was still wearing a waistcoat and of course, none of that mattered because it felt *so good*.

I moaned, my thighs trembling around his ears and my nipples pebbling in the cold air of the carriage even as I flushed hot. My hair was rubbing into tangles against the cushion, and Daniel was eyeing me hungrily from between my thighs as his growl vibrated against my pussy and his tongue fucked me with all the fervor of a cock.

"Oh stars, Daniel! Oh, fuck!"

And then the carriage hit a rut in the road, and Daniel grunted as my body bounced and knocked into his nose.

"Oh, fuck," I said, trying not to laugh as I scrambled back and Daniel covered his nose with his hand. I snorted and then slapped a hand over my mouth, my eyes wide. "Are you all right?"

Daniel grinned at me, rubbing his fingers over the reddened bridge of his nose. "Fine. Come here."

I wiggled back and shook my head, giggling. "No, that's bound to happen again. Save it for later. The bed will be stationary enough."

"But I like your taste on my tongue, Your Highness," Daniel said, sliding his hands back under my ass and squeezing my cheeks.

I leaned forward, cupping his cheeks in my hands and peppering kisses on his lips, taking a taste for myself. "Then you may have more later, my Chosen. For now, I have a better idea of how we might use this...additional movement to our advantage. Undress for me."

Daniel's eyes went an especially pretty shade of blue-green as he sat back on his haunches, ripping his own clothes away as we watched one another. If Daniel had been mesmerized by the reveal of me, it was nothing compared to my own interest as he stripped. He was so...thick. I'd only ever seen him dressed, and he somehow looked even *bigger* without all the wrappings. He was still trying to find a way out of his trousers, without falling out the door of the carriage, when I helped myself to touching. His muscles were dense but somehow soft in appearance too, rather than Thao's perfectly carved form. Daniel's strength was undeniable and animal, and he grunted as my hands tightened on his sides.

His hands gave up the battle with his pants at his ankles, and together our arms wrapped around one another. He dragged me from the seat down onto the small floor of the carriage with him. His cock was stiff between us, licking and sticking at my belly, and my memories hadn't done justice to his size. Perhaps we needed to revisit our judgment on cocks that rated above a ten, as I was sure Daniel's did.

Daniel groaned as our chests pressed together, his mouth covering mine, his arms squeezing tight around me. He held his breath as I stroked my hands over the planes of his back until I realized he was trembling.

I pulled away from the kiss and pressed my cheek to his. "I'm here. You're mine."

"Yes, Your Highness," Daniel rasped, squeezing even tighter until my ribs ached.

"You belong to me. You belong *with* me," I murmured, ignoring the ache of my chest in order to kiss his earlobe, his jaw, over his pulse.

"Yes," he said. He sighed and then loosened his grip on me just enough to lift me up.

Without warning, his cock was at my entrance, and then he was forcing me down onto his length in one endless, exhausting, shocking stroke. My nails dug into Daniel's back, my mouth open against his throat in a silent cry as he stretched and filled me relentlessly.

The carriage bumped, and we both shouted as he sunk in to the hilt. My legs tied around his waist, my hands sliding up the back of his head to knot in his hair, and still Daniel held me tight.

"Does it hurt?" he asked.

"No, Daniel, you feel *wonderful*," I said, even though it *had* hurt a little, at first. But it was exquisite now, the way he seemed to touch everywhere inside of me, encouraged by the little bumps and rocks of the carriage. Neither of us moved, just held our breath until the next sudden buck of the carriage, both of us gasping.

"Shiiit," Daniel hissed, and then he released a soft laugh, leaning back just enough to share his massive smile with me.

I leaned in, grinning too, nibbling on his bottom lip and then moaning as the rhythm of the carriage grew more persistent, Daniel shuddering and humming inside of me. "Oh, oh, I think Aric should make a bed that is a carriage," I whispered, leaning back into the cradle of Daniel's folded knees at my back.

Daniel loosened one arm, his hand stroking gently up and down my chest, fingertips gently brushing over my breasts. I watched as he swallowed hard, touching and watching, his eyes fluttering shut with the next jump of the wheels on the uneven roads.

"I know you ought to repair the roads, but I also really think you shouldn't," Daniel said with a low chuckle.

Thump, rock!

"Ohh!"

My moan fell apart into laughter, and Daniel drew me back to his chest, panting, searching for my mouth. The kiss was slow and deep, a constant sweep and lick and suck, our noses occasionally bumping along with the rhythm of the ride. It was constant pleasure, and somehow simple and silly and shy too. I came once, holding tight to the magic after not even realizing I was so close, and smiling through the soft orgasm as Daniel writhed beneath me, fighting his own pleasure in the wake of mine.

"Fuuuck, can you really make a man stay hard for hours?" Daniel rasped, his head falling back to the opposite seat.

"Yes, but—"

"Good," he grunted, and then he was shifting, holding me fast to his hips as he rose up on his knees. "Elbows on the seat behind you, feet up on the opposite," he hissed.

It took a bit of work, and my body strained at the position, balanced precariously between the two benches, Daniel's grip on my hips holding me up.

He has you skewered, I thought, blinking at the obscene position I was in. And then Daniel's cock retreated and snapped forward into me, and all embarrassment faded beneath the shock and explosive pleasure of the clap of him against my sex.

I hated to think of what Cresswell or Owen must've said to the carriage driver, but in spite of the great howls and groans and gasps of pleasure Daniel and I made loudly and profusely, the ride never stopped. It was absurd, and it was hilarious, and it was impossibly good between Daniel's relentless fucking and the carriage's endless motion.

I came again with a scream buried behind my lips, my whole body trembling under an attack of pleasure, and Daniel fell with me, holding me against him as he bucked and sagged back down to the floor, bundling me tightly to his chest. I spared a little magic, my hand on his chest, and he groaned, sweat on his brow and cock twitching inside of me with his release and renewed arousal.

"Just like this," I said, wrapping my arms around him again, pressing a kiss to his shoulder. "Just gentle like this."

Daniel's hands caressed my sides, his own mouth sucking a mark on my shoulder. We stayed like that for what seemed like hours, the world going dark outside, the shadows growing deeper in the carriage, our fingers exploring one another with tender curiosity.

"Call me yours again," Daniel rasped.

My hands drifted to cup his throat, his pulse pounding against my palm, his cock twitching inside me in anticipation of another release. He was close. I probably was too, for that matter.

I rode him a little, smiled at the hiss and tremble of him as I held his throat in my hands, thinking of the time I'd held a blade to it and rubbing over the spot with my thumb.

"You are mine, Daniel. My Chosen. Mine."

He came with a long, relieved groan, carrying me with him as he spilled hotly inside me and it splashed a little between us.

"Yours," he vowed against my mouth, the pair of us settling and going still, still wrapped around one another.

⚜

"WHAT A RACKET YOU MADE," Thao teased as Daniel and I stumbled out of the carriage in front of the Winter Palace.

I glanced up, blushing, and paused as my eyes snagged on Cresswell's broad shoulders retreating away from us, his horse left behind.

"It's hard to ride in that state," Owen said in my ear, and I wasn't sure if he meant himself or Cresswell.

"I hope you let us watch next time," Thao continued.

Daniel's hand on mine squeezed and then he shrugged. "As long as the privilege is returned," he said softly.

Thao grinned in triumph, and Wendell huffed and rolled his eyes. I looked between them all and then at Cresswell as he hurried away from us to the guard's dormitory. I was still soft and shivery, still weak limbed from so much satisfaction, my heart still full of the hours alone with Daniel.

Suddenly, my guilt vanished. I had a right to my feelings. For Daniel and for Cresswell. He would have to come to terms with his own reservations and where that left him in my life. I deserved the happiness I was finding. So did Daniel for that matter. Cresswell was his own obstacle, not Daniel or I.

The doors to the palace banged open, and Griffin rushed ahead of Aric and Cosmo.

"Well? Were you successful? Oh, for fuck's sake, you smell like sex," Griffin huffed as she neared, rearing away from me and waving her hand in front of her nose.

My laugh burst out of me as Griffin backed away, nose wrinkling.

"We were successful. Not only did Bryony smash the new proposal amongst the council, she demonstrated that she is a force to be reckoned with and must be taken with the utmost seriousness as future queen," Wendell said, lifting my hand in the air like a victor in a match.

"Thank the stars for that," Griffin said with a sigh.

"I have made friends with a viscount," I said, eyeing Griffin carefully.

She froze and then blinked with exaggerated slowness. "Who?"

It was probably too dark, but I thought I detected a blush on her cheeks. Instead of furthering the tease—Griffin would probably take to the air if I tried my luck—I caught her and the others up on what the council had been planning, the moment of celebration chilling beneath the reality of what had almost been made into law.

"That's especially brazen of them," Aric said, frowning.

"Even better then, that you were able to put a stop to it," Cosmo said, stepping closer. I slid into his arms, smiling as he pressed a kiss to my forehead. "Mm. You do smell like sex."

I pinched Cosmo's chest as he laughed. "Yes, all right, I don't know why you all insist on acting surprised."

"Because you were in a *carriage*," Griffin huffed.

Aric leaned in to where Cosmo held me against his chest. "And are you sated now, princess?"

Griffin gagged. "If I never hear you use that word again, it'll still be too soon. I'm flying back to Rumsbrooke. Good work, Your Majesty. You have the arms of the two-natured now."

"Wait. The *arms*?" I asked, pulling away from my Chosen. But it was too late, Griffin leapt into the sky, vanishing into the bird and taking off with a screech that I thought must've been the hawk version of laughter. "Does anyone know what she meant?"

"The shifter community has played it close to the chest the worse things have gone for them. You can try asking Sam," Aric said, resting a finger on my parting lips. "*Tomorrow*, princess. Tonight, you should come up to bed with your Chosen and get a very well-earned night's rest."

"She really was magnificent. By sheer display of strength, she was sure to demand support from some of the smarter nobles," Thao said cheerfully, heading for the doors.

"Demand support *and* win hearts," Owen murmured, smiling at me, following Thao.

I wasn't sure if that was true, but I bounced to my toes and pressed a kiss to his cheek as he passed, Wendell squeezing my shoulder on the way to catch up with Thao.

"There's a bath waiting for you, already," Cosmo said.

"And Cook Umber insisted on reserving your favorite treats," Aric said.

"In spite of Aric's best attempts to steal them," Cosmo added with a bark of laughter from Aric.

I paused in my steps and turned, my chest pounding at the sight of Daniel behind me, his expression shuttered and cool. "Chosen," I murmured, smiling as his eyes burst to sudden life. "What are you waiting for?"

Daniel's grin was slow and shy, Aric leaving my side with a brush of his fingers over my waist, making room for my new Chosen. Daniel approached slowly, and I held out my hand to him, Cosmo squeezing my fingers at the same time as Daniel did.

"I don't have to join you," he said softly, watching me carefully.

"Why shouldn't you?" I asked. "You are mine now."

"Bryony sleeps heavily after traveling, so we pass her around a bit at night," Cosmo said, grunting as I elbowed his side. "What? Like you haven't noticed falling asleep in one spot and waking up in another. We Chosen all deserve a little cuddle, don't you think?"

"I did wonder how you all managed it," Daniel said before I could answer.

I eyed Cosmo gratefully, and his smile stretched a little wider. "Oh, we handle most of the negotiations while she's distracted. And if Owen offers to arm wrestle you for the privilege, don't agree."

I laughed, bright and giddy, and my Chosen stepped in closer, their arms looping around my waist as they escorted me up to my bed.

EPILOGUE

I screeched and flailed as two arms hauled me up into the air and tossed me over a broad shoulder, air rushing out of me with a great *oof* of breath.

A hand clapped against my behind, muffled through the heavy layer of skirts and petticoats, and then my captor hauled me away, my breath fogging in the air and my ribs jostling against the muscle beneath me.

"Gentler, Owen," Cosmo called, but his warning was broken by his laughter, and I looked up and shot him a grin as Owen carted me off behind the trees into enemy territory. At his side, Aric, my betrayer and I suspected the one responsible for swatting my ass, was bent over with his obnoxious rowdy laughter.

Owen darted behind a great oak and then hauled me down from his shoulder, my boots sinking into a snowdrift as he pressed me between the tree trunk and his warm, solid frame.

"And here I thought I'd earned such loyalty from you all," I said, grinning and catching my breath.

Owen wedged his knees between my thighs, bending enough so that our noses were level and our misty breath mingled. "I think you've just been teaching a very strange collection of men how to cooperate, really," he said.

Which was very astute of Owen and deserved a reward. We both moaned as I took his mouth in a messy, hungry kiss, our bodies arching into one another and rubbing pleasantly together through all the layers of fabric.

"Here they are. Owen's converting her to our cause, I think," Daniel said, stomping through the snow with Thao at his side, the pair of them grinning wolfishly at me as I pulled away from Owen's lips.

There were snowflakes dressing Thao's hair, and he looked almost twice as broad and fluffy, decked in so many layers, I was surprised he could move about. "They'll come for her soon enough, but I say we grab Wen next. He'll be easily swayed to our side."

"Mm, it's Aric we'll have to worry about. He'll cheat and use magic," Owen agreed, standing straight again.

Capture the princess was the winter sport of the day, but I was working on a plot to declare myself an independent party and let them all be losers.

"Ah, is that a white flag? No doubt a trap," Thao said, glaring through the trees.

I twisted and peeked around the side of the oak to where Wendell, Aric, and Cosmo were facing away from us. And striding toward them was Cresswell with...

"It's a letter," I said, nudging Owen away gently.

He scooped me up with his hands around my waist and pulled me out of the drift, the three of them following at my back as I jogged back toward the palace.

"Is it from my grandmother?" I called.

Aric had the letter now, frowning at the seal and then up at me. "The queen."

I stalled, just for a moment, Owen bumping gently into my side. My mother didn't write to me, not more than a note added to my grandmother's letters, or her statement of confidence. I hurried to the group and Aric passed me the letter, my men crowding around me, even Cresswell remaining close when he'd been avoiding me for over a week.

I tore the seal and read the page, my stomach growing heavy and woozy, my heart aching.

"Bryony, love, what is it?" Wendell asked.

Owen's hand stroked my back, Thao's hand cupping my hip, all of their eyes focused on my face as I read the words and over and over again, wishing they might rearrange their order or disappear altogether.

"The dowager queen is ill," I said, voice too whispery and thin. But no one else was speaking, barely even breathing. "Gravely so."

Your grandmother is dying, dear heart. Please come home, I can't bear it.

The letters wobbled and there were a few puckers and smears of tears, my mother's open temperament brought to tears as she'd written. That same ache choked my throat now, but it was more than that too. My grandmother was ill, and I was full of the bitter edge of dread at what this would mean for me.

"I have to go back to the south," I said, looking up from the page, feeling the parchment twist in my tight grip. "I...please, I need you all to come with me, my Chosen."

I looked to Aric first, struck suddenly by the notion that he might refuse. His brow tangled as he met my eyes, one leather-gloved hand rising to cup my cheek.

"Of course, princess," he said, tight but reassuring.

Daniel looked surprised when I turned to him next but nodded quickly, as did the others.

"Cress," I said suddenly, searching for my guard. He was there of course, standing between Wendell and Cosmo, our gazes locking in a warm hold. "Cress, *please*. I need you all at my side for this."

He stepped forward, warm fingers closing around my cold and shivering hands. "Where you go, I will follow, Bryony."

Relief rushed out of me in one great breath, my knees shaking, and then Cresswell bent and my head tilted back automatically. Soft lips pressed to mine, once, and then again more firmly, a promise in the kiss.

"Then we have preparations to make inside," Aric said. "We travel south at the soonest opportunity."

TO BE CONTINUED...

ACKNOWLEDGMENTS

Thank you to my author world, full of incredible friends and encouraging readers and outstanding authors. I'm so lucky to be a part of the microcosm I've found and so grateful for the hundreds and thousands of amazing women making it richer with every word!

Now specifically onto the people who keep me on track and in the best possible shape-

Gorgeous cover compliments to Covers by Combs for the exquisite work on the cover!

Proof-reading amazingness thanks to Bookish Dreams Editing!

My alphas - wink wink - Chloe, Lana, and Desiree, who chased me down for more!

My beta babes who absolutely devoured and protected this story; Jami, Ash, Kathryn, and Helen - thank you so much for all of your input and for helping to shape my stories!

My author pack - most notably my babes Lana, Chloe, Aleera and Crystal

And thank you, lovely reader, for taking this journey with me, Bryony, and her Chosen. Hold on and get ready to weather the storm!

ABOUT THE AUTHOR

Kathryn Moon is a country mouse who started dictating stories to her mother at an early age. The fascination with building new worlds and discovering the lives of the characters who grew in her head never faltered, and she graduated college with a fiction writing degree. She loves writing women were are strong in their vulnerability, romances that are as affectionate as they are challenging, and worlds that a reader sinks into and never wants to leave. When her hands aren't busy typing they're probably knitting sweaters or crimping pie crust in Ohio. She definitely believes in magic.

You can reach her on Facebook and at ohkathrynmoon@gmail.com or you can sign up for her newsletter!